THE CRIMES OF
ROOKER FLYNN

LOCKE INSTITUTE TRILOGY

BOOK I

A. R. WITHAM

Nepenthe House

ISBN 979-8-9874072-3-3

Cover Art by Alejandro Colucci

Map by Erin Shales from sketch by Sara Ferrari

Minor Illustrations by A. R. Witham

Printed by Kindle Direct Publishing

First Printing Edition 2024 in United States

arwitham.com

For Brian Snyder,

Who Laughs.

TABLE OF CONTENTS

You do not have to read
The Legend of Black Jack
in order to enjoy this story.

Everything you need to know
is contained within.

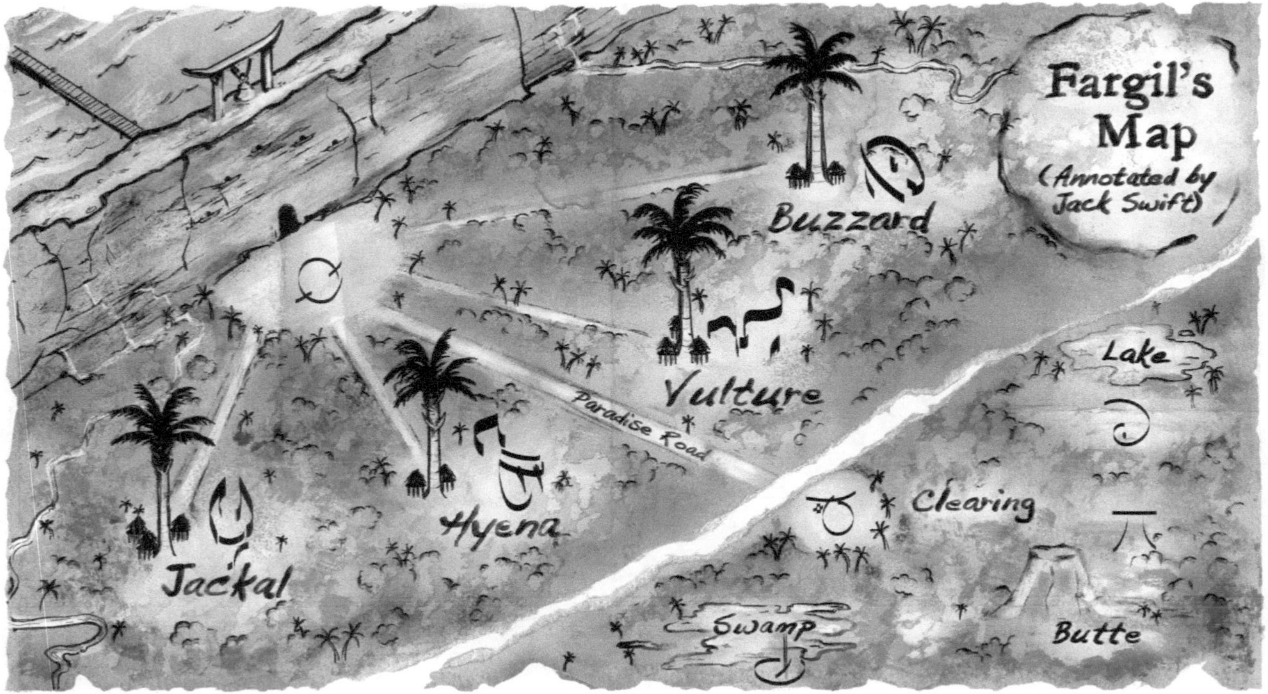
Fargil's Map
(Annotated by Jack Swift)
Buzzard
Vulture
Hyena
Jackal
Paradise Road
Lake
Clearing
Butte
Swamp

O nce upon a time there were two friends.

One was named Rooker Flynn, a pirate on the high seas of Keymark. The other was a fourteen-year-old boy from Chicago named Jack Swift.

In their shared journey across Keymark, the pirate's lies thrust the boy into the role of a century-dead folk hero named Black Jack.

Armed with the majik staff Nepenthe, Rooker and Jack resurrected the healing majik of the Great Bells, whose song heals every wound.

But it is rare for two eople people to tell each other the whole truth. Even good friends have their secrets. So it goes.

Jack never told Rooker he was from another world.

Rooker never told Jack of his innumerable crimes.

Prologue

GET
GOOD
GR!T

Uva Uvam Videndo Varia Fit.
We are changed by those near to us.
Juvenal

H is death was cause for celebration.

Addie Winegrad did not receive a solemn funeral or a drunken wake. No priest said a prayer over his corpse. There was no vigil of reverent mourners come to pay their respects or reminisce about their fond memories of the man. Not a soul in the world mourned Addie, he was unloved by all.

His life was spent in drink, women, and debt, often mingling several different brands of each. Addie was not wise enough to let go of the bottle, nor smart enough to avoid the debt, but the women were canny enough to leave him with the children, and so he found himself in possession of several on the day he died. Those who knew him well (and there were damn few who would admit they did) said those children were the only good Addie Winegrad ever did.

Some of them, anyway.

Pip found the body an hour after Addie was cold. The scrawny boy was ten and shaggy, a prickly thicket of midnight hair, dirty cheeks, and skinned knees. Pip thought his father was sleeping off another bender and so he made the most of it. The boy snatched a pear from the table and stuffed it in his mouth, poised to bolt the moment Addie moved.

Nothing happened.

Dead drunk as a skunk. Pip grinned. Barefoot, he climbed up on the counter. *Hello, Honey Bear.*

Honey Bear was forbidden. Only Addie was allowed to touch the cookie jar, a misshapen ceramic thing painted to look like a yellow bear with its face stuck in a beehive. Jasper, Pip's older brother, had tried to steal a cookie last spring and Addie broke his arm for it. But now...

Pip stretched for the jar on the top shelf. Balancing precariously on the counter, he stood on tiptoe and slipped one finger through the little handle of Honey Bear's arm. Grinning like a fox, Pip silently pulled his prize over the edge.

It tipped, spun on his finger, and the lid fell off.

Pip watched the lid tumble through the air. He saw visions of a thousand bruises awaiting him, a rainbow of reds, purples, and blues. The lid hit the ground and shattered, smashing the silence like a brass cymbal. Pip froze, wincing. *I'm dead, I'm dead, I'm—*

Addie didn't move. Not an inch.

"Da?" came Pip's tiny voice. "Addie?"

Nothing.

Pip stood on the counter, frozen. Realization dawned slowly. Cocking his head, Pip grabbed a tin cup from the counter and threw it at his old man.

The cup bonked Addie Winegrad's head, clattered to the floor, and hit his stiff hand with a soft *ka-tink*.

Nothing.

Pip blinked, slowly accepting the truth that Addie was dead. He threw his hands into the air. *"Yes!"*

All the kids lived nearby, most in the collapsed shed, the hayrick, or the privy. None of them were allowed to sleep inside the hovel—there was only one mattress and dear ol' Da wasn't sharing that. Sometimes Addie shared food, but most days the kids sucked eggs from the lopsided old henhouse where General Beauregard, the sole rooster, presided over his harem. The General squawked as Pip's bare feet pounded past him.

"Jasper!" Pip appeared in the doorway of the coop. Jasper, his older brother by thirteen months, glanced up from a threadbare hammock where he was whittling a shapeless piece of pine into a smaller shapeless piece of pine. Pip danced like a three-year-old who needed to pee. "Jasper! I got a secret!"

"You're a moron." Jasper growled. "That's not a secret, Pip."

"Ya remember what we was talkin' about the other day?"

"Whether you could eat a whole cake? You can't."

"Yes, I can."

"No, you can't."

"Before that."

"Before what?"

"Before the cake."

Jasper frowned. "What we'd do if Addie went away and never came back?"

Pip nodded, grinning like a fool.

Jasper cocked his head. "Did he...what? Did he go away?"

Pip shook his head no, still grinning.

"He's not gone. So he's—" Jasper stood like a lightning bolt had struck him. "He's—" Jasper ran out the chicken coop, headed for the house.

The two boys stood over their dead father, grinning. Pip started his little dance again. Jasper prodded Dad with his tattered sandal. He knelt, touched Addie's face, and jerked his hand back as if stung.

"Cold." Jasper stood up. "He's cold." He grinned. "Cold and dead." He kicked the body. "Dead!" He kicked it again, harder. "Dead!" He punted Addie's face. *"Dead!"* Jasper screeched and fell to his knees sobbing.

Pip ate a cookie while Jasper wailed on the floor, hollering curses at their father's corpse.

Jasper had always gotten the worst of it. The beatings, the burnings, the lockups, the starvation. He always had a black eye or a busted rib or an interesting new scar. His left arm had never worked right after that whipping last autumn. And of course, there was his time on the chain.

Addie did not keep track of their birthdays so none of the children knew how old they were, but when Jasper was around ten, he received the only present Addie ever gave him: an ax. Ten years old was big enough to fell a tree, and lumber was the Winegrad's only source of coin since the mill went bad. When Jasper proved unmotivated to produce timber, Addie bided his time until the next flood, never a long wait in their little gulch where mountain streams met to seek the sea. When the rain started, Addie chained Jasper's leg to the biggest juniper on the riverbank. "Lessee how slow ya go now, boy" slurred Addie, and left him there as the water rose. For six hours Jasper hacked at that tree, his fervor increasing as the Alaganset rose around him. The river was up to his knees when he finally toppled the juniper and freed his chain from the stump. When Jammy, the eldest girl, had the temerity to ask Addie why he had done it, her old man simply mumbled, "Boy needs to toughen up."

Pip got his turn on the chain early this spring. That flood had taken out half the valley. Pip lost Jasper's ax when the water got to his shoulders. Left with no means of escape, he was forced to climb the tree and cling to the branches. For two days Pip had been trapped like that, half-drowned in the Alaganset River. Since then, he hadn't touched water deeper than a frying pan and avoided the Alaganset like red iron.

Pip continued his excited dance. He did not have the patience to wait for Jasper's senseless caterwauling to end. "Can we do it?"

Exhausted, Jasper leaned against the body of his father and wiped snot on his tattered shirtsleeve. "Do what?"

Pip smiled. "Eat a whole cake."

Jasper stood up and hugged his little brother tight.

Half hour later, they sat together on top of the kitchen table with Honey Bear between them, crumbs littered around their bare feet, singing

Here comes the oxcart, oh, how slow!
It's pulled by an ox, of course, you know.
The wooden wheels creak as they roll along.
Creak, creak, creak, creak is their song!

Jasper shoved the last cookie in his mouth. "We're gonna run this place."

"You and me." Pip nodded.

"It's ours now."

"Yeah." Pip sprang to his feet. "We should tell the others!"

"Not until we decide who has what job." Jasper eyed him. "No freeloaders, right?"

"Cut the dead weight loose!" Pip agreed. It was an old family saying.

"You and me," nodded Jasper. "We'll get the mill working again. That's our job."

"Yeah."

"Jammy takes care of General Beauregard and the eggs."

"Yeah."

"Ferd handles cleaning."

"Ferd's six."

"He'll figure it out. And the littluns do whatever."

"But it's you and me, right?"

"You and me." Jasper clasped Pip's arm and together they stood side by side on the table like a pair of princes. "Ferd!" Jasper hollered. "Get in here! You need to go to the mercantile!"

"And Wint's bakery," squeaked Pip.

"And the bakery!" Jasper slung his arm around his little brother.

Six cakes lined the table: vanilla, chocolate, strawberry, red velvet, lemon, and carrot. To the Winegrad children, it seemed like every missed birthday had arrived at once.

Jasper started to give a speech about how he was in charge now but didn't get five words out before the fighting started over who got which cake. In the end, they settled for grabbing a fistful of whatever they wanted and stuffing it in their mouths, laughing.

Pip proved that yes, he could eat a whole cake.

All six of the Winegrad children remembered that day for the rest of their lives as the finest moment of their childhood. A sugar-coated world filled with rainbows of frosting, more cake than they could ever eat, and two big jugs of milk waiting to wash it down. Their little family screamed and laughed, cawing and hooting as they stuffed handfuls of treats into chocolate-ringed mouths. They sang songs. They swung from the rafters. When the inevitable food fight broke out, they assaulted each other with glee.

All the while, Addie's corpse lay in the next room, insensible to the joy it had created.

The next morning, Jasper and Pip went upstream to take a gander at the old mill.

It was a simple machine, not much bigger than a doghouse. The lever that connected the waterwheel had broken two years ago, but Jasper claimed he could fix it easily. He selected a branch and started whittling with Dad's hunting knife. "We should paint it," said Jasper.

"Why?" asked Pip.

"So everyone will know it's, like, under new ownership."

"Nobody comes out here."

"They will. When they see our mill, they will."

"Mill they will." Pip giggled. "We should put our names on it. Pip and Jasper."

"Jasper and Pip."

"Yeah."

"So they know about *us*. The Winegrad boys."

"Yeah."

That night they all had stale cake for supper. The atmosphere was less joyful; the novelty had worn off and Addie stank. Jasper, who could write a bit, put together a list of things they needed to fix the mill, including the paint, and gave it to Ferd to deliver to the mercantile the next day. They all slept in Addie's bed and had a pillow fight that lasted three hours.

The next day, Jammy scratched a hoop-a-three on the ground and played with the littluns while the big boys talked about construction plans and drank the last of the milk. Ferd came back from town with tools and paint; Jasper gave him a grocery list and sent him back.

The big boys went to work. At sundown, they came back spattered head to toe in white paint. Pip wore a big stripe of it across his smiling face.

When they wandered back inside, they didn't stay long. There was nothing to eat, and the hovel smelled rancid. One of the littluns prodded Addie with a stick, laughing as the green bottle flies jumped off his corpse. "Ugh!" screeched the littlun. "He's squishy!"

Pip was sitting with Jasper on the front porch when Ferd arrived empty handed. Mister Ito, the merchant, wasn't willing to extend the Winegrads any more credit. Jasper shrugged. "We'll get him the money when we have the mill working."

Ferd agreed, picking a particularly sticky booger.

They sucked eggs for supper and dreamt of cake.

Grease Liu showed up two days later, loping down the hill like a hungry wolf. Pip never liked Grease Liu. Didn't like his yellow teeth, didn't like his raggedy pants that smelled of fish guts, and didn't like how his one eye squinted through his pipe smoke at Jammy.

"Where's yer pa?" he croaked around the knobby pipe stem. None of the kids answered. Grease stuck his head in the hovel, smelled the rot, saw the flies on Addie's boot, and *hmphed,* wordlessly dismissing the corpse of the man he'd known twenty years. He worked his pipe, bringing the coals cherry red, lost in thought. Silent, he walked upstream toward the old mill.

Once there, he assessed the machine with one squinted eye. The mill was slopped with white paint, as were the bushes and dirt around it. Even the rocks in the stream looked covered in snow. The white roof was scrawled in red paint:

"Get gud grit," chuckled Grease. "Boy," he turned to Jasper, "You ain't gonna get far."

Jasper stuck out his chest. "We'll get it fixed."

Pip mimicked him, planting his feet.

"Not with that stick yer whittlin' ya won't. And once town hears yer old man's dead, they won't give you credit for a bag of beans." Grease squinted at Jasper. "Got any grain?"

"What?" asked Jasper.

"Grain. Fer the mill. Or corn?"

Jasper looked at him blankly.

"We'll get some," decreed Pip.

Grease eyed the boys and broke into a harsh, hacking laugh. A wheeze started in his chest and didn't stop until the last *hee-hee-hee* escaped in a whine of hissing coughs. He spat a hocker on the ground. "Heh." He wiped his chin and stabbed a bony finger at Jasper. "Five days from now, you meet me down the docks, after the tide goes out. I'll get you sorted." He limped down the path away from them, cackling as he went. "Get gud grit."

That week, the flies took over the house, along with a few crows and a family of raccoons. There weren't enough eggs to eat so they cooked one of the chickens, much to General Beauregard's ire.

The children ate happily that night, but Pip stared into the fire, thinking. *There wasn't enough eggs with three chickens, what happens with two?*

Jasper stole some milk from Miss Akawa up the hill. He'd done it before, but it was a long way to her house and most of the milk spilled out of the pails before he made it back.

That night, Jammy lost one of the littluns, Button, who disappeared into the forest. The kids wandered around in the dark hollering for her, then gave up when the wolves started hollering back. The next morning Jammy found Button down by the crick, shivering and pale. Her lips were blue. Jammy tried to warm her by the fire, wrapping Button in a blanket and hoping for the best.

Jasper and Pip shivered together in the coop, looking out at the rain. "Ya a-scairt a goin' down the docks tomorrow?" Pip asked, shivering.

"Naw." Jasper coughed. "I ain't a-scairt of no deep water, I's just pretendin'."

"Me too. I's just pretendin'." Pip peered through sheets of rain where Miss Akawa's dog, a bulky pit bull, padded out Addie's front door. It licked something from its greasy chops and disappeared into the woods. "We're gonna be all right...right Jasper?"

"Don't worry, Pip. I'll take care of you."

When Jasper went to town, he was gone a long time. It was hard to listen to Button hacking and crying all day, so the kids went down to the swimmin' hole. Pip kept well away from the water, whittling and thinking.

At sunset, Jasper returned home like a triumphant knight. He carried a burlap sack filled with tools for the mill, biscuits, a paper bag of rock candy, and a bottle of liniment for Button. He wore a new sailor's sweater and a big smile on his face. Button's cough got better that night, the smell of the liniment complementing the peppermint candy in Pip's mouth.

"Ya did good," said Pip.

"Yeah." Jasper nodded. "Real good. We gotta get the rest of that mill done before we go back. I got big plans."

Pip's heart beat faster. "We?"

Jasper smiled a long grin. "Yeah, Pip. I need your help. It's you and me, right?"

Pip grinned. Jasper's face was bright, his cheeks and nose red. In the flickering firelight, Pip thought his big brother looked a bit like Addie.

Even with the new tools it took four days to repair the old mill. They busted most of their fingers (and two toes) doing it, but it worked. Jasper and Pip hooted and hollered, slapping each other on the back. The Winegrads were down to their last dozen eggs and Button wasn't getting any better, but they had a mill.

A. R. WITHAM

They had a future.

On the final day, Jasper donned his sailor's sweater and Addie's hat, then set off to town with Pip close at his heels. Pip had only been to Moritoc twice and the port town seemed enormous. The trading post, the mercantile, the bakery, two stables, a common house, and at the end of it all, the dock. Pip heard the chatter of traders, smelled the fresh bread baking, and tasted the damp sea air. He saw a gigantic jug of lemonade in the mercantile window. "Can we get some of that?"

"We ain't got no money, remember?" Jasper sounded agitated. "C'mon." He led Pip down to the harbor and stepped on the long dock.

Pip stopped at the edge of the world and stared at the great Irridin Sea. *All that water.* He looked down and saw his reflection in the lagoon staring back at him. *I don't want to go over deep water, Jasper. Please don't make me.*

"Come on, Pip! Don't act a fool."

Please.

"Pip!" Jasper cocked his head. "I thought you was *pretendin'* to be a-scairt of the water."

Pip stared at the sea. It betrayed nothing of what lay waiting for him beneath. "I thought I was." He ducked his head. "But I wasn't."

Jasper leaned to whisper in Pip's ear. "I wasn't neither." He sighed. "C'mon Pip." He held out his hand. "We'll pretend together."

The harbormaster's hut was warm and bright, out on the end of the docks where the old brass watch-lamp shone all night, warning travelers this was the end. Jasper knocked on the wobbly window. Old Bert, the harbormaster, waved the boys to the freight platform out back. There, Grease Liu and two other men, sailors by the look of them, were drinking from a bottle and laughing. Near an empty barrel rested a wheelbarrow.

Pip's eyes grew wide at the sight of it. The thing was loaded with loot. Salt bread, pomegranates, a quarter-wheel of cheese, pickled pig's feet, jam jars, salt butter, a black pea coat, two new scarves and most miraculously, five sacks of grain.

To Pip, it seemed a fortune.

Jasper's breath spilled relief. "You got it."

"Ayuh. All here," nodded Grease. "Mill done?"

Jasper nodded. "Pip helped me finish."

"This is the brother?" asked the smaller sailor, eyeing Pip.

"Yep." Jasper nodded. "Pip's real strong. He helped me."

The big sailor chuckled. "Is that right? Yer a strong one, eh, boychick?"

Pip flexed like a circus strongman and the assembled company laughed. The smaller sailor poked him in the ribs. "Bet ya can't lift one of those sacks."

"Bet I can!" Pip showed off, hoisting the thing in the air.

"Not bad. How 'bout two?"

Pip hucked the first bag over his shoulder, then tried to get an arm around the other bag. He struggled to wrestle it out of the cart and fumbled it onto the dock with a thump. "Hang on, I—"

"Don't bother, boychick," said the big sailor, his voice dark and cold.

Pip looked up. *Why is everyone frowning?*

Something had changed while he wasn't looking, just as surely as something had changed the moment Honey Bear hit the floor. *Did I do something wrong?* Pip looked at their faces, confused. "I can—"

"Shut up, kid." The smaller sailor looked at Pip like he was something to scrape off a boot. He turned to Jasper. "Four bags is plenty."

Pip watched Jasper set his jaw, angry. "You said five."

"You said eleven." The sailor jerked a thumb at Pip. "He ain't eleven."

Pip glanced at Jasper. "Why did you tell them I'm eleven?"

"Shut up, Pip!" Jasper's voice cracked like a whip. "He *is* eleven."

"He's four bags of grain." The big sailor removed himself from the rail. "Take it or leave it."

Jasper eyed the sailor, then spat in his hand. "Deal." The sailor did the same and they shook hands, the deal done.

Pip stood, staring at his brother. "Jasper? What's happeni—"

"Bert." The big sailor hooked a thumb in his belt. "My ship ain't in the register, right?" He flicked a coin in the air.

Bert's old fingers snatched it quicker than Pip would have guessed he was capable. "You know, Roper Jon, I plumb forgot to write it down." He pocketed the coin. "Silly old man."

"See you in the spring." Roper Jon grabbed Pip by the neck.

Pip's eyes flashed panic. "Jasper?"

Jasper rifled through the contents of the wheelbarrow, fingering one of the scarves.

Pip struggled against Roper Jon's meaty grip but it was like fighting iron. The big man dragged him down the dock, his heels rattling over the boards.

No, no, no, no. He didn't. He couldn't—

Pip dropped out of his shirt and abandoned it in Jon's fist. He sprinted to his brother, who stood by the wheelbarrow in the last fading rays of daylight. "Jasper! What did you do?"

The bigger boy wouldn't meet Pip's eye. "There ain't enough food, Pip. And you was the only one big enough to sell." Jasper pulled on the new coat. "Addie said it was time to toughen up." He spat. "I did. Jammy too." He finally looked up, and what Pip saw in Jasper's eyes was as cold as their father. "It's your turn."

"But..." Pip stuttered. "It's you and me. Right?"

"I gotta cut you loose, Pip."

Rough hands grabbed Pip from behind and threw him down the dock. Scrambling to his feet, the shirtless boy backed up, trapped. There was no place to go. He stood at the end of the world.

Jasper's shadow disappeared behind two sets of burly shoulders.

Heart hammering, Pip eyed the gangplank leading up to the ship at the end of the dock, the two men closing in on him.

Toughen up. Chained to that old juniper tree, Pip had learned to fear the deep water. It surrounded him like a dark mouth waiting to swallow him whole.

He dove into the waves.

Pip's heart stopped. Icy fingers prickled their way down his flesh. He forced himself to swim underwater and dragged himself away from the dock, away from the men, away from his brother.

Perhaps an eleven-year-old would have escaped. Perhaps not. His shoes were too heavy. His arms were too weak. His skin was too cold. He made it twenty yards before he foundered and kicked to the surface, gasping for air. Even then he kept swimming, trying to get away.

The sailor's slingstone ricocheted off Pip's skull and skipped once into the waves.

Bloody, the water took him.

Down.

Dark.

Dying.

His breathing stopped. His lungs filled. His heart shuddered, and every nightmare came.

As he fell into the dark, Pip suffered from one last, desperate hope his brother would save him, then it was gone.

PART 1

NIGHT
&
DAY

Chapter 1

AFFAIR
OF
THE
HEART

No man is an island,
Entire of itself,
Every man is a piece of the continent,
A part of the main.
John Donne

Their bodies intertwined beneath the waves, her lips pressed against his. Bubbles cascaded over his beard and through his hair, tickling his scalp as she cradled him closer. Her chest pressed against him and he thought of love.

Water rushed past them as she gave another strong kick with her tail. Horizontal, she rode atop him, blonde hair curling past her waist, around his back, his arms, binding them, twin harpoons locked tight. She dove, and he felt a tipsy sensation in his belly as they dipped and spun. He laughed, bubbles gurgling from his mouth. She kissed him again, lending her air; he kissed her back, taking all he wanted.

Together again, girl.

She was six feet taller than him if you counted her tail. Green-gold scales surrounded her hips and arched down to a wide fin that moved a hundred gallons with a flick. They could go on forever like this, coursing under the waves, even down into the depths where the light could not follow.

We claim to choose love, but we lie. Love comes and takes us. It does not wait for us to weigh the consequences, consider our options, or make up our minds. You may love a woman for the way she adjusts her glasses, or a man because he gave you a kind word at the perfect moment. You may love a chair for the shape of its back, a ribbon for its color, a cat for the way it curls against your leg. When love calls, we obey. It does not ask our consent.

Schools of fish engulfed them like a silvery cloud. He laughed as they tickled his bare back. Cora laughed too. She inverted her dive and they shot upside down through an underwater cave, startling the sharks that rested there. As they scattered, she dove deeper into the tunnel, into the dark below.

Bioluminescent flowers, staghorn coral and bubbletip ferns waved in the dark, beckoning them, urging them onward. A neon panoply of purples, oranges, and pale greens sped past, growing thicker the deeper she went. He felt the pressure build, hugging against him, and still, he thought of love.

A thirty-foot nautilus covered in glowing mouths flicked its tentacles at them. Cora took a hard turn to port and now it was her turn to giggle as she darted into a tiny fissure. The space became tight, too tight, and he felt the reef scrape across his back. It was painful, but for love, he was willing to endure pain.

Cora kissed him again, filling his lungs with her endless air, then she shot upward, leaving a trail of bubbles in her wake. Moonlight returned to the world above, yellow and orange on blue. He squinted at the surface, searching, finding his purpose. As she approached the ceiling of the sea, Cora's lips broke from his, she arched her back and let him go. He floated upward, slowly, toward the boundary between sea and sky.

Rooker Flynn's head silently broke the surface. His long black hair spilled out around him, flowing like oil as his dark eyes settled just above the water, predatory as a crocodile.

When love is taken from us, it feels like losing a part of your soul. And if you are lucky enough to be reunited, it is sweet as oxygen.

Rooker took his first deep breath in a long time at the sight of his one true love.

The *Venture Brigand.*

His ship rested beneath the stars, surrounded by sea. Moonlight shimmered around her. Ripples of light danced across her curved sides as a puff of wind riffled her red silk sails. Her head nodded and he could hear the faintest sound of pleasure from her body as he returned to her at last.

Yes.

Of all the ships that traveled the vast Irridin, only the *Venture Brigand* sailed above the sea. Suspended twenty feet over the waves, her tall body was built in the shape of a Λ, balanced on slim legs like a tremendous water strider. At her feet were enormous outriggers that ran the length of the ship, twin skis that supported her above the waves. The *Venture Brigand* never touched the ocean—she skated atop it. Under her belly at the center, a rounded glass dome gleamed, offering those who sailed aboard her a panoramic view from beneath the ship, above the water. She was unique, she was perfect, and she was the only woman Rooker Flynn would ever love.

Floating, Rooker smiled up at his ship, the relieved face of a man who has traveled too far and waited too long to be reunited with his heart.

"Hello, girl."

Another head surfaced beside him. Cora's golden hair cascaded around his neck as the mermaid embraced him. "Hello yourself," she purred in his ear. "Is this what you wanted?"

His eyes twinkled. "O, yes."

"You're happy?"

"O, yes."

"And you love me most of all?"

His eyes never left the ship. "O, yes."

Cora's eyes grew narrow, jealous. "Are you listening to me, Rooker?"

He wasn't. "Swim me over there, would ya darlin'?"

For a year and a day he had pursued the *Venture Brigand* across the world. He'd lost her during a raid in Rimmy's Cull and had chased her ever since. He hunted down rumors of her in Caer Laverlock, bribed rum runners in Javernis Twist, and listened to the whispers of the merfolk of the Deep Blue South. The *Venture Brigand* was the fastest ship in Keymark, and following her scent was like trying to catch the wind. In the end, Rooker had greased the palm of an old sea witch who had pointed him here. All it had cost him was a lock of his hair, a drop of his blood, and the final year of his life.

She was worth it.

Ya wanted me to catch ya, didn't ya, girl?

The ship sighed, rocking in the gentle breeze. *Yes.*

Cora flicked her tail, propelling them to the outrigger, and at long last Rooker's fingers touched his love. He caressed the lowest peg and swung himself up onto the outrigger. He stroked the wood with his hand, looking up at her body. "O, I missed ya, girl."

The mermaid snorted. "It's a damn *boat*, Rooker."

He shifted his pack, resettled his sword, and made sure the conch shell was still inside. He'd won it from the lord of the merfolk by saving his son's life. Of course, Rooker himself had kidnapped the young princeling, but no one knew that. The conch granted him three boons from the merfolk. The first he had used to gain access to the sea witch's underwater grotto. The second he had used to summon Cora, and together they had spied on the *Venture Brigand* for the last three days. The third, he kept in reserve. Just in case.

Rooker realized Cora was still there, floating in the water below him. For the first time he looked the mermaid in the eye. "All right darlin', ya can go."

"Thanks a lot." Cora frowned. "You told me you loved me."

Rooker flashed his teeth like a weapon. "Now darlin', don't take it hard. We had *fine* times together. I couldn't have gotten here without ya." He rubbed the *Brigand*'s leg. "But I only have one love of my life. And it ain't you."

Cora folded muscular arms over her chest, pouting. "This stupid tub can't give you what *I* can give you."

Rooker climbed, ignoring her. "I can get that lots of places."

"*—excuse* me?"

But he was already gone.

One of the many reasons for the *Venture Brigand*'s success as a pirate vessel was the fact that it was damnably difficult to board her. The long, curved legs that connected her outriggers to her hull were the only way to reach the main body of the ship. It made a perilous path for sailors' feet. Few men could cross the top of the arc, it was too narrow and too slippery, like an oiled balance beam.

Rooker Flynn climbed it like a cat coming home.

He had lived, worked, and slept aboard the *Venture Brigand* since he was a child. For a decade he had served as pilot to the myriad pirate captains who came and went like moths. Once Rooker reached his full height, he had spent two years assembling a cadre of men loyal to him. At long last, he had challenged the last captain, Dagan Saltz, to a duel and won not only the saber in his pack, but the *Brigand* as well. After ten long years, he finally claimed the title of Captain Rooker Flynn.

His first act as captain had been to raid Rimmy's Cull, and that was the last time he'd seen the *Brigand*.

I'll never leave ya again, girl.

No, she sighed.

Whoever was crewing the ship these days didn't seem to have much initiative, fapping aimlessly up and down the channel near Outmost Isle like a cheap cargo ferry. It unsettled Rooker to see the *Brigand* used so badly; it was like watching a thoroughbred stallion strapped to a turnip cart. Rooker had wanted to seize his ship on sight, but her crew now numbered twelve and even with Lady Luck on his side, he couldn't take a dozen sailors. He and Cora had been forced to spy on the ship from afar, waiting for the opportune moment. For three days Rooker Flynn had felt like a child looking through a shopkeeper's window at a rack of sweets he couldn't have.

Until tonight.

Pausing halfway up the *Brigand*'s leg, Rooker slipped his brass rings from his finger, put one to his eye, and held the other at arm's length. Lining them up, he peered through the majik spyglass at the pier, two miles away. The *Brigand*'s crew had just arrived at the dock in pursuit of beer and company. Only two men remained aboard the ship, a skeleton crew.

Satisfied, Rooker threw one hip over the rail and his boots landed on the deck of the *Venture Brigand*.

Home.

Voices came from aft. The two sea dogs left behind to guard the ship were sharing a jug, bemoaning their lot in life. Rooker kissed his rings for luck and walked into the moonlight, singing:

> *A sailor's away all night and day*
> *And never the call to find me*
> *She was a sweet girl with a bobbly curl*
> *And she always knew just where to bind me.*

The sailors gaped as his lean shadow strode from the dark.

"Ey!" One pointed. "Who'zat?"

"Yeah!" shouted the other, drawing his pigsticker. "Who *you?*"

"Boys!" Rooker smiled. "Don't ya recognize me?"

They stomped closer, peering at him. Rooker eyed their feet as the bigger deckhand raised an accusatory finger. "No one's s'posed ta be back 'til—"

There. He tapped his rings on the deckrail. "Hard port, girl."

Red sails billowed in a sudden gust. Catching the wind, the jib swept across the deck. Neither sailor saw the tree-sized boom coming as it hit them square in the ribs with a merciless TUNK.

Both men were swept into the sea with a scream and a splash.

"So." Rooker smiled and tapped his rings on the deckrail. "I'm still yer captain, then?"

The *Venture Brigand* sighed happily. *Yes.*

He gripped the deckwheel. He could feel her beneath him, the lithe power of her, waiting to run. Her sails riffled with anticipation. "Then let's stretch those legs of yers, girl. Anchors aweigh."

A hundred feet of iron chain grew taut and the anchor rose from the depths. Her sails snapped full and she pulled away. The *Venture Brigand* left the little port town behind, skiing over the waves toward the mismatched moons beyond the horizon.

Rooker felt a grin cross his lips as he slid into a linen shirt from a locker. After so many months, he finally had his freedom back. The world was theirs. *We'll cut that chain and throw that anchor overboard, girl. We'll never stop.*

Yes, she sighed.

Now. Maps.

Rooker always had a knack for the sea. The Irridin was the living, shifting blood of Keymark and he could sense the tiniest ebb, channel, and winder. Moving with the current took artistry. That's what so few lubbers understood. You don't sail a boat; you sail the sea.

But for that, he needed the good maps.

As superstition demanded, Rooker popped one hand over his eye, kissed the other hand, and touched it to the little female angel carved on the inside of the door before he went belowdecks. *No sense jinxing my luck now.*

One of the many curious features of the *Venture Brigand* was the transparent half-dome that hung from the ship like a fat potbelly. The curved walls were clear as glass and hard as diamond, a long-lost elven majik. Suspended above the water, the dome offered a fantastic view, a good place to pilot in bad weather, and had a trapdoor that was excellent for rappelling onto docks from above.

Old Punch used to joke that the belly dome made the *Brigand* look perpetually pregnant with pirates.

Rooker deposited the conch shell in the captain's cabin and entered the catwalk that ringed the glass belly. He popped one of Saltz's cigars in his mouth and snapped his fingers. Flame ignited between his thumb and index finger, the only decent majik he'd ever learned. He lit the cigar with it, then popped it back out of existence as smoke curled around his head.

"I'm gonna get those scars fixed," he said to the *Brigand*. "They grow that rennel wood ya like here in the Deep Blue South. We'll get some. No spit-shine oak like Carnadale used, I'm gonna treat ya right." The boat creaked softly. "I know yer antsy, I know girl. We're gonna stretch yer legs a bit." The *Brigand* groaned. "I'm *not* lyin'. Right now, tonight. Hey, ya remember that blue in the Cape? Porpoises and sandy bottoms. Flat as glass. Ya skated it with barely a ripple. We'll go there."

She cooed.

Rooker grinned, thinking of the marooned sailors back at the port, wondering if they had noticed she was gone yet. "They needed a dozen sailors to crew ya, girl." He patted her bulkhead. "All ya need is the *right* man."

The catwalk around the belly dome offered an unobstructed vista of the sea, but whatever idiot called himself captain these days had planted the map cabinet at the foremost part of the glass and blocked the view. "Morons. I swear, yer never gonna have to put up with another captain but me, girl." Rooker strode the catwalk to remove the offending cabinet.

An unfamiliar creak.

He froze.

Bad luck.

"You realize you're talking to a piece of wood, right Flynn?"

Rooker turned as a figure descended the stairs. Cloven hooves thudded against the wood as the massive shape squeezed itself through the door. Atop the figure's sloping brow were a pair of horns curled like a ram, each bigger than Rooker's head. His chest was a grey wall of rippling muscle; his arms looked like they could rip a gorilla in half.

Rooker's face paled. A bounty hunter. And not just any bounty hunter. *One of the Naysayer Brothers. Bloody hell.*

Wont Naysayer, the brute in the doorway, was the fist of the Naysayer family. The blunt instrument, the closer. Rumor had it that Wont had knocked out a direwolf with one punch. If Wont was here, that meant another Naysayer couldn't be far behind.

Rooker felt a cold sweat break out over the back of his neck. He managed to force a smile, as if he had been expecting guests. "Heya, Wont. Where's yer brothers?"

"Hello, Flynn," came the Naysayer's rumbling voice. "Where's the dog?"

Rooker scowled. He'd forgotten Wont knew that old story. "I think he's stuck under yer fat belly."

A deep chuckle came from Wont's chest that rattled Rooker's bones. The bounty hunter reached into his belt and produced a pair of iron manacles. "You should put these on before you hurt yourself."

Rooker backed away along the catwalk. His eyes darted around the glass dome. His best exit was the stairs, but Wont was blocking them. "How'd ya find me?"

"Flynn." The brute shook his head. "We didn't need to find you. You came to us. All we needed"—his massive hands gestured to the *Venture Brigand*—"was the right bait."

Rooker ground his teeth. "Whatever they're payin' ya, I'll double it."

"You know that's not how we work. Come on." Wont threw the manacles at Rooker. "Let's do this the easy way."

The cuffs clattered to the catwalk at Rooker's feet, two rings of cold iron. He swallowed. "There's got to be *something* ya want."

"I want you to put those on."

Rooker fingered his saber's hilt. He was almost halfway around the circle, but Wont wasn't following; the bounty hunter was smarter than he looked. *So, make him come to you.* Rooker wrapped his fist around the sharkskin pommel and drew the blade.

He'd named it Bessie, after the woman with the sharpest tongue he'd ever known. As he released the saber, it buzzed in his hand like a nest of hornets, singing a violent, angry hum. He felt the power, the *wikk* of the blade's cursed majik, sting his palm. It always hurt to hold it, but it was worth the look of caution in Wont's dark eyes.

Rooker smiled, enjoying the sting. "Why don't ya come over here and mak—"

The map cabinet suddenly toppled on him. Five hundred pounds of wood smashed against his back. He felt Bessie forced from his hand as the impact bashed him off the edge of the catwalk. Crashing down into the glass dome below, the wooden case shattered against his body, leaving him a writhing tangle of pain.

At the bottom of the belly dome, Rooker fumbled for his sword and couldn't find it. He looked up on the catwalk to find Bessie in another man's hand.

The second bounty hunter was covered in black feathers like a giant raven. A long, sharp beak jutted between two eyes black as obsidian. Birdlike talons clutched the catwalk as Shant Naysayer slung Bessie over his feathered shoulder. He spoke to Wont with a chill voice. "I told you that would work."

"When you're right, you're right," came Wont's reply.

Rooker eyed the Naysayers from the bottom of the dome like a guppy in a fishbowl. *No. Not now. Not when I finally have her back.* He spat splinters. "Lo there, Shant. Yer ugly as ever." He managed to sound relaxed, almost breezy, as he staggered to his feet, wiping blood from his cheek. "So where's the third Naysayer Brother?"

"You won't see him coming." Shant cocked his raven head. "Like Wont said, put 'em on." His clawed talon flicked the manacles into the fishbowl. "Unless you want us to come down there."

"Please fight." Wont ground his fist into his palm. "I like it when they fight."

Rooker stepped sideways along the bottom of the belly dome. The trapdoor was only a few steps away. *Just a few more feet.* "Out of curiosity, boys, what's the bounty on me up to? I mean, if they're paying Naysayer prices, it's gotta be big."

Shant's beak twisted into an impossible grin. "Seventy-five thousand marks."

Hot damn, that's high. Good on ya, Rooker. "Too bad ya won't be getting it today." He grinned and kicked out the dome's trapdoor lock.

The door dropped open and Rooker fell through the hole. Plummeting toward the sea, for a second he thought he was free. Then his body collapsed in on itself, gripped from every side, tangled in a net. The webbing was whisper-thin and nearly invisible. It cut his skin, his face, his hands. Suspended in midair below the belly dome, he was caught like a fly in a web.

In the water below, a mermaid's sweet face looked up at him. Cora smiled wickedly. "I *told* them you would do that." She grinned. "Didn't I tell you?"

"You did, angel," called Shant from above. "And here's my thanks." Shant tossed down a small bag. Cora caught it in one hand and Rooker heard the clink of coins.

"Cora!" Rooker growled. He felt the net draw tight as Wont dragged it up through the trapdoor, hauling him in like a fish. *"Cora!"*

"Sorry darlin'." Cora grinned, counting her coins. "I only have one love of my life. And it ain't you."

The Naysayer Brothers pulled him aboard and Rooker was introduced to Wont's fists until they were tattooed on his eyelids.

He woke to something dripping on his face.

Rooker cracked one blackened eye open. The *Venture Brigand* was gone, as was the sea, and his shirt. He lay on his bare back against a cold stone floor, his head ringing like the inside of a bell.

Plip. Water from the rock ceiling dripped down and hit his cheek again. He struggled to sit up and failed, his body a bruise. *Plip.* Gingerly, he rolled over. On shaky hands, he pushed himself up to a sitting position, weak as a wet kitten. *Plip.*

Blinking, his eyes adjusted to the darkness. He was in a small stone room on a straw mattress next to a smelly bucket. *Where is this? A cave?* Groggily, Rooker sat up and spied a door, thick, wooden, and heavy. He lurched to his feet and grabbed the handle. It didn't budge, locked from the outside.

Rooker dug in his pockets for his lockpicks. *Gone. Everything is gone.* His picks, his blade, his boots, and the *Venture Brigand.* He glanced around the room hoping for something to use as leverage, but there was nothing.

He snatched up a pile of straw and stuffed it into the tiny gap between the door and the wall. As he did, he saw the rock walls were littered with graffiti. Fatlip was Here, one said. Baronet Ket

Rot in Hell, demanded another. Whips Got Kit Krax on Basque. Pirate cyphers. Thieves' cant. Gypsy runes. Useless.

He felt the stone walls closing in around him. "No, sir," Rooker shook his head, feeding more straw through the gap in the door. "Not me. Not today." There wasn't enough straw in here to burn the door down, but he might be able to roast the wood around the handle enough to weaken it. *No one's gonna keep me locked up, that's for damned sure. I'll burn it and—*

He stopped. There were no windows. The smoke from a fire would probably kill him.

He backed away from the door as panic crept in. Rooker Flynn had no fear of tight spaces; he'd once hidden in a barrel for a day and a half, happily munching on onions while the guards scoured the docks for him. But the idea of losing his freedom, of being caged...*that* was terrifying.

"I'm Captain Rooker Flynn!" he shouted. "I demand you open this door!" No one responded. Nothing moved outside. Just silence. *Plip.*

Dread leaked into his body like a toxin. "Now!" He hammered on the door with his fists. "Hey!" The door didn't rattle, solid as a fencepost. "Dammit, *get me outta here!*"

"Rooker?"

The pirate spun. "Who's that?" The room was empty. "Where are ya? Show yerself!"

Rooker looked around and discovered a tiny crack, almost invisible, low in the wall. From the crack came a soft voice. "God, I forgot how loud you are."

He dropped to his knees and scrabbled toward it. "Hey?! Get me outta here!"

"I can't get out," came the voice. "How am I supposed to get *you* out?"

Rooker knew that voice. "Who *is* that?" Kneeling on the rock, Rooker lowered his eye to the crack in the wall.

He found one blue eye staring back at him.

It blinked. "Hi, Rooker."

Rooker's eye went wide.

"Jack?"

Chapter 2

CHEM
509

*The love of learning,
the sequestered nooks,
And all the sweet serenity of books.*
Henry Wadsworth Longfellow

B asketball was an obsession this fall at Walter Payton High School.

The Junior Varsity coach had placed seven players on suspension for smoking weed at a party over Fall Break, and with only two days until the season started, the school was fighting for the open positions on the Grizzlies. Everyone wanted a shot at the team. Everyone except Jack Swift.

He walked down the aluminum bleachers behind the school, listening to a half a hundred sneakers squeak against the asphalt of the outside courts. The air was crisp as a honey apple, and he was glad of his new leather jacket. Before long he'd need a scarf. Winter came early in Chicago. Jack stood on the lowest step, staring at the courts, watching Arman Mirza.

Arman dribbled left and sunk one from the three-point line. He was tall, good-looking, popular, and in the National Honor Society. Jack was none of those things. He'd grown three inches in the last year, but he was still well under six feet, his face was blotchy with an exciting new round of acne, and he had always had trouble making friends. He had nothing in common with Arman; they didn't operate in the same universe. Jack had no idea how to start a conversation with him, so he raised his hand and stared at him.

Donny Butkus noticed and jerked his chin at Arman. Jack could just make out the words. "What's with this turd?"

Arman stopped playing. "What?"

"Him." Donnie scowled. "He's staring at you."

Arman locked eyes with Jack. He frowned, then ambled toward him, dribbling the ball. "You trying to get in on our game?" He chucked the ball at Jack.

Jack snapped the ball out of the air with quick hands. "No."

"Good." Arman opened his hands, waiting for the ball to come back. It didn't.

"Ms. Sargonetti says you have the keys for Chem 509 after school."

"Yeah. What of it?"

"I need that room today." Jack stepped down to the asphalt, still cradling the ball, shorter than Arman by a head.

"Use 407," snorted Arman.

"It doesn't have a vent hood. I need one."

Donny Butkus elbowed his way in. "Hey, you're the kid from the news, right? With the dad who was missing for like a hundred years?"

"Seven. Yeah."

"They thought he was dead, didn't they? Had a funeral and everything?"

"They sure did."

"Well, where was he?"

Jack didn't feel like explaining that his dad had been trapped in an alternate dimension where time moved differently, so he settled for the standard story. "Got hit on the head with a rock, lost his memory." He turned to Arman. "I need a vent hood."

"I heard a bunch of Indians found him in the desert," piped up Mitch Galiki.

Jack didn't bother looking at him, he'd been through this so many times he could play out the scene without them. "Sioux Tribe. Lakota. Badlands. Would you be willing to use 407 today? Just today? You've had 509 booked every afternoon for three weeks."

Arman shrugged. "That's my lab."

Jack stared him down. "It's the *school's* lab."

"And I'm the one with the key."

Jack's blue eyes narrowed. "How about a bet?"

A murmur of interest rose from the sweat-stained onlookers. "For the key?" asked Arman. Jack nodded. "You want to shoot for it?"

"No." Jack eyed him. "You're NHS, right? A Senior? Here's the bet: You pick any problem from your physics book. Whoever gets the right answer first, wins."

The assembly busted out laughing at him. Jack was used to that, too. As far as they were concerned, this was David challenging Goliath without a rock. "*Physics?*" snorted Arman. "You don't know physics, you're only a freshman."

"Sophomore," said Jack. "So you feel pretty confident about winning."

Arman laughed. "What do I get when I win?"

"I'll do your homework every day for a week."

"I'm on the Academic Decathlon, dipshit. You couldn't *understand* my homework."

"Name it then."

Arman grinned. "Okay. You win, you get the key. I win, you wash my car every week for a month. Top to tires, inside and out. And if I don't like they job you did..." He grinned. "You do it again."

"Deal."

Donny barked a sharp laugh. Arman stuck out his hand. Jack shook it.

Mitch grabbed Coletta's *Physics Fundamentals* from his bag and cracked open the cover. "Get one from the back," tittered Donny, leering through a crater-face of acne scars. "The hard ones." Mitch found a problem that looked nasty enough and winked at Arman. The big man reached into his backpack, grabbed his tablet, and called up a scientific calculator on the screen. "Ready?"

"Hang on." Jack reached into his JanSport and pulled out a ring notepad and a Dixon Ticonderoga No.2 pencil. "Okay."

The assembled group leaned in, anticipating the massacre.

Mitch looked at one man, then the other. "Locate the center of mass of a uniform solid hemisphere of radius R from the center of the base of the hemisphere along the axis of symmetry."

Arman went to work, his fingers flying over the calculator.

Jack finished writing, tore the page out of the binder, and handed it to Mitch. "Done."

"*What?*"

Dumbfounded, Arman looked to Mitch, who was equally awestruck by the solution in his hand. Scribbled out on the piece of paper was this formula:

$$Z_{CM} \frac{\int_0^R r^3 dr \int_0^{\frac{\pi}{2}} \sin\theta \cos\theta \, d\theta \int_0^{2\pi} d\phi}{\frac{2\pi R^3}{3}} = \frac{3R}{8}$$

"Uh," Mitch flipped to the answer in the back of the book. "That's correct."

Arman snatched the paper out of Mitch's hands and glared at Jack. "You cheated!"

"How?" Jack spread his hands and pointed at Mitch. "He picked the problem. I didn't know the question until you did."

"That doesn't...you didn't...how did you get it that fast?"

Jack smiled and held out his hand. "Key, please."

Rajiv is coming.

Jack hustled past the Halloween decorations that littered the hallway. Draculas, Frankensteins, and ghosts had been taped to lockers and classroom doors in a carnival of family friendly fright. Black-and-orange crepe paper hung across the ceiling with cardboard bats strung in a neat, orderly row. The anatomy skeleton was placed outside the door to biology with a big rainbow clown wig, white gloves, and a laminate printout that said: Why don't cannibals eat clowns? Because they taste Funny!

Jack Swift twirled the key to Chem 509 on his finger, whistling.

The memory game was an old trick, although it had been a while since he won a bet with it. Doctors called Jack eidetic, which most people think of as a photographic memory. It just so happened that Jack's particular interest was science. Medicine was the highest discipline (obviously so to Jack), and he had memorized as many of those textbooks as he could get his hands on. Two years ago he'd performed an emergency appendectomy which had worked out rather well. There wasn't much about medicine Jack didn't know, so during his first September at Walter Payton, he decided to read every STEM textbook in the school, including Coletta's *Physics*. No matter what question Mitch had asked, Jack could write the answer from memory.

It was an easy win, and he needed one.

For six weeks he had tried to fit in at Walter Payton High. Six miserable weeks of getting shut out, shut up, and shut down. It didn't bother him, Jack was used to being the new kid. But this time, he needed to come at the problem differently. This time, he wouldn't be moving on. Both Jack and his dad wanted to keep the same ground under their feet for a while. Explaining the disappearance and unlikely re-appearance of Dr. Alex Swift after seven years had required more work than they wanted to repeat.

The platinum coins Valerian Tsai had given the Swifts as a farewell gift from Keymark were enough for one good house, one good car, and one great lie. The house was a two-story mid-century brownstone in Lincoln Park. The car was from Detroit and made sounds that made both father and son feel joy in their gut when it roared. The lie took the longest to create and was the most important of the three.

Lee Whitehorse lived alone, way out on the Pine Ridge reservation, an old man winding down his days planting buckwheat and shooting groundhogs. He had no love of any government agency and didn't mind telling them a lie or two. When Alex Swift approached him about the lie, Lee had only asked Jack one question: "Is he really your dad, son?" Jack nodded and Lee pocketed the platinum. "Okay then." He blew a hocker into an old snot rag. "What's the story you want to tell?"

It took two weeks to set up. They built the camp way out on the Badlands ridge, tucked south of Oglala Lake in a green valley along a stream that fed the White River, a little nook hidden from prying eyes. After a few days of Badlands living, some reading on dissociative amnesia, and one packet of grey hair dye, they were ready. Lee called the tribal police and told them he had seen a man wandering around his property the last few months. The tribal police fingerprinted him and lo-and-behold it was the seven-year-dead archaeologist Dr. Alex Swift.

After that, it was just sticking to the story. 'No, I don't remember anything after the cave-in.' 'No, I don't know how I survived in the wilderness so long.' 'No, I don't know why my memory came back.'

Lee Whitehorse sold it all the way down to the bone. The Great Spirit, he claimed, had brought the good doctor through the wilderness, and he was to be revered as sacred. Lee also added some chanting at the deposition, which shut down follow-up questions from the insurance company.

It was national news for a half-second but it blew over quickly since Dr. Swift didn't tell much of a story and game seven of the World Series started that night. Back in Chicago, his former colleagues reacted with uncertain excitement, not sure what to make of it. And there was, of course, no family to lie to. No laws had been broken, no one was suing, and Dr. Swift waived his right to any insurance claims. After that, no one seemed to care.

In the end, he didn't even need a new social security number. The SSA keeps it for seven years after you are presumed dead. Apparently, this kind of thing has happened before.

After it all died down, Valerian's coin purchased one last thing: two weeks in Jamaica. After that, they were like any other father and son team, working their way through the world together.

The yellow GOTCHA sticker on Jack's new phone case vibrated quietly. He checked the screen.

Dinner @ 6, came dad's text.

I'll be there, he tapped back.

It was strange having regular meals. It was stranger having money. Dad had taken a job at the Field Museum (he was done with expeditions and wanted to spend every possible moment with Jack) which paid moderately well. With no big expenses, they had no money worries. Despite that, Jack still squirreled away half-eaten sandwiches for later, saved used batteries for emergency use, and always, always used both sides of a piece of paper. He still couldn't bear to waste anything.

If you've ever been poor, you understand.

Rajiv is coming.

"Hey Mr. Sackler," Jack waved to the old custodian mopping the hall. "I'm headed to 509. Rajiv Banerjee is coming soon too."

"Y'okay." Sackler shrugged, ignoring him.

Jack entered the lab and flicked on the lights. Four vent hoods lined the side of the room waiting to explore the mysteries of compound chemistry, and to play their part in creating the alchemical mixture that is a new friendship.

Jack didn't have friends. He never had. Sometimes he thought it was because he had moved so many times from one foster home to the next. Sometimes he thought it was because he was smarter than the other kids and it put them off. But lately, he had been wondering if he was just lousy at it.

Teenage boys have a particular method of communicating. No one has ever named it, but it goes something like this: the unexpected happens, and one guy reacts with a quote. Whatever is popular at the time, like *"You ain't playin' Sherm"* or *"I'll buy that for a dollar."* Some punchline to a movie scene or a meme. The other guys laugh, then do their versions of the line in different voices. This activity is like dogs sniffing each other's butts, a reliable way to confirm someone has been the same places you have. Proof of a shared experience. Sometimes, a particularly helpful boy will chime in with another quote from *another* meme. This is one-upmanship and considered the highest form of teenage male communication. The ideal conversation to most high school boys would be a string of memes that leaves them all laughing with Coke squirting out their noses.

Jack didn't know any memes.

He was out of step and the other boys could smell it on him. He hadn't been the same places, didn't know the same lines, didn't play the same games. He didn't watch shows, he just read books. Jack had spent forty days in a foreign sphere filling the shoes of a legendary folk hero with a majik staff. You don't get weirder than that. He was an oddball, an outsider, and they treated him as such.

Until Rajiv.

They had met in Driver's Ed. Jack had been paired with a kid who seemed a good bet to spend time in the Illinois State Penitentiary for assault. Rajiv had been paired with another boy who spent the first ten minutes in the student-driver car trying to tattoo his arm with a burned needle. Jack and Rajiv agreed it would be best to switch partners and suddenly found themselves in charge of a moving vehicle.

Rajiv didn't know memes, either. Jack mentioned the Hill equation. Rajiv came back with body plethysmography. When they both mentioned "Ontogeny recapitulates phylogeny" at the same moment, Jack knew he had found his match.

Raj was a junior. He'd skipped a grade in elementary school, so he didn't share any classes with Jack. Driver's Ed was over, and desperate for any excuse to hang out, Jack had offered to help Raj with his chemistry exam after school. They weren't quite friends yet, but this was the first time in years Jack stood a chance of making one. All he needed was a vent hood.

Jack dumped out his JanSport on the black epoxy resin countertop. Various instruments and books clattered out, some spilling into the table sink. In the other direction, a foot-long piece of pale bamboo rattled across the desk, rolling toward the edge.

He snatched it before it fell, and Jack felt Nepenthe's warmth in his palm.

The majik stick was made up of seven pieces, each separate and capable of connecting with the others to form one long staff, the weapon of Black Jack. In Keymark, it was a legendary majik artifact. In Chicago, it was...awkward.

In the beginning, Jack kept it with him at all times. The soft blue purr of Nepenthe's majik was addictive. He had wondered if the staff would work here, far, far away from her homeland, but she did. A little weaker, maybe. She didn't purr as much, and she never shone blue anymore. But if he held a piece of her in his hand and called her name, *takatakatak!* every piece flew to his fist.

But Chicago was far safer than Keymark, and a staff is a weird thing to walk around with. These days, Jack kept only one stick with him, tucked in his backpack. One little piece of her, just in case. The other six pieces were hidden beneath the floorboards under Jack's bed, in a little hollow Dad had helped him cut out. Sometimes he wondered if Nepenthe would come if he called her on the L train, and what people would think of six sticks of blue light rocketing through downtown Chicago.

He smiled at that.

Jack flipped open the secret compartment at Nepenthe's tip and his favorite pen slid into his hand. That's all she was good for now: a pencil case. He sealed her back up and flicked her in the bag.

Humming, Jack set out the instruments, the burners, the flasks, getting everything ready. It was going to be a good day. Safety First was the rule of chemistry lab, which meant washing up to make sure there were no chemicals left on the workstation.

Jack turned on the faucet. Water gushed out the nozzle in a powerful burst and splashed onto his hands.

The droplets burned as they struck Jack's skin.

Something sharp stung him, as if the water were acid. Jack looked down to see a green mark on his hand, a pale vermillion dot.

It winked at him, disappearing into his skin.

Did somebody not wash up after an acid test? The pain increased as Jack shook his hand and stuck it back under the faucet.

Kunk. The nozzle of the sink suddenly bucked. *Kunka-tank!* It jerked again, sputtering, then sprayed water like a sneeze.

"What the f—"

Kunka-kunka-kun—

ka-kunka-kun—

"—is with the pipes?" Mr. Sackler, the custodian, watched water flood from beneath the bathroom door marked BOYS.

"Damn kids, bet they packed it with paper towels again." He reached for the handle to the boy's bathroom and it burst open, breaking two of his fingers.

As he fell to the floor, Ernie Sackler did not notice the lenses in the hall cameras crack as the REC light died, nor did he notice the fluorescent lights flicker like the building was having a stroke. All he noticed was the monster standing in the doorway.

It was if someone had taken a man and stretched him. The figure was near seven feet tall, and not in a good way. Scarecrow thin, the man's legs were like toothpicks, his waist slim as a wasp, his chest narrower than a linebacker's thigh. He wore a wide-brimmed hat, a large ring of keys on his belt, and a long duster that flowed in the water around his heels. His face was covered with a black half-mask, but his eyes shone blue.

"Stay away from the outhouse," came a raspy rattlesnake voice from under the hat. "It's not safe." The scarecrow sniffed the air. It found the scent it was looking for and stepped over Sackler, flicking a bony finger. "Forget me."

Something landed on Earnest Sackler's face. Some kind of moth. It crawled over his nose, and there was a sudden *pop*. Sackler's eyes went pale as milk. His body went limp, and he collapsed in the water spewing into the hall, listening to the sound of the pipes.

Kunka-kunka-kun—

—ka-kunka-kun—

Jack shut off the faucet. It let out a metallic wheeze and shuddered to a stop. *That was weird.*

His phone pinged. Jack saw a message from Raj.

Running L8. Sry.

The lights in the room flickered and Jack heard the door handle turn. "Raj?"

The door to Chem 509 kicked in with a bang.

That is not *Rajiv Banerjee.*

The thing was taller than the door and lean as a fencepost. His strange odor washed over Jack, a pungent mix of curry and cinnamon, dry as a bone. The creature radiated *wikk* like a furnace.

Jack would always know that feel. That strangeness, that *otherness.* The subtle vibrant hum of focused intent, the majik music of it, the *wikk.*

In Chem 509.

"Black Jack," came a raspy voice from under the hat. "You're coming with me."

Jack felt his body spring to life, jerking to his feet. He glanced behind him, looking for an escape. *Storage room.*

The nightmare man drew a handbow and aimed at Jack.

O sh—

The bow fired as Jack ducked under the table. The bolt ricocheted, cartwheeled past Jack's ear and shattered the Erlenmeyer flasks he had been setting up.

Every faucet in the classroom burst at once, sending a dozen geysers of water into the air, splashing against the epileptic fluorescents as Chem 509 became a strobe waterpark.

Nope. Not doing this. Jack snatched his backpack and sprinted for the storage room.

"Halt!" came the thing's voice behind him but Jack was already through the door.

What is happening? Who the hell is this guy? Jack unzipped his pack, fumbling in the big pocket for Nepenthe.

The door slammed open behind him. A long-fingered hand snatched the bag out of his hands, but Jack already held the bamboo in his fist.

He called upon the staff. *"Nepen—"*

Spiders crawled out of Jack's mouth.

He tried to scream but couldn't. His windpipe was filled with a thousand spiders, all of them crawling from his throat, wiggling. In sheer terror, Jack's hands clawed at his mouth. He smashed himself with a fist, desperate to stop it *stop it stopit*—

The nightmare man plucked the bamboo from Jack's hand. "Now, now. None of that." He raised the handbow and fired at point-blank range.

Something struck a bullseye in Jack's chest. He looked down. A feathered dart jutted from his sternum.

He watched, wide-eyed, as a sick purple smoke escaped the wound and curled toward his face.

Jack ripped the dart free. More spiders climbed up his face.

He ran.

He made it two steps before his stomach flipped upside down; he needed to vomit. Jack careened sideways and struck his hip on a table. The room grew blurry. More spiders crawled over his face as he fumbled for the exit, running blindly into the nightmare man.

Fire sprinklers exploded water from the ceiling, blurring the tall man into a showered silhouette. The alarm bell sounded, hard and sharp over the indoor thunderstorm that had once been Chem 509.

One knee wobbled and he went down. Jack could not bring his heavy arms up to stop the fall and his head cracked against the floor.

A booted foot stepped on his wrist. "You're all very lucky, water wherever you want it." The man in the hat slipped a gold ring onto a gloved finger, then another, then another. Pipes exploded in the room, hemorrhaging water up through the drains. He uttered incognizable syllables, the rings glowed, and the water tripled, quadrupled, quintupled, flooding the room as it glowed purple, green, and red.

The tall man grabbed Jack's head and shoved it under. Water flowed into Jack's mouth, choking him, drowning him. Paralyzed, Jack couldn't do a thing to stop it.

The water boiled light, blinding the room in a flash of concentrated *wikk*. It smashed into the desks, the wallboards, the shelves, the tiles, all exploding at once into a Vesuvian eruption of majik.

The geyser stopped; the sprinklers shut off, and just like that, it was over, *ka-tunk*.

When the water fell from the air, neither man was there.

Rajiv Banerjee arrived in time to watch the door to Chem 509 break off its hinges, releasing a tsunami wave into the hall. He was knocked off his feet in the flood.

As the bulk of the tide coursed down the hall toward the stairwell, Raj staggered to his feet, dripping. Stunned, he took a cautious step and peeked into Chem 509. The room was wrecked. It seemed to skitter in yellow spiderwebs for a moment, but then his head cleared and all that remained was the dripping from the ceiling and the water trickling around his shoes.

Raj took another step forward into the room as one of the lights collapsed out of the ceiling and shattered on a table, making him jump.

The lab was empty.

"Jack?"

Chapter

3

STRANGE BEDFELLOWS

*The pain of parting is nothing
to the joy of meeting again.*

Charles Dickens

J ack?" Rooker blinked, dumbfounded. The kid's blue eye stared back at him through the hole in the stone wall. *Is that really him?*

Jack's voice came again. "It's good to see a familiar face. Eye, anyway."

Rooker's mind raced. *It's Jack!* He felt a sense of elation bubble through him. *My good ol' lucky penny.* Rooker pressed his eye closer to the wall. "Heya, boychick. What are ya doin' here?"

"Same as you, I guess."

"Locked in?"

"Yep." Jack's eye blinked and Rooker tried to remember what the rest of the kid's face looked like. It had been a year since they'd laid eyes on each other and Rooker had never expected to see Jack again. He heard the kid sit next to the crack, groaning like an old man. "Where are we?"

I don't know, kid. Rooker looked around his cell. *Nowhere good.* "Way down in the Deep Blue South somewhere. Probably some island out by the edge of the world." His hatred of captivity had threatened to ruin him a few moments ago, but with Jack here it was easier to keep his dark thoughts from getting the best of him. It almost felt like hope. "Can ya figure a way out?"

"No, that's what 'locked in' means."

Rooker snorted. "Did ya try?"

"Yes I tried!"

"How *hard* did ya try?"

Rooker heard an exasperated laugh on the other side of the wall. "I turned the knob, the door didn't open. What else do you want me to do?"

Rooker settled on his rump, rubbing his thighs. *Calm down, he's just a kid. Without me he's basically useless.* "Try doing something smart."

Jack let out a frustrated *humph*. "I can't batter the door down. My window doesn't open. Even if it did, the jump is fifty feet down into the ocean."

Rooker leaned in. "Wait. Ya got a *window?*"

"You don't?"

"If I had a window, I would've set my door on fire." Rooker glanced around his cell. *If I had a window I'd jump. Maybe. Depends on the rocks.* "Do one of yer Black Jack tricks."

"Like what?"

"Like fly out the window."

Rooker heard the kid snort. "What do you want me to do, make a parachute out of bedsheets? I'd smash on the rocks."

"How do ya know until ya try?"

"Nice," came the kid's voice. "You're the pirate. Can't you pick the lock?"

Nothin' to pick with. Nothin' to smash with. Nothin' to dig with. Rooker banged the back of his head against the wall. *Nothin'.* He bit his lip. *I got nothin'.*

The silence dragged out. Rooker watched the condensation form on the ceiling as another water droplet fell.

Plip.

"Anybody know yer down South?" Rooker rubbed his black eye. "How about yer da?"

He heard Jack snort. "I don't think my dad can get here from there."

Rooker spat. *Landlubbers.* A six-year-old girl could sail here. The Deep Blue South had the calmest waters in Keymark. "So he's useless."

"Hey."

Rooker chuckled. He'd forgotten how tetchy the kid could get about his old man. *He can be such a child sometimes.* "How about that runty trol who followed ya around? That Memphis fella? Or that little doxie-gal ya were in love with. Either of them know where ya are?"

There was a long silence from the other side of the wall. "I wasn't in *love* with her."

Rooker laughed to himself. *Right.* "What was her name? Lynne?"

"Leah," came Jack's wistful voice. "Leah Archer."

"Right," Rooker nodded. "Had a great nose."

There was no response from Jack's side of the wall. Rooker shifted against the rock and tried to get comfortable. He heard Jack doing the same thing. They sat back-to-back, a foot of stone between them.

The silence went on for a long time, each man contemplating their new place in the world.

Plip.

Rooker soon found himself rocking back and forth, restless. The walls were closing in, he could feel it. After ten years on the open sea, captivity was the same thing as hell. He couldn't stay trapped in here much longer, he felt like he was ten heartbeats away from losing his mind. Rooker got up and paced like a caged animal.

"Hey?" came Jack's voice from the crack. "Where are you going?"

"Nowhere." Rooker growled. "I'm goin' nowhere."

"Can you come back?" Jack sounded shaky. "I feel better if...if you're close."

Great. I'm baby-sitting a child. Rooker returned to the crack and peeked through the hole. "See? I'm still here."

Jack's eye was waiting for him. "Wow. That's one hell of a shiner. How'd you get that?"

Rooker realized he'd put his black eye to the crack this time. He put his fingers to the bruise. "Big bounty hunter took a couple cheap shots when I was down. How'd they get you?"

"They?" Jack sounded confused. "It was one guy. One...really scary guy."

"Heh," Rooker snorted. "Took *two* of 'em to get me." He tilted his head back, swiped the stray hair from his eyes and stared at the ceiling. "Let me guess, the one who came after ya was a tall, skinny fella with a hat. Mask over his mouth. Key ring on his belt."

Rooker heard a surprised noise from the other side of the wall. "That's him. You *know* him?"

"Cant."

"You can't know him?"

"Cant is his name." Rooker sneered. "Cant, Shant, and Wont. The Naysayer Brothers. Bounty hunters out of Chult." Rooker prodded at his black eye. "Nasty fellas. The one who got ya is the... warlock, wizard, whatever, I can't keep those majik-types straight. I got Shant and Wont, the sneak and the heavy. The Naysayer Brothers are the ones who took down Iron Chen and the Marauders. They're good. Expensive. Smart. Smart enough to use the *Venture Brigand* as bait."

The memory stung like a wasp. Thinking of losing his ship again was enough to make Rooker's blood boil. *I had her in my hands...*

He snapped his fingers and sparked an angry flame, distracting himself. "How'd Cant get ya?"

"Shot me with a poison dart," Jack grumbled. "At school."

"*School?*" Rooker snorted. The kid was smart, no question about that, but he had no education at all, an illiterate. Jack couldn't read sigils, kanji, or runes any better than an infant. The kid was one of those clever country bumpkins who couldn't spell *cat*. "What, are they teachin' ya to read?"

"Hey! I can read a little."

Rooker could hear the sting in Jack's voice, and that made it easier to forget his own troubles. *It's so easy to get under yer skin, boychick. If there's anything ya hate, it's feelin' dumb.* He couldn't resist turning the knife. "Tell me *one* thing it says on yer walls."

"There's writing on your *walls?*" Jack shifted closer. "What does it say?"

Rooker scowled, looking at the many cyphers carved in the stone. "What, ya got no graffiti in yer room? SPIKE WAS HERE or somethin'?"

"Graffiti? No, just some decorations."

Decorations? "Wait." Rooker frowned. "What's yer room look like?"

"I don't know. It's got...four walls. A chamber pot, a lamp. A dresser that's locked. A pretty decent bed..."

"A *bed?*" Rooker looked around his stone gaol cell. "And a lamp? All I got is a bucket and some straw. Yer livin' in luxury compared to me. What, is it wallpapered, too?"

"Actually—yes."

Jack Swift stared at the gold-and-green pineapples dotted in patterns on the walls of his room. Everything here was sparkling clean, brand new. The bed was soft with big fluffy pillows, the stonework inlaid in detailed filigree. A vase of tropical flowers rested on the teak dresser. Up until now, Jack had assumed he and Rooker were locked in the guest rooms of a castle. "What does *your* room look like?"

"It's a rock box!" He heard Rooker bark through the hole. "Why'd they give *you* the good room?"

Jack was wondering the same thing himself. "I don't know. Maybe they want us for different reasons."

"So I'm a prisoner and yer...what? A *guest?*"

Jack glanced down at his nearly-naked body. The only clothing he wore were his Fruit of the Loom underwear. Everything else was missing. Shirt, pants, shoes, and backpack, all gone. Jack fingered the little puncture wound in his chest where Cant Naysayer's dart had pierced him. *If I'm a guest, my host has a funny way of showing it.*

Rooker hawked and spat. "How long have ya been in yer little palace?"

Jack shook his head. He had forgotten how petty Rooker could be. *We're both locked up and all he can think about is how my room is better than his.* "Maybe half a day?" Jack looked out the window at the afternoon sun. "It was dawn when I woke up. I ate the last of the mangos about an hour ago."

"Mangos?!" Rooker shouted. "Well yer living like a little *prince* over there, aren't ya, boychick?"

My God will you shut up about the damn rooms?

"You want to trade places with me, Rooker?" Jack shouted. "Would that make you happy?!"

"I wouldn't mind a damn mango!"

"Will you stop yelling at me?!"

"Stop yellin' at *me!*"

Jack stood up and walked away from the crack. *I swear, it's like talking to a child.*

He had remembered Rooker fondly during their time apart, but like many fond memories, the ugly truth had been glossed over with nostalgia. Rooker Flynn was the most selfish and pigheaded man Jack Swift had ever met.

Jack wobbled across the room to his window. His legs still felt like rubber from the poisoned dart. As he leaned against the sill he saw a tiny yellow spider the size of a pinhead, waiting patiently in its web. His stomach flopped over, remembering the spiders coming out of his mouth.

Jack turned away from the window, sat on the edge of the bed, and took a long breath. *This isn't getting me anywhere. Focus.* "You said the Naysayer Brothers are expensive?"

"Too right," came Rooker's voice. "Top shelf contractors."

"So who paid them?"

There was a long pause from Rooker's cell. "I dunno. Law, more than likely."

Jack pulled at his lower lip, thinking. He didn't know much about majik, but he knew jumping between Keymark and his world was an outrageously perilous undertaking, and potentially lethal. Only a few Keymark wizards would even attempt it. "That's a *long* way to travel to serve a warrant."

"A long way? To Chee-ga-go?" Rooker sounded incredulous. "That's a milk run."

Jack paused, not sure what to say. He had never told Rooker the truth, that he came from another reality, another *sphere*. As far as Rooker Flynn was concerned, Jack was a Keymark kid from some podunk backwater called Chee-ga-go.

"Chicago," Jack corrected him.

"Yeah, that's what I said," Rooker said. "Chegago."

Now is probably not the best time to tell him the truth. Jack eyed the intricate hieroglyphs chiseled in his locked door. Rooker was accurate about Jack's illiteracy. Jack knew maybe fifty Keymark symbols by sight, like a poorly trained tourist. The deeper truth was Jack and Rooker didn't even speak the same language. The only reason Jack could communicate with Rooker, or anyone in Keymark, was the *wikk* translated the speech of anyone who wanted to be understood. It was like that story out of the Bible, where everybody heard words in their own language.

Writing, however, did not have a will. And so, to Jack's eyes, most Keymark symbols were incomprehensible scribbles.

"This doesn't make any sense." Jack banged his head against the wall and felt the frustration rise in his chest. He hated a puzzle he couldn't solve. *None of this makes any sense.* The only thing that made him special in Keymark was his knowledge of medicine, but the Great Bells had come back to life, and they could heal anyone of literally anything. *So why did someone attack me, kidnap me, and lock me up like a bird in a gilded cage?* "Who wants us this badly?"

"Yer not listening to me, boychick." Rooker growled. "I'm telling ya: it's the law."

Trapped, confused and angry, Jack felt his voice get louder. "Why the hell would the law want me?"

"Probably because we're criminals."

Jack scowled. "I am *not* a criminal!"

He heard Rooker chuckle. "Yer Black Jack, remember?"

Jack stopped. He had forgotten that part of the story. A hundred years ago, Black Jack had been an outlaw highwayman, the Keymark version of Robin Hood, stealing from the princes to give to the poor. Jack scowled. "I'm not *him*. That's a story we made up."

"Yeah?" Rooker snorted. "Tell that to whoever locked ya in."

Jack lurched up from the bed and stalked the room like a caged wolf. *They kidnapped me because they think I'm a freaking bandit?* "That's ridiculous! *Insane!*"

"Simmer down, boychick, yer gettin' hysterical."

If Rooker's words were meant to calm him (and that was a big if), they failed. Jack had always hated it when Rooker called him 'boychick'. It felt like having his nose flicked by some third-rate schoolyard bully. *I can't control the lock on my door or the pain in my gut or the hole in my chest, but I can damn well control whether I listen to your crap.* "Don't call me that."

"What?"

"You *know* what. We're done with that."

He heard Rooker laugh. "Whatever ya say, boychick."

"Dammit, Rooker!" Jack's anger bubbled over. "I've spent the last two years of my life without you in it. I forgot how lucky I was!"

"*Two* years?" Rooker chortled on the other side of the wall. "Ya really have gone crazy! It's *one!*"

"I can count, Rooker." Jack had been fourteen the last time he'd been to Keymark, he was sixteen now. "It's been two years."

"I-can-count-Jack, it's been twelve moons."

Realization hit him like a bucket of ice water. Of all the strange aspects of Keymark, from the lack of language barriers to the way the sun rose in the west, or the pair of mismatched moons, there was one feature that stood out. *Time moves differently here.*

Jack stared. "Wait. Rooker. What are you saying?"

"I never met a smart guy so dumb." Rooker huffed. "Some lucky penny you are!"

Jack stared at the wall. "It's only been a year for you—"

His sentence was broken by a sudden rap at the door.

Jack froze.

"Hello?" came a soft voice from outside.

"Who'zat?" Rooker's whisper was harsh.

"Someone's at the door," Jack whispered back.

"Hello?" It was a woman's voice, high and lilting. "Are you awake?"

Jack looked around the room, trying to find something he could use as a weapon. "What...what should I do?" he whispered.

"Get me outta here!" hissed Rooker.

Jack turned to the door, raising his voice. "Hello? I'm awake?"

"O, excellent!" said the woman. "There's a fresh set of clothing for you in the dresser."

Is she messing with me? "The dresser's locked."

"O, I'm so sorry, I forgot! The key is under the left front leg."

Rooker growled through the crack. "Ya didn't check under the *dresser?*"

"Shut up." Jack found the key and unlocked the drawer, revealing tan pants and an ivory-white tunic. "Uh, hang on!" He slid on the shirt and returned to the crack in the wall, hopping on one leg to get into his pants. He dropped to the floor and looked through the crack at Rooker. "I'll see what I can find out. I'll come back as soon as I can."

"Jack, wait wait *wait.*" Rooker's black eye was hard as flint. "Listen to me, boychick. Don't trust her. Don't trust anybody but me. Ya don't know these people." Rooker's voice was urgent. "Don't give 'em yer name. Don't give 'em *anything.* And don't tell 'em ya talked to me, or they'll know there's a hole between the cells."

"May I come in?" the woman asked politely.

"Figure out an escape plan," Rooker hissed. "Start thinkin', Jack, and start *now.*"

The door opened. Jack backed into the corner as a lone figure entered the room.

She was tall and wore a long seamless drape-front cloak of creamy silk. Around her head was wrapped a veil that looked something like an Arabian niqab. It covered her face except a single slit that revealed bright brown eyes. "Hello! I am so glad to see you are recovered," came her pleasant voice from under the veil. "It is such an honor to meet you...the real Black Jack."

Jack stammered. Every inch of the woman was a mystery, but the last thing he'd expected was her esteem. "I...It's a pl...I'm sorry, who are you?" He finally got out. "And where am I?"

She bowed her head. "I am called Portia, an acolyte of the Institute." Jack heard a touch of pride in her voice. "I understand you must have questions. Most of our new students do."

Students?

"So!" She clapped her gloved hands together. "I will take you to the one person who has all the answers." Portia held out her arm to escort him.

Jack glanced at the silent crack in the wall and took her proffered arm cautiously. "And who is that?"

Her warm voice chuckled beneath the silk as she patted his hand. "Why, the Headmistress, of course!"

Chapter

4

HEADMISTRESS

*It is impossible for a man to learn
what he thinks he already knows.*

Epictetus

P ortia led Jack through the corridors. The stone around him was dark and volcanic, like something you would see on Hawaii, but the walls were smooth-bored, and the floor was perfectly even. As they traveled, the hallways grew more intricate, carved in great detail, including picturesque scenes of men and women harvesting rice, felling timber, shipbuilding, milling, bootmaking, almost every labor imaginable.

It was as if someone had taken a mountain and turned it into a town hall.

As Jack walked, he heard the tiny *tink-tink-tink* of a dozen hammers ringing against the stone like bells announcing his entry. He followed Portia around a corner and saw a group of short men working the walls with chisel and mallet, borer and bob. Jack had seen hammerdwarves before but had never met one. They stood under four feet tall, their skin greyish and blue-veined, all with muscular, calloused hands.

Jack saw a few acolytes like Portia, men and women dressed in the head-to-toe pale cloaks, entirely veiled except for their eyes. As he passed them in the hall, they nodded, but remained silent.

The hallway began to slope upward, and Jack saw windows and balconies overlooking the Irridin Sea, Keymark's freshwater ocean. As the tunnel ascended, he saw apertures on the opposing side that offered a vista of vast jungle. It was as if he could see two entirely separate worlds at once, one blue, one green.

Portia came to a large door and opened it. Inside, ornamented bookcases filled a vast two-level library dominated by a huge mahogany desk the size of a Buick. Around the room were elegant statues of warriors, workers, and scholars. A crackling fire danced merrily inside a vast fireplace carved into the rock. Upon the floor, a lavish forty-foot carpet was decorated in green and gold pineapples.

"Headmistress," Portia announced with a smile. "I would like to present Black Jack."

A figure stepped out from behind one of the pillars and Jack was struck with a sudden familiarity.

The gigantic monster looked like a rhinoceros standing on two legs, tall as an upended truck. Leathery skin covered her massive body in natural plate armor, cracked and wrinkled in all the right places. Three horns grew from her long nose, the foremost nearly four feet long, ornamented in rings and gold chains that dangled over intricate etchings in the keratin. Her fingers were thick as bread loaves, most bedecked with gold rings and jewels.

Jack had only met one trol in Keymark, but he had never imagined one in a dress.

A blazing red polka-dot pattern peppered her bodice, accented with a white lace décolletage atop a tufted crinoline skirt. A little pillbox hat and a large brooch at her collarbone were the icing on the cake, making the trol appear as if she were a socialite attending the Kentucky Derby.

"O hello, dearie!" came her sweet voice. "You must be famished." She offered a silver tray. "Watercress sandwich?"

Perfect white tringles of bread, each spread with mayonnaise and topped with a sprig of parsley, adorned the platter.

Jack didn't know what to do. He'd been expecting...not this. With the appetizers presented before him, there wasn't much else he could do but take one. Then the last words he expected to say escaped his mouth. "Um...thank you."

"I *do* hope you are feeling better after your rest." The trol smiled. "I am told the jaunt can be quite draining. I have never done it myself, although I would dearly love to see the Tosh. You live in such a *fascinating* sphere."

Jack swallowed his watercress sandwich and felt it necessary to state the obvious. "You...kidnapped me."

"O, my dear boy, I am so sorry." She clasped her leathered hands. "It all had to happen so quickly, there was no time to explain." She shook her big head and *tsked*. "It is so dangerous in your sphere. So little room for error. I simply do not know how you survive in such a place. Those fast carriages!" She clasped her mammoth hand to her breast. "But forgive me! I am so excited to meet you, I forgot my manners. I know who you are, obviously, but I should introduce myself." The trol's red high heels clopped toward him and she bowed, her head two feet above Jack's. "I am Headmistress of the Locke Institute, Gerba Whipmarples."

Jack laughed. He couldn't help himself—the trol was ridiculous, too prim and precise for that gigantic body. He cut off the laugh, snorting it back into a cough. "Excuse me." He cleared his throat. "Gerba." He swallowed. She was being polite, the least he could do was respond in kind. "Pleasure to meet you."

She nodded delicately, dipping her horn.

Jack didn't know what to think of Gerba Whipmarples, or any of this. A trillion guesses ran through his head as he discarded one theory after another, finding it difficult to be suspicious of someone so polite. His recent imprisonment and Rooker's warnings still rang alarms in his head, but Jack had been kidnapped by a trol before. "I'm guessing you're Memphis Kubiak's sister."

"O, we are not all related because we are trols, dearie." Gerba smoothed her dress. "And no, Memphis Kubiak is of *much* better breeding than I. He is a mage. I know a bit of majik, but I am more of a scholar, myself. As I understand you are." She offered him an iced glass. "Cucumber water?"

Jack took it and drank. He eyed her over the rim. *Don't tell her your name. Don't tell her about Rooker. Don't tell her about anything. But get some answers.* "So. Why did you bring me here to..."

"Huánghūn, dearie." Gerba smiled prettily, or what passed for prettily on her monstrous face. "A lovely island, tropical and lush, you will enjoy it."

"And why did you bring me to Huánghūn..." Jack struggled not to laugh her name. "...Gerba?"

"Ah," she said, tilting her horn daintily. "It might be easier to explain up top. Would you care for some fresh air?"

Gerba Whipmarples led the way up a set of stairs, chatting pleasantly about the stonework, the tunnels, the workers. She took great pride in the aesthetic of the Locke Institute. Jack walked up a staircase to a clear blue sky and saw Huánghūn clearly for the first time.

He stood atop a thin rock butte a hundred feet high and eight miles long, a stone wall that divided the jungle from the sea.

The blue of the Irridin stretched on forever, split by a quarter-mile stone pier that jutted toward the ocean like a pointing finger. On the green side, a thick canopy of lush rainforest stretched as far as the eye could see. Above the jungle stood four gigantic palm trees, bizarre goliaths taller than California redwoods, that dwarfed the verdant jungle beneath them.

None of those things mattered. Jack's full attention was on the structure at the pinnacle of the cliff, the thing that took his breath away.

The Great Bell was big as an upended box truck, wide and fat-bottomed. Twenty feet tall, it resembled a Buddhist bonshō bell, suspended on two wooden pillars and hung from a gigantic crossbar.

Jack had seen one of them before. The power of the Great Bells was legendary. Blessed with healing majik, the bell would cure any injury, any ailment, any sickness. It granted instant health to anyone who heard it, a surgeon's dream. He'd seen it. He'd felt it. Jack felt his heart quicken. "Is that—"

Gerba Whipmarples spread one huge hand. "The Agrat-ban-Haifa, the Great Bell of the South." She smiled. "I thought seeing it might make you feel on more familiar footing, yes?"

A wave a nausea hit Jack out of nowhere. Maybe it was the strain of jumping between worlds, or the soured adrenaline pumping through his veins, or the pollution-free air of the tropical island. Maybe it was finding himself atop a hundred-foot cliff face with a talking rhino in a polka-dot dress. Whatever the reason, Jack toppled sideways as his knees dropped out from beneath him.

Gerba's huge brown hands caught him before he hit the ground. Jack could feel the warmth of her skin, the smoothness of her fingertips, the slow rhythmic beating of her football-sized heart. For a moment, Jack almost felt safe.

"O dear," came the rumble of her voice. "You *are* shaky. Such a cream-faced boy. Perhaps Mister Naysayer was too rough with you. Well, I have just the thing for that."

Gerba carried him toward the bell. As she walked, robed acolytes moved out of her path, bowing their heads. Jack's vision swam, his thoughts unfocused. He felt like a baby being brought down the church aisle for baptism.

The bell occupied the narrowest point of the ridge, a hundred-foot drop on either side. Gerba walked, unconcerned with the strong wind that threatened to topple them from the stone path. Arriving at the dais beneath the bell, the trol did not reach for the clapper but produced a tiny steel baton from her belt, held it delicately between her massive fingers, and gently rapped the bronze.

The sound was soft but reverberated to the marrow of Jack's bones. As the Agrat-ban-Haifa sung its low, solitary note, Jack felt the dart wound in his sternum close as if it had never been. Pink skin replaced it, tickling him. Jack closed his eyes and felt the healing majik of the bell wash over him. A dozen tiny scrapes and bruises across his body pulled shut. The headache behind his eyes disappeared. Even his *hair* felt invigorated. *Ahh.*

"Good, yes?"

Jack opened his eyes and stared at the bell. "It's like—" He paused, fumbling for the thought.

"Yes?"

Jack felt alive, like a child on a playground. "It looks like a prayer bell I saw in my dad's old videos. A monastery. In Tibet. Not nearly this big, but the shape...it had smaller bells, very heavy, hanging from chains around the rim. When the big bell rang, the smaller bells did too, and together they made a major chord, like a choir. It was beautiful." He shook his head. "Sorry. I got lost for a second."

"No, that sounds marvelous." Gerba smiled and lowered him to his feet, her sea-green eyes watching him kindly, almost lovingly. "Better?"

"Yes." Jack found his equilibrium, standing on his own. "Thank you."

"Now. Would you like me to address you as Black Jack? Or is that your..." She tapped a finger against her lips. "O, what is the word? I do try to study your sphere, it's from your French. *Nom de guerre?*"

Jack couldn't help but smile. "Just Jack is fine." *Don't tell 'em yer name.* He straightened, collecting himself. "I think it's time you told me why I'm here." He glanced at the bell. "Clearly you don't need me to heal anyone."

"Quite so. The Agrat-ban-Haifa makes your skill as a doktar somewhat irrelevant."

Jack couldn't help but be a bit hurt by that idea. "So what do you want from me?"

Gerba Whipmarples gestured to a stone bench. "Please, have a seat." Her considerable weight settled on the bench, legs crossed. "You are an intelligent man, a true genius." She spread her hands. "You talk to animals. You killed a jabberwok. You defeated the Fell Prince himself. My!" Jack found himself blushing. All those stories were half-true, an exaggeration of the facts, but Jack couldn't deny the pride filling his chest. Her sea-green eyes adored him. "You are a living legend. I apologize that you were injured on the way here. I would sooner shed my own blood than see a genius like you injured. All your wounds are healed now, I am sure?"

They were. Jack felt better than he had in months. He took a deep breath of ocean air. *Enough with the flattery.* "Gerba. Why did you bring me here?"

"I want you to be my teacher."

Jack's mouth opened. He didn't know what to say next, so he stood there and blinked. *What?*

"I am an academic, Jack. What you call a bookworm." Gerba ducked her horn, as if she were embarrassed. "I flatter myself to think I am a bit like you. I want to know everything that *can* be known. It is why I have studied so much about your sphere, your science, your tales, your songs. I know all the stories. The Pied Piper, the Tortoise and the Hare, the One Thousand and One Nights. Such colorful fables! And your people control so much. The earth, the sea, the air. You are masters of it all. But my people..." Her eyes dropped. "We do not possess such knowledge. We have rudimentary tools. Wheels. Fire. Steel. We are like children, with a child's intellect. We do not think." She sighed. "Knowledge. Health. Safety. These are but dreams to us. But you..." Gerba Whipmarples' sea-green eyes fell on him. "You can change all that."

Jack settled back on the bench, eyeing her. She was right. Keymark was a backward place, not much past the Middle Ages, powered by majik and simple machines. Pulleys, wheels, axles. No clocks. No eyeglasses. No printing press. Gerba Whipmarples' world was truly primitive. Jack felt a thrill go through his belly. *The things I could teach them...*

"All I ask is that you help me." She leaned in. "I will pay you whatever you like, for as long as you are willing, and take whatever instruction you will offer. I do not know if I will be able to understand your science, but if you would be willing to help me, I will do my best to learn your ways."

Jack hesitated. It was too much to digest, too vast an idea to wrap his head around. "Gerba, I don't—"

She held up a hand. "And I promise, when we are done, I will return you to the exact time and place you left the Tosh, so you do not miss out on *one moment* of your life there."

Jack stared at her. He couldn't come up with a single argument why it wasn't a perfect offer.

She looked at him, hopeful. "Please."

Jack pulled at his lower lip, thinking, cautious. "What do you want to know?"

Gerba's eyes sparkled like a child with a new toy. "May I show you?"

The vault door was made of iron, round, and nearly as tall as the trol. Built into the terminus of a hallway behind Gerba's study, the thing had no visible locks or bolts. Embedded in the side of the vault door was a round emerald the size of Jack's head. It glowed softly, radiating a gentle pulse of the *wikk*. Jack heard Gerba whisper something to the emerald and the vault door opened, rolling away with a rumble. "Please," said Gerba. "Come look."

Jack stepped inside. Incandescent crystals embedded in the ceiling sensed their presence and blossomed to shimmering light. The stone room was filled with barrels, boxes, and crates. The top of one was open and Jack saw the glint of silver coins inside. Several tapestries were rolled up against the wall, along with a varied assortment of tablets, scrolls, ledgers, and charts. A rack of odd-looking vials stood covered in dust, along with a head-sized jar containing some kind of murky green liquid.

"This is very exciting for me," Gerba tittered. "I have studied your sphere for so long. But this is the first time I have been in possession of some of your magnificent tools." She sifted through a box. "Mister Naysayer scouted your institute a few days ago in preparation for your jaunt and brought me back some marvelous artifacts. Such mysteries. Such potential." Gerba carefully plucked out an item. "This, for example."

Jack leaned in, curious. *What does she have? A phone? A laptop? A book?*

Gerba Whipmarples held a small black object in her hands, her eyes excited. "It comes alive when you do this." Her huge thumb flipped a trigger, and a low *brrrr* began to tremble in her hands, humming. "Isn't that amazing? Can you help me understand it? Is it angry? Is it hungry?"

It's ridiculous. Jack laughed. He tried to stop but couldn't. *A talking rhino shanghaied me to another universe to help her understand—*

"An electric razor."

The look on Gerba's face was priceless. "A razor?" Stunned eyes ogled the thing in her hands. "But it is not sharp."

"Right," Jack chuckled. "That's the idea, you can't cut yourself with it. Here." He took the Norelco and pulled it across the hair on his forearm with a buzz, leaving a strip of bare skin down the middle. "Like that."

"O, that is marvelous!" Gerba laughed.

Jack chuckled, shaking his head. *If you think that's something Gerba, wait until you see an internal combustion engine.* "You should turn that off, you'll wear out the battery."

"What is—" She fumbled with the Norelco until the thing turned off with a sharp *klak*. "What is a battering?"

"Battery. It's like a little power supply." Off her puzzled look, Jack tried to come up with a medieval analogy for a battery. "Like a coiled spring." According to Gerba's face, that didn't help. "It's... like..." *A millwheel? A forge fire? A lightning bolt?* He gave up. "It's like majik."

She nodded, satisfied. "Impressive. A majik razor." She glanced at him, then corrected herself. "A *science* razor." She stood up. "May I show you a few more things?"

Before he could answer, the trol rifled through another box. Jack peered under her arm and saw an assortment of school supplies, satchels, a soccer ball, and a jacket emblazoned with a Walter Payton High Grizzly. Then he saw—

"My backpack." His blue JanSport bag rested near the top of the box. He snatched it and reached inside, searching.

Gerba frowned. "Is there something I can assist—"

Jack dumped the bag upside down. Its contents spilled over the vault floor. Campbell's *Biology* tumbled next to his American History textbook. His laptop clattered out with a pack of C-cell rockets for chemistry lab. Some graph paper. His phone.

"Where's Nepenthe?"

Something changed in Gerba's face. She stopped cold, her eyes wide. "I beg your pardon?"

Nepenthe. Where is Nepenthe? Jack felt panic in his voice. "It's a piece of bamboo, with designs along the sides. It's not in my bag."

Gerba's voice was suddenly low, almost reverential. "Everyone in Keymark knows Nepenthe. You have it *here?*"

Jack could feel anger creeping into his voice. "No, that's what I'm saying, it's gone! Your thug stole it from me!"

"Jack." Gerba's voice was suddenly cold and formal. She straightened to her full height. "I will ask you to keep a civil tone while you are my guest." Jack stared up at her, suddenly reminded the trol could pound him to paste any time she wanted. He swallowed.

The headmistress folded massive arms over her polka-dot bodice. "Mister Naysayer would not have taken anything from your bag without my permission. So, either there is some mistake"—Jack opened his mouth, but she raised a hand—"or some misunderstanding." She nodded her head with an air of finality. "I will get to the bottom of this, I assure you. In the meantime, you will come with me."

Without another word, Gerba Whipmarples put her arm around his shoulder and led him out of the vault. Jack considered resisting, but her arm was thick as a tree trunk. She escorted him through the halls and into a small antechamber near her library, a cozy study with a little fire going in the hearth. "You will wait here." She seemed to remember herself, softening her tone. "Please." She smiled and spread her hands. "I will feel better if you are somewhere safe while I am gone."

"Safe?" Jack eyed the headmistress. "This is a school. What kind of school isn't safe?"

"The *majik* kind." She smiled sweetly. "Do not worry dearie, everything will be fine. You and I are going to become great friends." Gerba Whipmarples smiled and closed the door.

Jack breathed through his nose and listened to her footsteps pad down the hall.

Okay, what the hell just happened? Gerba Whipmarples seemed entirely in control, used to getting her way, and certain of what she wanted. His hostess hadn't threatened him or demanded anything; she had offered to pay him. In addition, Gerba had volunteered to find Nepenthe, and she had healed him with the Great Bell. All that, and her manners were impeccable.

Jack wasn't sure if he was being naïve or if Rooker was being paranoid.

It wouldn't be the first time he was wrong.

He waited until the trol's footsteps disappeared. He turned the door handle, hoping for a peek outside.

The door didn't budge. He twisted the knob harder. Nothing. She had locked him in.

Jack heard Rooker's bitter laugh in his head.

Chapter

5

DETENTION
HALL

I could carve a better man out of a banana.
Teddy Roosevelt

ater splashed Rooker's face like a wet slap.
His black eye stung as the water hit, and he shook his head back and forth, whipping wet hair out of his eye, plastering half of it to his face. Dripping, he glared at the man with the bucket. The veiled figure had taken him from his cell, never uttering a word. As he walked away, Rooker heard him speak for the first time. "That should take care of the smell."

Rooker fingered the iron manacles around his wrists. He was chained to a bench in a large stone room. Daylight streamed in from a domed cupola above. Ignoring him like he wasn't there, a crew of hammerdwarves worked the stone, *tink-tink-tinking* with their tools. They were busy transforming the big empty space into an official-looking hall, working the raw stone into more respectable shapes. The half-finished room was outfitted only with his stone bench in the center. Against the wall, a flat-front desk sat like a hulking beast, raised on a dais inscribed with the emblem of the Inquisition.

That's bad news.

Rooker turned at the sound of a footstep. An impossibly tall figure stepped into a shaft of light, his face a blank mask.

Of the troika that made up the Naysayer Brothers, Wont was the biggest, Shant was the sneakiest, but Cant Naysayer was the brains, and the most lethal of the three. The beanpole was still dressed in the same outfit Rooker had seen him in three years ago, when he'd single-handedly taken down Jawbone Kreel. *That long, no-color duster, that half-mask, and that ridiculous gambler's hat.*

"Hello, Flynn," came the rattlesnake voice that gave Rooker chills every time he heard it. "Where's the dog?"

"With yer mom," Rooker growled. "He heard she gives out free treats with every bone."

Black widow spiders suddenly appeared on Rooker's legs. He jerked away but the chains held him fast. He felt panic rise in his throat as he watched them crawl toward his crotch. Cant's blue eyes smiled. "You still have that nasty mouth."

They're not real, they're not real. Rooker knew Cant used illusion majik to terrify his prey, but it was difficult to ignore poisonous bugs crawling up his body. He spat, forcing himself to focus. "And yer still too ugly to take off that mask."

"I'm not the one with a black eye chained to a bench." Cant waved his hand and the spiders dissipated into smoke.

"Ya don't need these, do ya?" Rooker held up his manacles. "Yer a big-deal warlock, right? What're ya worried about, Cant? Do I scare ya that much?"

"I can roast you alive while you're sitting there," said Cant. "But if I do that I don't get paid."

Rooker felt a breeze come in through the cupola, bringing a whiff of sea air with it. He inhaled through his nose, drawing it in. His brows furrowed together. The smell was wrong. *We're too far south. Way too far. On the very edge of the world, out where things get weird.*

Tink-tink-tink was replaced by *tok-tok-tok* as the sound of bootsteps came like a metronome from somewhere down the hallway, echoing in the stone chamber. Hammerdwarves set down their tools and exited quietly, leaving Rooker alone in the room with the bounty hunter. *Tok-tok-tok.* Cant grabbed Rooker's chain and hauled him to his feet. "Stand in honor."

The bootsteps maintained their steady pace as a young woman emerged from the shadows. She wore a white blindfold over her eyes, bearing a set of perfectly balanced iron scales. Rooker wasn't surprised to see she was wearing Inquisition robes. *Well that answers that.*

"Heya, judge." Rooker cocked his finger at her. "Let me save the Inquisition some time." He spread his hands and flashed his best smile. "Ya got the wrong man."

The silent woman settled the balanced scales on her desk. Rooker knew she could see through the majiked Inquisition blindfold, but it still was unnerving to watch her move with such cold precision. Her thin fingers placed a small stone on either side of the scale. They counterbalanced, swaying back and forth, until they found equilibrium. When she spoke, her tone was flat, thin, and sharp, the very voice of dispassionate jurisprudence.

"Release."

Rooker's manacles fell free and clattered to the floor. *Dammit.* He rubbed his wrists. *They want me to go for him. Or her. Must have more muscle outside. Maybe I could go out the window.* He glanced at Cant and saw the bounty hunter finger the little handbow at his belt. *Yep. He wants me to run.* Rooker cocked his head and eyed the inquisitor. "Okay, lady. What ya got?"

The judge sat rigid, her mouth pursed like she'd eaten a rotten lime. Her loud voice filled the empty room. "You are the pilot of the outlaw vessel *Venture Brigand*, Rooker Flynn."

"*Captain* Rooker Flynn."

"My documents list you as pilot."

"Captain," Rooker repeated.

The inquisitor shook her head. "Dagan Saltz was captain until the incident at Rimmy's Cull."

"I tossed Saltz overboard the day before." Rooker stood tall. "Righteous mutiny. The *Brigand* is mine."

"Incorrect," the inquisitor snapped. "The *Venture Brigand* is registered property of Cant Naysayer."

Rooker's head whipsawed to Cant, his eyes livid. *"Thief!"*

The bounty hunter kept his face hidden beneath his stupid hat. His voice had all the humor of a years-dead corpse. "Legal salvage. Abandoned." Cant raised his head, revealing icy blue eyes. "By you."

Rooker barely stopped himself from launching a fist at the bounty hunter. The thought of Cant Naysayer in possession of his girl was unthinkable, insulting. "She don't belong to ya."

"It certainly doesn't belong to *you*."

Rooker glared at Cant. *Think. What's the smart play? What would Jack do?* He snorted. *Probably ask a bunch of stupid questions.* "Where is she?"

Confused, the inquisitor tilted her head. "Who?"

"The *Venture Brigand*."

"Irrelevant."

"What about my sword?"

"Ah, yes. The cutlass."

"Saber."

"Entered into evidence." She reached under the table, revealing the sharkskin scabbard that housed the singing saber. Rooker felt a pang of jealousy as the inquisitor's fingers closed around the grip and pulled the blade halfway free. Bessie hummed her low tune, vibrating three feet of curved steel, eager for violence. The judge appraised the weapon, staring at it from behind the blindfold. "This is not of elvish make."

"Nah. Just a mean hunka steel." The blade had been cursed by the same sea-witch who tried to kill Saltz. *Maybe the curse is rubbing off on me. Can't catch a scrap of luck.*

The inquisitor leaned in. "How many people have you murdered with it?"

Rooker scowled and bit his lower lip.

"Continuing." The inquisitor's thin lips parted as she brought up her quill. "Please state your true name."

Rooker looked at the inquisitor, then at Cant. *They're gonna sing this song whether I like it or not.* He took a quick step toward the judge's desk and enjoyed watching her flinch. "Captain Rooker Flynn."

"Your *true* name?"

Rooker grinned, his eyes sharp. *Who do ya think yer dealing with lady?* In the singsong voice of a lying seven-year-old, he said sweetly: "That *is* my true name yer honor."

The inquisitor's sigh was masterful, a true work of art. "State your true name and this can go better for you."

"Captain." He took a step. "Rooker." He took one more. "Flynn."

"Fine. Rooker Flynn. Pilot." She frowned and made a mark with her quill. "Aged twenty years."

Rooker didn't have any idea how old he was, but apparently his birth had been recorded somewhere. *Twenty years old. Seems longer than that.* "Sure, why not?"

The inquisitor leaned back in her chair. "One more question, Mister Flynn. Are you or are you not a confederate of Black Jack?" She lifted her chin. "Our records indicate you are his manservant."

Manservant? Rooker felt his blood steam. *Manservant? He's my lackey, not the other way around.* Rooker opened his mouth to say so, then remembered where he was. *She's trying to get under my skin so I talk. Don't be stupid.* "Who?"

The judge slumped in her chair, exasperated. "Mister Flynn. Every man, woman, and child in Keymark has heard of Black Jack."

"*Captain* Flynn." He grinned. "I thought Black Jack was long dead."

"Mister Flynn. You are a known associate of the most wanted outlaw in Keymark. I have been given the authority to lessen your punishment if you are willing to cooperate with the Inquisition on this matter."

Rooker raised an eyebrow. *A reduced sentence?* "In exchange for what?"

"His true name."

Rooker scowled. Asking an outlaw's true name was an old game, older than the Inquisition. But this was the first time he'd been asked for someone else's. *I don't remember what his surname is. Jack...Speed? Jack Quick? Something fast.* It didn't matter. Rooker wouldn't turn rat for the Inquisition. "I don't think I know the man."

"Very well, I shall pronounce your sentence." She stood, her back straight, her voice sharp. "Rooker Flynn, you have been tried *in absentia* and found guilty of the following crimes upon the Irridin and associated bays, gulfs, and straights. *Ahm.* Smuggling, bootlegging, trafficking contraband, fraud, blackmail, forgery, arson, extortion, kidnapping, graft, harboring wanted men, bribery of a city official, cat burglary, intentional scuttling of seventeen ships, impersonating a priest, stealing twenty-six pigs..." She finally took a breath. "Operating a city-owned crane without a permit, camel rustling, misuse of community sewage, commandeering a ship of the royal navy, and bringing a woman on board a Ysterian vessel. Multiple counts of plunder, pillage, and piracy."

"And I looked damn good doin' it." Rooker cocked a grin. *When they got yer number, might as well smile.*

"The punishment for all of these crimes combined is eighty-three life sentences and thirteen sentences of death."

Rooker shrugged, casual as a cat. "Unlucky number. Better wait until we hit fourteen."

"Hereby sentenced." The inquisitor took one of the stones from the scale and rapped it smartly on the desk with authority. "Justice always."

Though he gave no outward sign, Rooker felt the weight of that stone like a boulder on his chest. *Prison. Again.* The thirteen death sentences didn't bother him much; they were rarely carried out unless someone wanted to make an example. But the loss of his freedom felt like a knife in the heart.

Cant Naysayer approached the bench. "My reward?"

The inquisitor nodded. "Seventy-five thousand marks, minus fifteen percent for the Institute." She handed the bounty hunter a slip of parchment. "Take this to the bursar to collect your payment."

Rooker scowled at Cant. "I hope ya choke on it."

"Your bounty?" Cant chuckled. "That's chicken feed. We got a million for your pal Jack."

Rooker balked. *A million marks?* Black Jack, the real one, had robbed the nobles blind way back in the day; every fief in Keymark had placed a bounty on his head. *Some of those warrants must be a hundred years old.* Still. A million marks. *He's not worth more than me.*

Rooker felt a heavy hand on his shoulder and turned to find Wont Naysayer behind him. His black eye flinched involuntarily and the ape smiled. "Anytime you want to escape again, feel free."

Shant's beak poked from the shadows. "You're easy money."

Cant walked away through the shafts of light streaming down from the cupola. "I won't be seeing you again, Flynn." His brothers joined him, one on each side. "But know that when I'm done with that piece of junk you call the *Venture Brigand*, I'm going to run her aground and burn her to the waterline to make sure there's no trace of you left in the world."

Sonofabitch is enjoying this. Rooker wouldn't give them the satisfaction. "Just know that when I get her back, I'm gonna keel-haul ya from one end of the Irridin to the other."

"Make sure you get to bed early, Flynn," Cant called over his shoulder. "The Institute isn't the kind of place to get caught in the dark." The trio chuckled, their laughter echoing down the stone corridor long after they were gone.

Rooker popped his neck. *Okay. Time to go to work.*

"Hey judge." He offered the inquisitor his most dazzling smile, the one that never failed to work with the ladies. "Where I come from there's always a little...*wiggle-room* when it comes to serving time." The inquisitor's blindfolded face stared at him. She looked as interested as a rock.

Never met a judge who couldn't be bought. "Hey, I get how things work. Everything's negotiable, right?" She stared blankly ahead in silence. "Hey!" *Nothing.* Rooker snorted, looking around the empty room. He took a deep breath and hollered at the top of his lungs. "Who do I have to bribe to get outta this turkey farm?!"

"Me."

Rooker's eyes narrowed as a figure appeared in the doorframe. The silhouette was huge, bigger than Wont. Three long horns sprouted from its snout. As the creature stepped into the daylight, Rooker saw it wore a polka-dotted dress. A trol.

Rooker frowned. Trols were the worst when it came to bribes. Brownbellies *loved* rules. Law. Order. They had only one way of doing things and you can bet your last penny it was written down in a big book somewhere. Rooker scowled at the woman. *The odds of me buying my way out of this just went overboard with an anchor around their neck.*

"And you are...?"

"My name is Gerba Whipmarples, dearie."

Rooker stifled a laugh. *That stupid dress makes her look like a five-year-old. She should have a lollipop.*

"Look, Whipmarples." He cleared his throat. "I'm sure we can come to an arrangement."

"I agree completely." Gerba tittered, bubbling merrily as a mountain stream. "You will be happy to know I have already dismissed your death sentences."

Rooker felt a smile curl over his face. "Well, there we go. A reasonable woman." *Okay, this is someone I can work with.* "So. Gerba baby. How much do ya need to let me go?"

"O, we have not gotten to that point in our relationship yet, dearie." She tittered under one hand. "But the time will come, rest assured."

Mmph. She has to make a show of it. Fine.

Rooker had been a prisoner for two months in Xucong Gulag; it wasn't so bad. Three hots and a cot. He'd broken out strapped to the underside of an offal cart. He'd served three weeks in Misan River. The dungeon wasn't bad but the food there was terrible, little chunks of meat in the stew, all boiled grey. *If they send me up the River, at least I know which palms to grease.* Hanger House had only kept him two days before he literally just walked out the front door. *Maybe I'll get lucky and end up back there.* "So where am I gonna to serve my stretch, darlin'?"

She smiled prettily; at least, it *would* have been prettily if she had been pretty. "Why here, silly. You have been remanded to my custody."

Here? There aren't any prisons this far south. There's nothing this far south. "Here as in..."

"The Locke Institute."

Institute? Rooker lowered an eyebrow. "Sounds like a school."

"It is." She clapped like a little girl. "That is *exactly* what it is, Mister Flynn. We are going to teach you a trade, we are going to teach you to work, we are going to teach you to mind your manners...everything you need to become a useful, productive member of society."

"Reform school." He chuckled. *She's gonna teach me to be a good little boy.* "And where exactly is the Locke Institute, Gerba?" Prisons he knew, schools, not so much. "We're on the Precipice Archipelago, obviously, but which island?"

She smiled. "Huánghūn."

Rooker barked a surprised laugh. *She's crazy. This whole place is crazy.* "Huánghūn? Pull the other leg, sweetheart, this one's had enough. Where are we *really?*"

Gerba lowered her head, three horns lowering with it. They were engraved with strange etchings, decorated in gold chains, and swung too close to his chest. "O, Mister Flynn, I do not like repeating myself. I speak very clearly, I make certain of it."

She's not serious. "Huánghūn is uninhabitable." He frowned. "Everyone in the Deep Blue South knows that."

"Uninhabitable?" The polka-dotted trol stepped closer to him, her long horn nearly at his neck. "And why, do you think, is that?"

"Because it's overrun with spid—"

Something came through the open door behind Gerba Whipmarples. At first, Rooker thought it was a thick tree branch covered with spiky hair. Then it bent, like a knee, reached above the floor and attached to the stone with a *click*. Another branch followed, then another, coming through the door one at a time until four tree-sized legs splayed up the wall. A brown-furred head emerged. Eight black eyes. A mouthful of fangs.

A tarantula the size of a horse crawled up the wall.

Rooker stifled a scream. His flesh shivered with revulsion, every sinew in his body wanted to *kill it, kill it or run!*

His eyes searched for Bessie, but the inquisitor had locked the saber away. She sat in her chair motionless, blindfold fixed in place, ignoring the horror that crawled above her. The thing's hairy legs passed inches from her head.

Rooker ran.

Something hit his ankle and he collapsed. He spun to find a sticky sheet of webbing bound his feet to the floor.

"Overrun with what, dearie?" asked Gerba Whipmarples. The tarantula moved along the wall, touched the ground, and strode toward Rooker. He fell backward against the bench. As the spider passed the trol, her thick fingers brushed the spider's fur, stroking it like a beloved pet. "*Do* go on."

It passed by her, making a throaty *kek-kek-kek* sound as it came. Bound by webs, Rooker could do nothing but watch the thing come, its fangs scissoring against each other like knitting needles.

Gerba stepped forward and steepled her fingers. "That is the difficulty with little people like you, Mister Flynn. You *think* you know things. You think you know Huánghūn is uninhabitable. You think you know who you can rob and get away with it. You think you are important." She shook her head and *tsked.* "I am going to fix you. It may take a year. It may take twenty. But by the time I am done, you will know the truth." She leaned in and whispered in his ear. "You simply do not matter."

Webbing smashed against his face, sealing his mouth shut. Terrified, he tried to scrape it off but only succeeded in binding his hands in sticky gossamer. Another webline hit his ankles and he was reeled into the air by a second tarantula inside the cupola above. Rooker flipped upside down and dangled above the floor like a pig for slaughter.

Gerba Whipmarples ambled forward, her hands behind her back. The brooch at her collar glimmered ruby red in the shafts of sunlight. She came nose to nose with him, smiling her sweet smile. "I only have one question for you, Mister Flynn. Everyone we interviewed said you were a compatriot of Black Jack. A *friend.*" She said the word like it was poisonous. "Perhaps you believe that as well. But let me ask you this..." She tilted her head. "If he is your friend, why has he been lying to you?"

Rooker's eyes narrowed, but he couldn't make a sound with the webs gagging his mouth shut.

Gerba cocked her head and stroked the spider by her side. "Winston, I think our new student might still have a little fight left in him. Please show him the punishment for fighting here at the Institute."

The tarantula made a noise that sounded like a chuckle, a low gurgling *kek-kek-kek*. "You got it boss."

Rooker's eyes went wide. *Did it just talk?*

Winston's fangs plunged into Rooker's belly.

He screamed. He felt the fangs in his stomach, felt them moving inside of him, felt their poison flooding his gut. He gagged on the webbing and screamed again.

"No more fighting for you, Mister Flynn," Gerba wagged a finger at him as he was dragged up into the cupola, wrapped tight as a fly waiting to be sucked dry. "It is high time you learned to mind your betters."

Chapter

6

=PRIMARY= EDUCATION

There is now less flogging in our great schools than formerly, but then less is learned there; so that what the boys get at one end they lose at the other.

Samuel Johnson

Jack Swift could not sleep. Outside his window, Keymark's two moons shone, one pale, one orange, one waxing, one waning. Double moonlight filtered through thick clouds as warm winds blew from the sea. He could hear the Irridin faintly, waves brushing against the far side of the butte, muffled by a hundred million pounds of stone. Below his window, a jungle denser and lusher than the Amazon rainforest lay silent, holding its breath.

The darkness should have been a cacophony of sound. Keymark was a wild and untamed land, especially at night. Nocturnal animals should have called out to each other, looking for mates, looking for prey. There should be primates, amphibians, mammals, and birds. Nightjars, nighthawks, whip-poor-wills, frogmouths, oilbirds, potoos, even a damned owl. But no.

Nothing.

It takes time to notice something is missing. If you're not looking for it, nothing can be easy to miss. When Jack realized it, it was a slap to the face.

Where are the pixies?

On his last visit to Keymark, the air had been rife with little flying angels barely bigger than dragonflies. They were everywhere, bearers of the *wikk* that breathed life into Keymark's majik. They should have been drawn by the Agrat-ban-Haifa, feeding from its majik. But when clouds blotted out the moonlight and darkened the jungle black as pitch, Jack could not find one pixie-light. In the jungle, nothing moved. Nothing, at least, that could be seen.

A cold shiver ran down Jack's spine.

He got up, abandoning any hope of sleep. He paced the eleven steps from one side of the room to the other, crisscrossing his path a hundred times before the sun finally cracked the horizon. *Bird in a gilded cage.* He paced, pulling his bottom lip. *Gerba Whipmarples didn't bring you here to identify a Norelco.*

So what does she want?

All that talk and she didn't tell you a damn thing. What do you know? If this is a school, where are the students? All you've seen is servants and builders. It's like there's nobody here.

He pulled his lip harder.

You need to find Rooker.

A knock on the door startled him, followed by the sound of an acolyte's singsong voice. "Breakfast is served!"

"Good morning, young man! I hope you slept well!"

Gerba sat in a huge chair in front of a massive table filled with fruits, steaming hot bread, orange marmalade, sizzling bacon fresh from the pan, decanters of juices and milk, and a bowl full of buttery macadamia chocolate spread.

"Can you smell that?" She extended her hand at the large window. "The freshest air you have ever tasted!" This was the same library room Jack had seen yesterday, but the curtains were thrown wide over the jungle. Half the mahogany desk was covered with a long white sheet, the other half dressed for a tropical breakfast.

Jack couldn't smell anything but the bacon.

Gerba got up and offered her chair, a huge stone thing with six legs and two wide arms. "Come. Sit."

He did. As he settled himself into the chair, Jack felt it shift beneath him. The stone flowed like water, taking on a shape more suited for him, positioning him at the perfect height at the table. It scooted forward, bringing him closer to the meal. "That's an interesting trick."

"Ah, yes. A gift from an old friend of mine. Strawberries?" She used a dainty pair of tongs to place some on his plate. Jack realized he was starving, ate the strawberry, then chased it with a hunk of bacon. Chewing, he glanced at Gerba. Today's dress was a frilly coral-colored number with enough crinoline to stuff a Mazda. Her lips were painted in a nearly matching fuchsia, with complimentary jewelry on her collar, neck, ears, and horns. She looked like a pink nightmare. "I do hope you slept well."

Jack cleared his throat and kept his eyes on his food. "Did you find Nepenthe?"

"O, I nearly forgot, I am so sorry, dearie." A sympathetic look came into her eyes. "No, unfortunately your Nepenthe did not make the journey with you to Keymark." Her mouth turned to a small pout. "I would have dearly liked to see it. Its powers are legendary."

"Cant Naysayer took it from me." Jack controlled his voice. "It was just one piece of the seven, but he took it."

"Are you certain? The jaunt can have a strange effect on memory. Things tend to get a bit...fuzzy."

"I had it with me."

"Well," Gerba dabbed her lips with a napkin the size of a hotel towel. "There does not seem to be anything we can do about it now. Have you tried the apple tart? They are delectable."

Kidnap me, shoot me, steal from me. Just don't lie to me. Jack straightened his jaw. "Will any other students be joining us for breakfast?"

She giggled, delicately covering her mouth. "O no, they are such busy bees from sunup to sundown." She gestured to the room around her. "This is my study, students eat below. Have some fish."

Jack cleared his throat. He had thought all night about how to ask the question without revealing the crack in the wall, but he needed answers. "And will Rooker Flynn be joining us for breakfast?"

"I do not believe he will," she piped merrily. "Marmalade?"

Jack set down his silver fork. *Enough. Stop pretending.* "Gerba." He leaned forward, feeling the chair adjust beneath him. "I would *like* Rooker to join us."

Gerba placed her silverware delicately on either side of her plate. "Are you upset, dearie? Missing home already? Not enough sleep?"

"Where is he?"

She popped a grape in her gigantic mouth. "Well, if you must know, I have not seen him recently. I believe he is being sent down today."

"Sent down to what?"

"Why the school, of course, silly! You *are* such a Grumpy Gus in the morning. O! I know what would cheer you up. Marguerite!"

A silk-robed acolyte appeared from behind Jack like a ghost. Jack felt the chair spin slowly underneath him as she folded back the sheet and revealed the loot from Walter Payton High. Each item was marked and labeled like an archaeology exhibit. Phones, laptops, textbooks, tablets, notepads, headphones, fidget toys, sweatshirts, ball caps, car keys, a can of soda, pencils, pens, spare erasers and wadded up receipts.

"A touch of home, yes?" Gerba smiled. "Just the thing to perk you up." She rose, cleared her dress, and stepped to the display. "So many fascinating mysteries! I must confess, I am eager to learn what you will teach me." She picked up a phone, and Jack recognized the yellow GOTCHA sticker. *That's mine.*

"So many flat rectangles. And when I touch them...look!" The phone's home screen lit up, displaying a picture of Jack and his dad at a Bears game. "It's a little painting of you!"

Jack was not amused. All he knew was that he didn't want to play this game anymore.

Gerba fiddled with a laptop. "And this one opens like a book, but it has no pages. What does it do?" She set it down and picked up a Rubix cube, turning it over in her massive hands. "And this! A clever little puzzle-box! Is there a secret inside?" She set the thing down and faced Jack, bouncing on her toes like a little girl who could not wait for Christmas. "So many secrets! Are they valuable? Are they Toshan weapons? Treasure? Knowledge? I am so eager for you to teach me...everything!"

Jack scowled. He wasn't going to tell Gerba Whipmarples a damn thing. Not until he got some answers. He just had no idea how to go about getting them. *What would Rooker do? Probably be a cocky bastard.*

Jack folded his arms. "I don't think I'm going to answer any questions until I get Nepenthe back and Rooker up here."

Gerba's mouth soured to a disappointed moue. "O, please do not say things like that, dearie. We have so many exciting mysteries to explore together."

"You want me to help you? Then give me what I want."

"I am so sorry, dearie. But what you want is simply not possible."

"Then I'm done," Jack said. "You said I could help you as long as I wanted, then you'd send me home. Well I think I'm done helping you."

For the first time, one of Gerba's manicured eyebrows lowered into the barest hint of a frown, a crack in her armor. She blinked, then pearly pink lips curled back into a smile. "My dearest Jack, I think it would be best if you reconsidered."

Whatever last hope Jack had that Gerba Whipmarples would be true to her word disappeared like the carbonated spray of a soda can, atomized to nothing. *She's not going to send me home.*

Once hope was gone, he found it much easier to pretend he was Rooker. "My dearest Gerba," he mimicked her. "It's almost as if I can't trust you."

Her lips pursed. "Well, dearie." She spread her hands. "It is not as if I can trust you. After all, you *are* a criminal." She came closer and Jack was reminded of how massive she was. "I will give you one more opportunity to change your mind, doktar. I would appreciate your considerate assistance."

Jack squared his jaw. "I don't think so."

"Ah." Gerba fingered the brooch at her collar and frowned, a crooked line disfiguring her face. "Pity."

Jack's chair collapsed.

It did not fall over, it *collapsed,* folding in on itself, the stone turned to cold, hard liquid. Jack fell and the amorphous rock caught him, hardening around his body, gripping his thighs, wrists, and neck. He strained against it, but couldn't move, bound in stone.

Gerba waved one hand idly. Jack heard a sighing sound from several places around the room. He had spent enough time in Keymark to recognize the soft creak of a bowstring being relaxed. A dozen of them. He glimpsed a few acolytes between the upper bookshelves as they stood down.

Gerba sipped from her teacup, one pinky up. "Strip him, please."

The stone became rough. Sharpened edges dug into his skin. Jack tried to pull away but there was nowhere to go. The chair twisted around him, tearing his shirt, his pants, his flesh. He screamed as the chair rotated, shredding his clothes off, spitting them out into a pile of strips riddled with little drops of blood.

Naked and bound, cold stone prickled across Jack's flesh. *O God.*

"O goodness gracious, look at *you.*" Gerba touched her brooch and the chair flipped Jack over like a dead fish. He felt the trol's meaty fingers touch his back, tracing the four long burned scars, the ones he was glad he never had to see, the wounds even a Great Bell could never heal.

"Dæmon claws," came her quiet voice. "You *have* had an adventure or two, haven't you?" Jack winced as she touched them. "And it was such pretty skin, too. Well, that will make this easier."

Jack swallowed as the stone flipped him back over. He faced her, eyes wide, and started to hyperventilate. "Wait. Stop. Gerb—"

"*Oop!* No, no." She raised her finger like she was scolding a kindergartener. "Talking time is over."

Jack felt a tentacle of stone jam into his mouth. He thrashed back and forth, screams muffled against the immovable solidity of it. His teeth clicked on it as the living rock forced its way to the back of his throat, opening his jaws. Gagging, he could only suck air through his nose.

"I did have such high hopes, Jack." Gerba plucked her earrings off. "Although I am an optimist, so there always hope for tomorrow! Now. There are only three rules here at the Locke Institute... ah, thank you, Sun Hee." An acolyte arrived with a tray. It was shallow and filled with three things: steaming hot water, an upside-down glass cup, and a little wood-handled scalpel.

"You are a doktar, so you are familiar with cupping, I presume. A tool of your trade, yes?" She picked up the scalpel. "You may feel a slight pinch."

Jack's eyes went wide as Gerba slit his wrist.

It was impossible to scream with a stone fist in his throat, so Jack was forced to watch silently as blood sprayed from the cut, pumping arterial red.

Gerba plucked the glass cup from the steaming water and placed its mouth against his arm. The heat created a vacuum, suctioning against his skin. Jack watched, still unable to make a sound, as his blood geysered into the glass ball.

The stone tentacle sealed over Jack's nose and that was the end of oxygen.

"Now, do I have your attention?" Gerba's sea-green eyes watched him. "Good. There are only three rules of the Locke Institute." She raised a finger. "Rule One: Mind Your Betters." She tilted her horn, watching him like a stray dog. "You have already displayed a lack of respect for authority, so this may be difficult for you. But believe me, if you obey, you will have a much more rewarding experience. Do you understand?"

Tears streamed down Jack's cheeks as he strained against the stone, fighting against the immovable forces slowly killing him. His chest bucked, begging for air. He nodded.

"Very good. Now, normally we use a straight razor, but since we have this..." A sharp buzz erupted by Jack's ear and he watched a hunk of his hair fall to the floor. *The Norelco.*

"O that *does* work a trick," Gerba tittered. Another buzz and a wad of hair drifted past his eyes. "Look at that. Such marvelous inventions. We make it a policy to shave all jaelin before they're enrolled. Lice, you know. Since you humans are *so* similar to jaelin; we shall maintain the same policy." Jack Swift felt the Norelco dig into the side of his head again, again, again.

Deprived of air, Jack felt his head go light.

"Rule Two: Gather at Sunrise." Gerba ran the razor over his scalp. "Community is important. This is how we hold the bonds of society together. We do not want stragglers or outliers or malcontents, none of *those* people, you know? You are here to learn your lessons. Now, to save you some confusion, sunrise on Huánghūn is the moment the sun appears over the top of the Institute wall. This gives you a bit of extra time to get ready in the mornings. Understand?"

Losing blood and oxygen, Jack saw stars. His vision narrowed to slits; black crept in around the edges. His skin began to turn blue as brain cells died by the thousands.

"Stay with me. You humans have such tiny lungs." She clucked her tongue. "Rule Three: Be Inside by Sunset. This is, of course, for your own safety. There are many dangers on Huánghūn from which I will protect you. The jungle can be a hostile environment, and it is in your own self-interest to remain inside after dark. I do not want anything to happen to you, so please follow this rule carefully. I do not like repeating myself, but I will: Be Inside by Sunset."

Jack spasmed. He stared at nothing with bloodshot eyes.

Gerba smiled. "Lovely. That should do, Sun Hee."

The acolyte nodded and removed the cup from his arm. It came loose with a wet sucking noise as Sun Hee covered it with a lid and trapped the blood inside. She placed it carefully on the table as Jack's wrist continued to pump blood.

Gerba spread her hands, smiling. "And that is everything you need to know to succeed here at the Locke Institute! Isn't that a relief?"

The stone fist in Jack's throat suddenly became hollow. His lungs dragged air like a drowning man. He coughed into the tube, inhaling his spit. Jack's eyes sharpened in time to see another acolyte arrive with a small box. He could feel the heat of it, burning like a furnace as she moved it close.

Gerba opened the box, revealing a small, shapeless lump of metal radiating heat. "Now, this next part you may not like." She gestured with her finger and the red-hot lump levitated into the air, buoyed by her majik. "But. Black Jack *is* a criminal, so it must be done." The steaming metal drifted closer to Jack's skin.

"Uhh! *Uhh!*" came his strangled, panicked shout.

Gerba sighed, irritated. "O, very well. What do you have to say?" The stone snake withdrew from his throat and Jack found his mouth could move.

"Please." Tears streamed down his cheeks. "Please. I'm not Black Jack."

Gerba tilted her head. "No?"

"I'm just me." He drew in a ragged breath. "They called me Black Jack, but that's not who I am. *Look* at me!" he wheezed. "Do I look like I could have a hundred-year-old song written about me?

Gerba smiled. "O, I do like that song. *'Ol' Black Jack, the man with the knack, stole the people their money back.'*"

"That guy is long dead," Jack sputtered. "I'm just a kid who found his grave. I'm begging you, Gerba. God's truth. I'm not a criminal. I'm innocent."

"Oh, my sweet dove. I will tell you a little secret." Gerba leaned in. "It does not matter."

Jack's eyes widened. "What?"

"Whether you are the real Black Jack or not is unimportant. It is the story we tell the noble houses of Keymark that matters. *'Ol' Black Jack is trapped at last. Gerba Whipmarples holds him fast.'*" She smiled. "No point in confusing them with facts."

"Listen to me—"

"I *am* sorry dearie, but we need to get your bleeding stopped. Let us kill two birds with one stone, shall we?"

She brought her fingers up. The superheated hunk of metal sizzled white-hot, dripping molten steel on the floor. Manipulated by Gerba's majik, it transformed into a familiar shape.

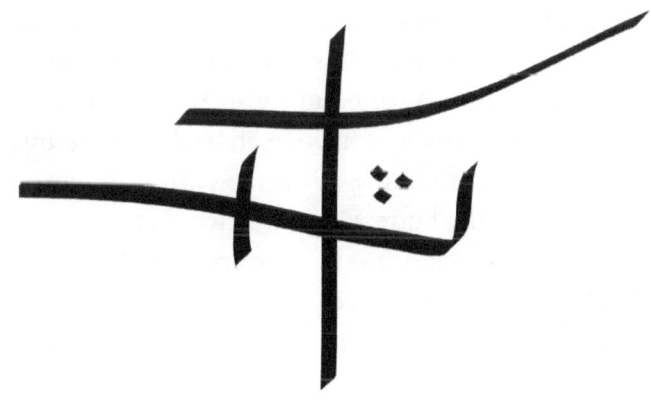

The symbol of Black Jack. Jack's eyes went wide as he realized what she meant to do.

"N—" The rock tentacle jammed down his throat again. Hyperventilating through the stone straw, he watched the brand draw closer.

Gerba winked at him. "Try not to break your teeth, dearie."

She lowered the sizzling metal onto Jack's forearm. He screamed as he felt his flesh bubble and melt. Jack heard his skin spit and hiss in agony. He bit down on the stone, splintering two teeth to shards, but that pain was nothing, *nothing* compared to the hell in his skin.

Gerba Whipmarples waited, watched the boy writhe in anguish, and relaxed her fingers. The metal cooled from white to red to silver, steam wreathing her head. "Cauterized, you see? Very clean."

Jack slumped in the chair, sobbing. After a time he forced his eyes open. The haze cleared and the violation of his body was laid bare.

The sign of Black Jack was burned into his flesh. Tendrils of smoke wafted from the molten steel that was now a permanent part of his body, fused to the bone. He would wear Gerba's brand until the day he died.

"Never deny who you are." She smiled satisfaction and called over her shoulder. "Winston, you may take him down."

Something pulled Jack from the chair. Shorn, bled, and branded like livestock, Jack was dragged to his feet and forced down a short corridor to a stone balcony. A panoramic vista of the jungle canopy came into view, then tilted as someone shoved him against the stone railing at the edge. Looking down the cliff, Jack saw a large dirt yard at the base of the butte, a hundred feet below.

Dizzy, Jack pushed back from the edge and saw the horse-sized tarantula that had dragged him here. Before he could scream, one of its hairy legs kicked him squarely in the chest and he fell over the edge.

Chapter

7

DINNER DASH

*And while the law of competition
may be sometimes hard for the individual,
it is best for the race, because it ensures
the survival of the fittest in every department.*
Andrew Carnegie

The freshest air Jack Swift ever tasted whipped over his naked body. He sucked huge gulps of it into his lungs to help him scream.

One last thought passed through his head: he would never see his dad again. When the clock turned 6:00 in Chicago, their dinner of hamburgers and tater tots would go uneaten as his dad waited for him, and he would go on waiting for the rest of his life. He would never discover what happened to his son. He would search the earth to find him, never knowing Jack's corpse lay on a tropical island in another world, splattered on the rocks like a wet red bag.

I'm sorry, I'm sorry, I—

Jack crammed his eyes shut and prayed he wouldn't feel the finale.

Something hit his arm, then something else, then a hundred more somethings. They pressed against his body, thin strips of pain. Jack's stomach kept heading for the ground as the rest of him decelerated, suspended by strips. His head came to a halt five feet above the rock.

Upside down and naked, Jack's eyes snapped open to see he was caught in white filament, a net made of flexible fibers that slowed him like a hundred little bungee cords.

They stuck to him like glue.

His heart hammered against his chest; his lungs thundered. He snorted in a shuddering breath, trying to get himself under control. Gulping air through broken teeth, he looked around and found he couldn't move his body, stuck to the net like a fly in a—

Web.

Jack blinked as he discovered the air around him crisscrossed in an interlocking mesh of spiderwebs thick as his thumb. Gulping breath, he glanced to the side and saw another figure tangled in a thick skein of glistening threads.

A man-sized cat.

A jinx. Jack had met a few of the cat-men before, but none so wretched as this one. Its orange coat was matted and dirty, its body limp as a noodle, nearly dead.

Terrified, Jack looked around and saw he was suspended at the base of the butte. Nearby was a wide dirt yard not quite the size of a football field. Beyond it were the four big monster palms, which looked much, much taller from down here.

"Help!" he shouted through broken teeth. The pain in his mouth was sharp as needles, the pain in his arm like fire. He could see the metal brand in his skin still cooling as the skin around it wept pus. *"Help me!"*

"Shaddup!" came a rough voice from above. Jack looked up the rock face to see the horror descending. His plummet to earth had wiped the giant tarantula from his mind, but now it came back in full force, descending the wall toward him.

That's not right, his perfect memory fought reality with facts. *Tarantulas don't spin webs for hunting, just for mating. They're also not the size of a horse.*

Eight soulless black eyes studied him. Spiky brown hair bristled over its body, standing up like the quills of a porcupine. Strange orange and black markings covered its chest, the death's-head pattern of a human skull.

Screams found him again as Jack twisted, but the filament held him fast, binding him tighter. He paled as the thing crawled right on top of him.

We were going to have tater tots for dinner.

"Help me! Help!" he screamed, looking for the source of the voice that had told him to shut up.

The tarantula's mouth opened, revealing twin fangs long as knitting needles. Jack felt his stomach shrivel inside him as every part of his body tried to draw away from this thing. The fangs drew close to his cheek and he felt the tarantula's hairs against his mouth. Jack screamed.

"I said shaddup!" yelled the tarantula.

Jack screamed harder.

"Keep it up and you're gonna get bit." Jack felt the thing's belly slide over his face, hairs scratching him like a repulsive beard. The tarantula pulled Jack's arm from the web, plucking the gossamer away with little claws at the end of its legs. "Shut your yap and don't move."

It released Jack's legs and he fell onto the rock. He tried to break his fall but found his hands were bound with silk. He hit his forearm and the skin around his brand shrieked pain. Nearly blacking out, Jack rolled on his back and stared up. The tarantula loomed over him, hanging upside-down. "Now. You gonna give me trouble or you gonna be civilized-like?"

Jack stammered. "Y-you can *talk*."

"Another genius." The spider emitted something like a laugh, a burbling *kek-kek-kek*. As it did, half its eyes turned upward. "Hey Winston!"

"Yeah?" A second massive tarantula crawled down the rock ledge, carrying the jinx-cat strapped to its back.

"Is this the last one?"

"Headmistress said ten, is that ten?"

"I dunno, I ran out of hands to count on." *Kek-kek-kek* came the burbling laugh of Jack's captor. It plucked a burning torch from a sconce in the rock wall. "Well, if there's one more, he's gonna have a *real* short stay." The tarantula threw the torch at the webbing. It lit up like it was made of paper, spitting and roasting into charred embers. Anyone who fell from the balcony now would have a much more final stop.

"Gimmie that burner." Jack's tarantula tossed the torch to Winston. He produced a gigantic cigar, put it between its jaws, and lit it with the torch. "We got time."

As the spiders lit up, Jack snatched a hunk of unburnt webbing and wrapped it around his forearm, a makeshift bandage to cover his seeping wound. It stung, but it was better than letting the wound get dirty. Keymark wasn't civilized enough for antiseptic.

Winston puffed the cigar, which smelled like a burned skunk. "Move it, frosh." He shoved Jack. "Party's waitin'."

Stumbling, Jack covered his arm, trying to shield it from further injury. He shifted his jaw, feeling the edges of his two broken teeth against his tongue. The giant tarantulas shoved him toward the open dirt field.

What kind of school is this?

Nine prisoners were pushed to the center of the yard by the big spiders. Jack saw three others who looked human, or jaelin, but the rest were creatures he would only see in Keymark. Two hulking beasts that looked like crocodiles flicked forked tongues between saurian teeth. Jack remembered they were called llystra, and their long, powerful tails were strong enough to knock a man down. There were two creatures Jack had never seen before, pig-faced men with tusks and hairy, bristled backs. There was only one jinx, the cat webbed to Winston's back. All the prisoners had fresh brands in their arms, their metal gleaming in the jungle sun. The jaelin were shaved bald. None had broken teeth. Jack was alone in that respect.

Awaiting them in the center of the field were four groups of hard-looking men. They stood apart from each other like opposing teams, each gang numbering roughly a dozen. They consisted of a variety of races, but all wore the same denim work pants, long since new. Some wore palm frond hats, most were barefoot, all of them had a dark look in their eyes that spoke of violence.

Jack scanned the faces, looking for Rooker Flynn. *She said he was being sent down today. He has to be here.* But there was no sign of the pirate.

Nine prisoners were shoved into the no man's land between the spiders and the gangs, naked and shorn like spring sheep.

"Listen up!" Winston shouted around his cigar. "Let's get this done without any bitching, dinner's on the way. Vulture camp, you're up!"

"Him," said the team leader immediately, pointing at the biggest croc, a llystra that must have weighed three hundred pounds. Winston shoved the llystra forward and threw a pair of denim pants at him. The Vulture leader snatched the croc around the neck and walked him into the group, whispering harshly in his ear.

"Jackal camp," shouted Winston, his head wreathed in cigar smoke. "Go!"

"That one." The Jackal pointed out the next biggest croc. As the man got his denims, Jack had the strange sensation of being on the playground, being picked for dodgeball teams. The strong ones went first.

"Buzzard."

Unsurprisingly, the Buzzards picked the next biggest guy, one of the tusked pigs.

"Hyena."

A big jinx that looked like a striped Bengal tiger did not answer immediately. He whispered with a young blond human. *No. Not human. Jaelin.* There was a brief argument between the man and the tiger, then the big cat thrust a clawed finger at Jack. "Him."

Jack blinked. It was the first time he hadn't been picked last for a team in...well, ever.

"Move it," growled Winston, and threw a wad of denim into the back of Jack's head.

Hauling the pants over his hips, Jack buttoned them up and joined his gang. Most of them were jinx-cats, and they stared at him with cold eyes, friendly as a pack of panthers. Only the blond man offered half a smile. Jack went to the back of the group, rubbing at his bald head. His attention went to his used denims. Blue fabric, yellow stitching, brass grommets. *Add a patch on the back and they'd be Levis.*

As the rest of the teams were picked, Jack glanced up at the rock wall from which he had been pushed. From here, Jack could see the volcanic butte was carved with balconies, terraces, windows, and parapets. Under different circumstances it would have been stunning, an edifice to rival the rock city of Petra in Jordan. Not one opening was lower than thirty feet off the ground. At the base of the wall was a great round stone door, sealed tight.

At the end of the gang selection only the jinx-cat remained unassigned. "Vulture!" Winston shouted. "You get the skag."

"We don't want him," growled the big leader.

The big tarantula blew smoke. "It's your turn, Eightfingers."

Vulture's leader scowled. "One more mouth to feed is one more mouth to feed. We ain't doin' it."

Winston extended his hairy legs, standing nearly twice as tall as Eightfingers. "I said no bitching."

"We'll take him," said the Jackal leader, sudden and sharp. "We could use some entertainment tonight."

Jack flinched as all four gangs broke into harsh laughter. There was no joy in the sound. It was the laugh of a group of bullies on the school playground yanking the lunchbox from the nerdy kid. Jack knew that laugh well, and hated it.

"Done." Half of Winston's eyes angled toward the sun. "Get in position. Food's on the way. Move it." All four gangs exchanged hard looks and retreated toward the edge of the dirt field where the jungle began.

Jack followed the Hyena gang. Glancing over his shoulder, he saw tarantulas head for the great stone door at the base of the cliff. It seemed to be the only way in or out of the Institute. Above, the balconies were empty. Not a soul watched or cared what happened below.

He ran his tongue over a broken tooth and felt blood trickle down his throat. His steel brand hurt like fire, but the webbing was glued tight to his arm, and Jack didn't want to imagine how much it would hurt to peel it off.

The Hyenas stopped in the shade of a palm tree and lounged against the trunk. A few lit foul-smelling cigarettes. None of them talked to the new recruits. Jack scanned the assembly yard they'd just left and noticed a big dirt road at the back that cut into the trees and disappeared into the jungle.

"So..." Jack cleared his throat. "Where does that road go? To the school?"

Hyenas burst out laughing. "School." One jerked a thumb at Jack. "You hear him?" Another spat at him, scowling. "Damn stupid frosh."

"Don't worry about them," said the blond man. "We'll get you straightened out after dinner." He extended his hand. "I'm Ransom Adare."

"Ja—"

Don't give 'em yer name. Don't give 'em anything.

Rooker's voice hit him like a slap. Jack had flirted with breaking the pirate's rules, and this is where it had led. Jack felt the webs covering the Black Jack symbol on his arm and finished the thought with the only name he could think of.

"—sper. *Ahem.* Jasper."

"Welcome to the Locke Institute." Ransom smiled dirty teeth. "What'd they get you for?"

"Get me for?"

"Your crime."

"Crime?" said Jack. He looked around the assembly and realized the brands of the Hyenas' arms were words. He couldn't read many, but those he could said things like *bandit, pirate,* and *thief.*

I'm surrounded by criminals.

"I'm...um..." Jack stammered. "I didn't do any. Crimes, I mean."

"Me too," chuckled one of the Hyenas. "Innocent men, every one of us," said another. The assembled gang laughed like it was an old joke.

Jack glanced at the leader. The Bengal tiger was well over six feet and broad-shouldered. "Sir?" He held out his arm. "Do you have anything for our burns? This is killing me."

"No." The tiger's voice came hard, striking with a military sharpness.

"How about a shirt? Or some shoes?"

"Only jaelin need shoes," the boss cat growled. "Weak feet." He abruptly sat up. "Dammit! They're already running!"

Confused, Jack spun to see the three other gangs race across the dirt field, sprinting toward the wall at a dead run. At the base of the cliff, the big stone door was slowly rolling open. The Bengal growled. *"Move!!"*

He took off and several Hyenas sprinted after him. Jack started to follow, but Ransom grabbed him by the arm. "No." He jerked his chin at the Bengal. "Boss West wants the fastest guys."

Jack eyed the footrace. "What's going on?"

"The dinner dash."

Each gang sprinted inside the door, reappeared with something in their hands, and darted back toward their base. As the Hyenas returned, Jack saw each carried two balls that were purple as eggplants. The runners dumped them at their tree, then returned for another load. Jack eyed one of the things and found it looked like a perfectly spherical potato the size of a volleyball. "What is that?"

Ransom licked his lips. "Galt."

Each of the thirty-two convicts ran flat-out, trying to grab the purple spheres before the other gangs could. Jack edged forward. "Should we help them?"

"Only if you want to start a war." Ransom spat. "Each camp only gets eight runners. It gets nasty if we send more. Hey, where are you from? You look like a mainlander."

Don't tell them anything, came Rooker's voice. "Um." Jack picked an area he knew from Keymark. "The Eynrys Plains."

Ransom smiled. "Hey, me too. Sawzer Ranch."

Jack leaned in to Ransom. "So, um, if this isn't a school, what is it?"

"Hell."

As another round of runners dropped off more galt, Ransom pulled two long bamboo poles from the jungle. They were lashed together with palm leaves, forming a crude travois. Ransom collected the purple balls and dumped them onto the sledge. Jack joined in, grunting from the heavy galt.

Jack jerked his chin at the wall where the tarantulas watched the footrace and smoked their big cigars. "What the hell are those spider things?"

"The attercops? Don't worry about them. They're like any other prison guards. All show." Ransom turned back to Jack. "They told you the rules, right?"

Prison. Jack stared, his mind blank except for one word. *I'm in prison.*

Ever since Jack had been kidnapped from Chem 509, he'd been lying to himself. Maybe Gerba Whipmarples was okay. Maybe the Locke Institute was a school. Maybe he could go back home. He'd held on to the illusion until it at last evaporated, and he felt like a child for letting himself be so naïve.

"Hey, look, don't worry about the 'cops," said Ransom. "And don't worry about the galt. Just follow the rules. The most important thing is—"

"Ransom." Jack turned to find the big Bengal standing over them. The other seven convicts were still on their way back, winded and panting, but the boss cat wasn't even breathing hard. "They're bringing down a tenth man. Let's get out of here before we get stuck with him."

"Okay, boss."

Jack took his cue from Ransom and packed the galt quickly as he could. As the other runners arrived with their haul, Jack saw one of them had a bloody nose, freshly broken. Jack walked to him. "Do you want me to take a—"

"Get away from me, frosh!" He threw Jack to the ground where he sucked air through his broken teeth and gripped his burned arm, trying not to scream.

"Enough," said Boss West. He dragged Jack to his feet and shoved him toward the path. "We have to go."

Jack turned to see the tenth prisoner enter through the great stone door. The late arrival was a lean and rangy man with olive-toned skin, a shaved head, and a loud mouth. He shouted at the tarantulas as they shoved him across the yard, spewing curses in a never-ending stream of blistering profanity.

Jack recognized the voice.

Shaved of his oil-black mane, Rooker Flynn looked diminished of his power, like the story of Samson and Delilah. His face was barely recognizable as the cocksure pirate captain Jack remembered, but the fury in his voice was unmistakable.

"Rooker!" Jack called out, but the pirate was too preoccupied with fighting the 'cops to hear him.

"Let's move out," came West's command. "Double time it, boys."

Jack turned to Boss West. "That's my friend! Over there!"

"He's not your friend anymore. He's a Jackal." West shoved him down the trail. "You're a Hyena now."

Chapter

8

DAY CAMP

Come to the sunset tree!
The day is past and gone;
The woodman's axe lies free,
And the reaper's work is done.
Felicia Dorothea Hemans

Wishing for a pair of boots, Rooker padded on naked feet along the dirt path into the jungle. The black eye Wont Naysayer had given him still ached and his gut throbbed from the attercop bite yesterday, but the paralytic poison was long gone and the fang marks had scabbed over. The real pain was from his prison brand; his skin was inflamed, and the metal had started to itch.

Frustrated, he ran his fingers against his stubbled scalp. He found a dirty bandanna in the pocket of his denims and tied it into a head scarf, leaving the tail long. *I miss my hair. I had such great hair.*

The Jackals tromped through the jungle toward one of the four monster palms. After a half mile of walking, Rooker realized how big the things were. He could barely make out massive nests in the branches near the top of the big palm, but he did not see any birds. There was, in fact, no sign of wildlife at all. Insects whirred in the thick jungle air, but during the walk he didn't see a single animal bigger than a dragonfly.

Halfway between the Institute and the big palm, the gang stopped by a stream to cool off. The crocs rolled around in the shallow water, covering themselves in mud. Shirtless and shoeless, Rooker waded past the party and into deeper water. He found a dropoff where the streambed suddenly fell away and dove in head-first. Bubbles drifted up around him as the stream cooled the skin on his brand. He remained underwater, enjoying a moment of silent luxury.

Unbidden, a face appeared before him in the liquid darkness. It had the familiar sharp eyes and cruel smile of a boy he had known a lifetime ago.

(I thought you were a-scairt of the deep water, pip.)

Rooker Flynn had long since put that face behind him, along with his fear of water. Neither held any horrors for him anymore. *Go away, Jasper.*

(How long do you think it will be before your new friends cut you lose?)

Shut up.

(I bet you a sack of grain you don't make it a day.)

Rooker surfaced and took a breath. He snatched off the bandanna and wiped down his face and body, trying to ignore his own thoughts. He glanced down into the water, but the phantom was gone as if it had never been. Wordlessly, he strode out of the water and joined the crocs heading up the path.

Soon the jungle revealed the colossal system of the monster palm. Most of the roots were taller than Rooker, festooned with what looked like large green seedpods. Closer to camp, the seedpods grew much bigger, from the size of a dog to the size of a bear. Most were closed, but Rooker saw a few standing open, red and glistening on the inside, and realized they were gigantic flytraps awaiting large prey.

The afternoon sun touched the jungle canopy by the time they made it to Jackal camp. Rooker first saw a wooden hut raised on stilts, then another and another. The huts were primitive, handmade from bamboo and dried palm fronds, lifted ten feet into the air on poles to protect from flooding. Twenty huts ringed the base of the big palm, some of them in advanced stages of disrepair. A few lay on their sides, legs broken and collapsed. The intact huts had no windows or openings of any kind save a door at the top of the stairs. Rooker couldn't fathom why the residents would forego windows or roof vents. It was hot enough in the jungle; inside the huts would be an oven.

The strangest thing about the camp was how new it was. All the timber was fresh, absent of the rot and moss that grew so easily in the jungle. *It looks like this place hasn't been here half a year.*

At the center of the camp stood a badly constructed water tower that tilted as if it were in immediate danger of falling over. This is where most of the prisoners gathered.

Rooker counted a hundred and sixty jailbirds milling around camp, some cooling off under the water tower, some resting in the shade beneath the huts, lethargic, ragged, and dirty. Every single convict wore a metal-inscribed Institute brand on their forearms, bearing symbols that read *poacher, arsonist, rapist, murderer.* Their numbers consisted of three dozen jaelin, a few hammerdwarves and handful of tusked razorbacks, but the camp was utterly dominated by llystra. The man-sized crocs were everywhere; Jackal camp was filled with reptilian teeth.

As Rooker's group moved between the huts, he realized how badly the camp stank. There was no evidence of a bath or an outhouse. The air reeked of disease, filth, and urine. He lifted a hand to his nose.

It's not a school. It's not a jail. It's a penal colony.

Rooker scanned the Jackal prisoners. There were a few landlubbers, but the camp seemed dominated by diverse pirate crews that normally wouldn't be caught dead together. Shavers. Kubla Clan. Red Tigers. The Rimmy's Cull cartel. Dirty hands from all over Keymark. All looked the same, all malnourished, all with the same *pirate* brand burned into their arms, all moving with a hopeless, leaden despair. Rooker recognized many of the faces, but he had no friends here, and more than one enemy.

At least now I know who I'm up against.

Covering his face with his hand, Rooker watched several convicts come to fetch the galt. They ferried the purple balls to a thirty-foot barbeque made of baked clay, sliced them into manageable pieces with stone knives, and threw them on the dented metal grill.

Rooker's stomach rumbled at the smell and he wondered how long it would be until they ate.

He strolled over to the water tower, followed closely by the other new inmates. The gaze of the camp was upon them. No one met their eye, but everyone was watching. Keeping one hand over his face, Rooker walked past a few dirty troughs and leaned against the water tower. He lowered his head and let the other fresh fish take the lead.

One new inmate, a mustachioed jaelin, turned the spigot to drink from the pipe. He was immediately smacked in the head by a group of inmates. "Whacha think yer doin', frosh?" One of the convicts leaned in, smiling broken teeth. "No fresh water for you."

Rooker folded his arms. This little dance was nothing new. The trick was to stay invisible until the hazing crew found a weak sister. All Rooker had to do was stay out of the spotlight until they picked one.

Mustache scowled, unwilling to back down. "I want a drink."

"Pray for rain," the con shot back. That got a laugh from the prisoners.

"Excuse me, sir?" Rooker was surprised to find a second newcomer, the jinx-cat, had spoken. Llystra, as a rule, hated jinx; the crocs and the cats had been at war since forever. Rooker didn't think much of jinx either, but he expected one with the word *counterfeiter* newly branded on his furry arm to be smarter than this. If the idiot had been paying attention, he would have noticed there were only four or five jinx in the whole camp. *Where does he think he is?*

The counterfeiter held up his freshly branded arm and spoke slowly, as if to a servant. "We are obviously going to need to *treat* our wounds with something cleaner than that trough-water. We wouldn't want to get infec—"

The toothless outlaw lashed one clawed hand and shredded the jinx's face. The counterfeiter screamed pain as blood tricked down his furry cheek. The crowd laughed as the jinx grasped his face, trying not to cry. Rooker ignored him and walked to one of the troughs, knowing it was the only drink he was likely to get today.

He eyed the brackish, stagnant water. Something foamy floated on top. Several chipped clay cups lay along the rim of the trough, which meant other prisoners drank here. Rooker took a cup, splashed away the gunk, and filled it. He screwed up his courage and drank. It felt like swallowing warm sweat. *Better than nothing.*

He glanced at one of the convicts sitting in the mud nearby. He spoke softly, making sure no one else heard. "Outhouse."

The man spread his arms, indicating the camp. "You're looking at it."

Well that explains the stink.

Rooker dabbed his shirt in the water and wetted the brand on his arm. The wound might get infected, but at least the cool water felt good.

Somebody rang a triangle dinner bell and the camp leapt to its feet. They ran for the barbeque, shouting and whooping. Surprised, Rooker watched them sprint for the food. *Never seen anybody that excited about galt.*

Wringing out his shirt, he approached the throng with Mustache and the counterfeiter. Most of the galt had already been taken; there were only a few scattered slices left on the grill. As Rooker moved toward the food, the prisoners closed ranks in front of him, showing him their backs. Rooker tried to make his way around them, but the men closest to the barbeque suddenly started throwing punches at each other, fighting for food. Desperate, Rooker forced his way toward the grill. A fist boxed him in the ear and he got knocked to the ground. He covered his head, buried under a mass of fighting convicts. A piece of galt bounced into the dirt. Rooker grabbed it, but a foot came down on his hand and yanked it away.

As suddenly as they had come together, the convicts dispersed. Breathing through a bloody nose, Rooker staggered to his feet and looked at the empty grill. Not one sliver of galt remained.

A prisoner walked over him, flicking a slice in his filthy mouth. "None left for you, frosh. Too bad."

Getting to his feet, Rooker rubbed his ear. He'd been in plenty of fistfights before, but nothing so primal. Only starving men could be that desperate. Rooker felt the growl in his belly as he realized the cold truth of the Locke Institute. *There isn't enough food for everybody.*

Before the fight, Rooker had seen two crocs fill a wicker basket with galt. He scanned Jackal camp and found them walking up the highest hill. Atop the rise was the largest hut in camp. The crocs mounted the steps and carried the basket inside. Rooker's eyes narrowed. *But plenty for you.*

He rubbed his empty belly and got to his feet. "Fine." He scowled. "Galt tastes like crap anyhow." Not one passing prisoner looked his way or said a word. Rooker had never been ignored by a hundred and sixty people at the same time; it was a new and unnerving experience.

Abandoned at the empty barbeque, the frosh rubbed their bruises. One saw a familiar face and disappeared into the crowd.

"The three of us should team up," Mustache stated. "Strength in numbers, that kind of thing. You know, until we get situated."

"I'm all for that," said the jinx. "Maybe we can...you know... make a break for it."

Idiots. Rooker scowled. This camp had no walls, no fences, and no guards. Any Jackal could escape any time they wanted, which meant there was no place to escape *to*. As for Mustache's idea, it proved he had no clue the jinx counterfeiter was Jackal's new whipping-boy, which made Mustache too stupid to keep.

"Sounds good," said Rooker. "I'm in."

Mustache nodded. "I'm Two-Time Tom."

"Tinker Voss." The counterfeiter extended his hand.

Rooker forgot their names immediately. "Vaughn Waumsley."

"All right frosh, listen up," said the beefy croc walking toward them. Rooker recognized the outlaw immediately. This was one of the cartel boys, an axe-for-hire known as the Leech. "Let's get three things straight." Leech put his hands on his hips. "One, you don't eat until we say you eat. Two, you don't drink until after you work. Three, all of you work for Boss Mamba now. Get me?"

Rooker felt the blood drain from his face. Boss Mamba Crait, the Crime King of Khandun, had once controlled the cartel territory from Rimmy's Cull to Caer Laverlock. He was gargantuan, easily the biggest croc Rooker had ever seen. Ruthless and vindictive, Mamba had made his bloody reputation by tearing the heads off his enemies and nailing them to the doors of their homes.

Boss Mamba knew Rooker Flynn's name very well. The crime king was, in fact, entirely aware that Rooker had robbed his safe two years ago. More pointedly, he had put a price on Rooker's head.

And I'm locked in with him.

Rooker lowered his head, wishing he still had some hair left to cover his eyes.

"You find anything on a worksite, you give it to Mamba," continued Leech, pointing at the big hut on the hill. "You get an extra ration of food, you give it to Mamba. You steal anything from the Institute, you give it to Mamba. If I find out you're holding out, I'll rip you to strips and cook you." He tossed a piece of galt on the grill where it sizzled. "Stick to the rules if you want to stay alive. If you don't, it's no skin off my back." He plucked the galt off the grill and tossed it in his mouth, glancing at Rooker. "Hey, do I know you?"

"Rooker?" came a new voice.

Rooker's head snapped to find a prisoner behind him. His face looked like a pig, or, more accurately, a boar. Rooker blinked. "Puck."

Tusks jutted beneath Puck's snout. A mohawk of bristled hair ran down his spine. The big razorback had never looked so thin, his time in the Institute had not been kind. Puck hitched up his filthy denims. "It *is* you. Wow, you look so different without the hair, Rooke—"

Rooker launched himself at Puck.

There is an old prison adage that says, on your first day, you should fight the biggest guy to prove you're not afraid of anyone. Rooker knew that tactic was a great way to get your teeth knocked in. You don't want to fight the biggest guy. You want a fight you can *win*.

Rooker drove his fist into the razorback's jaw and sent him reeling. Puck tried to run away but Rooker grabbed the boar's hairy shoulder and spun him around. "Where ya goin' Puck? We got some catchin' up to do."

Puck snorted, scared. "Hey, c'mon R—" Rooker rattled him until his teeth shook. Puck shouted, his eyes squeezed shut. "I paid you back for what happened in Junai!"

"Ya paid me back in stolen cargo that had *tracker majik* on it!" Rooker hollered. "I had to outrun yellowjackets for three days after ya stuck me with that junk."

"That's not how it—"

Rooker belted him in the snout. He felt a few outlaws watching, so he did it again, harder. Puck was perfect for this little dumbshow, just big enough to look intimidating, like most razorbacks, but Rooker knew the pig was all butter. Rooker popped him a third time and Puck went down blubbering.

"Ya wanna keep that other tusk?" Rooker leaned over him and cocked back his fist. "Gimmie yer galt."

Puck threw up one hand to ward him off; the other dug in his pocket. "Here, take it! It's all I got!" He offered a dried slice of galt no bigger than a coin. Rooker snatched it out of his hand and kicked the razorback running. As Puck scuttled off, Rooker posed, his bare chest stuck out, gut sucked in, biceps flexed, giving his audience the right impression. *Won't be long before I get skinny like the rest of 'em. Might as well take my chances now.*

He flipped the galt in his mouth. Dry and crunchy, it had no flavor at all, bland as boiled rice. "Ya owe me!" he hollered at the razorback.

"Who is that guy?" asked Leech.

The counterfeiter wiped dried blood from his chin. "That's Vaughn Waumsley."

As the sun touched Huánghūn's horizon, Rooker sat high in a tree at the perimeter of Jackal camp. He could see the big escarpment of the Locke Institute less than a mile away, the carved balconies, the Great Bell, the flickering lamps inside. Only the part of the wall near the assembly yard seemed occupied; the remaining miles of stone were featureless save for a few attercops on patrol. The cliffs glowed golden in the setting sun, pretty as a picture.

I gotta get outta here.

The other two frosh milled around in the jungle foraging for fruit, but Rooker knew they wouldn't find any. If there were bananas out there, the prisoners wouldn't be fighting for food.

From his vantage point in the tree, Rooker considered his situation. Getting tossed in a penal colony with Boss Mamba was the worst kind of bad luck. Surely some of the outlaws had recognized him, and his name would snake its way to Mamba before long.

Once that happened, Rooker's chances of staying alive fell to long odds.

He closed his eyes. His arm hurt. The stings in his abdomen hurt. His stomach ached, empty.

I gotta get outta here.

Rooker imagined the *Venture Brigand* beneath his feet, the sea wind in his hair. He could feel it, the infinite blue stretched out ahead of him. Perched upon the *Brigand*'s prow he cut through the air like a bird in flight. There, he was free, unbound by the world.

All I gotta do is get back to her, one way or another. Once she's mine, no one's gonna trap me again.

Rooker opened his eyes from his daydream and looked to the sky. The purple and gold clouds of the Huánghūn sunset were magnificent, lit by the fading sun.

Rooker turned to find Jackal camp empty. Everyone had gone inside but the three frosh.

Right. He remembered the acolyte's words. *Rule three: Inside by Sunset.*

It was a stupid rule, there was no point to it. *Still, best not to rock the boat. Not yet.* "Hey," Rooker called down from the tree. "We should get going."

"Yeah." Mustache sneered. "Don't want to get in trouble with Boss *Mamba*."

"It's too early to go to bed," grumbled the jinx. "And too hot."

As Rooker climbed down the tree, he heard a sudden bray of laughter from a group of convicts inside the huts. Several were hanging outside the door with stupid grins on their faces, watching the frosh with a predatory look.

"I need some food," grumbled Mustache. "There's gotta be s—"

In the jungle, something *churred.*

Rooker turned toward the sound. A shiny-smooth stick rose from the undergrowth, yellow with a reddish tip. The two frosh turned to watch as the stick was joined by another, and another. Rooker took an inadvertent step back.

Mustache cocked his head. "What the hell *is* th—"

A yellow spider the size of a dog emerged from the jungle. It was different than the attercops, much smaller, and had no hair whatsoever, covered in shiny chitin with pale markings down its back. It stared at Mustache with eight soulless eyes.

He backed up. "Guys? Maybe we should get insi—"

As the sun disappeared below the horizon, another spider emerged from the jungle, testing the air with its hooked forearms. Another came behind it. Another.

Rooker saw the jungle ripple with yellow bodies.

Mustache turned to run. An alien *churr* burst from the spider as it jumped. It landed on the man's hip and wrapped around him. Mustache hollered and bashed its head in with a fist. Before he could move, another yellow body latched around his legs and sunk its fangs into his calf. He cried out in pain, then a third spider was on him, a fourth, a fifth, a dozen. Swarmed by a nest of moving legs, Mustache went down screaming.

Rooker ran.

Hoots and hollers came from the huts as prisoners leaned out to watch. Rooker and the jinx ran, hearing the *churr* rise in pitch behind them. The jinx sprinted past Rooker on quick paws. Bare feet pounding, Rooker tried to catch up, feeling the spiders closing in behind.

"Go that way! *That* way!" A prisoner waved him on, indicating the next hut. The jinx cut toward it on quick cat's feet. Rooker was never going to catch up. "Yeah!" laughed a convict as Rooker passed. "That way!"

As the jinx sprinted past the hut something long and thin whipped around his ankles. He hit the ground jaw-first, screeching a cry of pain. Shouts and hollers erupted from the hut as the jinx went down. "Got 'im!"

Rooker watched as the cat tried to remove something lashed around his ankles. A homemade bola, used by cattlemen to entwine a cow's legs.

Rooker heard the prisoners inside the hut giggle.

Churr.

Rooker looked up to see spiders close in on him, dozens of them, flowing over the compound.

"Help me!" the jinx begged him with panicked eyes.

Another bola whipped from the hut. It missed Rooker's legs, but one stone clubbed him in the knee. He spared a single glance at the jinx. "Good luck." Stumbling, Rooker turned and ran.

He heard the spiders devour the counterfeiter, heard his gibbering last shrieks as the jinx was buried beneath a swarm of squirming yellow bodies.

Rooker ran on alone.

All around Jackal camp, spiders swarmed from the tree line.

"Rooker!" yelled a voice. Puck, the razorback, stood in the doorless entry of one of the half-broken huts, waving for him. "Come on!" Rooker sprinted for him.

Puck disappeared inside. As Rooker ran up the steps and came through the doorway, he saw a cluster of six-foot flytraps around the walls of the hut, their stems growing through the floorboards. Inside the flytraps, Rooker could barely make out the shapes of shadowy bodies, outlaws encased within. One of them wiggled his fingers at him. *What the hell?*

"Oops. Not enough beds." Puck shot Rooker a cruel smile and stepped into the last open flytrap. The plant came alive and swallowed him. As yellow spiders came through the roof,

Puck disappeared inside the flytrap's spiraling green venules, leaf blades wrapping around him like a cocoon. The spiders descended, parting over the flytraps, refusing to get near them. Rooker heard Puck's muffled voice inside. "Shouldn't have hit me, Rooker."

Churr.

A spider appeared in the doorway. More crawled through the hole in the roof, skittering down the walls. One leapt at his face. Rooker felt it claw at him. Blood trickled into his eye as Rooker shoved the spider away with both hands. The creature was remarkably light; it flew across the room, landed on the wall, and scuttled at him sideways.

Another spider came through the door and jumped on Rooker.

His body reacted like a frenzied animal, exploding in every direction as the spider held on. Revolted, his mind abandoned rational thought and the shrieking part of his brain took over, leaving nothing but panic as he tore at the thing.

Stop! Stop! N—

Rooker smashed the spider against the stout wooden door jamb and heard it crunch, splattering as he ran out the door.

He caught a heel and fell down the steps, tumbling. He hit the turf hard, a severed yellow leg in each hand. A sticky goo spattered him as the spider legs spasmed.

Churr.

Rooker watched a dozen spiders scuttle over the roof of the hut. As he rose to his feet, he realized Jackal camp was overwhelmed by yellow. They were everywhere, crawling over the cabins, the grill, the water tower. Bodies skittered on silent legs all around him. The only place left within the spiders' tightening noose was an old collapsed hovel tilted on three broken legs.

He ran for it.

Rooker's lungs ached as he fled across the compound. Drawn by the movement, the spiders closed the distance, faster than he was. Rooker ran for his life.

I'll never make it.

Ten heartbeats. He had ten heartbeats until they were on him. Spiders came by the hundred, by the thousands. Hopeless. *Hopeless.*

He ran, alone.

The first spider hit him as he reached the broken hovel. His skin crawled but he managed not to scream as he kicked it away. Another was on him, tangling his legs. He fell and smacked his head against the broken hut leg.

The thing crawled up his body. Flailing, Rooker grabbed a rock and smashed it. He roared at the top of his lungs, fighting off the next one. They came from every side. He crabbed his way under the gap near the leg and found a hole in the bottom of the hut. He wiggled his way through it, entering from the bottom.

A skull's hollow eye socket stared at him blankly. The broken hovel was filled with denuded, rotting corpses.

He had found where Jackal camp kept its bodies.

Now he screamed.

A leg came through the gap and touched his bare foot. Terror filled Rooker's mind, an empty, hollow fear nothing could ever fill, a yawning chasm of blackness. Another spider wedged its way through the gap. Fangs bared, it sunk them into Rooker's calf.

Die, just die!

He smashed its head with both fists and got to his feet. Pain seared his back as another spider sunk its fangs in. He spun, feeling a third spider climb his leg. It bit him on the thigh. As poison flooded his blood, Rooker stumbled to one knee, his leg numb. The spider crawled onto his head, legs scraped over his scalp and brushed against his eye.

Die!

Rooker's eyes went wide as—

A leaf. Amid the corpses, Rooker saw a big flytrap, open, unclaimed by the dead.

He crawled for it.

Arachnid legs flickered over his bare back as he shoved corpses out of his way. He crawled inside the flytrap. As its sticky leaves closed around him, Rooker turned to find the crooked hovel teeming with yellow. It was like being inside an egg sac as it hatched. The world was spiders. All of it.

They bit him, clawing at his skin, prying at the flytrap, holding it back from closing. He punched at them, his arms leaden, screaming, poisoned, dying. The thick leaf closed slowly as his struggles became more cramped. Fangs pierced his chest, but he could not feel it. His body was numb. His arms were bound by the plant as it closed around him like a boa constrictor. Rooker screamed, unable to move, as a spider bit his face.

Overwhelmed by the weight, the flytrap fell partway through the gap in the floor. The stem almost snapped but barely held on as it slid into the hole, leaving Rooker inverted, face to face with a corpse. Smaller spiders were crushed by the plant as it gripped Rooker like a fist.

Through the translucent leaf blade, Rooker saw and felt the pitter-patter of spider legs crawling over his paralyzed face.

And that is how Rooker Flynn spent his first night on Huánghūn: cocooned, eye-to-eye with death, upside down in a graveyard.

PART 2

WORK
&
PLAY

Chapter 9

MORNING
ANNOUNCEMENTS

Experience keeps a dear school,
but fools will learn in no other.
Benjamin Franklin

erba Whipmarples blew steam from her ginger chai and took a delicate sip.

The porcelain cups were a gift from the Sultan of Thaj, a polite thank-you for collecting the leaders of the rebellion against him last summer. The snow-white cups were made for small jaelin hands, and required a delicate touch, but the little blue mountains painted within the glaze reminded her of home.

Portia finished buttoning her up in back and Gerba examined herself in the looking glass. The emerald dress was imported from Highyon Garde, made especially for her, and still smelled faintly of lavender. She eyed the line of her waist, the length of her hem, the way it showed off her leg. "Mm. What do you think, dearie?"

"You look striking, headmistress," Portia said from behind her niqab. "Very elegant. Even a noble lady would be jealous."

"O, I do not know about that." Gerba twirled the dress. "But Madame Grès is quite the designer." Gerba smoothed the bodice, admiring the beadwork. With any luck, she would have an opportunity to wear it soon. "Are we quite ready to begin?"

As always, Gerba had woken well before dawn. Juttlander trols do not require much sleep, but she made sure to get a few hours beauty rest each night. She woke every morning in darkness, did her exercises, checked the accounts, and wrote several letters to a variety of noble houses before sunrise. *As the Toshan saying goes, the early bird gets the worm.*

"Almost ready, headmistress," Marguerite said from the other side of the modesty screen.

Gerba lowered an eyebrow. She prided herself on running the Locke Institute like a well-oiled machine; it simply would not do to slip a cog. *Not today.* "Is there a delay, Marguerite?"

"No, headmistress," came the immediate reply. "Our featured student was...unruly last night. We are giving him the proper correction."

"Very good. You may unbutton me, Portia." Her teacup was smaller than her thumbnail and delicate as a soap bubble, miniscule in her huge, leathery hands. Gerba kept it perfectly steady as she disrobed to her chemise. "I think I shall wear the kimono today, Portia. The white one."

She watched the sun peek its head over the Irridin Sea. The clouds were pink today and looked as happy as they could be. In a few hours, the sun would rise high enough to crest the Locke Institute wall and fall upon the assembly yard. By then, Gerba was certain, everything would be prepared.

It is best, after all, to keep a positive outlook on these things, she thought, smiling at the sunrise. *Every obstacle can be overcome.*

She held the teacup by the barest tips of two fingers and took another sip.

On the jungle side of the wall, the loud *churr* that dominated every Huánghūn night slowly faded away as the island's native denizens retreated before the sun.

"Well." Gerba took a final sip from the cup. "Let us begin a new day, shall we?"

Rooker Flynn woke with a scream on his lips. His dreams told him he was still covered in spiders, but his eyes told him otherwise. He swallowed his panic before anyone could hear him shout. Inside the hut, it was quiet, dark, and humid, filled with the snores and farts of a dozen sleeping outlaws.

Rooker held his breath until the scream went away.

Toughen up.

He breathed out slowly. Checking the walls, he made sure the yingcao leaves were intact. There were no rips. No spiders had gotten through during the night. No arachnid feet pattered over the surface, nothing tried to get in from above. The spiders were gone with the sun, just like every morning. He was safe.

Safe.

Rooker exhaled.

On Huánghūn.

Mind your betters. Gather at dawn. Inside by sundown. As long as I follow the rules, I'm safe as houses.

Rooker rocked in his hammock, wondering which rule he could break first.

Yingcao, the big flytraps that grew from the roots of the big palm tree, offered the only defense against the nightly swarm. Yingcao loved the taste of spider, and the eight-legged beasts knew to avoid them. The raised huts, called cliques, were covered in layers of yingcao leaves that protected them from infestation. After dark, the inside of a clique was the only safe place on the island.

Having a clique meant staying alive.

Rooker checked to make sure none of the Red Tigers were awake. They were stacked three deep inside the cramped hut, snoring as only pirates could. Rooker swung a leg out of his hammock and eased one foot onto the floor.

After that first horrific night, he had tried to join a clique, any clique, but had no luck. During his piratical career, Rooker Flynn had stabbed half the Jackals in the back, and was not greeted with open arms. He spent three miserable nights in a sticky yingcao cocoon before the Red Tigers approached him. Smiling yellow teeth, Jape, their leader, had explained the Red Tigers could offer their clique as protection from the yellow spiders, what the prisoners called 'shiq', in exchange for half of whatever food Rooker could get his hands on.

Every prison has its currency. Smokes, booze, tools, clothes, weapons, sex; it was different everywhere. At the Institute, the only currency was food.

Nothing else mattered when there wasn't enough to eat.

Rooker eased out of his hammock, silent as a mouse, watching Jape snore. He eyed the floorboards. *Ya always put yer foot...there.* Rooker eased down, hoping his knees didn't pop and give him away. Squatting, he ran his nimble fingers over the floorboards and discovered an uneven spot. He glanced at Jape and eased up the false board, revealing a secret stash beneath: a dozen dried slices of galt, each the size of a fat coin.

It took all his self-control not to gobble it down. He'd been in camp six days and had only eaten twice. Starving, his stomach felt like it was collapsing on itself. Instead of giving in to temptation, Rooker pilfered a single slice, slipped it in the pocket of his denims, and left the rest where they were.

One.

If this were a straight robbery, he would have taken it all, but this way Jape would wonder if he'd gotten his count right. *No need to carve the whole goose at once.*

Resisting the urge to eat, Rooker silently slipped out the front door and left the Red Tigers snoring.

Shiq had plenty to eat; they were cannibals. They fed on each other all night long, the strong feasting upon the weak. They were also prey to the big raiptars that nested high in the yingcao tree. At night, Rooker heard the birds swoop in and carry the spiders aloft, screaming. But sunlight was their worst enemy. It melted shiq like candle wax. Rooker saw a few scattered puddles of yellow, but he knew by noon all traces of the dead spiders would be boiled away.

A fresh corpse lay in the dirt near the water tower, the smeared remains of a highwayman called Razor Nick. The shiq were efficient when it came to picking over a man's bones, but some of Razor Nick's sinew remained, along with his eyeballs. Shiq would eat your face, feet, hands, and liver, but they wouldn't touch an eyeball.

Picky little buggers.

Rooker dug through the corpse's clothes. Nick's denims were shredded, but there was a hidden pocket sewn into his bloody workshirt that contained a slice of galt. Rooker tucked it into his pocket along with the one he'd stolen from Jape.

Two.

Walking toward the water tower, Rooker saw his old pal Puck coming to examine the corpse. Rooker intentionally shoulder-bumped him as he passed, making sure it hurt. The razorback snarled something at him, but Rooker shot him a deadly look and kept on walking. Puck was a coward; his attempt to feed Rooker to the shiq had failed, and the pig wouldn't dare tangle with him in a straight fight.

Rooker tucked away the piece of galt he'd pinched from Puck's pocket.

Three.

He scratched the metal brand on his forearm, which had gone from painful to itchy, and glanced up at the big clique on top of the hill. In six days Boss Mamba had yet to make an appearance. The crime king had not left his clique. His door remained closed, and the only people who went in and out were his underbosses.

Rooker kept scratching at the brand, knowing it was only a matter of time before Boss Mamba came for him.

Maybe I'll get lucky and the shiq will eat him.

"He knows you're here," came a silky voice.

Damn. I thought she hadn't noticed me yet. "Heya, Patch." He turned and smiled at the jinx. "Ya look good."

For once, Rooker wasn't lying. In the real world, Patch Pica-roon had always been a cat-next-door kind of pretty, blessed with golden eyes and razor-blade cheekbones. But here among the filthy prisoners, the jinx looked better than a five-tier birthday cake. Her coat could not have been shinier if she ate eggs every morning and had a handmaiden brush it every night. *How does she pull that off?* The only hint of imperfection in her fur was the metal brand on her arm that said *pirate*. Patch leaned against a fence rail as if she owned it, a bit of sassafras between needle teeth. "And you look like a man who owes me a thousand marks."

Rooker spread his hands. "Patch. Junai wasn't *my* fault. It was Saltz who—"

"I only know you're lying because your mouth is moving." Patch's golden eyes narrowed. "Fork over your galt."

Rooker palmed his three slices into his waistband as he turned out his pockets. "Fresh out."

"Heh." Patch grinned. "That's a good trick. You'll do well in here." She detached from the rail and ambled closer, her sharp teeth white. "Tough being a frosh, isn't it? You gotta be starving by now. Tell you what...how about I give you some galt?"

Give? Patch, I've seen ya steal candy from an actual baby. He held out his palm. "Great, hand it over."

"In trade for your pants."

Rooker blinked. "My...what?"

"Wear a grass skirt until you pick up another pair." Patch smiled. "Call it a kilt. Nice breeze. I'll give you ten slices of galt for them right now."

So they're worth thirty. "Patch, ya need to be a lot more creative if ya wanna get in my pants."

"Not from what I heard."

He hid a grin. He and Patch had gone head-to-head more times than he could count, but at least she had a sense of humor, which was more than he could say about the rest of Jackal camp. "Tell ya what, I'll give 'em to ya for *free* if ya help me."

"Help you what?"

"Break out."

Patch Picaroon laughed, sharp and harsh. "Be my guest. Jungle's right there, Rooker. I'll give you a tip." She leaned in and whispered, "Go at night."

Cute. "There have to be more yingcao trees out there somewhere, right? More of those big flytraps?" Rooker gestured at the vast jungle. "All we gotta do is find 'em."

A surprised look came over Patch's face. "My God, Rooker, you're a genius. No one ever thought of that."

Rooker Flynn realized how desperate he was when he allowed the word "Really?" to escape his lips before his brain caught up.

Patch shot him a look cold enough to freeze lava and walked away. "Idiot."

"Hey!" Rooker trotted to catch up.

Patch's tall leather boots tromped across the yard. "I've been here four months, Rooker. Every con in the joint has come up with some harebrained scheme, so let me save you some time. The flytraps only grow under the four big trees. That's why the Institute made four camps."

Rooker scowled. "There's gotta be a way to make it through the jungle. What about that big road at the back of the assembly yard?"

"Try it." Patch picked her teeth. "The attercops will bring back what's left of your corpse."

Rooker frowned. "Boats then."

"Half the cons in here are pirates, Rooker, you think we haven't tried the *sea?*" She spat. "The breakers are too big for a raft."

"So we swim around to the dock and steal one of their ships."

"A four-mile swim through a razorsquid nesting ground. Have fun bleeding out."

Razorsquid. Damn. "So we climb the wall."

Patch laughed. "You realize the Institute is guarded by giant *spiders*, right? Climbing is kinda their thing. Mumbling Mads is the only idiot to ever try it. Attercops tossed him back and forth on the cliff face like a rag doll, laughing the whole time." She bunched up her face, imitating the harsh laugh of the attercops. "*Kek-kek-kek*. Took half an hour before they got bored and threw him from the top."

Rooker grimaced.

"There's gotta be someplace to get to. A fishing village or—"

Patch cracked up laughing. "I love frosh the first few days. This is the best entertainment on the island right here, I should sell tickets." She spat. "Get it in your head, Rooker. This is hell, and you're stuck here with the rest of us."

Rooker frowned. He'd never met a prison he couldn't beat, but Huánghūn had him stumped. As he scratched his stubbled scalp, one of the female inmates, a razorback, came up to Patch, whispered in her ear, and headed back to the women's clique. Rooker watched her go. "How does that work, exactly?"

"What?"

"The women's clique. Seems like that would be a problem."

Patch scowled. "Women always were a problem for you, Rooker."

Ya want me to spell it out? "It's in a *penal* colony, Patch. You know what these guys do to women." He pointed. "I saw Cozy Harry in that clique, I saw Liceboot in that one. I see Hambone Jon, right there. You wanna tell me those guys aren't a problem?"

Patch spat out the sassafras. "You know Dag Raban?"

"Another raper." Rooker nodded. "Cuts women for fun."

She reached behind her ear and pulled out a home-rolled cigarillo. "You see him here?"

Rooker scanned Jackal. There were plenty of cons he recognized, but Dag wasn't among them. "No."

"Neither does anyone else. Not anymore." Patch lit the cigarillo. "The gals stick together, Rooker. Dag got what was coming to him. We made sure it was real painful, and real public." She exhaled a puff of smoke. "The other boys caught on quick. You come at one of us, the rest are gonna tear you to pieces." She took another drag. "Am I going to have a problem with you?"

She has to ask? Rooker put on his most charming smile. "No worries, Patch. I've never really seen ya as a woman."

"That's fair, I never thought of you as a man." She blew smoke in his face.

Turning away, Rooker spotted a familiar face under one of the cliques. The bum was caked in a thick layer of dried mud. He banged his head against one of the support beams making a 'buh-buh-buh-*buh*' sound, staring at nothing like he'd been struck feebleminded. Rooker wouldn't have recognized him if it weren't for a bit of orange hair sticking through the mud. "Is that Billy Pilgrim?"

Patch glanced at him. "Not anymore."

The last time Rooker had seen Pilgrim, he had been onstage at a packed Windward Theater, a troubadour adored by thousands. Rooker could barely believe this was the same man. *Filthy, broken, and mad as a hatter. Buh-buh-buh-*buh. "I saw him sing." Rooker couldn't help but smile at the memory. "He was hilarious."

"Now he's hysterical." Patch chucked a rock. "People crack in here, Rooker. One of the girls in my clique got all dark last month. Stared at the jungle a lot. Then she walked in and never came back out." She gazed out at the palms and Rooker saw a hint of longing in her eyes. "Some of us...go to the green."

Great. Rooker spat. *There's no way out unless we go crazy or kill ourselves.*

Patch glanced up the hill to the big clique. Rooker followed her eyes to see one of Mamba's underbosses give her a nod. Something went cold in his gut. "What's goin' on, Patch?"

She stubbed out her cigarillo and tucked it behind her ear. "He's ready for you. Head on up."

Rooker tried to mask his surprise with no success. "Yer workin' for Boss Mamba?"

"Me and every other Jackal who wants to stay alive."

Rooker snorted. "A jinx with a llystra boss. I never thought you'd stoop so low."

"Me and the girls have a bet going." Patch smiled at him. "Two-to-one odds he kills you this morning. Don't let me down, Rooker." She slapped him on his shoulder and walked away, flicking her tail. "I've got dibs on your pants."

Rooker watched her go, then glanced up at the big clique. *Might as well get this over with. Maybe I can bribe him.*

He reached into his waistband for his three pieces of galt. He stopped, searching his denims. *Gone.*

He spun around in time to watch Patch disappear into the women's clique. *Damn. She picked me clean.*

As Rooker stepped inside the boss clique, he was hit with a wall of smells. Sweat, decay, swamp water, and blood, all mixed together with a thick miasma of bitter incense that filled the room. Through the smoke, he saw an immense shadow. "Rooker Flynn," came a familiar deep voice. "Where's the dog?"

Three people in a tenday who know that story. My luck just won't turn.

"Inquisition found him innocent." Rooker flashed his teeth, pretending he didn't expect to be eviscerated momentarily. "He's drinking rum on a beach 'til I get back."

A shadow emerged from the incense smoke and towered over him. Boss Mamba Crait stood well over eight feet; his tail alone was longer than Rooker. Black scales covered his monstrous body from his clawed feet to his crocodile head. His saurian mouth grinned bladed teeth. "Why haven't you come to see me?"

Think.

Boss Mamba was one of the old-school llystra, a believer in the bloody warrior code that when you killed a man you took his power. He'd murdered Boss Ito, Governor Spiner, and impaled poor Duke Stiglitz on his own pike. The greater the enemy, the more power Mamba took.

So look small. "I figured ya wouldn't have time for me. Looks like yer the big man in here."

It worked. Mamba puffed himself up. "I've been here since the beginning. Nearly a year now. Before there *were* cliques."

That explains why the camp looks so new. Nothing in Jackal was a year old, including the cliques. Rooker had an image of the Crime King of Khandun squeezing himself into a yingcao pod. He covered his laugh with a cough. "Ya got arrested with Mace and Fourblood, right? You three were cozy as lice. They still around?"

"I had to kill them. They weren't cooperating." Rooker felt a clawed hand close around the back of his neck. "But *you* want to cooperate with me, don't you Rooker?"

Rooker felt his flesh go cold. "Mamba, look, that thing with yer safe—"

"O, that's all over. Water under the keel." Mamba led him out the door. "We're going to make a new arrangement, you and I."

Rooker swallowed as they descended steps that creaked under Mamba's weight. "You're a good thief. I can use someone like you. Supplies are hard to come by on Huánghūn. Knives, shoes, boots, soap, rope, khef, coffee, you name it. There's a rumor someone's got a few bottles of moonshine hidden away somewhere." Mamba took Rooker's hands; they looked tiny in the llystra's giant claws. "I don't know how you got inside my safe, Rooker, but I want those greedy little fingers working for me."

He wants a scrounger. "Sure, Mamba." *Not a chance in hell.* "I'll holler when I got somethin' to trade."

"*Trade.*" Mamba chuckled. "You know what I like about sailors? They understand rank." He gestured to the camp. "You see all these men? They work for me. The women? They work for me too. I *am* Jackal. To put it in your terms: I am your captain." Mamba led Rooker to the top of the rise. "So here's your orders. Tomorrow, you're going to bring me something on that list I just told you. The day after tomorrow you're going to do it again. I'll give you one guess what you're going to do the third day."

Rooker had never liked being told what to do, and he didn't take to it now. He unfurled his best wicked grin. "Be careful, Mamba, ya could choke on that much swag."

Mamba frowned. "I'm not someone you want as your enemy, Rooker."

"Ya don't make much of a friend, neither. Ask Mace and Fourbloods."

Mamba fixed him with a hard stare. "Your cooperation is expected."

Rooker had had enough. *What's mine stays mine, ya big lizard.* "Ya know, Mamba, I been hearin' a lot of high-minded ideas lately. Education. Reform. Cooperation. None of 'em seem to mean what they *seem* to mean." He thumbed his nose. "I'll stay my own captain."

Mamba gave an exaggerated shrug, displaying his vast, muscled shoulders. "Your choice, of course. There's one thing you should know."

"I already know plenty."

Mamba leaned in, eye to eye. "If you don't bring me something I want tomorrow, I'll know we're not friends. And if we're not friends, then you're just some thief who stole fifty thousand marks from me."

Mamba slung his giant arm over Rooker's shoulder, letting him feel the weight of his muscle. "Tomorrow, I'm going to have some of my boys pound a big stake down into the dirt, six or seven feet. Then I'm going chain you to it. I've got a good iron chain, Rooker. And then I will sit right there on my porch with a little fruit drink and watch the sun set." Mamba smiled knives and pointed one scaly finger. "Get me?"

There was a fresh carcass on the far side of the hill. The shiq had picked it clean, leaving only some guts and eyeballs. The corpse's ankle was manacled to six feet of good iron chain, attached to a stake like a dog on a leash.

"Think about it." Mamba slapped him on the back. "I'm sure you'll make the right choice. O, and Leech?" The assassin suddenly appeared at Rooker's side. "I hear sailors have queasy stomachs on land. Any food he gets his hands on, I want you to eat it. Make sure he doesn't get sick."

Mamba finally released the weight of his arm and smiled hideous teeth. "See you tomorrow, Rooker."

He watched the croc mount the stairs and disappear into the big clique. He eyed Leech. "Don't worry, pal. I ain't had a bite since I got here." He slapped the man on the gut and turned away.

As he did, he flicked the slice of galt he'd lifted from Leech into his waistband.

One.

All students at the Locke Institute gathered at sunrise, obeying the Second Rule like holy writ. As the sun crested the butte, Jackal, Buzzard, Hyena, and Vulture stood waiting. Each pack kept their distance, each wary of the other. Most prisoners would kill a member of a rival camp as soon as look at them.

Attercops walked the wall, keeping near the great stone door, smoking their khef and chatting. Atop the wall, Rooker saw a shape move toward the Great Bell, silhouetted against the dawning sun.

Gerba Whipmarples.

"Good morning, students! It is wonderful to see you all looking so ready to learn!" The headmistress was dressed in a tidy white kimono, her voice amplified by whatever majik she used. Rooker snorted. *She looks ridiculous in that tiny white hat.* "Today you take another step in your journey to become an obedient, trained, and useful part of society. This is what we all strive for here at the Locke Institute. To better ourselves. To excel. And today is your opportunity to do that!" She smiled and nodded, as if her students were applauding.

They were not.

"Here are your assignments for today! Vulture and Buzzard, to the mines. Hyena, the rice paddies. Jackal, timber." A communal groan rose from the prisoners as Rooker frowned. *Same work assignments as yesterday. And the day before.* His back was sore from dragging trees through timber camp. *Does it ever change?*

"Now, now!" scolded Gerba. "Practice makes perfect! And I have more good news, students. Hyena will return to the Institute an hour early today for a healthy bloodletting!" Rooker wasn't paying attention. He scanned the other camps, checking for faces he knew. Unsurprisingly, he was familiar with most of the outlaws on Huánghūn, but there was only one face he wanted to see.

There.

Jack. Rooker only caught part of the kid's shape, but he knew that nose, that chin, those skinny legs. What little he saw of Jack's silhouette was sunburnt, shaved, and scrawny.

He had been trying to find the kid for days, but the crowds were so big and morning announcements only lasted so long. *My lucky penny.* Rooker clicked his tongue. *Yer my ticket outta here.*

He leaned into Patch. "How do you switch camps?"

"You're not going to get rid of Boss Mamba that easy," she chuckled. "Once you're in, you're in. Nobody takes a new prisoner unless they're forced to. One less mouth to feed is one less mouth to feed."

Rooker scowled. *There's got to be a way.*

"Now, before you continue to your assignments..." Gerba raised her hand. "I have some unfortunate news."

The chatting suddenly quieted and Rooker felt the assembly lean in, expectant. Gerba had their full attention, like an animal trainer with a treat. "One of our students was caught trying to leave the school without permission yesterday." Behind Gerba, two acolytes led a bound prisoner toward the Great Bell. Rooker couldn't make out what the con was saying, but he was sobbing, dragging his feet. *Is that Shifty Haan?*

One of the acolytes reached up into the Great Bell and something fell out.

A noose.

Shifty started screaming again. The acolytes led him up a small platform and placed the rope around his neck. "Please!" he cried. "Please!"

Cheering erupted from the convicts in the yard. Rooker had attended public executions before, but he'd never seen a crowd quite so eager for one. *Vicious bastards.*

Gerba straightened. "You are here to learn your lessons. And learn you shall." She turned to Shifty. "We complete our studies at the Locke Institute, Mister Haan. And if you *refuse* to learn, you shall teach by example."

An acolyte removed a pin from the platform beneath Shifty and it collapsed. Shifty screamed right up to the moment his neck snapped. As he jerked at the end of his rope, the crowd went berserk, hollering like barbarians charging to bloody war.

As the hanged man kicked and twitched, the Great Bell rang, pulled by his weight.

Kong!

The soundwave rippled over the camp. Rooker felt his body come alive with delight as the healing majik of the Agrat-ban-Haifa washed over him. The wounds in his abdomen healed over, his bruises faded, and the gnawing hunger in his belly went silent. Even the brand on his arm repaired itself to a healthy brown as the burn wound became a memory, leaving only the metal brand. All around him the prisoners healed, suddenly filled with vitality. Rooker watched in amazement as a convict's recently severed finger grew back, healed and whole.

But Shifty healed too.

Choking and gasping, his arms tied behind him, the hanged man regained his strength. He kicked out, still strangling, still dying.

Rooker watched, appalled. He had seen men hang, but this was something else. The more Shifty struggled, the more the bell tolled, and the longer it went on. But that wasn't the worst of it. Every time Shifty swung the bell, another chime of physical exhilaration washed over the crowd. They rejoiced in it, eager for more. The depraved assembly cheered for Shifty, hollering for him to kick once more so they could feel that sensation again.

Rooker felt a dark longing overwhelm him. With each new toll of the bell, he found himself cheering louder, roaring like the animals around him. It became an all-consuming passion, the perverted joy of pleasure drawn from death.

It took a long, long time for Shifty Haan to die.

When he finally kicked his last, Gerba raised her voice and adopted the crowd's passion as her own. "Yes! Work will make you free! Rehabilitation leads to graduation!" She raised her massive hands. "So get to work and have a *magnificent day!*"

Roaring cheers erupted from seven hundred prisoners over-flowing with the vigor of the healing *wikk*. Attercops hollered and hustled the camps toward their work assignments, knowing the thrill of majik would only last so long.

As Jackal marched toward the logging camp, Rooker glanced up at Shifty's limp corpse.

Gerba Whipmarples' Locke Institute was horrifyingly effi-cient. He almost had to admire her for it. *That's why she doesn't give us enough food. As long as she keeps ringing that damn bell, starvation won't kill us. Sickness won't kill us. We can go on working forever.*

As he was herded toward another day of labor, Rooker glanced up at the bell, secretly wishing Shifty would kick one last time.

Chapter

10

ACUILLO

The vilest deeds like poison-weeds
Bloom well in prison-air:
It is only what is good in Man
That wastes and withers there:
Pale Anguish keeps the heavy gate
And the Warder is Despair.
Oscar Wilde

J ack Swift flinched as the knife dug into his arm.

Every time they bled him, it hurt a little more. This was his tenth session of bloodletting at the Locke Institute, and while he feared the knife, the promise of the sting was far worse than the blade itself. Much like the anticipation of the spiders at dusk or the apprehension of yet another hanging, the wait was more painful than the event. Forty days he had spent in Hyena camp, and the suspense was killing him.

The acolyte pressed a cup to his arm, made sure the vacuum held, and leaned back in her chair. Her face was covered by the niqab, but Jack saw her eyes watching him as he bled. Her gaze was draining, almost vampiric, and drew as much out of him as the cup.

The flap of the tent billowed as another acolyte entered, the hem of his robe wet. Today's rain refused to stop. Jack's denims were soaked, his feet caked with mud. It was too hot for a shirt, but he wore one anyway, one sleeve covering the wrap that hid his prison brand. No one in Hyena camp had yet seen his mark, and Jack still clung to the only piece of advice Rooker had given him. *Don't tell 'em yer name.*

It was the only thing left he could control.

"Why..." His voice scratched his throat. "Why are you doing this?" He knew the acolyte wouldn't respond; Sun Hee rarely talked during her visits to the work camps. Winnifred was chattier, but none of the acolytes would engage the prisoners in discussion, their dialogue was restricted to empty pleasantries.

"Very good." Sun Hee capped the cup and put it with the others in the crate. "All done. Next."

Jack tried to stand and failed. A normal hospital would take maybe 100ml of blood; the Institute took five times that every session. The combination of anemia and near-starvation was deadly, or would have been, had the bell not healed the prisoners every ten days.

God help me, I can't wait to hear it ring again.

Jack let the dizziness pass, rose shakily, and exited the tent. Ransom was waiting for him outside. He'd already had his blood-letting, and looked paler than usual, but his smile seemed intact. "Hey Jasper." His eyebrows furrowed. "You don't look so hot."

"Imokay," Jack slurred his words together. "Jus' tired."

"Here." Ransom checked to see that no one was watching and slid a bit of galt into Jack's hand. "I got you half a piece." Jack would probably be dead without Ransom's help. The man had taken him under his wing from the first day; he made sure Jack had food, clothes, and most importantly, a clique. He thumped Jack on the back. "We Eynrys Plains boys have to stick together, right?"

"Stop running your mouths," said Boss West. The big tiger did not put up with laziness and ran the work camp with military efficiency. Hyena was full of jinx, and West was good at herding cats. "You two wasteka scabs can't jabber all day."

Jack had learned 'wasteka' was a shortened form of 'Waste take you', which loosely translated as 'worthless asshole, die and burn in hell'. It was a convenient, all-encompassing profanity that packed ten curses for the price of one.

"Ransom, you're with me." West pointed Jack toward the rice paddies. "Jasper, back to work."

Jack nodded and trudged from the blood tent.

He walked the ridgeline of a hill layered with twenty-seven ter-races, tiers of shallow grassy curves, each containing about half a foot of water and long green grasses. It was beautiful or would have been under different circumstances. Twenty-seven layers of con-victs worked the rice paddies, bent double, calf-deep in the water, as they had the last tenday, and the one before. It was simple work, and backbreaking. The attercops gave out scythes at the beginning of the day, which the prisoners used to cut the base of the mature panicles, a loose cluster of grains at the top of the stem where the rice grew ripe. Those stems were gathered and handed off to another set of Hyenas, more senior than the reapers, who whacked the panicles into a wooden box, separating the rice from the plant, then used string-grid sifters to remove the hulls, chaff, and immature rice. The finished product was laid out on wooden tables to dry in the sun, then bagged in burlap and loaded into wagons by the prisoners with the most seniority.

All frosh were assigned to the reaping.

Jack picked up his little dented scythe and bent to his work. Instantly, his head felt light. His body had been flirting with exhaustion for days; the combination of starvation, anemia, and hours of manual labor was taking its toll. His mind didn't work at all anymore, and the only thing he could think about was the sun trying to roast him from above while trench foot slowly ate everything below his knees.

I should have listened to her, he thought. *Gerba Whipmarples. Not such a joke anymore.*

Lightheaded, he toppled sideways and caught himself in a three-point stance like a football player. Jack shook his head, trying to clear it without success. He threw the rice panicle at the box and missed, nearly stumbling with the exertion. *Starting at center for the Chicago Bears, Jack Swift.*

Stop.

He didn't dare think of Chicago. Or worse, his father. That life seemed a dream to him now.

(just a dream)

A dream too painful to remember. A dream when he had been worth something.

(all you're good for now is sweat and blood)

Jack stumbled to his knees in the water of the rice paddy. He felt the scorching sun blocked by a cold shadow cross his back. He heard the shadow's footsteps in the water, padding around him. It crept unseen, circling him, waiting. Its wolfish voice, the voice of his fear, grew more insistent, stronger.

(you're just a slave)

Jack felt the wolf creep the perimeter of his mind, predatory, searching for weakness.

(and you will never be anything else)

Jack did not realize he had blacked out until he found himself face-down in the water. He sputtered and rose to his feet, but he could not get off his knees. On all fours like a dog, it was all he could do to keep breathing. *I don't even control my body any more.*

(or your mind)

Jack's brow furrowed. *Go away.*

(you are so weak)

Jack spotted a bucket of fresh water on the rise. *You're only heatstroke. I just need water to get rid of you.* He took a step toward the bucket.

(give in)

Jack took another halting step through the paddy. *Leave. Me. Alone.*

(what will you become without me)

Jack's bare feet hit something sharp hidden at the bottom of the paddy and he fell face-down in four inches of water. He tried to push up, but his arms didn't respond. His knees didn't bend. His body had quit. Panicking, Jack tried to summon his strength, but he felt his limbs were separate things, miles away.

For a moment, he considered not getting up. Somewhere, his wolfish shadow laughed.

"Don't make me bite you," said an attercop. The guard poked him with the butt end of his spear. "Do you think he's gonna get up?

Another 'cop's voice came. "Nah, look at 'im, he's done. He's gonna drown."

Jack felt his face sink into the mud.

"So put your money where your mouth is, Jamedi. Bet me a khef."

"That he drowns? Nah. He's a frosh, he's still got some fight left. Might rally."

Jack felt an attercop's leg push him away from the edge, out into deeper water. "How 'bout now?"

Jamedi made a considering sound. "You're on."

Jack struggled to get up, but his body simply wouldn't. Maybe the sharp thing in the water was a dusk-spider fang, and he was slowly being paralyzed. He tried again, not so hard this time. It was nice, the dark. He didn't need to worry about his body. Or breathing. Those things would take care of themselves. All he wanted right now was to sleep. Little by little his brain started to go. *It's okay,* he thought. *I can go.*

(yes)

Something grabbed him by the arms and hauled him out of the mud. It slapped him in the face, hard.

Jack opened his eyes to discover a jinx-cat dragging him from the mud. "Geddup!"

"Hey, no fair!" yelled one of the attercops.

The jinx hauled Jack out of the muck and threw him against the bank. "Hey!" She slapped Jack again. "What's wrong with you?"

"...sleeping..." murmured Jack.

"Damn it." The woman turned to the attercops. "Hey, boss! Give us some food."

THE CRIMES OF ROOKER FLYNN

The attercops laughed. "That's Hyena's job," snapped one. "Get him back to work."

The other 'cop nudged him. "Is she in Hyena? I ain't never seen her before."

"They all look the same to me." The tarantula lit a khef cigar and turned to its partner. "Now pay up."

As the pair argued, the jinx woman dumped a gourd of water down Jack's throat. He sputtered and coughed, then drank. She held the back of his neck and whispered in his ear. "You're the one they call Jasper, right?"

Jack felt the water cool his throat and he shook off some of the brain fog. He checked the shallow pool but there was no wolf lurking in the rice paddies. *Of course there isn't.* He glanced at his rescuer. "Thank you..."

"Patch," she said. She had golden eyes and looked entirely too clean for a rice paddy. She thrust a handful of raw rice at Jack. "Here, eat this."

Jack shook his head. "I can't. *Bacillus cereus.*"

"What?" She blinked. "You're not making any sense, dingus."

"B. cereus."

"I *am* serious."

Jack shook his head and the definition spilled out from a medical journal trapped somewhere in his brain. "It's a toxin-producing facultatively anaerobic bacterium in raw rice."

"More words. Eat it."

Jack shook his head. "Emetic syndrome, nausea, vomiting, diarrhea. I'll die barfing it up."

"You'll die either way. This way you don't die *now*. Eat it." Patch jammed her hand to Jack's mouth. He struggled a moment, then realized the jinx wasn't going to stop until he ate, so he did. The rice was disgusting, like eating crunchy dirt.

As he chewed, Patch leaned in close. "I have one job here, and that's to make sure you make it back to assembly with this."

Jack felt her palm something tiny into his hand. Surprised, Jack glanced at it. A macadamia nut. "Who sen—"

"They catch you with that, you found it." She moved away from him. "Mention my name and I'll cut a hole in your clique." With that, she was gone.

Jack felt the macadamia shell between his fingers. Big and perfectly round, it seemed hollow. Eyeing the attercops, Jack split the shell open along the seams, hoping to find a nut, but inside was a miniscule piece of paper rolled into a tiny tube. He unrolled it to discover a bright red leaf inside. The paper was scribbled in Keymark kanji. Jack was able to translate some of it, although it didn't make much sense.

Hope you can read.
Get to ◯
→ leaf in mouth.
Bite. Quit.

He couldn't decipher the signature at the bottom, but there was only one person it could be. "Rooker," he whispered. Jack read the note again. *Get to where? Quit? What the hell does that mean?* Jack thumbed the note into his waistband as the attercops' attention came back to him. "Get back to work or get back to drownin'. Cost me a cigar, ya lousy frosh."

"Yes, boss. Sorry, boss." Jack took another drink and waded back into the rice paddy. "I'm on it, boss."

Jack slogged his way back into the water, finding his scythe. His belly felt better from the rice, but he knew it wouldn't be long before it came back up with a vengeance. As he chopped the heads off the rice, he glanced over his shoulder to make sure the spiders weren't watching, then opened his hand.

One red leaf. That's all he had.

Still, it was hope.

On the way back to assembly, Jack hunched over on the side of the road in a slashing thunderstorm, vomiting out his guts.

Indigestion hit him on the way back to camp, followed immediately by a geyser of rice and stomach acid. Hyenas marched past him, hair and fur plastered to their skin from the driving rain. No one offered to help him or support him. They silently slogged along, wet shadows moving through the jungle palms. Jack fell twice. The first time he got up on his own. The second he stayed down.

"You done?" asked one of the attercops as the rest of the camp moved on.

Jack dry-heaved until there was nothing left to barf up. He rolled onto his back, rain spattering his face. "Help me up."

The attercop grunted. "Got any khef?"

"No."

"Then no." The tarantula plunked his spear in the ground and waited. Jack forced himself to his feet, gripping the red leaf in white knuckles like a talisman against Huánghūn. He walked, rain trickling down his shaved skull.

Thunder rolled overhead as Hyena joined the other camps at the base of the Institute for assembly. As grumpy attercops counted heads, Jack's vision blurred and he tumbled to the ground. His stomach compressed involuntarily, pain shooting through his core, and he knew he wasn't getting back up again.

Wherever I'm supposed to get to, this is it.

Jack shoved the leaf in his mouth and bit down.

Whatever hope he had that the leaf was some special majik that would fix him was dashed as the weed flooded his mouth with a bitter shot of poison that turned his tongue instantly numb.

"Ya son of a bitch!" came a shout from the other side of the assembly.

Jack clawed at his tongue, trying to get the taste out.

He looked up as the shouting man strode into the no man's land between Hyena camp and Jackal, a rangy figure with stubbly black hair. The man thrust one accusatory finger right at Jack. "*You!* I'd know that ugly, fish-eyed, wasteka face anywhere! C'mere ya runty little quim!"

Rooker Flynn hauled Jack to his feet, his eyes ablaze with fury.

Jack had half a second to open his mouth before Rooker broke his nose.

He hit the ground like a sack of rice. A thrill of excitement went up among the assembly. All four camps drew close to watch the violence.

"Back off, Flynn!" bellowed Boss West, his fur soaked to his skin.

Rooker threw a hard look at the tiger. "Ya know me?"

"Yeah," grumbled West. "I've heard of you."

Rooker bared white teeth. "Then ya know not to stand between me and what's mine."

Boss West was a foot taller than the pirate. He leaned in and put a claw on Rooker's chest. "He's not yours."

Rooker grinned like a madman. "Ya get that paw offa me or I'm gonna shove it down yer throat." He pointed at Jack. "*That one* put a hole in me in Baruni." Rooker ripped his tattered shirt aside revealing an old, jagged scar on his lean gut. The audience reacted, a rippling wave of disgust and admiration. Rooker let the rain glisten on his wound as he glared at Jack. "I'm gonna return the favor."

The assembled prisoners edged closer. Jack watched Boss West take a step back, understanding that revenge was the wrong train to stand in front of. The attercops eyed them from the edge of the yard, pretending to continue the head count. A ring of convicts formed around the two men. Murder was an old friend, and always encouraged.

Jack staggered to his feet, nose dripping blood. He wiped it and looked at Rooker, not understanding.

...what the hell is happening?

A wave of dizziness passed over him and he realized the numbness had spread to his face. The nausea was gone, and so was the pain. He didn't feel anything at all.

"Nobody pokes a hole in me, lubber! Unless they're sick of breathin'." Rooker lunged at him and Jack threw his arms up as Rooker attacked.

What The Hell Is Happening?

Jack stumbled under the blows. Rooker suddenly hooked him under the arms and held him up. Jack felt heat from the red leaf pouring down his throat, oxygen flooding his body, eyes dilating to saucers, heart thudding like a Detroit piston looking to burn rubber.

Rooker's fierce eyes were locked on Jack's, an inch away. "*Hit me, boychick.*" Jack swallowed as rage coursed through him in waves of red. "Wh—"

"Hit me or we're *both* dead—"

Jack slammed his fist like a hammer into Rooker's exposed ear. Rooker staggered back, dazzled by the pain.

Laughter erupted from the crowd as the pirate lost his footing and almost fell. Jack felt blood boil in his ears, his heart too fast, too powerful, too big.

WHAT THE HELL IS HAPPENING?

Jack lunged at Rooker with an animal roar. He slammed into him, knocked the pirate into the mud, and straddled his chest. His right fist nailed Rooker's nose. His left smashed the other ear.

Hollers of encouragement spewed up from the crowd, cheers for each side rising. Bets traded more quickly than the punches.

Jack's head was nothing but screaming violence, a cacophony of killing drums.

Rooker broke away, got to his feet, and stared at Jack with hate in his eyes. The pirate was stronger, but Jack was indomitable, feeling no pain. Rooker lunged. As Jack dodged out of the way, Rooker's feint disappeared as he shifted his weight and came in low, taking out Jack's legs. Bellowing like a bear, Jack went down in the mud to thunderous approval from the crowd.

You can't beat me! Jack's brain burned fire. *I'll kill you! I'll kill you!*

He hooked his leg through the back of Rooker's knee, brought him down, and rolled on top of him. Jack jammed his knee in Rooker's balls and hammered his face like an anvil.

Jack felt all his frustration of the last forty days blast from his fists like a volcano. *Trapped in prison!* Wham! *Starved!* Wham! *Giant* wham *sonofabitching* wham s*piders!* WHAM. He wailed on Rooker in a berserker rage, blaming him for everything, everything, everything.

"Crikey!" Rooker hissed. "Stop!" Jack didn't, blood streaming from his knuckles as he took more skin off Rooker's face. "That acuillo is gonna wear off in about ten seconds and yer gonna be weak as a kitten."

Jack couldn't stop. There was nothing in his mind but revenge. Revenge for everything on this stupid island. They had kidnapped him, taken his hair, violated his body, and starved him. They had taken away his freedom. Jack took it all out on Rooker; there was no one else to hit.

Shouts came from the prisoners surrounding him, egging him on. Jack gave Rooker another shot to the face, then suddenly sagged, his muscles lax, his eyes unfocused. Rooker spun and threw Jack off, reversing their positions. Jack groaned as he went down in the mud. He struggled to get up, but Rooker put a knee on his neck.

Jack's breath bubbled water, then he went limp as a dead fish.

Rooker stood and staggered as blood streamed down his chest. He threw his arms up in victory, rain spraying from his body. Shouts of approval and disdain went up from the crowd while galt changed hands. As Hyena and Jackal fell to hurling insults at each other, Rooker grabbed Jack from the mud and flung the kid over his shoulder like a felled deer.

"I'm takin' him back with us!" Rooker roared at the top of his lungs. "I ain't done with him yet!"

Jackal camp hollered their approval. Boss West stepped forward to stop him, but Rooker turned on him with a furious glare. "You wanna fight about it? Let's go *right now!*"

West glared at Rooker, then eyed the hard men of Jackal camp. The big cat uncoiled, relenting. "One less mouth to feed is one less mouth to feed."

Jackal camp cheered, laughing, and welcomed Rooker back into their fold with his prize slung over his shoulder.

Attercops lazily ushered the convicts apart, driving them back to their respective camps as insults flew back and forth in the rain like volleys of arrows.

Rooker hocked up a wad of bloody phlegm and spat. His mouth tasted like copper. He nodded to his campmates as they slapped him on the back. They moved toward camp, looking to get out of the rain and inside the cliques before the sun set and tonight's nightmare began.

Rooker hucked the unconscious kid up on his shoulder. "Damn, Jack." He shot a wad of blood from his nose. "Somebody forgot to teach ya the meaning of the word *quit.*"

Chapter

11

CHICKEN
LEGS

*Of all possessions
a friend is the most precious.*
Herodotus

A railroad spike was driven through his skull, Jack was certain of it.

Pain split his forehead right down the center. Somewhere, he heard singing, but he wasn't sure if it was real or not. Jack tried to move, but his limbs felt like steamed noodles. Staring up at the palm fronds, he realized the rain had gone. He turned his head sideways to discover he was flat on his back on the jungle floor. Yellow light drifted across verdant green. The singer was close.

Jack roused, focusing. The singer sat on a mossy log, whacking a stick against it to the rhythm of the old Boy Scout marching song.

Great green gobs of greasy grimy gopher guts
Mutilated monkey meat, chopped up parakeet.
Deep-fried eyeballs rolling down a dirty street—

Jack's raspy voice joined in for the final line, singing together:

And me without a spoon.

Rooker Flynn smiled a grin that said all was right with the world because he was in it. "Hey."

"Hey."

Rooker handed him something that looked like a green bean. "Bite and pull."

Jack stuck the pod in his mouth and pulled out the first seed. It was about the size of a raisin, and half-bitter, but it was the only food in Jack's stomach. It tasted like heaven.

"Thank you." Jack tried to deliver every ounce of gratitude he felt.

"Yeah." Rooker grabbed his hand and pulled him to his feet. The two men stood face to face for the first time on Huánghūn.

Rooker raised an eyebrow. "Yer taller."

Jack nodded. *Right. It's only been a year for him.* "Growth spurt." Jack took a shaky step and had to grab a tree for support.

"Come on, kid." Rooker spat between his teeth. "Toughen up."

Jack didn't have the strength to be offended. "I *am* tough."

"No, yer fallin' down, ya look like a starved rat, and I had to rescue yer bony ass."

Same old Rooker. Jack screwed up his mouth, smacking his lips. "You got any water?"

"No."

"Got any food?"

"No." Rooker leaned in. "So what's the plan?"

Jack dragged a sweaty arm across his lips. "What plan?"

"For gettin' us off this rock."

Jack stared at him. "A plan?" He felt heat build inside his ears, a sudden echo of the acuillo. "A *plan?* This place is like Devil's Island...or Australia."

Rooker scowled. "What's a Strailia?"

Jack ignored him. "We're trapped on an island of endless jungle and if we step foot outside after dark, we get eaten by giant spiders. The only boat I've seen is on the other side of a hundred-foot wall that has no way to get through, over, or around, plus we're surrounded by criminals who will murder us for a handful of food because everyone is *starving.* Either we get killed trying to escape, killed by prisoners, or killed by spiders. Am I missing anything?"

"They could hang us."

Jack snorted. "So far I've been kidnapped, interrogated, stripped, shaved, bled, branded, beaten, and starved. Plus drugged by you. So I'm sorry Rooker, no, don't have a *plan* yet."

Rooker pursed his lips, disappointed. "I thought ya would know how to, like, fly or something."

Jack glared at him. "You think I can fly."

Rooker shrugged. "Okay, maybe not fly, but something. I seen ya do a lot of weird stuff." He leaned in. "But I know ya got *somethin'* up yer sleeve."

"Well I don't. I was hoping you would."

"Mm." Rooker chucked a stick into the woods. "Well we better come up with something fast. Jackal camp thinks I kept ya alive so I could take you out here and kill ya."

Cold ran up Jack's spine. "What?"

Rooker suddenly hollered at the top of his voice. "All right ya yellow-bellied cuss! I'm gonna slice yer eyeballs outta yer head and make ya wear 'em as a necklace! Eat a pickle ya chum-guzzling fudge-juggler!" Dropping out of character, Rooker jerked a thumb over his shoulder. "Got to keep 'em guessing. Now—"

Jack busted up laughing. He snorted air through his mouth, cackling like a jackass. "Eat a pickle you chum-guzzling—"

"—fudge-juggler." Rooker smiled. "Ya never heard that one?"

Jack couldn't stop laughing. He held his belly, feeling it, unstoppable, deep in his gut. Rooker snorted and joined in. For a moment, the two of them were lost together, seized by laughter in a cascading river of rolling joy that made Huánghūn disappear, even if only for a moment.

Eventually the pair recovered from their hysterics and gulped down enough breath to regain their composure and fall to a series of low chuckles.

Rooker grinned, watching him. "Ya okay?"

"Yeah, I..." Jack gulped and wiped a tear from his eye. "It's been a rough month."

"Yeah, well, life's tough. Laugh or cry, you pick." Rooker clicked his tongue. "Better now?"

Jack looked him in the eye. "Better."

They sat together in a moment of contented quiet, the only sounds the babble of a nearby stream and the cry of the raiptar birds far above. Sitting there with Rooker was the closest thing in a month Jack had had to a moment of peace. Just a few precious minutes of tranquility, a brief respite from the horrors of Huánghūn. He said nothing, not wanting to break the silence, wishing it could stretch a little longer. In the end, it couldn't last.

"So."

"So."

"No one's ever made it through the jungle." Rooker spat. "The shiq get everybody."

"Shiq?" Jack glanced at him. "Hyena calls them dusk-spiders. You guys call them shiq?"

"Yeah, like '*Holy shiq, I'm being eaten alive.*'"

Jack barked another laugh. "Yeah. The shiq are...terrifying."

Rooker blew through his lips, staring at the trees. "They are."

"What about the cliques? Can we use the yingcao leaves to make...I don't know, a shelter or something?"

"No, ya can't make some kind of half-assed spider tent." Rooker scowled. "Yingcao doesn't travel. Didn't ya *talk* to anybody in Hyena?"

Jack shook his head, realizing how long it had been since he'd had a real conversation. "Nobody would talk to me. Except one guy, Ransom, but he wouldn't *discuss* breaking out. He was too scared to consider it. And I'm pretty sure everyone else in Hyena wanted me to die so they could have my food."

"Boo-hoo. Yer not a puppy." Rooker cracked his neck. "What else?"

Jack scowled. "*You* don't have a plan. That means swimming and boats are out?"

"Too right." Rooker eyed him. "Are ya out of questions now?"

"Not even remotely." Jack leaned in. "Where does the great stone door go?"

Rooker lowered an eyebrow. "Ya haven't been down in the mines yet?"

"No. Just rice, and the one where we made boots. Fabrication."

"It's a tunnel. Three paths, all guarded. One goes down to the mines, one goes up to the Institute, and the third fork." Rooker eyed him. "The one with the screaming. The one people go down and don't come back up."

Jack scratched his steel brand, thinking. "Why do they take our blood?"

"I don't know." Rooker cricked his neck. "Maybe she drinks it."

"Gerba," said Jack, his voice dark.

"Gerba *Whipmarples.*" Rooker's eyes met his. They shared a long look.

"I thought it was funny when she first said it."

"Not funny now."

They stood in silence, thinking of the headmistress.

Jack shook his head. "I gotta tell you, Rooker, it's one hell of a prison."

"It's not a prison." Rooker held up a finger. "It's a *school.*"

Jack snorted.

The pirate stood. "Let's move. The camp will want to see your dead body before long. Not sure how to fix that."

Jack cocked an eyebrow. "So why are you smiling?"

"Because now I got *you*," Rooker slapped him on the back. "So get thinkin', Black Jack. Figure out how to fly."

Rooker led the kid down to the stream. *He looks like hell.*

He tried to keep it off his face, but with the growth spurt, the kid was all skin and bones with dark circles under his eyes, more skeleton than man. As Jack drank from the stream Rooker felt his body become tighter, his shoulders creeping up around his neck. He shifted back and forth, gripping his hands. *This ain't gonna get any easier. Better get going.*

"C'mere, I gotta show ya something." He slung his arm over the kid's shoulder and led him through the jungle toward Jackal.

Jack followed, wrinkling his nose. "Does it smell like urine *everywhere* in this camp?"

"There's a midden pit out back for dumping cargo, but when it comes to having a slash, everyone's lazy as hell." Rooker shrugged. "When ya gotta go, ya go."

"It's disgusting."

"That's what yer worried about? No privy?"

"It's unhygienic."

Another big word I don't know. "Listen." He pulled the two brass rings off his middle finger. "Put this one to yer eye." He handed a ring to Jack. "And put this one—"

Jack held the ring up. "What is this? Did you steal this from a prisoner?"

"They're mine, ya seen 'em before." He handed the second ring to the kid. "Here."

Jack put the ring to his eye and held up the other, peering through both. Rooker watched the kid take a half-step back, like most people did. The enhanced view through the rings was a strange sight when you weren't expecting it. "Line up the rings, they're like a spyglass. Get it?"

"This is awesome!" Jack squinted, playing with the distance. "How did the Institute let you keep jewelry? And how did the *convicts* not steal these, they're spectacular."

"The rings have a forgetting spell. Nobody remembers they exist but me." Rooker had long since figured out the fewest number of words to explain the spyglass rings. *Every damn time.*

"Rooker." Jack dropped his arms. "I remember *everything*. I think I'd remember these."

"That's great. Now shaddup and look."

Jack peered through the rings at Jackal camp. Rooker watched Jack dial the far ring slightly, bringing the camp into focus. *How'd he know to do that?* "Okay. Jackal camp. Water tower, cliques, grill, flytraps. And no privy. Now. Look up the hill. The big clique."

"Okay I see it. There's a...*woah*."

Boss Mamba makes an impression. "Big llystra outside?"

"He's huge. He doesn't look anything like the others."

I forgot how sheltered you are. Everybody knew the big alpha crocs were the only fertile male llystra. There weren't many, but they sired all the rest. *Everybody knows that but some half-smart kid from Chegago.*

Unbidden, Gerba's voice drifted into Rooker's mind. *Why has he been lying to you?*

Rooker shook her off. *Bigger fish.* "That's Boss Mamba. He's our real problem."

"He's eight feet tall."

"Ya wanna fight him?"

"Um. No."

"Good call. Yer no fighter."

The kid glanced at him. "I'm not bad."

"Ya stink."

Jack scowled. "I'm fast with Nepenthe."

"*Nepenthe's* fast. You run away pretty good. I'm fantastic and I couldn't take Mamba." Rooker stiffened. "Hey? Ya didn't tell anyone yer name, right?"

"No, you told me not to—" Jack looked at the rings in his hands. "What are these?"

"Forget it." Rooker took the rings away from him and slipped them back on his finger. He pointed at the shirtsleeve wrapped around Jack's forearm. "Hiding that brand was smart. Let's see it."

Rooker watched Jack's brain try to fill in the memory gap. He had never been exactly sure why the spyglass rings had a forgetting spell, but it kept them from getting stolen. The kid struggled with it longer than most, but in the end it was the same. Rooker had to admit a sense of satisfaction watching the kid with the perfect memory suddenly forget his rings. Jack sneezed, and the work was done. "Sorry, what?"

"Your brand. Let's see it." The kid rolled up his sleeve to reveal his mark. The metal glinted in the sun. "*Black Jack.* That's pretty good. Heh." He slapped it. "Check mine." Rooker thrust out his arm. "'Pirate.'" He blew his lips. "I'm gonna change it when we get outta here. Add three stripes."

"Why?"

"So it says, '*Boss* Pirate.'" He flicked a fingernail against Jack's brand. "Wrap that. Don't let anybody see it."

"I don't get it, why's my name so important?"

Sometimes he's utterly useless. "Ya notice not one convict uses their real name? Scar Miller or Benny the Hat or Snowball Zhao? They're all masks."

"Masks for what?"

"Names have power, Jack, ya know that. Ya know a dog's name, he'll come. Ya know a woman's name, ya got an in with her. Ya know a man's name, ya can call him out, ask for help. Knowing a name is having control over someone." He gestured at the Jackals. "And these boys don't wanna be controlled."

Jack raised an eyebrow. "So...is Rooker Flynn your real name?"

(heh) He heard Jasper chuckle in his mind. *(where's the dog?)*

Rooker forced a grin. "Far as ya know. Now listen. Out of everyone ya don't want to give yer name to, the top of the list is Boss Mamba."

"Why?"

"Because as far as Mamba's concerned, the man who kills Black Jack will take his power. Word gets out, yer not gonna last long." He watched Jack swallow, hard. *Good. He gets it.* "Yer gonna need a different handle."

The kid sighed. "Every time I'm around you I have to change my name."

"Hell, I don't remember yer real name."

Jack blinked. "Jack Swift. I told you."

"Jack Swift? Black Jack? Neither one of 'em suits ya." Rooker scratched the stubble on his head. "Yer not black and yer not swift."

"Thanks." Jack scowled. "I've been going by Jasper."

Rooker felt his heart skip a beat.

Somewhere in the back of his head, he heard his brother chuckle. *(jasper. heh. you can't get rid of me, pip)*

"That's a stupid name. I got the perfect outlaw handle for ya." Rooker snapped his fingers, popping a tiny spark of flame. "Chicken Legs!" He took great delight in watching the kid's face fall. "It's perfect." Rooker gestured at Jack's denims. "Look at 'em!"

"Rook—"

"So what's the plan, Chicken Legs? Go."

"Rooker. I. Don't. Have. A. Plan."

Rooker felt his jaw clench hard enough to strain tendons. *Dammit, kid. I spent a month stealing every bit of food I could get my hands on to get ya that acuillo leaf, and this is what I get?* "Nothing?"

"Dammit, Rooker, I'm in the same spot as you! I don't know what you expect!"

"I expect ya to wake up, Jack!" Rooker smacked his hands in front of Jack's face. *Time to straighten him out.* "No knight in shining armor is coming to save ya! Not yer trol pal Memphis or yer little chippie-gal! There's no wizard waiting to jump out and majik ya away someplace safe. Yer *alone*." He jabbed a finger in the kid's face. "Either ya fix this or it don't get fixed, and ya ain't gonna last long with that scrawny bod and that big mouth." He kicked at the dirt. "Yer all brains and no smarts. Without me, ya'd be dead."

The kid scowled. "I said thank you."

"Cram thank ya. Yer either strong enough to survive or yer not. The rest is excuses and whining. Toughen up, Jack."

"I *am* tough."

Rooker punched him in the nose. Jack hit the ground with a stupid look on his face. "If ya were tough ya would have seen that comin'."

Jack spat. "That was a cheap shot."

Rooker stepped closer, drooping his shoulders. "Come on." He extended a hand. Jack took it. Rooker pulled him up and kicked him in the nuts. He dropped back to earth. "*That* was a cheap shot." Rooker paced while the kid figured out how to breathe. "Here's the deal, Chicken Legs. Ya got no idea how to handle prison. I do. I'll keep ya alive in here. I'll make sure ya get fed, I'll give ya protection from the cons and the screws. All ya gotta do"—he met Jack's eyes—"is use that fat brain of yours to get me outta here."

Jack wiped blood from his nose. "I should have known. It's always a bargain with you, isn't it Rooker? I thought we were friends."

"We are." Rooker leaned in. "And toughening up means knowing friendship doesn't count for much in prison, boychick."

"Don't call me that."

Yer gonna listen to me or yer gonna die. Both of us are gonna die. "Don't try to pretend yer tough, kid. That mark on yer arm doesn't make ya Black Jack. I *gave* that name to ya." Rooker stood straight. "The only reason yer Black Jack is *me*."

"Black Jack," came a voice from the jungle. "Really."

Rooker spun and glimpsed Patch Picaroon's face. The jinx grinned like the cat that ate the canary. Rooker raised his hand. "Patch, wait—"

She turned and darted toward Jackal.

Toward Mamba.

Rooker crashed between trees, his bare feet pounded through the mud. *Can't let her get there. Can't let her—*

"Patch!" he yelled as he jammed his toe on a root. "Patch wait!"

She flashed through the trees ahead, and he heard her laughing. *Never gonna catch a jinx, I gotta—*

He burst into the camp clearing to see two dozen Jackals turn his way. Patch stood with her arms held high. "Ladies and gentlemen!" she hollered at the top of her lungs. "We have a new development!"

"Patch!" Rooker hissed.

She half-turned to him, whispering. "Ten pounds of galt, Rooker, or I tell Boss Mamba."

"Ten *pounds?!*" Rooker hissed. "I can't get my hands on that!" Rooker heard Jack come through the trees behind him and skid to a halt in the mud, staring at the crowd.

Patch shrugged as only a cat could. "Too bad." She turned to the crowd. "It looks like Rooker's not gonna kill the kid after all." Angry sounds bubbled up from the men. She flashed two fingers at Rooker. *Twenty.*

"Dammit Patch! I can't—"

"It's another rook from Flynn!" she hollered and jerked her thumb at Jack. "These two are cozy as lice! The Rook just wanted to bring his little boyfriend over and he expects *us* to feed him!"

Grumbling simmered among the outlaws. Not only had they been deprived of a good murder, now it was costing them food. Rooker gritted his teeth. *Three,* he signaled. *Three pounds.*

Patch snorted. "Guess it's time to bring it to the bossman. Let's go see *Mamba!*"

Shouts rose up from Jackal camp. Rooker's heart pounded like a trapped bird as Patch marched up the hill toward the big clique. *This is going bad fast.* He hustled to keep up with her.

"Come on, Patch, please, don't—"

She strode like the cock of the walk. "What's in it for me, Rooker?"

"Ya know I don't have anything." For once, it was true. *I spent it all smuggling Jack outta Hyena.*

"Well *I'm* gonna get something outta this, bet your wasteka ass. I'm sure Mamba will reward me for *him.*" She jerked her chin at Jack and tromped up the hill. Rooker turned around to find the kid limping, a crowd of Jackals trailing behind him.

Rooker snatched the kid's elbow and forced him to walk faster. "Don't do that."

"Don't do what?"

"Limp." Rooker straightened. "Makes you look weak."

Into the dark they went. Every clique was dim, there could be no cracks in the yingcao leaves, but the big clique was twenty layers thick. The only light came from the doorway, cutting across a huge rattan chair the size of a throne. In it sat the massive shape of Boss Mamba, his face hidden in shadow. "Makin' a lot of noise, Patch."

"I—" Patch slapped Rooker's hand away. "Rooker's crooked as a barrel of fish hooks. He's not gonna kill this wasteka frosh, they're in cahoots. The fight's a hoodwink."

A growl came from the shadows. "That right, Rooker?" Mamba leaned in, revealing his saurian jaw. "You pickin' who comes into my camp now?"

Five, Rooker gestured at Patch. *This silent shakedown is killing me.*

Patch shook her head. "That ain't half of it," she grinned at Mamba. "You're gonna love the new kid's name."

Rooker swallowed and glanced at Jack. *He's dead. And if the kid goes, so do my chances of getting off Huánghūn alive.* He caught Patch's eye. *Please.*

She opened one hand, showing five furry fingers and flicked her thumb. *Fifty.*

Mamba leaned in. "What's his name?"

Rooker shot breath through his nose. No choice. *Fifty.*

Patch grinned and spread her hands. *Deal.*

"Chicken Legs," cut in Rooker.

Mamba snorted. "Suits him. Scrawny little wasteka. But—" He flexed his huge hands, showing claws. "Skinny or not, one more mouth to feed is one more mouth to feed. So I guess we're gonna have to get rid of one mouth." Chuckles rippled from his underbosses as Mamba's eyes fell on him. "And Rooker Flynn's got the biggest mouth I know."

Rooker swallowed. *So that's the end of me, a corpse chained to the stake.*

Mamba turned to Jack. "You look like you're gonna die any second, little pink frosh. Tell me one reason I should let you live."

Jack straightened. "Because I'm going to make you the richest man in Huánghūn."

Rooker masked his surprise. Like everyone else in the clique, he watched Jack's eyes. They didn't blink, didn't duck, didn't cowtow. They stared Mamba down.

The big lizard leaned back in his throne. "And how's that, Chicken Legs?"

Rooker had to hand it to the kid, he eyeballed Mamba without a trace of fear. "In a month, I'm going to bring you more food than you can eat."

Silence in the clique. Rooker could almost hear the prisoners drooling over the thought. Mamba shifted his gigantic mass. "How?"

"Give me a month and find out."

Mamba chuckled. His gaze fell back on Rooker, who felt a bead of sweat trickle down the side of his eye. "So you're the one I get to kill."

Jack shook his head. "You can't do that."

Mamba growled. "Can't?"

"I need his help."

Mamba looked from the boy to the pirate and suddenly began to laugh. "I gotta say, it's fun to watch you squirm, Rooker." He eyed Jack. "And I like the way Chicken Legs thinks. But"—he raised a clawed finger—"not a month. A tenday." He stood. "I'll give you one tenday to bring me more food than I can eat, Chicken Legs. Either way it will be entertaining, and I still get fed. Because if you don't deliver"—he flicked his tongue over sharp teeth—"I'm gonna eat you both."

Descending the steps outside the big clique, Patch patted Rooker on the back. He gave her his blackest look. "This worked out well. I'm so glad we came to terms." Patch smiled. "I'll expect your first payment tomorrow. Otherwise..." She winked and flicked Jack's nose. "Mamba's having chicken legs for dinner."

She skipped down the stairs. Rooker went the other way, dragging Jack behind him. Some of the cons grumbled, moving toward him, but he shoved the first man back, barking, "Mamba says we're square! Ya wanna take it up with him, go ahead!" He cut his way through the disappointed crowd.

As soon as they were out of earshot, he turned to Jack. "Stop limping, it makes me look weak."

"I have a cut in my foot," Jack murmured. "I can't just stop limping because you want me to."

Rooker scowled. Whatever power Black Jack had summoned to face down the Crime King of Khandun, it was gone now. The kid looked tired and sick. All Rooker Flynn saw were the blue eyes of a frightened child. "So how are we gonna do this? What's yer plan?"

Jack straightened. "The plan?"

"Yeah." Rooker leaned forward, eager. "How are we gonna get him more food than he can eat?"

Jack's mouth opened.

Nothing came out.

Rooker's heart sank. "Jack?"

The kid shook his head. "I have no idea."

Chapter

12

COUNT TO TEN

*Nothing is particularly hard
if you break it down into small jobs.*

Henry Ford

By his third day in Jackal camp, Jack realized Rooker Flynn was born for prison life.

The scoundrel pickpocketed, conned, bamboozled, and lied his way through every minute of the day, and stole galt like a little girl picking blueberries. He distracted the outlaws with well-timed misdirection, often starting fights between convicts while he walked away with their swag in his pockets. He traded in galt, denims, knives, and leverage. Rooker knew to stay clear of Mamba's underbosses and paid Patch as little as he could. At dinner, he split the day's take with Jack, chewing it while eyeballing another mark. He brought food, he provided a clique, and he frightened off anyone who got too close to his partner in crime. Without him, Jack wouldn't have made it a tenday.

If either of them was going to live longer than that, he'd need to think fast.

Jack was a scientist at heart, and started looking for systems, patterns in the world around him, something he could use to make good on his lie or escape before the hammer fell.

The rhythms of the Locke Institute were simple: up with the sun, gather at the bell, work your assignment, go home, gripe, eat, sleep. Rinse and repeat. Each day the same as the one before, divided into segments broken down into manageable chunks of time with defined expectations and a boss to make sure you didn't screw around. Next verse, same as the first, a little bit louder and a little bit worse.

The expectations of the Institute were uncomfortably close to the rhythm of his days at Walter Payton High School. Up, bell, work, eat, sleep, up. The sameness, the repetition. Jack didn't think it was much of a stretch to think that this is what an average blue-collar or white-collar job looked like. Tomorrow will be the same, and tomorrow, *mañana y mañana*. Up, bell, work, eat, sleep, up. The beat goes on.

Sundown was the first pattern prisoners of the Locke Institute developed. Every single con on Huánghūn could tell you the exact position of the sun at any moment, even from the darkness of the mines. They could tell you within the minute of when the sun would wink out. It was the immutable pillar around which every day revolved.

Jack had learned to cope with the shiq. As long as you followed the rules, they were predictable as Christmas. But sleeping with them, hearing the *tika-tika-tick* of their legs pattering over the thin shield of Rooker's clique every night, hearing them *churr* looking for a way to get in and eat you alive...no one gets used to that.

Starvation was familiar. Of all the prisoners in Jackal or Hyena, Jack never met one who didn't look hungry. Galt was delivered every day like clockwork. The great stone door opened, the attercops dragged out a palate of purple gourds, and eight runners from each camp tried to grab more than the other guy. If anybody started trouble, the attercops broke a few legs. Once back at the camp, the galt was rationed out like gold. Mamba got the most, frosh got the least.

And of course, the most important pattern: every tenday another outlaw rang the Great Bell from the hangman's noose.

Then the bloody cycle started all over again.

Patterns are easy to fall into. Rooker and Jack fell into one of their own. Every night they stared at the ceiling from their bunks. And every night, Rooker would ask him the same question.

"So what's our plan?"

Jack watched spidery shadows crawl over him. "I don't know."

Nine days left.

Gerba Whipmarples never surrendered her illusion that the Locke Institute was a school. Every dawn she would make her morning announcements, invariably upbeat, invariably positive, encouraging the outlaws to excel in their education.

Jack soon discovered rice picking wasn't the worst job on the island.

Lumberjacking was mindless muscle work, hauling whole trees through the jungle and dumping them off the cliffs into the sea for a waiting trawler. Attercops encouraged students with whips made of webbing and broken glass.

Jack thought he might steal some tools from the timber camp to trade for galt, but there were no tools to steal, no axes or saws for the prisoners to turn on their captors. When he asked about it, the other Jackals laughed at him. Jack finally got the joke when Patch Picaroon showed him how the trees were felled.

He had never seen a ringslug before, and they were something to watch. Not many living things survived on Huánghūn, but the big toxic gastropods weren't on the shiq menu. The things looked like giant banana slugs, yellow and sticky, and spent their sluggish lives eating the island's palm trees. When a ringslug got big enough, it formed a circle around the trunk like a tightening belt until it finally cut through the center. Normally, the digestion would take weeks, but some clever devil had figured out a way to speed up the process.

"All right, now watch this." Patch handed Jack two wooden mallets. "Smack 'em together, make a big, sharp noise." Jack did so, producing a loud *SMAK!* The slug's underside came alive with a flurry of teeth. It chewed right through the center of the tree at a mind-boggling speed until the ringslug met itself at the center. The trunk was clipped in a matter of seconds, faster than a chainsaw.

The slug's fat body hung out around the tree like a belt of yellow flab, bloated with fresh sawdust. Patch reached out and flicked the slug's distended body. It ballooned under her finger like a puff-erfish defending itself. The tree toppled away from the bulge and crashed to earth right next to the sledge. Fat and dazed, the ring-slug lolled off the stump and burrowed into the ground to digest in safety.

Jack blinked. "This island's got some jacked-up animals."

"Yeah," said Patch and slapped a mucus-covered ringslug in his hand. "Cut ten more."

As bad as lumberjacking was, the mines were worse.

Jack despised the mines. Two camps, almost four hundred pris-oners, filled the black void below the Institute, packed tight into a dozen tunnels. He got the feeling that Gerba had only invented the other work camps because she couldn't fit more prisoners into the mines. Jack hated the dark, the crowded conditions, the smoky air from the guttering lanterns, the echoing cacophony of steel.

But what he hated most were what the mines did to Rooker.

The pirate had spent his life under a full sail cutting the line between open water and blue sky, freedom upon freedom. For someone like Rooker Flynn, being trapped down in the caves was the same as being buried alive. Steel picks rang on rock walls all day, and Rooker reacted like each one was a jolt to his head. Jack watched Rooker grip his pick handle like he gripped his sanity, holding on as tight as he could.

There was no pattern to the tunnels, just a mad spiderweb that quested through the mountain in a chaotic explosion. Sometimes they would excavate a vein of black diamonds, which were imme-diately carted up to the Institute. Any student caught stealing was next in line for the bell.

The strangest part of the mines was the great stone door that joined the Institute to the assembly yard. The interior of the door, all twenty feet of it, was transparent as frosted glass. Some strange majik allowed the guards to see if any prisoners were waiting in ambush on the other side. The great stone door reminded Jack of those old TV cop shows where the one-way mirror looked into an interrogation room.

On his way out, the numbered pickaxe that had been chained to Jack's wrist all day was unlocked and thrown into a bin. The attercops were lazy as union dockworkers, but they kept close count of the tools, and no convicts were released until every single pickaxe had been accounted for and locked away.

None of this offered a solution to Jack's problem.

That night, Rooker shaved using one of the few mirrors in camp, a broken glass the size of a watch face. He used a stone knife to carve his goatee with meticulous precision. The pirate was more handsome with a bit of scruff, and he knew it.

He eyed Jack in the mirror. "So what's our plan?"

Jack stared at the ceiling. "I'm thinking."

Seven days left.

Patch Picaroon was the toughest woman Jack had ever met. There is nothing meaner than a hungry cat, and Patch was ravenous. She collected her blackmail galt from Rooker every day, and every day they would argue, loudly. It was difficult to out-shout Rooker Flynn, but Patch went toe-to-toe with him and won every fight. After all, she held the trump card and lost no opportunity to press her advantage.

Being a woman in a penal colony dominated by men was tough, but Patch had the dubious honor of being one of the few jinx in a llystra camp that recruited her race just to watch them get eaten by shiq. The crocs thought it was a hoot. Jack wasn't sure why Boss Mamba would protect one of the hated jinx, but rumor had it that Patch ran a quiet smuggling operation between Jackal and Hyena for her boss. Whatever the truth, Patch must be damn clever to still be alive.

She was prison-rich, there was no doubt about that. Jinx are notoriously fastidious, but Patch's furry coat was cleaned to a glossy shine, her boots constantly polished, her whiskers ramrod straight. Compared to all the other Jackals, who were covered in mud and filth, Patch Picaroon was the black diamond in the rough.

She kept Jack at a distance the first few days until she suddenly demanded to see the brand on his arm. The two of them stood outside the women's clique, where Patch ruled supreme, and he was in no position to refuse. Jack uncovered his mark, making sure no one else saw. Patch drew smoke from her little cigarillo. "Huh." She ran a paw over his brand and her golden eyes met Jack's. "You're not him. Unless you age backwards or something, you're too young. I mean, that won't stop Mamba from killing you, but you're no Black Jack." She flicked his brand with a nail and the metal clinked softly. "I was a real fan of those stories though. Ever since I was a kid." A rare smile flickered over her feline face.

I've got a secret admirer. Jack took advantage of the moment and risked a question. "Patch isn't *your* real name, right?"

"Just like your name isn't Chicken Legs and Rooker's name isn't Rooker." She puffed on the cigarillo. "By the way, you might want to be a little more cautious of your boy. He'll use you up and sell your corpse the moment you're dead."

Jack smiled. "Yeah, that sounds like him." Despite herself, Patch smiled, giving Jack the courage to dare a second question. "Why do they call him Rooker?"

"Probably because he's a wasteka con artist who's always rooking somebody." She eyed him narrowly. "Like you telling Mamba you can get him more food than he can eat. That was a whopper."

Jack sighed. "What would you do if you were me?"

"Pay me before you die." She tossed her cigarillo and moved toward the clique.

"Hey, what did you get arrested for?"

She padded up the steps. "Cat burglary."

"Really?"

She rolled golden eyes. "Lord of sea and sky you're dumber than him." She ascended the stairs and waved adios. "Have fun getting eaten."

That night, Jack listened as the shiq crawled over the Red Tiger clique.

"So what's our plan?"

Jack exhaled, watching the shiq crawl over his roof. "I'll figure something out."

Six days left.

Jack and Rooker sat on a cliff at the edge of Huánghūn and watched the tide roll in. They had snuck away from timber camp to get a better look at their options for a sea escape, but the Irridin was nothing but another dead end. The island was edged with cliff faces that dropped straight down into jagged rocks. As far as Jack could tell, the only way to get to the sea was to jump and pray you hit water. Getting a raft down there without shattering it would be impossible.

Beyond the shallows, half a football field out, huge breakers formed a white wall of foam that crashed over a ridge just beneath the surface. The waves were violent and eight feet high.

"There's no way to get a raft past that?" asked Jack.

"Not a chance. The Irridin will wipe out anything that tries to go over that breaker."

"But you said you could swim it."

"I could, it's easy to slip under the waves. But..." Rooker pointed. "There. See that hammerhead shark?" Jack looked into the shallows and saw a tall fin move through the turquoise lagoon. "See the pink?" Jack peered closer; the shark left thin tendrils of rosy fog behind it in the water. Jack realized the hammerhead was surrounded by a pack of semi-translucent squid; the only thing he could see was their dark tentacles. As he watched, another stream of something pink sprouted from the hammerhead; it was leaking blood.

"Razorsquid don't kill ya all at once. Nasty little buggers. They take ya slow, one cut at a time, and wait for ya to bleed out." Rooker jerked his chin at the shark. "He'll be dead by dinner. And then they'll go to work on him."

Jack scowled. "Maybe we could climb down there and catch some fish."

"Some cons have tried it. Rotten climb. Takes too long, attercops notice. Then ya get dumped in solitary, down in the cooler." Rooker settled on his haunches. "Besides, we'll never carry up more than Mamba can eat."

"No."

"So what's our plan?"

Jack stared at the sea.

Five days left.

"Are you Fargil Fleet?"

The runner lounged in his cot, giant rabbit-legs hanging over the edge. His hairy toes brushed the floor as his voice croaked, "A galt for a map."

Jack heard Rooker *hmph*. "A whole galt?"

"That's the going rate." The runner was so caked in mud it was impossible to tell if his fur had ever been anything but brown. Flies buzzed around his head as he cocked up on one lanky elbow, his eyes narrowing. "Wait, are you Rooker Flynn?"

"I am."

"*Five* galt."

Rooker spread his hands, oozing an unctuous smile. "Hey, don't be like that Fargil, we just met."

"You poisoned my Auntie Min. Knocked her cold for three days."

"I did?" Rooker's blinked. "O, the one who got off that freighter with the daimyō. Yeah. I couldn't let him send a message. She's fine though, yeah?"

"And unemployed."

Jack had only met one of the rabbitfolk before, and that one had behaved like a bag of coiled springs. Fargil was the opposite. The long hare was lethargic; he'd barely raised his head since they came in. Smoking a khef cigarette, Fargil was sprawled out over two hammocks. *His legs must be six feet long.* "So you've already scouted all along the—"

"Sixteen circles around all four camps. Three tours." Fargil shrugged. "What else am I gonna do with my time?"

Jack couldn't contain his curiosity. "So what's out there?"

"It's all in this convenient piece of paper called...a *map*. Six galt."

Rooker growled and clenched his fist. Jack intervened again. "You've got maybe twelve hours of sunlight on a free day. What's your average speed? Call it thirty miles an hour...so you've searched a hundred and eighty miles out?"

Fargil glanced at Rooker and jerked his thumb at Jack. "Who is this guy?"

Rooker grinned. "Rabbit legs...meet Chicken Legs."

Fargil turned back to Jack. "Huánghūn's not a hundred and eighty miles long, kid. Maybe forty-five."

"Forty-five miles. That's forty-five miles for a mango tree, papaya, avocados. A patch of strawberries, right?" Jack felt a headache coming on. "Tell me there's something out there."

"You might as well ask for a cow." Fargil stretched, a symphony of laziness. "The shiq eat fruit, too."

That's when Jack knew for certain. There was no food in the jungle. Fargil had run the length and breadth of Huánghūn searching for anything edible, but he was still starved and surrendered to apathy, just a mud-covered bunny waiting to die.

Still, I need to see that map. "I can't give you six galt. But I can get you one."

Rooker scowled. "Hey, don't—"

Jack reached into the pockets of his denims. "Today, I can give you...four slices, another four tomorrow, and the rest—"

"Deal. Here." Fargil snatched the galt from Jack's hand and replaced it with a cracked tube of parchment. Opening it, Jack saw Fargil's drawings of the Locke Institute, the great stone door, the assembly yard and the four camps laid out around the big yingcao trees. The dirt track that led out of the assembly yard led to a clearing deep in the jungle, at least twenty miles out. It was labeled in symbols Jack could read. "Paradise Road? What's that?"

Fargil grinned. "It leads to paradise, because no one who goes there comes back." Fargil smoked his khef, his eyes bloodshot. "The Institute cleared some trees but it's nothing. I don't know what they're doing out there but whatever it is, it ain't done yet." He pointed out the other areas of the map. "The bog's a nightmare, the rock formations are sharp as hell, and the pond is occupied by some kind of octopus-thing that eats the shiq and anything else that comes within reach. Damn near got me twice already. And no, there's no yingcao out there."

Jack pointed at the rock formation. "What's this? Down near the bottom, there's...what is that?"

"Old hunting cabin. Probably built a hundred years ago, before the shiq ate everyone on the island. It's got holes in the roof, you couldn't spend the night there. The only place on Huánghūn you can do that is right here in good ol' Jackal."

Jack frowned. "How long would it take to get to the hunting cabin?"

"For me? A quarter of a day. For you? Day and a half."

Rooker glanced at Jack. "That does us no good."

Jack pulled his lower lip. "Maybe there's a place you haven't found or—"

"Let me give you a piece of advice." Fargil scratched his ear. "Everyone who buys the map says the same thing. 'Maybe.' Then they go out there. To the clearing, to the bog, to the pond. They all see the same thing. There's nothing to eat, nowhere to go. Then they get caught. Then the attercops show off their bodies at assembly. Then they turn their skulls into a puppet show." Fargil lazily held up his hands, miming the puppets. "'Hey Lance, I think we should go this way.' 'Well I don't know Logan, I think we should go that way.' 'Oh no, the sun's going down, what do we do? Ahh!' Then they rip the puppets apart." The runner leaned back in his hammock. "You'll get to see that show sooner or later."

Fargil closed his eyes. "You want to go into the green, that's your business. That map's accurate, I swear it on my thirty children. If you want to pick where to die out there, be my guest. If not, I'll see you for my galt tomorrow."

As they walked away, Rooker leaned in. "So what's our plan?"

"Stop it."

Four days left.

"*Buh-buh-buh*-buh. *Buh-buh-buh*-buh."

Jack sat in the shade of a clique, listening to the rhythm of Billy Pilgrim's skull bonking against the support post. Most convicts knew there was only one way out of the Locke Institute: death. The orange-haired troubadour had found a secret passage: madness. Billy Pilgrim had become unstuck from reality. He attended work every day in blank-eyed catatonia, silent as the grave. He followed orders, but he never met anyone's eye or spoke, staring at nothing. When he got back to camp at the end of the day, Pilgrim took his seat under the clique and started his lonely concert again, murmuring his only word and hitting his head on every fourth beat. *"Buh-buh-buh-buh."*

I guess the Agrat-ban-Haifa only cures the body, not the mind.

Attercops liked picking on Billy Pilgrim because he made an easy target and never fought back. Jack couldn't make out much of his face through the layers of dried mud, but what he could see was layered in purple bruises. His orange hair looked like a muddy fright wig. Jack didn't know how long Billy had been in Jackal, but he wouldn't survive much longer.

Damn 'cops.

Rooker claimed all prison screws were lazy and mean, but the 'cops had raised it to an art form. If someone got out of line they'd just web him up. While their victim was immobilized, they would go to work on them, bashing them around with club-like legs and laughing *kek-kek-kek.* The 'cops' favorite game was to web a convict down half an hour before sunset and take bets on whether he would break out before dusk. Every night by sundown, the 'cops were halfway up the Institute wall. Jack couldn't prove it, but he had the feeling the attercops were scared of the shiq too.

Are the attercops indigenous to Huánghūn? Or did Gerba bring them from somewhere else? And how does the Locke Institute not get overrun by the shiq? Those balconies and halls are all wide open. And full of food. He felt his stomach grumble. *Maybe we can rob the Institute.*

Impossible. Jack blew through his lips and started banging the back of his head on the support beam, keeping time with Billy Pilgrim. *Buh-buh-buh-*buh.

Bribes had their place, with both convicts and 'cops alike. Rooker had discovered some Jackal outlaws harvested khef from the jungle; Mamba had a cigar-rolling operation to manufacture the bribes that kept the attercops from forcing him to work. The attercops were addicted to the stinky weed and could be bought for a price. But between Mamba taking half of what Rooker stole, and Patch taking the other half, there wasn't a ton left over for bribes.

It would take a month for Rooker to steal enough galt to buy a single cigar. And even that would only buy us a day off work. There's no way to get food out of that deal.

*Buh-buh-buh-*buh.

Rice? Too heavily guarded, and the attercops empty pockets.

*Buh-buh-buh-*buh.

(you're going to die here)

Jack heard the wolf's chilling voice, felt the creeping fear that accompanied it. He forced it out of his mind, keeping the rhythm.

Jack opened his eyes to find Billy Pilgrim looking at him like he was a lunatic. Neither of them lost the rhythm, perfectly in time, a madman's duet. *Buh-buh-buh-*buh.

Rooker's head ducked under the clique. "What the hell are ya doin'?"

"The beat goes on," Jack muttered. He glanced at the crazy troubadour, then at Rooker. "Maybe there's a way to help Billy—"

"Stop thinkin' like that!" Rooker barked. "Ya need to help us, not him."

Jack shot back. "Well I need to do *something* that makes me feel human."

Rooker cocked a furious eyebrow. "What's *human?*"

Jaelin. I should have said jaelin. Jack stopped beating his head against the post. "Nothing. Forget it."

"Focus on helping you and me. He's gone with the faeries." Rooker pointed at Pilgrim. The troubadour's vacant eyes stared, seeing right through them. "At least Pilgrim figured a way outta here." Rooker turned to Jack. "How about you? Got a plan?"

"Yeah. Prayer."

Two days left.

"Axie?"

"Yeah boss?"

"I got a...what do you call it? Conundrum."

Mamba and a pair of underbosses wandered past Rooker's clique. Jack and the pirate sat on the steps, watching Mamba stroll by, keeping their mouths shut.

"What's a codrumdum, boss?"

"I'm having dinner tomorrow night," Mamba addressed the air. "Roasted long pig. Two of 'em, nice an' juicy." The big llystra pondered, hands behind his back. "My only problem is what to scrve. What's a nice wine that goes with white meat *and* dark meat?"

"Hawhawhaw! Thassa good one boss!" the second llystra pretended busting a gut. "Cause one's dark and one's white!"

Jack's scowl paired nicely with Rooker's as the flunkies ambled off. Mamba spared them one look over his shoulder, licking his chops.

Rooker leaned back against the steps and watched the sun descend toward the horizon. One of the little earthquakes so common on Huánghūn rumbled beneath them, then stopped. "One day left."

"Yeah." Jack nodded, scratching the ground with a stick.

Rooker squinted at the sun. "Should I ask?"

"No."

Rooker blew out through his nose. "Well our goose is cooked." He spat. "Wonder how we'll taste." Jack didn't respond, pulling on his bottom lip and scratching at the ground. Rooker glared at Mamba's scaly back. "Remind me to poison myself so he chokes on me."

"*Ha.*" Jack's laugh escaped without permission. "Maybe he'll serve us with nice roasted potatoes. A little gravy, a little butter."

Rooker chuckled. "There ain't enough meat on ya for a full meal. Maybe he'll serve ya skewered, get him some Jack-kabobs."

Jack's eyes went vacant as Billy Pilgrim's. His stick stopped moving.

"What?" Rooker leaned in. Jack's head came up, staring a hundred yards into the jungle at nothing. "What is that?" Rooker tensed, coiled like a spring, leaning in. "I know that look. Ya got something."

Jack continued staring, the solution running through his head. "It's a bad plan. It might not work and we can't do it alone. We need help, and no one is going to..."

"*You* figure out the plan. Let me worry about a crew." Jack started scratching in the dirt with purpose. "What are ya doin'?"

"Math." Jack frowned. "We don't need the fastest guys to get the most galt. Just the strongest." He pulled his lip. "How are you going to get people to help? No one likes you."

"There's more than one way to skin a cat." Rooker slapped him on the shoulder. "So what's the plan?"

Chapter

13

STRING OF PEARLS

> *No one can whistle a symphony.*
> *It takes a whole orchestra to play it.*
> **H.E. Luccock**

S ilhouetted against the sun, they leaned against the fence by the water tower, two shadows joined together as one. Both whistled, sometimes together, sometimes separately, a single, lilting tune. After a while, Rooker broke off into a low harmony, then fell into a round, backing up Jack's melody like a mischievous echo.

A musclebound croc walked past, hauling water buckets to his clique. He was one of the biggest llystra in camp, his biceps thick and ropy. Jack raised an eyebrow at Rooker, who nodded and began singing:

> Great green gobs of greasy grimy gopher guts
> Mutilated monkey meat, chopped up parakeet.
> Deep-fried eyeballs rolling down a dirty street—
> And me without a spoon.

The croc laughed at the last line. "Without spoon! Is good!" He lowered the buckets and folded his arms over the little macaroni necklace around his neck. It was an ugly thing with a pink heart at the center that looked like it been made by a little girl. In Jackal, only someone so big could get away with wearing something so childish. "Why you two not kills each other?"

"We were thinkin' about it." Rooker shrugged. "Came to terms. Mates now."

"They talk about you. Smiling pirate man. Devil man." He pointed a claw at Jack. "What is him?"

Rooker ignored him. "You're Copper Dave. You're a big deal. The Hammer of Bego."

"We have met?"

"If we'd met you'd remember it. Rooker Flynn. He's Chegs." Rooker jerked his chin at Jack, who said nothing. "He was just sayin' you couldn't lift that rain barrel." Rooker cocked his head. "I said he was wrong."

Copper Dave eyed the rain barrel under the water tower. "Could lift easy."

"Prove it," said Jack, not looking up, whittling a piece of bamboo to a point.

The big croc scowled. "I don't need prove."

"Hey Pierce!" Rooker shouted at a passing man.

Pierce, another strong-armed bandit, stopped, annoyed. "What?"

"You think Copper Dave can lift that?"

Pierce cocked an eye at Rooker. "Hey what's that song you two was singin'?"

"Can he lift it?"

Pierce eyed the barrel. "No."

"I can lift," repeated Copper Dave.

"*I* can lift it," said a third man, a bruiser from the Shavers. He hooked his arms around the rain barrel, flexed his knees, and lifted. His neck strained, his arms trembled, and he heaved it up, biceps flexing. He sneered at Copper Dave. "See?"

Rooker stood on the fence rail, applauding and whistling, loud enough to catch the attention of a few nearby convicts. A few of them wandered over, wondering what was going on. Jack kept his head down, whittling his stick.

Copper Dave scowled, moving to the barrel. "My little girl could lift. Is almost empty."

The Shaver stuck his chin out. "I could lift it half-full, you ugly lizard."

If Copper Dave had sleeves, he would have rolled them up. "Fill half."

Spectators began trickling in from nearby cliques, checking out the action. Boredom was the eternal problem of off-days, and the commotion soon drew a crowd. One of them filled the barrel half-full, making bets with other convicts. Copper Dave hugged the barrel and lifted it two feet in the air, easy as if it was empty. He set it down, gesturing for the smaller man to try. The Shaver spit on his hands and bent his knees. He gave his best, but the barrel only wiggled as he strained from the weight, then gave up.

Copper Dave grinned. "Go home, ugly man." He flexed, showing off the goods. "Anybody else?"

Before the last word was out of his mouth, Rooker yelled like a carnival barker. *"Copper Dave's takin' all comers!"*

Under the dripping wetness of the water tower the outlaws gathered, cooling off from the heat and watching the show. Men challenged each other, arguing. Nearly everyone in camp had a go. It became a gambling opportunity for the ones who dropped out early, betting on each contestant, cheering or heckling when they failed. The women showed up as a group, and shortly began catcalling the contest. One of them, a broad-shouldered razorback named Yolanda, lifted the sloshing barrel to the *oohs* and *ahhs* of the crowd.

Soon enough, the barrel was full. Nine convicts proved their mettle by lifting the thing to the sound of applause and cheers. Copper Dave was the last to go, lifting the thing up over his head to show off. He lowered it to the ground, grinning white teeth. "Is too bad no more water. I lift more than this."

"You can add more." Jack spun his knife on the bamboo and drilled a hole.

"How?" asked Yolanda.

"Lash another barrel to that one, with a rope between the two." Jack pointed. "Throw the rope over that crossbar, pull it out to about there." He pointed to a spot thirty feet back from the water tower, which just happened to be marked with a rock. "And we see who wins."

Yolanda scowled. "We ain't got no rope."

Rooker answered as if he had been expecting the problem. "Braid some of those skinny jungle vines together and you will."

The outlaws looked at each other. Copper Dave shook his head. "Sounds like work."

Rooker tilted his head. "What's the matter, Dave? You think Bofongu is stronger? Or Yolanda? I bet she is." Copper Dave glanced at Yolanda. The razorback stood a foot shorter than him, but flexed biceps big as skulls, ready to throw down.

"Get vines."

"Hey boss?"

Mamba Crait, the Crime King of Khandun, spread his galt with butter, a rare luxury smuggled in from his two-face at the docks. "Yeah?"

Leech stared at him. "I think you might want to see this."

Mamba growled. He didn't like leaving the big clique. It was better to keep out of sight and rule by reputation and fear rather than prove it every day. But having eyes and ears in camp was crucial to keeping Jackal under a tight fist. "Fine." He popped the galt in his mouth, savoring the depravity of warm salted butter. "Let's go."

He stepped on the balcony to see a crowd gathered around the water tower. Copper Dave dragged on a vine rope attached to two water barrels, hauling them off the ground as the surrounding Jackals cheered and hooted, singing a strange song.

Great green gobs of greasy grimy gopher guts
Scab sandwich with pus on top, vulture vomit, camel snot
Chunky boogers soaking in a chamber pot—
And me without a spoon!

203

"What is this? Some kinda carnival?" Mamba had been smoking khef all morning and his speech was slightly slurred.

"It's a contest, boss. To see who's the strongest."

Mamba growled. "Well we can settle that right this second." He strode down the steps, tail dragging behind him as he stormed toward the water tower.

As Boss Mamba approached, Rooker edged around the back of the crowd, fading from sight. Jack did the same, disappearing around the other side.

"What's this? Eh?" shouted Mamba. "You playing footsie or what?"

"It's a throwdown!" shouted Pierce. "We only got six cons left who can lift them two barrels! Copper Dave, Yolanda, Bree—"

Mamba's tail swiped Pierce off his feet. As he hit the ground, Mamba shoved Yolanda out of the way, grabbed the slim rope and wrapped it around his wrist. "Fill 'em up, Corky! All the way!"

Water sluiced from the bamboo pipe, filling the barrels to the brim. Mamba backed up, pulling the vine rope taut. "You wanna know who the strongest is?" His massive biceps flexed as he curled his arm and dug his claws into the dirt. With one arm, Mamba lifted both barrels. The rope creaked, drawn tight against itself, trembling. The Boss stood firm and grinned crocodile teeth. "Anybody want to try and beat that?"

Not one convict in camp spoke, most of them carefully scrutinizing their feet.

"Didn't think so." Mamba let the barrels drop. They hit the ground and shattered, staves tumbling in an explosion of water. "You've got work tomorrow, so save your strength." He pointed at Copper Dave with his tail. "And don't *ever* think you could ever come *close* to matching me." He towered over the big llystra. "Got me?"

Copper Dave matched his stare for a half-moment, then dropped his eyes. He fingered the ridiculous heart necklace around his neck, mumbling assent. Mamba snorted and stomped back up to his palace on the hill.

Grumbles rose from the men as they departed, the game ruined. As the crowd broke up, Rooker and Jack reappeared, positioning themselves in front of the six toughest thugs in camp.

"So." Rooker grinned. "Ya wanna prove him wrong?"

Every crew needs a nickname, so Rooker dubbed them the Big Six. The weightlifters liked the sound of it and traded friendly insults as they sat together under a palm tree at the edge of the assembly yard.

To the north, Hyena, Buzzard, and Vulture gathered with their eight men, waiting for the dinner dash to begin. Rooker and Jack crouched together, going over the plan with the six muscleheads one more time. Each wore a crooked smile, eager to go.

"Stay focused," Rooker said as his stomach rumbled loud enough to hear. "Don't panic, don't quit. Stick to the pla—"

Attercops emerged from the cave as the great stone door opened, revealing the crates of spherical galt, stacked on top of each other. One bounced free and hit the ground, sending all four camps racing across the assembly yard.

The Big Six were a ridiculous choice for a dinner dash. None of them were quick. They lumbered toward the crate, dead last. By the time they arrived, each of the other teams had already come and gone, heading back with their first round of loot, hooting at them.

Rooker, the fastest of the bunch, kicked the crates apart, scattering purple balls all over. Copper Dave arrived next. From his belt he pulled Jack's sharp bamboo stick. The vine rope was tied through the hole Jack had whittled, making a long needle and thread.

Copper Dave stabbed the needle through a galt. It came out the other end and Yolanda was waiting for it. She jerked the needle, yanking the rope through the center of the galt. A third Jackal grabbed the purple ball and dragged it down the rope away from the needle. At the far end of the rope, the other half of the Big Six operated their needle in the same manner. "Again!" Rooker shouted.

"What are y'all doing?" a Vulture shouted, picking up his second round of galt. "Makin' a little girl's daisy-chain?" He snatched another two galt away and elbowed Copper Dave in the back of the head. "Thanks for the free food!"

"Wasteka," Dave growled, stabbing another galt. He cast an angry look at Rooker. Twenty galt were already gone and all Jackal had was five on a string.

"Faster!" Rooker yelled as he handed Copper Dave another ball.

By the twelfth galt, the needles had gone dull. Copper Dave struggled to jam his through. "Is too thick!"

"Get it done!" barked Rooker in his captain's voice. "Three more each!"

The quickest runners from the other camps returned for their third round, taking more galt with them. Some of the Bix Six started to panic. "Eyes on your line!" yelled Rooker. "I'll tell you wasteka scabs when to quit! Move!"

Copper Dave's needle shattered, broken in half inside the galt. "Dammit!" he yelled. "Stupi—"

"That's it!" hollered Rooker. "Spread 'em out!" The Big Six dragged the heavy strand of galt like a string of pearls. Their giant necklace encircled the remaining galt.

"Now!" They ran south, dragging the string of pearls tight around the remaining galt. A few slipped outside the necklace, but the rest started rolling, collected like sheep trapped in a pen. *"Go!"*

The other camps looked to see all their food escaping. "Hey! *Hey!*" they yelled, but they were running in the wrong direction. Some of them dropped their galt and pursued their hijacked dinner.

The Big Six ran, three hundred purple balls of galt bounding merrily behind them, picking up speed as they went downhill. Rooker laughed, tossing a stray galt back inside the chain.

"They're going the wrong way!" pointed a Vulture. "They're not going back to Jackal!" It was true. The Big Six ran along the Institute wall, due south. "We can get 'em! C'mon boys!" Hungry convicts sprinted after the Jackals.

Eyeing the oncoming charge, Rooker gritted his teeth. "Faster! *Faster!*"

Jackal camp was too far away. Their galt would be picked clean by the other camps before they got home. But Chicken Legs had figured a way around that.

It all came down to a footrace. The Big Six dragged the herd of galt down the slope, all three tons of it. The other three camps caught up just as the stampede reached the stream.

Copper Dave splashed into the water with his end of the line and dozens of galt bounced in after him. The purple balls bobbled to the surface, shiny as a greengrocer's grapes. Caught in the current, the galt sped away from the shore and cruised downriver. Shouting, the other three camps watched hundreds more follow suit as they plopped into the water like a pile of lemmings.

The runners splashed into the water, trying to grab what they could, but in a matter of moments, all the galt was gone, rushing downstream and picking up speed.

Copper Dave bellowed a loud yawp while the rest of the Big Six stood in the water, panting like dogs and laughing, splashing each other.

Hip-deep in the stream, Rooker saw Jack come to the edge, the weakest of the bunch and last to arrive. Rooker jerked his chin at the kid. Jack nodded back.

"Come on boys and girls!" Rooker yelled at the Big Six. "Let's *eat!*"

They returned as heroes. Jackal camp exploded into cheers and applause when they arrived, a cacophony of frenzied voices from every outlaw in camp.

Patch and her girls had captured the cornucopia of floating food from the stream. Their nets of galt rolled through camp and collected in a pile under the water tower, an embarrassment of riches.

Dozens of prisoners slapped the Big Six on the back, hooting and hollering. Copper Dave held his chin high, flexing as Yolanda was embraced by cheering women.

Rooker snapped his fingers and fired up the grill. Knives came out, chopping the galt into slices and they went on the metal grate, sizzling. "Axie!" yelled Rooker. "Tell Boss Mamba we made good on our deal!" He spread his hands. "More than he can eat!"

"I think he knows!" yelled Axie, biting into a galt like it was a big purple apple. "*Everybody* knows!"

Never before had the prisoners of the Locke Institute gathered for a meal without needing to worry if they would get fed. Starving, they tried to eat it all, shoveling slice after slice down their throats, but it simply couldn't be done.

"Rook-er *Flynn!* Rook-er *Flynn!*" the Big Six chanted, slapping the pirate and his skinny companion on their backs.

Somebody struck a rhythm on a hollow log turned into a drum. As a rule, there was no camaraderie in Jackal camp, but the rare combination of too much food and a bit of music went a long way. A few pirates sang familiar shanties, joined by rival crews. Nobody ever saw the flask, but a few men got drunk on contraband moonshine. It was a magnificent party, the kind that only starving men with full bellies can truly appreciate. Soon enough, all of Jackal camp sang.

> *Great green gobs of greasy grimy gopher guts*
> *Mutilated monkey meat, chopped up parakeet.*
> *Deep-fried eyeballs rolling down a dirty street—*
> *And me without a spoon!*

RATE OF EXCHANGE

*Money, not morality,
is the principle commerce of civilized nations.*

Thomas Jefferson

Gerba Whipmarples nibbled a hot cinnamon roll and looked in the mirror, wondering which scarf went best with her dress. The chiffon was superb, gauzy and elegant, but the shade of red was just a bit off-color for her sari. The purple and gold shawl made a stunning contrast, but it made her appear a bit older than she would like. *Ah well,* she thought. *Perhaps bare shoulders are best.*

She caught the tall man's shadow as it appeared in her mirror. "I did not expect you back so soon." Gerba smiled, rubbed off a lipstick smudge, and popped her lips. "Hunting must have been good."

Separating from the shadows of her library, Cant Naysayer produced a sheaf of wanted posters. "Twenty-six bounties including Bloody Bao and that rabble-rouser from Highyon Garde. Your information was good." The bounty hunter idled at her bookshelves, examining her extensive collection. "One hundred sixteen thousand gold marks."

"A small price to pay to put rebels in their place." Gerba checked her reflection, satisfied. "Marguerite?" The acolyte stepped forward. "Please inform the bursar he may pay the Naysayer Brothers and send the Locke Institute's bill to the relevant noble houses." Obedient as ever, the acolyte disappeared down the steps while Gerba did the accounting in her head.

By the time she was thirty, a mere slip of a girl in trol years, Gerba Whipmarples had learned that taking gold from nobles was easy if you give them what they want. Once she took the criminals off their hands, off their streets, and off their seas, they had been only too happy to keep the money coming. They'd pay the bounty, they'd pay her fifteen percent fee, they'd pay to keep the outlaws locked up, they'd even pay for the galt to feed them. As long as the Locke Institute kept the outlaws away, the nobles would keep on paying. *I have all the labor I want, and I'm paid for the privilege. If the excavation continues at this pace, I may return home sooner than I expected.*

"Your new contracts are on my desk." Gerba powdered her nose, checked her reflection one more time, and took up her notes for this morning's announcements. "Some very exciting new prospects. I do wish you success on your upcoming journey, Mister Naysayer. Good luck and good hunting." Gerba straightened her brooch, preparing to mount the steps to the roof of the Institute.

"Such an extensive library." Cant's voice came dry as a snake. He hadn't moved.

She paused, curious. *Now that's unusual. Cant is not one for idle chit-chat. He has something on his mind.*

Cant Naysayer walked to the next row of books. "I keep looking through your collection, headmistress. But I wonder one thing: why don't I see the Book of Kos?"

Gerba stiffened. *So that's his game.*

She enjoyed playing chess with Cant Naysayer. He made an excellent opponent, and she had not anticipated this gambit. Gerba turned, keeping her polite mask in place, playing for time. "I beg your pardon?"

"I made some inquiries, wanting to know more about my employer." Cant ran a finger along the spines of her collection. "Eleven years ago, you were a stable hand for the Summer Mage, Crocius Wei. Just before he passed away." Cant's raspy voice was flat, emotionless. "His prize possession was one of the few remaining copies of the Book of Kos. That book went missing after his sudden murder."

The memory of Crocius Wei's death always brought a warm feeling to Gerba's heart. She had not killed her master. Nothing so crass. She had simply arranged for Wei's wife to discover the old wizard in bed with his mistress while all three of them were drunk and armed. The two women had done the rest. The Book of Kos was currently hidden in a secret compartment in the wall behind Gerba's desk.

She arched an eyebrow. "Are you suggesting *I* killed Master Wei? The Inquisition would disagree."

"I am suggesting you are one of the few people in Keymark who has read the Book of Kos." The Naysayer slid one of the books from the shelf and opened it. "I read it myself, many years ago."

Gerba considered the bounty hunter, impressed. The Book of Kos was written in the tongue of the elves, and nearly impossible to translate. It had taken her years to decipher the script. If Cant Naysayer had read it, the man was smarter than she gave him credit for. *But I am not playing this game with you.* "How very interesting."

"The Book of Kos has quite a bit to say about this island. But you know that, don't you?" Cant turned. "In fact, I would assume that book is the reason you took up residence here. It's not a difficult puzzle, headmistress." He snapped the book closed. "You're digging for the Heart of Huánghūn."

The words hit like a slap in the face. Gerba had never heard anyone say it out loud. No one but the acolytes knew her purpose out here at the edge of the world, but Cant Naysayer had sniffed her out. The thought unnerved her.

She regained her composure. Gerba Whipmarples did not like being behind in a negotiation, and she was in the middle of one right now. Her mind worked furiously to get ahead of Cant. She eyed the bounty hunter up and down, weighing how much of a danger he represented. *He has read the Book of Kos, he knows about the Heart, and he knows about Black Jack. So stay ahead of him.*

"If what you say is true"—she turned—"then you are aware that Nepenthe would aid my search."

"I am."

"And since you are bringing the matter to my attention, I will assume you are, in fact, in possession of Black Jack's staff."

"I am."

Gerba straightened. "You lied to me."

"I did."

"Then you are in breach of contract." Gerba managed to keep the scowl off her face, hearing the voice of her mother. *Wrinkles, dearie.* "You will recall that Nepenthe was included in our agreement regarding Black Jack's capture. Paragraph fourteen states that the Naysayer Brothers are to turn over the staff if it is found during his apprehension. Nepenthe is mine by law." The Naysayer Brothers were utterly without scruples, dependable only as far as their contracts demanded, but there was a simple remedy for that. *You should be careful, Cant. You just might wind up inside the Locke Institute yourself before this is all over.* Gerba's eyes narrowed. "I am afraid I must alert the Inquisition."

"I already have." The bounty hunter leaned against the railing. "Unfortunately, the doktar was in possession of only one *seventh* of Nepenthe at the time of his capture." A cunning smile touched his blue eyes. "I queried the Inquisition, and they ruled that a hand's length of bamboo is not, in fact, a staff."

Such low cunning. A legal loophole. I can outplay you. Gerba arranged the pieces of the puzzle as she mounted the steps toward Cant. "Since you are discussing the matter openly with me, I will assume that you have already tried to summon the other six pieces of Nepenthe from the Tosh." She tilted her horn. "And failed."

"Correct." Cant met her halfway down the library steps. "It seems Nepenthe will only respond to the call of its master."

Excellent. "Then the staff is useless to both of us. What a pity." Gerba waited. She knew what Cant Naysayer was after, but she would make him say it. Once he confessed what he wanted, she would have the upper hand, as was proper. She smiled, refusing to speak. *I have spent more than a decade getting where I am, Mister Naysayer. I am in no rush.*

Cant finally spoke. "Perhaps Black Jack should be given the opportunity to summon Nepenthe." The bounty hunter spread his hands, his voice unctuous as a courtesan. "And let it guide you to your destination."

Perhaps he needs a little push. "I have the man. You have Nepenthe." Gerba lent her voice a twist of coy. "I presume you have an exchange in mind?"

"I do." He produced a piece of parchment between two long fingers and handed it to her.

The payment was painful, but not impossible. It would mean harvesting more lumber for sale, increasing rice production, and constructing more boots and uniforms, but it could be managed. *Nepenthe would save me years. Years.* She imagined the Heart of Huánghūn in her hand, her long search finally at an end. Cant's demand was a bargain.

"A tidy sum." She walked away and moved down the passage that led to the rooftop of the Institute, forcing Cant to follow her. The wind picked up as the Great Bell came into view. "And what, as they say"—Gerba turned on him—"is the catch?"

Cant's duster blew in the breeze. "After you find the Heart, I get Nepenthe."

Ah. So there it is. Boys and their toys. Gerba Whipmarples had little use for a weapon, even an elven artifact. Her purpose was far greater. Once Nepenthe pointed the way to the Heart, the staff would cease to be of value to her. *Still, no point in making it too easy.* "In that case, half your suggested payment would be the most I would willingly pay."

The bounty hunter's rattlesnake voice came too quick. "Done."

I should have offered him less. Portia arrived, offering Gerba a steaming cup of chai. She took the cup and considered the negotiation. Despite being taken off guard, the terms were entirely in her favor. "Do you mind if I have a look at Nepenthe?" Gerba

Whipmarples let her voice lilt. "Just to confirm it is in your possession?"

"Now Headmistress Whipmarples." Cant Naysayer's voice adopted a mocking tone. "You have enough respect for me to know I wouldn't bring it here, where you might try to take it by force."

"Perish the thought." She smiled. *Pity.* "When may I expect delivery?"

"It will arrive on the *Venture Brigand* in a tenday." Cant spread his hands. "Plenty of time to show it off to your guests when they arrive next month."

So he knows about that, too. I need to keep a closer eye on the old warlock.

"That will be acceptable." Gerba added a squirt of lemon to her chai. "I believe we have an accord. The contract will be drawn up for your signature." Cant Naysayer gave a stiff half-bow and turned on his heel, exiting for the docks. "And Mister Naysayer." He paused. Gerba blew steam from her chai. "If you ever lie to me again, you will find yourself alone on Huánghūn at night." She let the words hang. "It would be an unfortunate conclusion to our mutually beneficial relationship."

Cant said nothing. His footsteps descended the stair.

Gerba Whipmarples took a deep breath, enjoying the cold of the morning air.

Nepenthe. At last.

Gerba Whipmarples felt her heart thrill. It was almost too much to hope for. The door she thought was closed had finally swung wide. The trick, of course, was getting the young doktar to summon the remainder of his staff. *And there are so many ways to make that happen.*

"Miss Whipmarples."

Gerba turned to find Portia at her elbow, offering a tray of plums. "Thank you, Portia."

"Would you like me to bring up Black Jack?"

"O no, dearie. We have plenty of time. Remember our goal for the students at the Locke Institute is for them to understand the right thing, and to do it *without* being told." She plucked one of the plums from the table and popped it into her mouth. She bit down and felt the pit crack between her teeth, dripping juice down her throat.

"When the time is right, the good doktar will come to me."

Chapter

15

FREE ENTERPRISE

If you want total security, go to prison.
There you're fed, clothed,
given medical care and so on.
The only thing lacking... is freedom.

Dwight D. Eisenhower

Why has he been lying to you?

Rooker Flynn stood with every other con at assembly, waiting for the hanging. Every outlaw in the yard, now over eight hundred men and women, leaned forward in anticipation, knowing that the convict's execution would make them whole, cure their ills, salve their injuries, and replace the incessant exhaustion of Huánghūn with the energetic vigor of a child. Every one of them silently begged for the death delivered by the noose beneath the Great Bell, anticipating the only good feeling they were likely to experience at the Locke Institute.

Every outlaw but Jack Swift.

As the executioner's mallet knocked the pin from the scaffold and another outlaw did the dance, only Jack refused to cheer. He turned away as the healing majik washed over the camp. Rooker ignored him, closing his eyes to relish the experience. He breathed deep, not even trying to keep the smile off his face.

When the final toll died, Rooker opened his eyes, and he could swear Gerba Whipmarples was staring directly at him.

Why has he been lying to you?

Rooker glanced at Jack. Gerba's question had rattled around in his head for the last few months like a pebble he couldn't get out of his boot. He couldn't figure out what the question meant. Rooker assumed everyone was lying all the time, but the kid wasn't good at it. *He's got a terrible poker face. Look at that sourpuss.*

"Don't get bent out of shape about it." Rooker slapped Jack on the shoulder. "He's dead, yer not."

"Look, it feels just as good to me as it does to you." Jack scowled. "I just wish—"

"Toughen up."

"The hangings don't bother you?"

"Not enough to want it to stop."

Jack shook his head. "You need a Jiminy Cricket."

Rooker blinked. "What's a Jimmy Cricket?"

"Jim*iny*. It's a story we have. Pinocchio. Jiminy Cricket is his conscience, sits on his shoulder, tells him right from wrong."

"I'd squash him like a bug." Rooker scratched his head. His hair had grown out some, but not long enough for his liking. *Gonna need to figure out something for the lice soon.* "Pinocchio. Is that a Chegago story?"

"Hello, gentlemen." Patch slid between the two men, throwing her arms over their shoulders. *She's lookin' healthy. As always. And she's loosened that belt a notch.* Everyone in Jackal camp had gotten well in the month since Jack's string of pearls scheme. Other camps had tried similar tactics, but without a stream all their efforts were wasted. Jackal had become the dominant camp on Huánghūn, and nobody had taken more advantage of it than Patch Picaroon. She had developed into one hell of a hustler since Jackal got wealthy. She leveraged jinx connections in Hyena and Vulture, trading galt for knives, sewing needles, denims, boots, and whatever else she could get her hands on. She had taken charge of Mamba's two-face on the docks and smuggled in contraband in exchange for stolen black diamonds. She traded after dusk, spending the night in Hyena, coming back with all kinds of interesting items, including a flask of cheap whiskey. "I've got a lead on something you want."

"I want a lot of stuff, Patch." Rooker squinted at her. "Is it a three-pound beefsteak?"

"I was trading with some Vultures and a little birdie told me there's a pickaxe in camp."

Jack stopped cold. He'd been obsessed with laying his hands on some digging tools for nearly a month now. Rooker kept walking, ignoring Patch. "Yer lyin'."

She eyed Jack, flicking her tail. The kid's expression was too eager. *No poker face at all.* Patch leaned in, whispering. "Rumor has it the twins smuggled a pick up from the mines."

Rooker spat. "What twins?"

"From the Red Dwarf clan."

"How can ya tell dwarf twins? They all look the same to me."

Jack piped up. "Barney and Yenrab?"

Rooker eyed the kid. "How the hell do ya remember everybody's names? They're not even in the same camp as us."

Jack frowned. "There's not much else *to* remember around here."

Rooker spun to Patch and pointed a finger in her face. "The attercops search every miner before they come up. Ya can't just sneak a pickaxe past 'em."

Patch yawned, stretching. "I'm just telling you what I heard." *Now there's a poker face.*

Jack touched her arm. "Can you set up a meeting with Barney and Yenrab?"

Patch grinned white needles. "Give me three galt and I'll think about it."

It took half a month to set up the meeting. Open hostility was the only thing the camps shared, but Patch was one of the few who could move between them without getting murdered. She greased the right palms, made the right friends, and soon enough a message came that the twins had finagled their way out of their work assignments for the day and were ready to meet. On their turf. Now.

Rooker never liked walking through the jungle. There were no paths between camps, and the way was overgrown with ferns and dead palms. It was eerie, silent, and motionless save the wind. There was nothing alive in the jungle but insects too small for shiq to eat. Every once in a while, a raiptar bird squawked overhead, but that was it. Rooker knew he didn't need to worry about the shiq, it was still hours until sunset. Still, he kept checking over his shoulder, scanning for yellow legs.

At the edge of Vulture camp, Rooker loosed the brass rings from his finger and set them to his eye.

"What are those?" asked Jack, eyeing the rings.

"Forget it," said Rooker. "There they are."

Vulture camp had no water tower. Their collection system consisted of dozens of wooden troughs the size of bathtubs The common area was virtually deserted, but Rooker saw two of the baths were occupied. *A matching set of Red Dwarves.*

Rooker slipped the rings on his finger. "Okay, keep yer guard up, it might be a trap."

"Why would they want to trap us?"

"Does everything have to make sense to you?"

As Rooker and Jack cautiously entered Vulture camp, Barney and Yenrab Bialik lounged side-by-side in the tubs. The twins were nearly identical, with long beards and dented hats, their skin an angry red, as if afflicted by permanent sunburn. The only real difference was one wore an eyepatch.

Rooker had never liked Red Dwarves. He'd attempted a botched robbery of their citadel last year and hoped they didn't recognize him.

"Hoo-*hoo!*" called one, his accent thick. "If it ain't the Jackals, come to bring us some purdy purple galt!"

"And give us the day off!" The other gave a smile that was more gaps than teeth.

"Must be real peachy to eat breakfast while everyone else starves," said the first.

"Must be." The second nodded. Together, they spoke in unison. "Rich pricks."

Rooker cocked a sneer. *Damn rednecks.* "Rumor has it y—"

"Galt," both demanded at once.

"Now look—"

"Nowish." The dwarves stared at him. Rooker sighed and nodded at Jack, who reached into his bag and handed a round galt to each dwarf. They snatched them and dunked them under their butts, sitting on them like eggs. "I'm Barney. He's Yenrab. Don't fret 'bout gettin' us confused, we're used to it."

Like I wouldn't notice Yenrab's missing eye? "Rumor says you've got a pickaxe."

"Two pickaxes." Yenrab nodded. "And a shovel."

"Ya mind tellin' me how ya smuggled all that past the attercops?"

"Well, I'll tell ya, whippersnapper." Yenrab leaned forward in the tub, whispering. "Can y'all keep a secret?"

"Yeah."

"So can I." Yenrab sunk down in the tub up to his nose and blew bubbles, his one eye twinkling.

Jack sat on the edge of Barney's tub. "We'll buy the pickaxes. Ten galt each."

Barney eyeballed him, wary. "And what d'ya need a pickaxe fer, little feller?"

"Digging an escape tunnel."

Rooker bit his tongue. *Dammit kid. Can't you lie just one time?*

Barney laughed like a drunken duck. "Tunnelin'? You hear these hee-haws, Yenrab? Tunnelin'!" He chortled. "Y'all would have better luck paintin' a purdy face on grandma. Tarnation! Sellin' it to y'all would be a waste of a perfectly good pick!"

Jack frowned. "What's so funny?"

"Ain't no place to dig, boy!" Barney threw up his hands. "You think we ain't tried? It's all granite two feet down. It would take ten years to get ten feet."

Rooker opened his mouth but Jack piped up again. "It's not granite everywhere."

"We done picked over every inch of this place, believe me, Freckle."

"You've been over every inch of Vulture camp. Not *every* camp."

"So? Everyone's got the same dirt."

Jack leaned in. "I saw basalt."

Rooker watched the twins straighten, water sloshing over the edge of the tubs. *Well that got their attention. What the hell is—*

"Basalt?" Yenrab's eyes were greedy.

Jack nodded. "Basalt. Obsidian. Some pumice. All igneous." Rooker watched the twins glance at each other, a slow smile creeping onto their faces. *Never saw anyone get so excited about rocks.* Jack faced the dwarves like a man encouraging a horse to take a bite of a carrot. "Do you understand what I'm saying?

Rooker folded his arms. "No."

Barney nodded slowly. "I hear you, Freckle."

"So what?" growled Yenrab. "It's just gonna be another dead end."

Jack smiled like a gambler revealing his last card. "They've got pahoehoe."

The twins stopped cold. "You're pullin' my pick."

Jack nodded. "I've seen it."

Barney looked at his twin with hopeful eyes. "Now that there's a light—"

"—at the end of the tunnel," finished Yenrab.

Rooker glared at Yenrab, then Barney, then Jack. After a moment, he finally erupted. "What the hell is *pahoehoe?*"

Jack smiled. "You know those little mounds of grey rock?"

Rooker squinted at him. "*Every* rock is a little mound of grey rock."

"They're crossed over each other, like a...like a pile of snakes." Jack crossed his fingers and wrapped them around each other. "You know?"

Rooker gave him a look that would peel paint. "I know what a nest of snakes looks like, Chicken Legs. I just never seen one made of rock." He scratched his scalp. "So...what, snakes are good?"

Barney leaned toward Rooker, water sloshing. "Igneous is brittle. Digs pretty easy with the right setup. And..."

"Pahoehoe," said Yenrab, "means pyroducts."

I swear they're just making up all these words. "What's a pyro duck?

"Lava tubes," said Jack. He pointed at the butte wall. "That thing used to be a volcanic plug, you can tell by the sheer face. When it was active, the lava made tunnels under the rock. If we can get into one of those tunnels..."

"...we could break into the Institute..." said Barney.

Yenrab finished the thought. "...and from there, we can get to the boats."

Rooker knew Jack had a vague plan, something to do with digging out of Hyena, but he'd never bothered to think of it as a real possibility. *Damn, boychick. Ya just might pull this off yet.*

Yenrab looked at his brother. "Still."

Barney nodded. "Still."

They both got out of the water buck naked.

"Aw *c'mon*!" Rooker growled and turned away.

Barney hooked one dripping arm around his galt, holding it like a baby. "So. Y'all got a plan. But y'all need our help."

"I reckon we just turn you two in to the 'cops." Yenrab grinned gap teeth. "Get us a purdy re-ward."

This is why I shouldn't let Jack talk. "Try it," threatened Rooker, leaning in. "I'll give ya a lot more missing teeth, ya half-pint hillbilly." He allowed the old smile to creep across his lips. The dangerous one. "But yer not gonna do that, are ya, boys?"

"Why not?"

"Because if ya tell the 'cops about the plan, we'll tell them about the picks." Rooker stared them down. "And we *all* get a trip to the hole." The twins glanced at each other. "Now. What's a pickaxe gonna cost?"

Barney eyed his twin. "Still."

Yenrab agreed. "Still."

"Stop saying still!" Rooker barked.

The two naked twins laughed. "You ain't listenin', bucko." They said it together in harmony. "Still."

Rooker blinked as the light dawned. *A still. The damn shrimps are talking about a distillery.* "Somebody's cookin' moonshine?"

The twins nodded. "Buzzard camp."

"And ya want the still for a measly pickaxe?" Rooker spat. "Forget it."

The twins stood with their hands on their naked hips, dripping. Barney lifted his chest. "Y'all want the pickaxes. We want the still."

I'm not negotiating with a pair of naked dwarves.

"Fine," came Jack's voice. "We'll bring you the still."

Rooker glared at him. *So much for negotiation.* "Just...put some damn pants on!" As the twins jiggled into their palm-frond kilts, Rooker eyed Barney, who seemed to be the leader of the two. "Who's the moonshine man in Buzzard?"

"Woman," said Barney. "Fancy Nan. Some kinda alchemist. They say she makes moonshine from actual moons."

"An alchemist?" Jack smiled. "That sounds like someone I can talk to. What's she like?"

"Cracked."

"Everyone on this island is cracked." Rooker snorted. "What's this one's problem?"

Yenrab shrugged. "She murdered her husband, her son, and her three daughters."

"With a hatchet."

And a"—Yenrab made a stabbing gesture in the air—"what are them things called? Chopsticks." He made one final stab at Rooker and grinned. "Have fun."

It took sixteen pounds of galt, nine khef cigars, and one more hanging to get to Fancy Nan.

Buzzard camp was on the far north side of the island, furthest from Jackal. It took a quarter of a day to navigate there through the jungle, avoiding Vulture and Hyena altogether.

Rooker swatted a stinging bug on his neck and peered through his spyglass rings. Buzzard was hillier than the other three camps, and the biggest clique was raised so high it required a ladder to reach the entrance. The top of the clique was peaked with a clever hatch over the top that closed like a lid at night. It was open now. A thin stream of white smoke luffed from the top.

"That's a distillery all right." Rooker nodded at Jack. "C'mon. And let me do the talking."

Jackal and Buzzard were unified in one regard, they were the only camps at the Locke Institute than took women. Several guarded the hooch hut, each armed with a stone knife. They took no chances, and patted Rooker and Jack down for weapons.

"Send them up," came a voice from above. Rooker and Jack clambered up the ladder and were ushered into the clique.

Sitting proudly in the center of the room was the still. It was the simplest one Rooker had ever seen, a gourd-shaped vessel nestled over a bed of embers. Atop the gourd was a domed plate of glass with a spout running out one end, which funneled to the jug that collected the white lightning.

The smell was intoxicating. Literally. Alcohol lingered in the air, along with the odor of watermelon and something that smelled like ship tar. Jack coughed, his eyes watering at the stench. Rooker breathed deep. *Ah, that's the stuff.*

Civilization was the farthest thing from Huánghūn, but Fancy Nan looked like she would be at home at a polo match. An older woman, her hair was stone-grey, braided down the back in rolling plaits. Lace tatting rimmed the neck of her dress, and real brass buttons dotted one side. Her ears were adorned with several thin chains and a variety of colored stones.

It was difficult to imagine this woman killing her children.

"Sit," her chipper voice came with an easy smile. "Please." Rooker and Jack obeyed as Fancy Nan produced three clay shot glasses, filled to the brim. "To your very good health, gentlemen." She quaffed her shot like water.

The men glanced at each other and took their medicine. Alcohol hit Rooker's tongue and he felt every sore in his mouth pucker shut in pain. Wincing, he tried to swallow, and had the poison halfway down before Jack upchucked. Moonshine sprayed from the kid's mouth and hit the coals, igniting an instantaneous fireball.

What a waste. Rooker swallowed his down with an audible gulp. *"Ahh."* The fumes alone were enough to kill a dog. "The watermelon's a nice touch."

Fancy Nan frowned at Jack for wasting her hooch. "So." She turned to Rooker. "You're the one I'm talking to."

Rooker winked and toasted her. "Believe it, sister."

"One more crack like that and I'll have them throw you off the balcony." Fancy Nan snapped. "I'm not sister, sis, miss, ma'am, missy, honey, babe, darling, tootsie, twist, chick, or chippie, and none of us here are ladies." The young women around her chuckled. "I am Nancy Guinevere Mannus, née Fondlaw, or

Fancy Nan if you must, but that is the only liberty I will allow you to take, sir."

"Fancy Nan. I misspoke." *Give her the old pearly whites.* He produced his most charming smile. "I was flummoxed by your beauty."

"Unlikely. The only reason I am considering a trade is because you Jackals have stolen all the galt. That's a dirty stunt you keep pulling." She raised a waxed eyebrow. "Whatever you want, it's not coming cheap."

Rooker eyed the girls. They looked tired and gaunt, especially the young one, the dark girl. *I bet she doesn't weigh seven stone.* For a moment, he almost felt bad for her. *Shut up Jimmy Cricket.*

"Nan. Sweeth—" Rooker stopped just in time. "Sweet setup you've got here." Jack rolled his eyes. "Aren't ya afraid the 'cops will shut ya down?"

"You let me worry about that. How many jugs do you want to buy?"

"Well now Nanny—" She scowled at Rooker but he continued. "How much would ya take for the whole kaboodle?"

Nan's eyes widened. "All twenty-two jugs?" She glanced over her shoulder. "I—"

"No, ya aren't followin' me, hon. We want the whole thing."

She followed his gesture, looking at the still. "You want Thunderbuck?"

Rooker snorted, laughing. "Thunderbu—"

"Are you out of your mind?" Nan shot to her feet. "That spout was shipped to me, a gift! It is a finely crafted piece of art! Irreplaceable! You think I am going to part with *this*, the one thing that makes sure I don't get shanked in this God-forsaken place?" She jabbed a finger in Rooker's face. "You must have been born a few cards short, buster."

No Nan. Yer gonna trade ol' Thunderbuck because ya ain't got a choice. He raised his hands. "Now don't get yer panties all bunched up, sweetheart, we're just—"

"Throw him out."

Rough hands grabbed Rooker's arms. Before he knew what was happening, he was shoved through the door, smacking a shoulder into the wooden frame. Someone grabbed the waistband of his denims and he was suspended over the twenty-foot drop from the balcony.

Jack shouted. "Please, you've got to listen to us!"

"You're going with him young man." Rooker heard more women grab Jack as he stared at the earth below. *O this is gonna hurt.*

"I can replace it with something better!" came Jack's shout.

Fancy Nan held up her hand and the guards paused in mid-grapple. Rooker looked to see Jack with his face pressed against the floor, a knee buried in his cheek. Nan cocked her head. "Something better? What's better than Thunderbuck?"

Jack's mouth moved like a hummingbird's wing. "Your condenser isn't cooling efficiently, you need a thump keg and a proper thermoscope, plus a fractionating column to make use of Raoult's law. Off the top of my head."

Rooker blinked. *What the hell did he just say?*

Fancy Nan's eyes narrowed. "Who *are* you?"

"Someone who appreciates your skill," said Jack, his face mashed by a boot. "I assume before you got the glass you were using a clay d—"

"Clay dome, yes." Nan eyed the kid like she had discovered a new species. She jerked her chin at the woman holding Rooker. "Let him back in. If he talks, punch his mouth." Rooker was released as Fancy Nan let Jack sit up. "What is Raoult's law?"

"It's French." Jack panted. "And it can double your yield."

Fancy Nan stared at him, then glanced at her assistant, the dark girl who hadn't said a word. She nodded. Nan turned to Jack. "This is some kind of a trick."

"It's not," said Jack.

"You're lying."

"And yer starving." Rooker's guard punched him in the mouth. "Heh." He spat away blood. "We'll give ya fifty pounds of galt." He heard the women inhale as one. "Plus ya get the design for a new still. A *better* still."

Nan considered. "No."

Rooker felt his stomach drop. Without Thunderbuck, there was no pickaxe. And without a pickaxe, they were never tunneling out.

Fancy Nan eyed her assistant. "However." Her eyes caught Jack. "I will accept your proposal if you include one final item."

"Name it," said Jack before Rooker could speak. *Worst haggleman on Huánghūn,*

"My journal." Nan leaned in. "My theories, my experiments, my notes. Forty years of my life's work. Gone." She snapped her fingers. "Lovely green leather. Gilt engraving around the edges. A little brass lock on the side. If I had my journal, to pass on to future generations like Farah"—she glanced at her silent assistant—"then you would have something worth trading."

"Green leather," said Jack. "And a little burn mark on the right top edge?"

Fancy Nan blinked. "How in the world did you know that, young man?"

Jack sighed. "Because I've seen it."

Rooker frowned. "Where?"

Jack leveled a cold eye at him. "Gerba Whipmarples' vault."

Rooker stomped through the jungle, swatting at stinging bugs both real and imagined. *This corkscrew keeps getting twistier. How the hell are we going to get into her vault?*

But another problem kept picking at him. He slapped a bug on his neck. "Hey?"

"Hey?" came Jack's voice.

"What's the French?"

"Huh?"

"You said it discovered Raul's Law."

"The French." Jack laughed that great laugh of his, but this time Rooker didn't join in. "They're not an 'it', they're a...group of people."

"Where?"

Jack picked up a little speed. "Near Chicago."

Rooker kept pace. "Did the French teach ya all that stuff?"

"What stuff?"

"The...whatever-that-was with the still. Raul's Law. Fractioned columns. Pahoehoe. Nobody knows all that stuff. Not unless they apprenticed to an alchemist in a mining camp." Rooker smashed another bug. "How'd ya learn all that in some little podunk village?"

Jack laughed over his shoulder. "Just a lot of books. Come on, we need to get back to Jackal."

Books. Rooker slowed, letting the kid get ahead. *Ya can barely read, boychick.*

"Don't worry, Rooker," came Jack's voice, further away now. "We're gonna figure a way out of here, you and me."

Rooker stopped walking.

You and me.

He heard Jasper's cold, dead voice in his head.

(yeah. you and me)

Sure, Rooker thought. *A team. Maybe we'll build a mill together.*

(you and me, pip)

Something cold crawled over Rooker's spine. Long-forgotten fingers wrapped around his heart. Cold water. Darkness. And her voice.

Why is he lying to you?

Chapter

16

GUESSING
GAME

*The cobra will bite you
whether you call it cobra or Mister Cobra.*

Indian Proverb

235

J ack tickled his fingers into Rooker's back pocket, hoping he'd get lucky.

"No." Rooker slapped his hand. "Try again."

Jack frowned. "You didn't *feel* that."

"Damned if I didn't, yer gentle as a walrus. Again."

Rooker Flynn was a lousy teacher. He had attempted to instruct Jack in the subtle arts of pickpocketing, thievery, and sleight-of-hand over the last tenday, and Jack wasn't sure he'd learned a thing. Today they practiced behind the fabrication workshop, and it was frustrating for both of them. If Fancy Nan's journal was still in Gerba's vault, they had to figure out a way to steal it. The problem was the only thing Jack had ever stolen in his life was a tin of Altoids from Mariano's grocery. As it turned out, his hands were steady enough for surgery, but too rough to pick a pocket without giving himself away.

Rooker slapped his hand again. "No. Go easy. Quick, but easy. Ya gotta make yer hand part of the pocket."

Jack drew a breath and tried again.

Winston had taken two khef cigars to deliver Jack's request to see the headmistress. Some part of Jack believed Gerba Whipmarples had been waiting for him to ask, that he would be ushered upstairs immediately. That was a tenday ago. No word, no message, no special look during morning announcements. Only silence from the headmistress's office.

Two months had passed since their first string of pearls dinner dash. While Jackal camp had been ecstatic with the feast, Boss Mamba grew angrier by the day. The big llystra didn't like his underlings having more than enough. That status was the exclusive honor of the camp boss, and Mamba did not enjoy sharing it. The Crime King demanded the galt be stored in his big clique, where he hoarded it like wheat for the winter until his hut bulged purple.

In the meantime, the other camps had grown desperate for food. Originally, Jack intended to pull his little trick once every few days, but Mamba insisted Jackal use the strategy every time, forcing the other camps to starve. Most of them would be dead if it wasn't for the regular hangings. The attercops hadn't done anything to fix the uneven distribution, and the atmosphere at morning assembly had become murderous. Jack knew it would not be much longer before things erupted into violence.

Even if I get Fancy Nan's journal, I'm still going to need Hyena on my side to try tunneling.

Rooker slapped his hand again. Jack winced, gripping his red knuckles. "*Ugh*. I'm trying!"

"Ya got hands like an ape." Rooker dragged the galt slice from his pocket and threw it at Jack. "Forget it. Where is this vault anyway?"

"In a hallway behind her office."

"How are you going to get it out of there?"

"I don't know."

"Well what the hell *do* ya know?" The pirate's attitude had turned foul since they came back from Fancy Nan's. A dark cloud hung over him, a scowl permanently etched on his face. "Ya got nowhere to hide it anyway, what're ya gonna do, stuff it down the front of yer pants?"

"You tell me! You're the expert!"

"Yer backside's flat as Aunt Possum's pancakes." Rooker scowled. "I dunno. Maybe cover it with a shirt."

"So jam it down my crotch? That's the plan?"

"Black Jack," came the sudden voice of an attercop. Winston. The big spider stood on the roof of the workshop directly above them. He dragged in a lungful of khef smoke. "Come with me."

"Dammit, I said gimmie my shirt back, Chegs!" shouted Rooker. He grabbed Jack's shirt and yanked it off. "Stop stealin' my threads!" He pulled off his shirt and thrust it in Jack's hands. "Lousy wasteka thief!"

Jack pulled on Rooker's larger shirt, leaving it untucked over his waistband.

"*Kek-kek-kek*," the attercop chuckled. "Let's go. She's waiting."

Inside the mine, Winston blindfolded Jack at the third fork. *The one where no one ever goes. The one with the screaming.*

One hundred and seven steps later the screams were louder. Jack heard banging metal, like bars rattling in a cage or a broken washing machine whanging in the dark. The air smelled of sulfur. Something shouted nearby, howling some guttural language he didn't understand. He heard several bleating animals...*Or are those voices too?*

Hairy legs grabbed him and he was hauled upwards. Jack's feet dangled as the attercop climbed...something...and the noises fell away below. Soon enough the sounds of the mine were replaced by the *tink-tink-tink* of hammerdwarf masons sculpting the inside of the butte, building Gerba's school. Jack's feet touched smooth stone and they walked sixteen paces, ascended one hundred twelve steps in a spiral, turned right, took eighty-eight steps, and stopped. Something that sounded like a wooden door opened, creaking on its hinges, and Jack felt the pressure change.

Beyond, he heard the ghostly sound of a harp.

His blindfold was removed. An acolyte stood before him, masked in her niqab. She took his elbow and ushered him into an elegant dining room.

Eight stone arches soared to a twenty-foot ceiling, carved with amazing detail work in bas-relief. Marble tiles lined the floor in neat interlocking shapes that shone with fresh polish, reflecting light as if wet. The center of the room was dominated by a twenty-guest dining table. The room had a formal, intimidating aspect, complete with a too-big fire crackling in the elegant fireplace next to the veiled harpist.

"Welcome back, doktar!" The headmistress of the Locke Institute smiled cue-ball-sized teeth. She wore gold bracelets and a lime green gown that looked like it might be at home at a dinner party for the Seattle Seahawks. "Please"—she gestured—"have a seat."

The stone chair was waiting for him. Jack instantly felt his throat grow tight, remembering the tentacle in his mouth, the knife at his arm, and the smell of his burning flesh. A phantom pain rippled through his metal brand and he felt the heat of it, the sizzling metal in his arm. He stopped, nearly tripping over his feet.

Gerba blinked at him. "Or would you prefer to stand?"

Toughen up.

Jack swallowed hard and sat in the stone chair.

"Back where we started." He leaned back, pretending to be comfortable. "Just you and me."

"You and *I*, dearie. You and *I*." Gerba gestured an acolyte forward; she came bearing a metal tray. "So. May I ask why you have requested this meeting, doktar?"

Jack found his voice. "I have an offer for you."

"An offer. How very interesting. Portia, bring supper if you please." The acolyte nodded and disappeared. Gerba lifted the lid off the tray, revealing two glass cups resting upside-down in steaming water next to a bamboo scalpel. "Are you going to sit still for this, dearie, or do you need help?"

Jack felt the stone chair shift underneath him. He gritted his teeth. "I'll be good."

"How delightful." She stuck his vein with the scalpel. Jack drew a sharp breath and Gerba clapped a hot cup over the wound.

The harpist continued playing a sweet melody from the corner of the room, hidden behind her niqab.

As the cup filled red, Jack blinked. "Why do you take our blood?"

Gerba cocked her head. "That is not an offer."

"No, I was just thinking I could show you an easier way. Cleaner, less painful." *Like basic phlebotomy instead of fifteenth-century bloodletting.*

"Ah, neither of those things interest me, I am sorry to say. Now if you are determined to waste my time, I shall have the acolytes escort you back to class."

Jack eyed the purpling sky. "It's almost sundown."

"Yes." She tucked her napkin into her bodice. "Pity."

Jack took a breath. *Give her what she wants.* "I'd like to play a game."

Gerba Whipmarples' eyebrow arched. "A game?"

"Each of us picks three things from your vault. I'll identify all six and show you what they do. In exchange, I get to pick one item to keep."

Gerba leaned back in her chair. *She's curious.* "Any three items?"

"Any three."

Her rhinoceros face broke into a smile as she clapped her hands. "O, this sounds like fun! Which ones do you pick?"

Jack described the items and one of the male acolytes took notes. Gerba whispered in his ear with her selections, then he was off to collect the treasure.

She eyed Jack, excited as a little girl. "So! The metal charm the size of an apricot...what is it?"

Jack forced a smile. "You'll have to wait and find out."

"O, secrets! I like it." She patted her giant hands. Portia returned with a tray of ripe plums, sliced mango, kiwi fruit, a soft white cheese, steaming golden brown crescent rolls dripping butter, and a crystal decanter of white wine. Jack felt his mouth water like Pavlov's dog. His stomach rolled over and begged.

Gerba tossed a handful of plums in her mouth and bit down, crushing the pits like ice cubes. She dabbed her lips with a linen tablecloth, eyeing the cup on his arm. "I think that is full." She pressed a cloth against Jack's arm, popped off the cup, and deftly replaced it with a fresh one. "O! Where are my manners? Here you are, be my guest." The headmistress handed him a glass of wine.

Jack licked his lips and drank a sip. Tart, buttery, and cold. He felt an involuntary *ahh* escape his lips. "Thank you."

"You are so very welcome. And please, have some food, of course."

The smell of salted butter demanded his full attention. He picked up a thick slice of bread, warm and soft in his hand.

She's not looking at me.

Three months ago he never would have noticed it. The way she turned her head aside, the way her eyes watched a corner of nothing in the room, pointedly looking anywhere *but* at him, making certain he knew how little she cared about what he was doing. Jack had spent enough time with liars and thieves to catch it, and he realized how badly Gerba Whipmarples wanted him to eat.

A little scopolamine or burandanga in the food, maybe a light poison...not enough to kill him, but something to help him lose his focus, make a bad decision, get him off his guard. He watched Gerba chew the plums. *She outweighs you by more than two tons, a little bit wouldn't phase her. But you're dehydrated, malnourished and...*

He looked down at the wine glass in his hand. The second cup of blood leaking from his arm.

Jack suddenly realized he was in a chess game for his life, and he was losing.

"I'm sorry, I'm not very hungry." He set the bread down.

If he hadn't been looking for it Jack would never have seen the scowl flicker across Gerba Whipmarples' eyes. The headmistress forced a smile. "Well, dearie, I will just leave it there in case you get peckish."

The acolyte returned and laid six items out on the table. One of them was a green leather book with gilt edges and a tiny clasp. Fancy Nan's journal. *Okay. It's out of the vault. Now all I have to do is get it home.*

Jack adjusted Rooker's shirt and reached for the first item he had requested. "This"—he took hold of the metal thing the size of an apricot—"is a pocket watch." Some retrophile kid at Walter Peryton High had it strung to his satchel on a chain. Jack clicked the button and the watch face popped open.

Gerba smiled. "Delightful! What does it do?"

"Hold it to your ear." She did. "Hear that ticking? It tells time."

"Ah." She looked vaguely disappointed. "A small hourglass. How interesting. And what about this one?" She revealed her first selection: a flashlight. A big black Mag-Lite, the kind cops used. Jack thumbed the switch and turned it on, making sure he got Gerba right in the eyes. She threw up her hands and sputtered. "O, I do not like that at all."

Jack handed it to her. "It's a flashlight. A torch."

Gerba swept it around the room, following the beam. "Hm. A bullseye lantern. What else?"

Jack's second item was an old audio player with attached earphones that looked like it had been handed down several times. Jack flicked the button and the screen lit up. *7% power.* "Here, put this in your ear."

"Really? All right." Gerba put one bulb in her ear. Jack hit the button and he heard Taylor Swift singing 'Shake It Off' inside Gerba Whipmarples' skull.

Jack stifled a chuckle as Gerba yanked the earphone out, scowling at it. "That is *much* too loud." She tossed the headset on the table and frowned. "A small music box. This is not what I was hoping for. Let us try this."

Her second selection was a quad-propeller drone barely small enough to fit in a backpack, probably from one of the Media Club kids.

Jack looked it over, switched the on/off button and got nothing. *Good.* "It's dead, but it used to fly. You could control where it went."

"And how do I make it alive?"

Get a 120-volt socket. "You'd have to take it to the Tosh."

Gerba frowned again. "And what about this?" She held out something small. Jack saw a familiar yellow GOTCHA sticker.

My phone.

Jack took a breath. It was still plugged into the external battery and lit up immediately. *98% power.* Gerba nodded. "It has the painting of you. Right there. It makes light when I touch it, but when I try to do anything else, these symbols come up."

The keypad lit up, asking for his passcode. Jack swallowed. "Um..."

"It is not dead." Gerba leaned in. "You cannot claim to not know how to operate it. And you told me you would show me how it worked. So. Make it work."

She had him. Gerba Whipmarples had already violated his body, and somehow this felt almost as horrible. "Go on."

Jack frowned, knowing he didn't have a way out. Reluctantly, he typed in his code, Sw1ft#.

"Show me again, please." Jack frowned, went back to the lock screen, and typed in his password again. The main screen popped up. *Too bad I can't call 9-1-1.*

"Well isn't that delightful?" She plucked the phone from his hands, but not before Jack saw his last text with dad.

Dinner @ 6

I'll be there

Gerba Whipmarples took it away from him and tapped at the screen, fascinated. "O, I could play with this all day. But! Before I do, let us discuss your final item, shall we?" She slipped Jack's phone into her pocket and placed one finger on the green book. "What, my dear, is so interesting about Fancy Nancy Guinevere Mannus, née Fondlaw's journal?"

Dammit. Jack stammered, caught flat-footed. He fumbled for a lie and couldn't find a good one. "I heard a rumor. That...she stumbled on something interesting."

"Fancy Nan stumbled on something interesting." Gerba cocked her head. "New and interesting ways to murder children?"

"That's horrible."

"She is a horrible person, Jack. Mistress Fondlaw is a monster. So what could be in her journal that you might possibly want?" She took the book. "Let us take a look, shall we?" She flipped open the cover to the first page, which was scrawled in incomprehensible symbols. Gerba frowned. "What is this?"

Jack leaned in and looked at the writing. "Can I just—" Gerba handed it over and let him leaf through the pages. He kept going, looking for anything useful. One page after another, the book was filled with nonsense and gibberish. Scrawled doodles, crazy scrawls, jagged kanji. It couldn't even be code, it was so chaotic. There were some words Jack recognized, and every few pages there was something resembling a chemical formula or a botanical experiment, but most was just the scattered ravings of a madwoman.

"Worthless," said Gerba. "Utterly worthless."

"Wait, there's got to be—" Jack flipped through the pages, desperately looking for anything that made sense. Half-filled grids. Senseless scribbles. Tangled drawings of birds. *Nothing.*

He reached the final page and stared, his face blank. Gerba snapped the book shut. "Well. So much for that." She straightened her dress. "There is no place at the Locke Institute for such nonsense." She snapped her fingers, and the pages went up in green flames.

Fancy Nan's journal glowed jade embers for a moment, and Gerba tossed it into the fireplace.

Jack's eyes went wide as it burned. *Gone. The distillery, gone. The pickaxe, gone. My tunnel, gone.*

"Let us take the air together, shall we?" Gerba smiled white teeth, dusting off her hands. "I do hate to miss a good sunset."

Atop the Locke Institute, the four camps were laid out at Gerba's feet as if she were a goddess surveying her domain. Purple clouds threatened rain as the sun mellowed toward the horizon and Huánghūn was touched with golden light over a green carpet of lush palms blowing gently in the tropical wind. It looked like a tourism photo for some island in the South Pacific. *Come to the Isle of Huánghūn for the sandy beaches, tropical drinks, and giant vampire spiders*, Jack thought bitterly. *Once you arrive, you'll never leave.*

"Black Jack," came Gerba's voice. "It is so odd to call you by your pseudonym. Black Jack is just a teensy bit silly, is it not? Lovely for songs and all, easy to rhyme, but cumbersome for an actual conversation. Tell me your surname so we can know each other better."

Jack had learned to play this game. *You've taken enough. You're not getting my name.* "Just Jack."

"Just Jack." Unperturbed, Gerba folded her arms behind her back. "I want you to understand that your contributions do not go unnoticed here at the Institute. I enjoy your new ideas. In fact, do you remember the first day you arrived? You mentioned there was a bell in your Tibet that had smaller bells dangling all around the rim. I thought that idea was so charming that I have made your suggested modifications. See?" She gestured at the Agrat-ban-Haifa and Jack saw hammerdwarves fastening slim chains that dangled from the rim. A series of bowling-ball-sized bells were arranged on the ground, waiting to be attached. "More to ring! You had a particularly good idea there." She turned to him. "But if all you have for me now is dead machines and music boxes"—Gerba shrugged massive shoulders—"it would be so disappointing for things to end there, don't you agree?" Gerba Whipmarples gazed out over the island, watching the sun settle behind the trees. "Ah, the show is about to start."

As the sun set, Jack felt his heart beat faster and faster as panic welled up inside him. He'd been on Huánghūn for three months; the fear of the dark had become instinctual, a survival necessity dug in bone deep.

From atop the Institute, Jack watched yellow bodies swarm the jungle, keeping pace with the shadow of the setting sun. The shiq were everywhere in the trees, flowing like the rising tide. Jack shuddered as they poured over Jackal camp. He watched his clique, with Rooker inside, overrun with yellow spiders.

The shiq broke toward the Locke Institute. They stampeded across the assembly yard, yellow legs scissoring across the empty field. They hit the Institute wall and came straight up it. Jack was overwhelmed with the need to flee, but Gerba Whipmarples' huge hand on his shoulder was immobile as the stone chair.

Shiq climbed toward him, a rolling curtain of skittering legs and dripping fangs. Jack felt a shriek rise in his throat, a tea kettle coming to boil.

"And stop...right...there," said Gerba, and the spiders did.

Jack swallowed. Thirty feet above the assembly yard, the shiq paused. The bottom third of the Institute wall looked like a giant had painted it yellow, but not one spider crossed that invisible line. The shiq milled about and turned, replaced by the next group behind them, who did the same. Over and over and over.

"You see? They do as they are told. Very good students." Gathering his courage, Jack leaned out a little further. Embedded in the wall, he could see a faint series of red markings, each pulsing gently. *Spider stop lights.*

Gerba nudged him closer to the edge. "Now. I recognize you are willing to help make the Locke Institute a better place. And I look forward to many more meetings like this one, for an honest exchange of ideas. So." She reached into a pocket. "As a gesture of goodwill, I have a gift for you." She extended her fist and opened it, revealing a tiny stick of pale bamboo.

Nepenthe.

"One of the acolytes found it a few days ago. Misplaced in the commotion."

Jack wasn't listening to her. His heart swelled.

Power. He'd been without it so long, helpless, weak, starving, outnumbered. Nepenthe was all the power Jack could ever want. He imagined the *wikk* tingling up his arm, the blazing glory of the elven majik in the palm of his hand.

He did not see the dark smile in Gerba's eyes. "I thought you would like to have it back." She extended her hand, offering it to him.

Jack reached for the bamboo. Power. *I could beat any man in camp. I could beat Gerba. With Nepenthe, I could knock her off the wall.*

(she knows that)

Jack's hand froze. The cold voice of the wolf rose within him.

(she's counting on it)

Jack didn't move. He wanted it. More than anything, he wanted it.

His lupine shadow chuckled bitterly.

(so does she)

Jack looked at Gerba's face and saw the hunger in those sea-green eyes. "Please, doktar, take it. It is yours."

The invitation, the game, the wine, the food. It was all for this moment. "If I summon it"—Jack swallowed—"Nepenthe becomes just one more of your collectables."

"O my dear Jack. You think too much of me," the headmistress tittered. "I am no match for Black Jack with the power of Nepenthe in his hands. There is nothing *I* could do to stop you. You can do as you like, go where you please." She leaned in. "Once you have summoned all seven pieces."

Jack grit his teeth. *She can't take it from me. She's not strong enough.*

(she is)

She can't.

(she will)

Jack stared longingly at the bamboo in her hand, then looked Gerba Whipmarples in the eye.

Toughen up.

He dropped his hand, empty.

Frown lines crossed the headmistress's face, canyons in her leathery skin. Her eyes went from hopeful to angry, her pretty smile twisted to a snarl. The first pats of rain fell, running down her bejeweled horn.

"I think I have had quite enough games for today." She touched the brooch at her collar and Jack saw a faint reddish glow pulse from within. "I was hoping we would be able to learn from one another. But how in the world can we be expected to do that if you refuse to share?"

"Gerba, I—"

"No, no, dearie. Class time is over."

Jack never heard the thing rocket up the wall behind him. He only felt it, a pressure wave of air that shuddered his body. He turned around to watch something black and long as an airliner speed straight up in front of his face. Scrabbling backwards, Jack watched the gargantuan shape fly up over the wall and shoot into the sky.

Two moons shone through the membrane of its black wings. They eclipsed the heavenly bodies, a diaphanous film drawn tight between eight legs as wide as a ship's sails. The arachnid dragon beat its wings once, twice, thrice, as its eight-eyed head stretched toward him on an elongated neck. Its mandibles opened wide, revealing fangs the size of lances. It shrieked; a cacophony of diamond fingernails dragged over a chalkboard, a sound that tore through Jack like broken glass inside a car crash.

Gerba Whipmarples stepped between him and the spider-dragon. Her polite mask was gone. Her eyes were hatred, eyes that lusted for bloody murder, eyes that wanted to rip out his throat and stomp on his skull until it popped like a red grape under her pretty green shoes. For a moment, he was convinced she was going to do it, then the mask slipped smoothly back into place with a smile. "I am offering to share my vast experience with you, in a school that can provide a *remarkable* education. You may elect to reciprocate." She gestured to the beast. "Or choose to be expelled."

The spider-dragon landed on top of the Agrat-ban-Haifa, eight legs surrounding the Great Bell like a cage. Jack stared at the horror, his face white. Rain fell in earnest now, dampening Rooker's shirt. The thought of stealing Fancy Nan's journal seemed like something from a million years ago, an idea long extinct.

Gerba presented the bamboo once more. "You will summon Nepenthe. Now."

Rain streamed down his face and Jack heard the wolf's cold voice.

(she will kill you)

Jack swallowed his fear. *She'll kill me either way.*

"You're right." He straightened to his full height. "This is a school. You've taught me. I understand what you are." He stepped into Gerba. "And the only part of Nepenthe you'll ever get is the one in your hand."

The spider-dragon shrieked, dragging nails down Jack's ears.

Gerba Whipmarples gestured to the thing perched atop the Great Bell. "And if I let Xeusia have his way with you?"

"Then you will never get what you want."

Gerba sighed. She made a shooing gesture and the black monstrosity launched backwards off the bell in a reverse swan dive of mythic proportions. It dropped below the edge of the wall then arced upwards, wings outstretched. The spider-dragon curled away from the cliff and sped out to sea, to hunt.

Jack started breathing again. Gerba smiled sweetly and walked to the stairs, opening a small parasol to defend herself from the rain. "I will allow you the evening to reconsider. You will rest here tonight in absolute comfort and safety." The headmistress of the Locke Institute paused at the stairwell, posed with her parasol over her shoulder. "In the morning, we shall see if you would like to remain here or prefer to go back down to the camps. To the criminals. And to the things climbing the wall." Gerba offered a sweet smile. "Come along, dearie. It is time to rest." She descended into the dark.

Rain pattered on Jack's face and he found his legs would not move.

Chapter

17

THE
HARD
TRUTH

*The liar's punishment
is not in the least that he is not believed,
but that he cannot believe anyone else.*

George Bernard Shaw

I swear if he's dead, I'll kill him.

Rooker glowered at the attercops flanking him, wishing they would curl up and die. Jack hadn't made it back to camp last night. Or all day today. *And now they're taking me down the same track they took him.*

An attercop pushed him from behind. Rooker stumbled, reaching out with manacled hands. *Damn tunnels. Damn hood. Damn Jack.* Rooker kept walking, feeling the cave walls pressing in on him. *Probably got caught trying to pick her pocket. Maybe she didn't kill him. Maybe he's still up there. And maybe a griffin will show up and fly me to a tavern.*

A spider bumped him again. "Easy, longlegs!" Rooker snapped. "Ya want to make this simple, take my hood off. And these chains. And give me a sword."

"Stuff it, skag."

Why do we keep going down? Gerba's up top. Rooker had heard screaming from the third fork further back in the tunnel, but he was far past that now. *And we ain't gone up one step yet.* "Yer gonna hafta—"

Fresh air washed over Rooker. It riffled his clothes, his skin. He felt sunlight wash over his arms, heard the familiar call of a gull. His breathing quickened as a gust of wind pushed against him.

The Irridin.

Only the sea smelled like that. The freshwater ocean he had called home since he was ten, clean, flat, and blue. As he walked, he heard the susurrus of waves on the shore, the long slow breath of the sea. Rooker smiled under his hood. *Home.*

A 'cop ushered him down the wooden slats of a dock. He felt them buck under his boots, lending a familiar bounce to his step. *O this is more like it. There's only one thing mis—*

He felt his manacles unlock, heard them hit the planks, and the hood was ripped off his head. Rooker blinked in the sudden sunlight. A large shape in front of him resolved itself into a ship, a big catamaran settled on two massive pontoons, its belly lifted above the water, a silhouette he knew better than his own face.

The *Venture Brigand.*

Rooker stared at her, not believing it.

Hello girl.

"It is a good-looking boat," came a rattlesnake voice.

Rooker turned to see a narrow shape standing on the docks beside him. He blinked and saw the long duster coat, the wide-brimmed hat. *"She."* Rooker stabbed the word at Cant Naysayer like a knife. "Not 'it'."

The bounty hunter ambled toward him. "They say it used to be the fastest boat on the—"

"Ship. *She* is a *ship.*"

Cant laughed under his mask. "Your mouth never quits, does it, Flynn?"

Rooker stared at him without saying a word. He waited. A long time. *This'll drive him nuts.*

Cant finally got the gist. He sighed. "Even when you shut up, you talk. Get aboard."

Rooker didn't need to be told twice. He bounded to the outrigger and flung himself up the arch of the *Venture Brigand*'s leg, climbing her pegs. He ran his hand over her leg as he went, looking for damage. *A few new nicks. Outriggers need a scrub.* In moments, Rooker climbed twenty feet up the arch and slid one hip over the rail. He turned, knowing the bounty hunter would be lucky to follow half as fast. "Try to keep up, ya shi—"Cant came up the *Brigand*'s leg floating in the air. He touched one foot on a peg and lifted ten feet, as if gravity had forgotten him. The bounty hunter levitated over the deckrail and touched down on the deck beside Rooker.

He tried to look unimpressed.

"I hate this boat," came Cant's voice from beneath the hat. "Never sailed a ship so hard to handle." Rooker ignored the insult. He was too busy eyeing the *Brigand*'s deck. Unscrubbed, untidy. The cargo nets were in the wrong place, and nobody had given her a polish in months. But worst of all was what they'd done to her sails.

Rooker Flynn's girl only wore red, and only wore silk. Cant had fouled her rigging with golden-colored canvas, sunshine-bright. Inquisition colors.

He felt heat boil in his neck. "Maybe if ya dressed her right, she'd do what ya ask." Rooker gestured to the corn-colored sails. "Those are yellowjacket colors. Get 'em down."

Cant glided across the deck and took a seat at a fancy little table on the foredeck. "As I was saying, this boat has a reputation for being quick. But even with a twenty-man crew she dragged like a trawler up to Werrun Fell."

Rooker turned. "Ya took my girl to Werrun Fell?"

The warlock nodded. "Long before we picked you up. There was a piece a collector wanted." He pulled a cloth to the side, revealing a bottle of wine and a basket of fruit. "Sit."

"The Fell's a nasty haul at the end." Rooker tried to ignore the food as his stomach twisted into hungry knots. "Did ya scuff my girl's skids on that hidden shoal?"

"No. But you're right, those rocks are nasty as hell. *Sit.*"

Rooker eyed the clustered berries, papayas, pineapples, and ripe red grapes big as his thumb. He took a seat and reached for the basket. A long skinning knife drove into the table an inch from Rooker's hand.

Cant sat relaxed in the deck chair, as if he'd never moved. "Once you answer some questions."

Rooker leaned back in his seat. "I'll give ya two."

"You were pilot of the *Brigand* for how many years?"

"Don't remember."

Cant's casual hand tossed the ship's log on the table. *Dammit*. Rooker turned away, feigning disinterest. Cant eyed him like a mouse in a trap. "You want to try again?"

"No. That's two." Rooker reached for the grapes and this time when the knife jammed into the table it almost nicked his hand.

Cant's blue eyes glared at him. Rooker enjoyed every second of it. "According to the log, the *Venture Brigand* is only ten years old," the bounty hunter continued. "That can't be true. This boat...this *ship*...was made by the elves. I can tell by the line of it, the shape of the wood, the *wikk* at the heart of it." The bounty hunter leaned in. "And the elves haven't made a ship in over a century." Cant flipped open the ship's log. "The first page has the original crew, right here. You see that?"

Rooker saw Yuzé's handwriting scrawled across the parchment. *What a third-rate pillock he was.*

1. Capt. Yuzé Jay Maas (owner, 20 shr.)
2. Mate Kestrel Shankar (3 shr.)
3. Mate 2nd Masie the Bloodless (2 shr.)
4. Nav. Brewster Liu (1 shr.)
5. Pilot Rooker Flynn (0 shr.)

"Ten years ago"—Cant pointed at the book—"at the beginning of the *Venture Brigand*'s existence. You were listed as pilot." Rooker kept his face carefully blank. "Most ships don't *have* a pilot. Pilots stay in port with the harbormaster, navigating the dangerous local terrain. It's odd they would have one listed on the *Brigand*. And even more odd to have one who has no shares in the spoil, not even a half point."

"Yuzé was a cheapskate." Rooker eyed the grapes.

"And look." Cant flipped the pages. "The captains change every year or so, commandeered by another crew, won at gambling, taken in mutiny. And with every captain, a new crew. Except for just one person. You."

Rooker shrugged. "What can I say? I'm well-liked."

"But then I found this. Five years and seven captains later."

The masked man opened the book and slid it toward Rooker.

Captain Vryce Tandil ~ 38 yrs. (25)

First Mate Liam Buckleburr ~ 31 yrs. (2)

Second Mate Peg-Leg Patel ~ 42 yrs. (1)

Nav. Reena Wezu ~ 51 yrs. (½)

Pilot Rooker Flynne — 16 yrs. (0)

"Sixteen years old." Cant leaned in. "Which leads me to my question: what kind of captain hires an *eleven-year-old pilot* for a ship's maiden voyage?"

"A lucky one."

Cant closed the log. "You want to know what I think?"

"I'm barely interested now."

"The *Venture Brigand* is an aräs windjammer."

Well hell. I should have burned those logs. "What's an are-house jindwhammer?"

"Aräs," said Cant. "Elvish for 'air'. Legend says the elves made three of them, back in the beginning. Their sails were full even when there was no wind. Ships that never needed to tack or jibe. Created to ferry the gifts of the elves to the farthest reaches of Keymark. Legend has it that the aräs would give a key, a part of itself, to one man or woman, and would sail for that person without a crew to hoist a sail. But you know all that, don't you, Rooker?"

Rooker said nothing, waiting for the inevitable.

"The *Venture Brigand* chose you when you were a boy, didn't it? I don't know how, and I don't know why, but I think that's why this damn boat doesn't sail right without you. One by one, your captains figured that out, and made sure to keep you close. Which means you, Rooker Flynn, are in possession of the only key to the fastest ship on the Irridin."

And here we go again. Rooker had had this conversation with thirteen captains, and it always ended the same way.

"What key?" Rooker patted his pockets. "I ain't got one on me. I got a snot rag, ya can have that. How 'bout some fruit?"

"Not until you tell me how to control the *Brigand*."

Rooker forced a sigh. "All right, Cant. Ya got me. I'll tell ya the secret." He pointed at the endless sea. Cant followed his lead. "Ya see out there? I mean waay out in the distance. That horizon. It's callin' to ya, right? Ya can hear it. Listen to the waves. *Mwah cha gra mm.*"

Cant turned back to find Rooker's mouth stuffed with grapes as juice cascaded down his chin and neck. He grinned purple teeth.

The skinning knife whickered a quick arc, there was a sharp *tak* of the blade striking the table and a spray of juice hit Rooker's face. The grapes dropped to the floor, scattering and bouncing in every direction.

Rooker watched a little brown stick hit the deck with the grapes. It bounced, flipping over in midair. The stick dripped red, sprayed crimson across the floor, splashed dotted blood on the fruits as they rolled away.

My finger.

He raised his hand to find his left pinky gone, severed at the knuckle. He blinked, dumbstruck. Blood poured from his hand.

He didn't feel the pain yet. It had happened too fast. The shock struck him stupid. *My fing—*

Cant was on him in a heartbeat. The chair toppled backwards, Rooker's head cracked the deck like a hammer. Cant kneeled on his chest, a knee on one elbow, pinning him to the ground.

He held the skinning knife to Rooker's eye.

"Watch that mouth of yours Flynn." A drop of Rooker's blood dripped from the brim of Cant's hat. "It's going to get you into trouble."

Rooker stared at his missing finger. "Son of a bi—"

Cant seized his neck. "Tell me how to sail it."

Pain consumed Rooker's hand. He felt the ship's empathetic groan beneath him. Rooker's rage suddenly eclipsed the pain, and he thrust his chin at the bounty hunter. "Take a running leap off the crow's nest and call her name on the way down."

"I'll give you ten heartbeats to tell me or you lose another finger."

Rooker felt the *Brigand* groan beneath him, frightened.

It's okay, girl. He's bluffing. Just like the rest of 'em. Yer mine. Nobody else's.

Rooker Flynn straightened his spine. "I can't count to ten, ya took my finger. How 'bout nine?"

"Eight." Cant sliced through the knuckle of Rooker's index finger cleanly as a twenty-year butcher. Rooker clenched his teeth as Cant flicked the knife and his bloody finger went overboard.

Rooker stifled his scream. He sucked air through his nose, crushing down the urge to wail. *Laugh or cry, you pick.*

Rooker extended his middle finger. "Try this one."

Growling, Cant raised the knife.

"Now, now boys." Rooker turned to find the headmistress standing at the prow of the *Venture Brigand*.

She shook her thick finger at them. "I simply cannot leave you two alone, can I?"

Belowdecks, Gerba opened the door to the belly dome and looked inside. "Well. This is just stunning." She walked in, circling the catwalk around the bowl of glass. "I can see the appeal. A real-life windjammer. If you ever consider selling it, Mister Naysayer, I will make you a lovely offer. My, my."

Cant shoved Rooker through the door. He stumbled sideways and grabbed a rail with his good hand. Blood pattered over the rug Saltz had stolen from a mansion in Junai.

"Sit down before you fall down," growled Cant, shoving him into a chair. He threw a rag at Rooker. "Bind that up."

"Nah," Rooker growled. "I'm gonna bleed all over yer stuff."

"You may be the single most difficult man I have ever met." Gerba tilted her head. "It is quite an accomplishment." Rooker tried to ignore his hand. *That's a lot of blood.* "So bullheaded, so intractable. Switching Jack to your camp, defying Boss Mamba, stealing all that food from those poor students. I understand why the nobles want you reeducated." She settled upon the edge of the table. It creaked under her weight. "I have been wondering, Mister Flynn...have you given any thought to the first time we spoke, when you arrived at the Institute?"

Why is he lying to you?

"Doesn't ring any bells." Surreptitiously, Rooker wrapped the stubs of his fingers in the rag.

"O, the lying." She paced around him. "It is like breathing to you people. Jack lies. You lie. Where does it end?"

Don't. Don't show any interest or she'll have ya. "How about some more of those grapes?"

She turned to face him. "Have you ever heard of a place called Meldetosh?"

The Tosh? Rooker blinked, caught flat-footed. *What is this, story time for ankle-biters?* "It's made up. A folk tale."

"So you do know it. A land of—"

"Skience."

"Science, that is right, dearie. Very good."

Rooker glared at her. "It's a bedtime story for children. Flying carriages and mile-tall buildings made of mirrors. A stupid fantasy."

"O, it is a real place, I can assure you. Cant has been there."

Rooker glared at the bounty hunter then faced Gerba. "Bilgewater."

"It is true. I will prove it."

She slid a shallow black box onto the table. It was perfectly made, almost elvish in its symmetry, crafted of a metal he didn't recognize. The top side was a glass rectangle, reflecting the *Venture Brigand*'s lanterns. "What is this? Some kinda mirror?"

"Touch the glass."

Rooker eyed the box suspiciously, then pressed it with a bloody finger.

The glass came alive. Images swam through it, noises came out of it, then the images evened out and Rooker saw mile-tall buildings made of mirrors. Strange sounds came out of the box, talking, roaring, crackling, sharp noises that sounded like gigantic geese.

Rooker flipped the thing over, thinking the strange little world might be on the other side, but the rest of the box was just a box. Then he heard the voice.

"We are heeeading downtown! To Navy Pier and the Bean!" Rooker didn't understand the words; they were in a garbled, unknowable language. But the voice was familiar.

Rooker flipped the box over and there he was, walking among the strange mirror-buildings. *Boychick.*

Jack had a full head of hair and was dressed in a bizarre costume, a style Rooker had never seen. Strange horseless carriages sped nearby, making goose noises and roaring like lions, but Jack didn't seem scared of them at all, he just kept smiling.

"And what's after that?" came a new voice. Rooker recognized it almost immediately. *That's his da.*

"Right here!" Jack lifted up a colored parchment. It showed real-as-life paintings, a skeleton of some big animal propped up like it was alive, and a shiny metal machine that looked almost like a ship. "We're going to see the Mirror Maze, and the Great Train Story, and the Whispering Gallery and—" Rooker didn't understand why Jack was speaking in a private language, but what puzzled him more were the symbols on the parchment, the buildings, the carriages, the benches.

He couldn't read any of them.

He couldn't read.

Gerba touched the glass again and the world inside the glass stopped cold. Jack's mouth was half-open, frozen like a statue. He looked hideous.

Ugly.

Unreal.

"This is one of his memories, his science box preserves them." Gerba nodded. "I knew you would never believe me if I simply told you. But now you see for yourself. Your friend Jack is *not* from our sphere." Gerba tilted her head, watching Rooker's face. "But he never told you." She arched an eyebrow. "Isn't that something a *friend* would tell you?"

Doesn't matter. It doesn't matter.

"He is not a jaelin, like you," came Gerba's voice. "They call themselves 'human' in Meldetosh. Similar, but only on the outside.

Not the same kind of creatures at all, really." She leaned in. "So. It all comes back to my first question. Why do you think he has been lying to you?"

Rooker said nothing, trying to figure out how he'd been so blind.

"I, myself, always tell the truth." Gerba rose from her perch. "So much easier to make good decisions when you are properly informed. I have revealed one truth, and already you see so much more clearly. Here is another."

She leaned in until her horn was inches from his face. "Your *friend* Jack came to me last night. He offered me a deal. An appealing deal."

What the hell is she talking about?

Gerba circled him like a shark smelling blood. "He offered something I want...in exchange for his freedom. It was a bargain I was happy to accept." She smiled. "The doktar will be returning home. Isn't that nice? Back to the Tosh, with his books and his fast carriages and his bedtime stories for children. Perhaps not today, perhaps not tomorrow, but soon he will be gone."

Gerba came over his shoulder, her voice quiet as a serpent. "He failed, however, to make any arrangement for you."

Rooker stared at the wall. He felt the *Brigand* rock beneath him. As it swayed, he felt like throwing up.

He's leaving me behind.

Rooker felt like he was falling, an emptiness in his chest, the screaming, hollow panic he hadn't experienced since he was a boy.

He's abandoning me.

(he already has)

"In a few days you will be all alone." She moved in for the kill. "Wondering how you could be so foolish as to trust a man I *told* you was lying."

Rooker heard Jack's voice in his head, his sweetest lie of all. "You and me, Rooker."

(you and me)

"However." Gerba lifted a finger. "Before he returns to his land of science forever, there is something of his that I need. Nepenthe. So far I have been unsuccessful in persuading him to summon it from the Tosh. But you—"

Rooker shifted in his seat, feeling his heart pound in the stumps that used to be his fingers. *Nepenthe. That's why she's telling me all this.*

"You are his boon companion. It seems to me that you could leverage your...friendship...to persuade him. All you need to do is convince him to summon it. I will take over from there." Gerba leaned in. "And if you help me get Nepenthe, *well.* I would release you from your obligations to the Locke Institute the very same day." Rooker raised an eyebrow. "In fact, if you succeed, Mister Naysayer has agreed to take you on board as pilot of the *Venture Brigand.*"

Rooker's heart stopped.

Yes, the ship sighed.

He glanced at Cant. The man stared at him, dead-eyed. Rooker looked down at his bleeding fingers. *If he lets me back aboard the* Brigand, *he can take the whole hand.*

"You want to be free, Mister Flynn?" The trol spread her thick fingers. "All you have to do is give me what I want."

Rooker swallowed, shaking his head. *She's playing you.* "Yer lying."

"Why would I? I want Nepenthe. Much more, my handsome vagabond, than I want you." She steepled her fingers. "You see, Mister Flynn, the hard truth is that you simply don't matter to me at all."

Rooker felt the steel come back into his spine. He cocked his jaw. "Yer gonna cut my throat the moment I deliver Nepenthe."

"Possibly. Although if I wanted you dead that could happen immediately. I prefer to place my faith in gentle encouragement." Cant fingered the skinning knife. "Mister Naysayer prefers the direct approach. Would you like him to continue?"

Rooker stared at the floor. He heard the water lap against the outriggers, the sound of the gulls outside, his ship calling to him. *Come.*

"I want it under oath," Rooker whispered.

"I beg your pardon?"

"The geas curse." His voice was dark. "I want to know if ya break yer word, the geas curse will kill ya for it."

Gerba's eyes twinkled. "Why Mister Flynn. It is almost as if you do not trust me."

Rooker extended his hand, spat on it, and thrust it at Gerba. "Trust is for children and dead men."

Gerba chanted hard syllables under her breath. As her sea-green eyes turned emerald, Rooker felt the thrum of the *wikk* pulse around her. Gerba Whipmarples' voice rose full. "Under geas curse and with the will of the *wikk*, I swear by my life: if this man delivers me Black Jack's stave Nepenthe by the Summer Solstice, I will release him from the Locke Institute to pilot the *Venture Brigand*."

Rooker glared at Cant. "You, too."

Cant glared back, then placed his hand on Gerba's, his blue eyes glowing bright with majik. "Under geas curse. This I swear."

There was a sizzling hum of majik and Rooker felt his hand bound fast to them, as if they shared flesh. He felt a sharp *snap* on his palm. The pain stung like a snake bite, and he let go.

Rooker Flynn raised his head, eye to eye with his new partners.

"You have thirty days," Gerba said. "At some point before the solstice, you may find Nepenthe within your grasp. I trust you will do the right thing if the time comes." Gerba Whipmarples stared him right in the eye. "I wish you the best of luck, Mister Flynn."

"Luck." Rooker nodded. "Put me with the *Brigand* and I'll show ya luck."

Rooker walked the dock, his head down. He stared at the water, gazing at his broken reflection in the rippling bay, trying not to think of anything at all.

Home.

He turned to face the *Brigand*. She bobbed in the water, beckoning him to *come back, come back.*

I will. I'm comin', girl. There's just a little someone I gotta do first.
(you and me, right pip?)

Rooker raised his head to find his brother waiting for him at the end of the dock.

For a man seven years dead, Jasper Winegrad looked young and fresh-faced, exactly as he had on that dock ten years ago. He still held his left arm close, the one that had never worked right after Addie broke it. Next to him was a wheelbarrow filled with goodies, including five sacks of grain. Jasper's new peacoat collar was turned up, hiding a bit of his face, but Rooker saw the nasty gleam in his eye.

(about time you got wise)

"Shut up Jasper." Rooker's voice came higher than usual, a hint of a child inside. "Yer dead, remember?" Jasper Winegrad had been moldering under the ground for a long, long time, knifed in the eye for a pair of candlesticks. His corpse was probably all bone now. But his shade remained to haunt him.

(dear ol' da had it right, pip)

"Leave me alone."

(gotta cut loose the dead weight)

Rooker walked, his boots thumping the boardwalk. "Ya taught me that a long time ago, Jasper." He refused to break his stride. "Taught me pretty damn well."

(da taught us both on the end of a chain, pip)

Rooker walked through Jasper and felt a deathly chill crawl over his flesh. A flood of cold memories assaulted him. The old mill, the sign they had painted, the kitchen full of cake. Their last moments on the dock. The moment Jasper abandoned him.

Rooker Flynn couldn't bear to look at his brother any longer and left him behind.

(time to toughen up)

Upon the foredeck of the *Venture Brigand*, Gerba Whipmarples poured a glass of wine. She raised it to her lips and savored the bitter pinch of tannin on her tongue. "Well. I should say that went well, wouldn't you?"

The bounty hunter faced the pier, watching Rooker diminish in the distance. "I bet you a thousand marks he cocks it up."

"I will take that wager." Gerba took another sip. "The proper leverage has been applied. All it will take now is time."

Cant shrugged, eyeing the *Venture Brigand*'s yellow sails. "It may almost be worth putting up with him if he can get this bucket running right. For a while, anyway."

"You can lock him up belowdecks for all I care." Gerba smiled as Rooker Flynn's shadow disappeared through the dock gate into the Institute. "Just remember not to accidentally kill him until he gives you the key. Otherwise, this ship will be useless."

"And why do you care?"

"The *Venture Brigand* is a thing of great beauty and greater majik." Gerba ran her fingers along the deckrail. "There is a soul deep in the heart of an aräs windjammer. You know this. All that power, waiting to be tapped. And I am serious about my offer, Mister Naysayer. When you tire of the *Venture Brigand*, please come to me first. I would love to see what she could do with the proper motivation. Winston?"

The big attercop climbed down out of the ship's rigging. "Ma'am."

"We will need to arrange for the doktar to stay another night. Send Winnifred to tend to his requests and report to me. I want to make sure he takes a few things back to camp with him."

"Yes, ma'am."

Gerba smiled, satisfied.

A productive day, indeed.

"What did he offer you?" Cant's voice came cold and rough.

Gerba blinked, touching her brooch to summon her mount. "Beg pardon?"

"Black Jack," said the bounty hunter. "He made a bargain with you to return home." Cant's blue eyes narrowed. "If he didn't give you Nepenthe...what did he offer?"

"O my dearest Mister Naysayer. Black Jack didn't offer me anything." Gerba Whipmarples smiled and wiped a dab of blood-red wine from her lips. "He didn't offer me anything at all."

TURTLEBALL

*Serious sport has nothing to do with fair play.
It is bound up with hatred, jealousy,
boastfulness, disregard of all rules
and sadistic pleasure in witnessing violence.
In other words, it is war minus the shooting.*

George Orwell

Y ou keep making that face it will freeze that way." Patch idled up beside him, unbidden, uninvited, and unwelcome.

Rooker ignored her, leaning on the fence. He had stood that way a long time, staring at the Institute, thinking dark thoughts. All around him, the convicts griped and carped. He heard them, their little problems, and hated them all.

Three days had passed since Rooker swapped shirts with Jack, and there was still no sign the kid was coming back.

Maybe he's already gone. Left me in the lurch.

"Is your hand okay?" Patch asked. "You might want to change that bandage."

Rooker ignored her like he ignored his two missing fingers. "It'll be fine with the next hanging."

"You've got a puzzlement on your face." Patch Picaroon's golden eyes narrowed. She almost looked beautiful just then. Almost pretty, almost healthy, almost friendly.

But not quite. "I'm puzzled why yer talking to me."

Patch crossed her furry arms and examined one paw. "I need six pounds of galt."

Rooker frowned. *She's thinkin' the same thing.* He shook his head. *I can always trust ya to look after yerself, Patch.* "Six? Right now?"

"Yeah."

"Because if Jack doesn't show up that means he's dead." Rooker eyed her. "If he's dead, you've got nothing to sell Mamba. And if you've got nothing to sell Mamba, ya got no leverage on me."

"Where's the trust?" Patch grinned and puffed her cigarillo. "You see all the angles, don't you Rooker?"

"Angles and luck, that's all there is." Rooker kicked at the ground. "I bet ya haven't trusted one person since yer boobs came in...or whatever happens to jinx when they turn on."

"Heat. We go into heat, Rooker. And yes, I trusted one person."

"How'd that go?"

"Mariska." Patch stared at sky. "Partnered up with her for two years, cutting purses on shore leave, running short cons: sick mother, helpless femme, quailing kitten stuff. Basic, but it was pretty slick."

"And?"

"Turns out she was picking my purse the whole time. Milked me for two years, then took the lot." Patch sighed. "Ran off with my man, too."

Rooker's chuckle was dark. "Ya think ya know somebody."

Patch looked toward the butte. "You think he's coming back?"

"Who's that?"

"Black Jack."

Rooker paused. *Black Jack. Sure.* "Who's that?"

Patch frowned. "I know it's not him. Unless he ages slow like a trol or a Border Knight. But still..."

Rooker nodded, staring. *It's all a lie. Just like everything else.* "Maybe his name's not Jack."

"Wait, what?" Patch cocked an eyebrow. "You told me he was—"

"Maybe his name is Ben." Rooker's voice was too sharp, but he didn't stop. "Maybe he's Kristofer. Or Xiang-lo. Maybe he's not jaelin. Yer name ain't Patch, you could be anybody. Maybe yer spyin' for Mamba. Or West. Or Whipmarples, for all I know." Rooker spat. "Nobody knows anybody, Patch."

He lifted his head and saw a familiar figure coming down the path. "And here comes nobody now."

Rooker edged forward to observe Jack's arrival. He was flanked by two attercops dragging a large sledge. On it were strapped a dozen clay pots a yard tall. Jack wore a new shirt, new pants, and had a bulging cloth bag slung around his shoulder.

Rooker's eyes narrowed. *Looks like he earned a few treats.*

The attercops quickly unloaded the jugs and headed back for the wall. As they left, Jack dragged one of the jugs into a little fissure and wedged it in. Some of the outlaws moved closer, curious at the commotion. Jack slid a three-foot bamboo pole from his bag and lowered it into the mouth of the jug. Rooker hung back, his arms folded, watching. *What kind of Toshan majik does he have now?*

"Whuzzat?" said one of the convicts, eyeing the long jug. A few more gathered around, curious.

Jack smiled. "The solution to half our problems."

The convict blinked. "A big straw?"

"This camp stinks. There's urea everywhere, which is why Jackal camp has so much Staphylococcus and Streptococc—" The kid coughed. "I mean, throat and skin infections. But all that's over because now we have"—he gestured to the bamboo—"urinals!" He looked out on blank faces. "You whizz in it."

One man cocked his head. He walked up to the pole, unbuttoned his fly, and let nature takes its course. "Huh," he said, nodding.

"Anyway," Jack said, moving away. "We set up these around camp and dump them in the midden pit when they get full. No more infections. No more stink."

"That ain't gonna work for us." Yolanda eyed the device. Several women agreed emphatically.

"Yeah," agreed Patch. "What do we get?"

"Privacy," said Jack. "Every guy in camp is going to use the urinals, it's a shorter walk. Which means—" He made a wide gesture toward the foliage. "You now have a very big ladies' room."

He got a few nods out of that one. As more prisoners checked out the new devices, Jack spotted Rooker and jogged over. As he came, all Rooker could see was the kid surrounded by fast carriages and mountains made of mirrors. He forced a smile. "Look who comes bearing gifts."

"Yeah, I—" Jack stopped cold. "What happened to your hand?"

Rooker glanced at his bandaged stumps. "I hadn't noticed."

"Do you want me to take a—"

"They'll be fine. How'd it go with Gerba?"

"I got a few"—Jack spread his hands at the pots—"concessions from the acolytes. I haven't seen Gerba in three days."

Now that's the worst lie I ever heard. Rooker nodded. "Did ya get what we were lookin' for?"

"Not exactly." Jack glanced at Patch. "I'll talk with you about it later. But...look at *this*." Jack pulled something from his bag.

The thing was perfectly spherical and patterned in a way that reminded Rooker of an ice tortoise. Its smooth skin had been sewn in alternating tiles, little patterns of black-white-black-white.

What is that thing?

Jack threw the sphere to the ground and it bounced back up into his hands. Rooker took a step back and gave it a wary eye. Jack grinned. "It's a soccer ball. Look." Jack kicked it to Rooker, who stopped it under his foot.

"An air bladder." He rolled it under his heel. "A toy."

"I thought we could use some fun." Jack grinned. "Kick it back."

Rooker did; Jack trapped it with his feet. "It's a game. You can't use your hands, but you try to get it past the other guy into his goal." He kicked it to Rooker. "Get it?"

Yeah. Rooker punted the tortoise right at the kid's nose. Jack's head snapped back and he hit the dirt. *"Agh!"*

Rooker grinned. "Good game."

"Ow." Jack got to his feet. "Not so hard next time."

The ball bounced into Copper Dave's leg. He grinned and kicked the thing at Sykes, who ducked. "Hey!" Sykes turned to chase it, but another outlaw already had the ball. He kicked it to another man but Yolanda intercepted it and booted it into Sykes' crotch. "Ha!"

As other prisoners focused on the round turtle shell, Rooker leaned in, conspiratorial. "So tell me how it went."

"I'll tell you tonight." Jack's hands went to something in his pocket. "I have something I need to do real quick but get the camp divided into two groups, pick goals, and I'll be back in a few minutes. We'll play teams."

"Yeah." Rooker turned and walked away. "One side against the other."

Jack blinked. "Are you okay?"

"Right as rain, Chicken Legs." As Jack ran off, Rooker strode to the assembled outlaws. *Let's see who outplays who.*

Jack trotted to one of the cliques, unable to keep the smile off his face. The urinals would go a long way toward making Jackal more livable. The soccer ball would ease the boredom and provide a sense of camaraderie between the convicts. But of all the things he had been allowed to bring back to camp, Jack looked forward to this one most. *He's gonna love this.*

He had been trapped up in the Institute for three days, locked in his room like a naughty child. Every few hours, Winnifred would come to ask him if he would summon Nepenthe, and every time his answer was the same.

Jack wasn't sure why Gerba had never returned and he didn't understand why Winnifred had been so generous when he was sent back down, but he suspected the gifts were a bribe. A little taste of how things could be easier for him if only he gave Gerba what she wanted.

Which is a sure way to get myself killed. But if they're giving me bribes, I'm gonna put them to good use.

He ducked under the clique and dropped on his haunches. "Billy?"

The mud-caked troubadour sat under the porch, bonking his head, rocking back and forth. "Buh-buh-buh-*buh*—"

"Billy. Hey." Jack waited a moment for Billy Pilgrim to look at him, but it didn't happen. "I got you something. Can you hear me?" Billy gave no sign, continuing the rhythm.

"They said you used to be a musician, is that right? Billy? What instrument did you play?"

"Buh-buh-buh-*buh*—"

"Yeah. Okay. I like that one too." Jack produced the last item Winnifred had allowed him to take: the audio player. He held it up in front of Billy's eyes. "This plays music. It only has about four hours of battery left. Pop songs, folk songs, a little bluegrass, some classical. I don't know if this is going to help, but...well, I figured you could use it more than me." Jack placed the earbuds gently in Billy's ears.

"Buh-buh-buh-*buh*—"

"I just, I'm just trying to help...something."

"Buh buh buh *buh* "

Jack clicked the button.

Billy's head snapped up like a startled horse as Jack heard the Doobie Brothers sing the opening lick to 'Jesus Is Just All Right With Me'.

Billy's mouth hung open, his buh-buh-buhs at an end. He tilted his head to the sky as if he expected to see singing angels descending from heaven.

When the electric guitar kicked in, Jack watched Billy's eyes light up in shocked amazement and he couldn't help but laugh. The troubadour smiled like a child, and for the first time since Jack met him, he stopped banging his head on the post.

Everyone else would get well with the next bell ringing. Like Rooker's fingers, they would heal. But Billy was sick in the head, and the Great Bell couldn't cure that. *If a Toshan music box helps him feel good, for a little while, well, at least I helped somebody get better.*

Billy Pilgrim still stared at nothing, but now there was a spark behind his eyes.

"Okay." Jack patted the filthy troubadour on the back. "Enjoy."

Rooker watched Jack stroll back to camp. *Okay, let's wipe that smug little smile off that smug little face.* "Chicken Legs!" Rooker waved. "Your goal is the grill! We got the water tower!" Rooker gathered his team, the Big Six and about forty others. "All right, boys and girls...here's what we're gonna do..."

And so, the game of turtleball was introduced to Keymark.

Not quite soccer and not quite rugby, the game was a travelling scrum of violence, like cavemen playing fútbol. Nearly a hundred prisoners chased the black and white ball across the compound, kicking it away from each other and tackling opponents without provocation. There were no referees, but if someone picked up the ball they got punched until they let go. Each team had as many goalies as they wanted, but points were scored not only by kicking the ball into the goal, but into another player's face.

Turtleball was an instant hit.

Spectating prisoners hollered and hooted from the sidelines, forming a boundary for the abuse as Rooker's team kicked, punched, and tackled their way to victory over Jack's players. Copper Dave used his tail to punt the ball, giving them a huge downfield advantage. Point by point, they drove the turtleball home, turning the barbeque into their personal victory celebration.

Jack responded by getting Fargil Fleet on the field. The big ugly jackrabbit was unbeatable. With his giant legs and enormous feet, Fargil scored three times in rapid succession, skipping a victory lap around the arena before Rooker's team could mount a defense.

When Yolanda threw off three attackers and booted the ball for a goal, the women's camp went berserk with cheers. Every faction whooped for their heroes, the Shavers, the Cull Cartel, Kubla Klan, each trying to outshout the other. The Red Tigers sat on the fence, hollering for Rooker's team:

> *Kick the turtle to the cookout*
> *We're never gonna stop*
> *We put it through in front of you*
> *You'll chase us 'til you drop!*
> *Bash their heads and bash their brains*
> *Kick like a billy goat*
> *Grind up the brew and make a stew*
> *And shove it down your throat!*
> *Turtle, turtle boys!*
> *Turtle, turtle boys!*

Rooker drove toward the goal; Jack came out of nowhere and kicked the ball away. Then they were both in the hunt. Rooker pushed the kid, who came right back and slammed him in the side.

Okay, let's go. Rooker attacked Jack with a relentless enthusiasm that bordered on criminal. He kicked his leg and elbowed Jack in the ribs, hard. He heard a cry of pain from the kid and cut away.

He drove toward the goal with an open field in front of him. *Yer the one getting left behi—*

Jack tripped him.

Rooker hit the ground rolling. The ball skittered off, captured by another player. Rooker sprang to his feet and stood over Jack, fists balled into angry knots.

The kid's sharp blue eyes were on him, furious. Rooker spat. *Come on. Get up. Ya wouldn't stand a chance, boychick.*

"Lighten *up*, Rooker! It's just a game."

Sure. Just a game. For an instant, Rooker felt torn in half. He didn't know if he wanted to pound the tar out of the kid or beg him not to leave. *Just a game.*

Rooker dropped his fists and stormed off the field.

He walked under the water tower and yanked the pull, drenching himself. He tilted his head back, filling his mouth, filling his nose, letting it drown him.

"Rooker!" came the kid's voice.

Shut up, Jasper.

"Rooker!" Jack planted a hand on his shoulder spun him around. "What the hell's wrong with you?" The kid's face was red, furious.

Rooker flashed a smile. "Thought I could scare you off, but ya hung in there. Yer gettin' tougher every day, boychick." Rooker grabbed Jack's chin before he could think too much. "Ya okay? I didn't clip ya that hard."

Jack jerked away and wiped blood from his nose. "You looked..." The kid's eyes narrowed. "Really, really angry."

"All part of the act kid." Rooker clapped Jack around the shoulder, grinning white teeth. "Gotta sell the show."

Rooker mended fences that night in the clique. He gave Jack extra galt, laughed at his jokes, and listened to his cock-and-bull story. Rooker couldn't fathom why Jack would expect him to believe he had spent three days in the Institute but only spoken to Gerba once, but he pretended to buy it. The kid was obscure about the details of their conversation, and his story had holes big enough to drive a cart through. Now that he was looking for it, Rooker saw Jack's deceit like it was marked with red paint. *He's a bold liar, I'll give him that.*

Rooker pretended to be surprised by the news about Gerba wanting him to summon Nepenthe, but her dragon was a genuine shock, and possibly another lie. The only dragons Rooker had heard of this far south were aquatic and couldn't fly. Whatever Gerba had conjured seemed like a nightmare. *An eight-legged spider-dragon. Never heard of anything like it.*

Finally, they arrived at the reason Jack had gone up there in the first place.

"So. Fancy's Nan's journal is gone." Rooker stared at the ceiling, watching the shiq. "So much for tunnelin' out of here." He took a breath and planted the first seed. "Ya shoulda summoned the stick."

"She had a dragon."

He grinned. "So what? I've seen ya fight with Nepenthe. Ya could take on *three* dragons, and they wouldn't stand a chance."

Jack chuckled. "Thanks, Rooker."

Human. They call themselves human.

"But—" said Jack. "It won't come to that. Look." Jack produced his final gift from the Institute: a crisp new journal bound in blue leather with a short quill attached. He opened it and Rooker saw the cover page was inscribed: 'Nancy Guinevere Mannus, née Fondlaw.'

"What is that?"

"It's Fancy Nan's journal."

Rooker blinked. "I...what?"

Jack grinned like a cat. "Gerba and I went through every page looking for some big secret." He picked up the quill and started scribbling in the notebook. "I might have trouble with the drawings, but I think I can get close. The hard part is all the symbols around the edges, you know, in case they have some hidden meaning or coded message. That'll take a while."

"You...memorized the journal?"

Jack grinned. "Every. Single. Page."

Rooker blinked. *Of course you did. Damn, boychick.* He laughed in spite of himself. "So we're still in the escape business?"

"We'll be digging tunnels before you know it."

Huh. Rooker rolled back into his bunk, not quite sure what to think. *Playin' both sides of the fence. I never would have given him credit.* Rooker stared at the ceiling. *He's got a deal with Gerba to let him go. If she reneges, I'm his backup plan. Either way, he wins.*

Rooker Flynn leaned back in his bunk, fingering his brass rings. *I wonder if all Toshans are like him. Just a buncha smartasses lyin' to each other.*

It wasn't the lying that bothered him. Rooker Flynn assumed if a man was talking he was lying.

No. It wasn't the lies. What kept Rooker up the rest of the night was the revulsion that he'd allowed himself, for little while, to believe them.

Somewhere on the rooftop of the Locke Institute, Gerba Whipmarples sipped her chai and waited.

PART 3

YOU & ME

THUNDERBUCK

There is no friendship in trade.
Cornelius Vanderbilt

Huánghūn's storms now came in earnest. Dark clouds appeared more and more often, roiling like a dark witch's cauldron. Rain was a constant companion with a thousand faces: fat drops that plummeted down in a symphony of plops, misty particle rain that hung in the air like a wet ghost, hissing razor rain that stung bare skin, sheets of blowing rain that appeared as a series of translucent curtains, and always, always the thunder.

Jackal camp transformed into a swamp. Water pooled everywhere, turning paths into filthy creek beds. The stream overflowed, and Jackal was forced to halt the string of pearls strategy after they lost a day's galt down the river. Outlaws unlucky enough to go without shoes were overcome by rashes, infection, and ringworms. Convicts with boots didn't fare much better.

Jack treated as many jungle-rotted feet as he could, but without terbinafine, clotrimazole or talcum powder, he was stuck prescribing soap, which was nearly impossible to get. The mood soured as prisoners were trapped inside their cliques with nothing to do. Turtleball wasn't fun in the rain. A periodic fistfight would break out, a five-minute wonder, then the camp would settle back down into an angry ember of constant irritation, bearing the rain until nightfall and the coming of the shiq.

Rooker's mood worsened. Jack was forced to walk away from him more than once, sick of listening to his bellyaching. The pirate ran hot and cold, alternating between surly accusations lashed out at anyone around him, or wild revenge fantasies involving Jack, Nepenthe, and Gerba's face. As the days wore on, Jack wondered if Rooker was right. Maybe he should have summoned the staff. His tunnel escape plan was certainly going nowhere.

Floods made it nearly impossible to communicate with Buzzard camp, and it was fifteen days before Jack received an invitation from Fancy Nan to prove he had her journal. Getting there was a four-hour slog through mud; Jack was exhausted and soaked through when he and Rooker finally arrived to reveal their precious cargo.

"That isn't my journal," said Fancy Nan.

Jack curled his body over the parchment, protecting it from the rain, cheek to cheek with the murderess. One of Rooker's few useful suggestions had been to tear out a sheet from the journal to offer as proof. "It's the closest thing left. The headmistress destroyed the original."

A sharp, painful sound escaped Nan's throat. "Then it's gone. All my work..."

Jack scowled. *I've seen your work. The ravings of a lunatic with a few bad ideas thrown in.* "I managed to make a copy before she destroyed it." He heard Rooker stifle a *hmph.* "My copy is the only version there is." Fancy Nan glanced at her assistant, the dark girl who stuck to her like a silent shadow. "Look. It's exactly the same." Jack shoved the paper into Nan's hands.

She reviewed the familiar equations, scribbles, and notations. She blinked and flipped the page over to find more writing. "How did yo—"

"Word for word, drawing for drawing, it's all there. I tried to get all the"—Jack choked the phrase *crazy scribbles*—"annotations right."

Fancy Nan's eyes darted to her assistant again, then Jack. "You promised me an improved distillery."

"The diagram is on the last page of your diary," said Jack. "With all the red clay you've got in Buzzard, it should take less than a month to get back up and running. Thunderbuck Part Two."

Fancy Nan looked at her distillery, then her guards, then the journal page. "I don't know..."

"That's fine." Rooker snatched the paper out of Nan's hand. "We'll just burn the diary."

Dammit. Jack snapped at Rooker under his breath. "Don't—"

"Shut up." The pirate thrust a finger at Nan. "Ya want this deal or not?"

Nan stared at Rooker. Her eyes blazed a white-hot hatred that had once consumed her family. Her hands curled around the paper, crushing it in her fist. "Deal."

"Outstanding." Rooker spat. "Meet us in the gap between Buzzard and Vulture in five da—"

"No." Jack raised his hand. *You're not thinking this through.* He glared at Rooker. *Like always.* "We'll be in touch on where to meet. You bring Thunderbuck, we'll bring the journal."

Minutes later, Rooker followed him through the jungle. The pirate flung rain from his hair. "What's eating yer liver now?" he growled. "We got what we wanted."

"Could you just once keep your trap shut?" Jack shouted over the rain.

Rooker scowled. "Yer slowin' this thing down. Fifteen days already."

"Think, Rooker! We get Thunderbuck and trade it to the twins for the pickaxes. But the only place we can *dig a tunnel* is Hyena!"

Rooker stopped. "But we're in Jackal."

"And the light turns on!" Jack exclaimed. "We need to figure out—"

"Move the twins to Hyena." Rooker stated the idea like it was obvious. "Let 'em do the digging for us."

Jack blinked. *That's not bad.* "How?"

"I'll talk to Bocephus."

Jack stopped. "Who's—"

"Boss West," said Rooker. "Formerly Major Bocephus West. I know how to convince him."

Jack didn't know which part rattled him more, that Rooker knew Boss West or that his name was Bocephus. "We'll pull the ol' double-pop on him." Rooker raised a wet finger. "The *real* problem is the damn jinx stick together...Hyena never trades with anybody but Patch. And I'm not lettin' her in on this deal. Those redneck twins already know, and the only way four people can keep a secret is if three of 'em are dead." Rooker spat rain. "We need somebody else as a go-between."

Jack cracked his first smile of the week. "I might know somebody."

"Ransom."

It was an hour to dusk, the time of day most outlaws stuck close to the cliques. Hyena stood virtually deserted, but Jack knew Ransom's habit of walking the perimeter at the end of every day. The blond outlaw placed his hand on his hat, peering into the rain. "Is that you? Jasper?"

Rooker flinched. Jack caught it out of the corner of his eye. It didn't make sense; there was nothing threatening about Ransom. *Why's he so twitchy?* "Hi Ransom. Good to see you."

"You, too!" Ransom grinned like he'd won the lottery. "You look so different!"

Jack realized how much he had changed in the four months since he arrived on Huánghūn. His body was transformed. His muscles had become prison-hard, his chest defined, his arms wiry and taut. He wasn't big, but he looked like a man capable of bloodying a nose or two. "I don't have much time. Can you help me?"

Ransom stepped into the jungle. "Yeah! Sure, what can I do?"

"I need to see Bocephus."

"The boss? But you're in Jackal now."

"I know, but I need to—"

Ransom shook his head. "He doesn't want us talking to you. Not to *any* other camp. Jinx only."

"He trusts you. And you're not a jinx." Before Ransom could argue, Jack slipped seven galt slices into his hand. "You're working timber camp tomorrow, right?"

Ransom eyed the galt. "Yeah..."

Jack glanced at Rooker, who still hadn't uttered a word. *I don't know what finally shut his trap but thank God for small favors.*

He slapped Ransom's shoulder. "Here's what I want you to do."

Ringslugs chewed though another tree trunk and down came the hundred-year teak. Men went to work lashing strops around it, preparing to drag it to the sea cliff, which was getting further away every month as the timber gang cleared the jungle. Boss West threw a strop over his shoulder, ready to put his muscle to work.

"Boss."

West turned to find Ransom with his hands nervously picking at each other. "Yeah?"

"'Cops wanna see you."

The big cat sighed and crawled out of the mud. Ransom led him into the trees, just far enough outside camp to not be seen.

"How'd ya like a stiff drink, Major?" Rooker Flynn stepped out of the rain.

Boss West scowled. Jack had forgotten how big the jinx was, a six-and-a-half-foot Bengal tiger with teeth and claws to match. According to Rooker, Major West had won twenty-seven battles against the llystra in the Pipen Wars before he went on a kill-crazy rampage that left hundreds of civilians dead and got him sentenced to Huánghūn by his own people.

The cat's yellow eyes stared Rooker down. "You took the kid off my hands. I don't do refunds."

"I said: how would ya like a stiff drink?" Rooker's dexterous fingers snapped, produced a flash of flame, and suddenly he was holding a stoppered flask.

Major West's mad marauding had touched every llystra hamlet in the Pipen Gulf. Mothers were mown down with their men. Children were burned alive. And after every pillage, the major confiscated gallons of alcohol for his personal consumption.

West's greedy eyes lit up at the sight of the flask. "What is that?"

"Exactly what ya want it to be." Rooker tossed it to him. The big cat eyed him warily, sniffed the flask, and drank it down. He breathed in slowly through his nose and a grin crept across carnivorous teeth.

Rooker tilted his head. "I always wondered, are the sharp teeth in a jinx's mouth called canines? Or felines?" As the big cat exhaled, Rooker snapped his fingers and ignited the major's breath into a half-second fireball. He grinned. "Good hooch."

West scowled. "No."

My turn. Jack stepped up. "Major West, I can give you the means to create that stuff right in your camp."

"*Boss* West," the tiger growled. "I'm no major. And Boss Mamba wouldn't take kindly to me stealing his still."

"Mamba doesn't know it exists." Rooker eased forward. "All ya need to do is bring the Vulture twins to Hyena."

West lowered an eyebrow. "Those redneck hammerdwarves?"

"They cook moonshine for ya now. All the mulekick ya want." Rooker shrugged. Jack couldn't help but grin. *He has the best shrug.* "And if Chicken Legs and I *happen* to show up every once in a while, during work, when everyone is gone..." Rooker spread his hands. "All ya have to do is nothing."

"No." Boss West turned and walked away. Jack shot Rooker a worried glance.

"O wait, look." Rooker's fingers flashed fire and another vial appeared. "Where did this come from?"

Ransom stifled a laugh. West shot him a hairy eyeball then glanced at the flask. "What's the catch?"

"No catch," said Rooker. "Goodwill."

"*Hmph.*" West turned away. "My old Tom said if a deal sounds too good to be true, it is."

"Now Majo—"

"I'll think about it. Give me a few days."

Jack looked at Rooker. *We don't have a few days.*

Rooker shrugged, nonchalant as a cat on a midnight fence. "Yer right, Major. Tell ya what, we'll just give the still to Boss Mamba. I'm sure he wouldn't mind having all the booze *and* all the food to himself."

Jack recognized his cue. He pulled a round galt from his bag and pressed it into Boss West's palm. "We'll feed the twins. Every time we come, we'll bring more galt. For them *and* you."

Bocephus stared at Jack, then Rooker. Wary. Skeptical. Sour.

"Boss," said Ransom. "This is a pretty sweet deal." He leaned in. "I wouldn't mind a little hooch. And food."

Boss West snarled at Ransom. The blond man took a step back and dropped his head. The big cat turned his glare on Rooker. "You're cheating me somehow."

"Major." Rooker clapped him on one furry shoulder. "By tomorrow night, yer not gonna care."

"I don't like it," grumbled Yenrab Bialik, pacing the mud.

"What's to like?" muttered Barney, pacing the opposite direction.

Jack blew rain off his lips. The twins had been carping for five days straight. "I'll tell you one last time, you're *getting* the still."

"In Hyena," complained Barney.

"I didn't sign up fer no dang *catbox*," agreed Yenrab.

"Will ya shut up?" snapped Rooker. "She's comin'."

Palms rustled as Fancy Nan and her ten-woman retinue emerged from the trees. They carried a jerry-rigged palanquin bearing Thunderbuck.

"O sweet Elvira," said Barney under his breath. "We're gettin' booze brought to us by wimmin. Kill me now, Yenrab, life ain't gettin' better."

Fancy Nan stepped froward. She looked nervous, jittery. "If you don't have it, boy..." she raised a stiletto. "I'll start with your eyes."

"Easy." Jack raised the journal. "It's right here." Nan snapped it out of his grip like a cat snatches a bird. She flipped it open to check the pages. Jack heard Nan's low sigh of relief, as if she had been reunited with a long-lost lover.

"Farah! Farah, this is it!" Nan grabbed her assistant's hand. "It's all here!"

Rooker clapped his hands. "Great! Let's get the damn thing to Hycna camp. Ladies, follow me." He tromped through the jungle, not waiting for a response.

"We're not carrying this thing to Hyena," said one of Nan's guards.

"I'll help you, purdy young thing," said Yenrab, staring at her, smitten.

"You'll do it for this, right?" Jack swung his bag around, revealing his last clutch of galt.

"What's the holdup?" Rooker's head reappeared from the bush. "Move it ladies."

Sweat and rain formed a waterfall down Jack's brow as he helped Nan's team carry Thunderbuck. His hair was plastered to his face, his boots were soaked through, and every inch of his skin felt bloated and white as a dead fish. He closed his eyes, shoulders aching from the weight.

"Stop." Boss West emerged from the palms. Hyena camp lay just beyond, but the tiger blocked their path. "I want to get terms straight."

Rooker fell into negotiations with West, but Jack knew it was just last-minute dithering. He walked away, getting some space, and leaned against a tree. All the pieces were in place. Tomorrow morning, they would be digging.

For the first time since he arrived on Huánghūn, Jack Swift was convinced he might escape.

The rain stopped. It didn't peter out or taper off, it shut off abruptly as a water faucet. Just like that, after nearly a month, the downpour was gone. Jack leaned his head back and watched dark clouds slink toward the horizon. Sunlight streamed through the drifting remains. Jack smiled, listening to the last raindrops from the trees.

Splish-splish-splish.

No. He blinked. *That's not right.*

Splish-splish-splish.

The sound came from the camp. Too big, too regular.

Jack edged through the trees and peeked through the palms at Hyena.

A gigantic hairy leg passed in front of him. Jack flinched backward, forcing himself not to run.

Attercops crept into Hyena. Four of them, Alfred, Jamedi and Jeeves. Winston brought up the rear. The tarantulas moved like a pack on the hunt, stealthy, quick. None smoked khef.

They know we're here.

The attercops moved in silently, checking empty cliques.

Jack slipped back to the negotiation. Rooker's finger was pointed at Boss West's face. "Don't give me that load of horsesh—" Jack threw a finger over his lips. Rooker was smart enough to shut up instantly.

The convicts fell silent as mice in close proximity to a hungry cat.

"Spread out," came Winston's voice. "I want every clique searched."

Jack looked back to discover Fancy Nan and her retinue were disappearing into the trees. "Nan—" he whispered.

"Good luck, young man." Nan melted into the palms, gone.

Jack turned. "Barne—"

He saw one stumpy foot disappear into the underbrush, crawling away.

"You brought this on me," Boss West hissed in his face. "*You* did this." His whiskers shook, enraged. "Damn you both." He turned and strode into camp, back straight, head up, marching toward his clique.

Rooker eyed Thunderbuck, abandoned in the mud. "If they find this thing they'll kill us all."

"Hey?" One of the attercops, Jeeves, noticed Boss West. "Hey!"

"O, hello officers," came West's calm voice. "I didn't see you there."

Leaning forward to watch, Jack felt a branch under his feet break with a *SNAP.*

Winston's head snapped up.

Rooker hissed at Jack. "Are you loud *on purpose?*"

The big spider padded toward them. "Show yourselves!"

No choice. Jack grabbed the stick and hurled it through the trees. It clattered against a trunk and splashed into a rut.

"Hey!" Winston charged into the trees, chasing the sound.

Rooker jammed his hand in Jack's chest. "Not yet. One-two-*three.*"

They broke through the jungle running.

"Hey!" came Winston's voice. "Hey guys! They're over here!"

The half mile run between Hyena and Jackal was made longer by the muddy slop that used to be the ground. Rooker was quicker and Jack fell behind. The 'cops were too big to manage the palm trees easily, smacking against them like giant pinballs. Winston climbed higher into the branches and scouted from above.

Jack tripped and stumbled jaw-first into a rock, rolled, and ducked under a gigantic fern. He had ten heartbeats to get his breath under control as one of the big 'cops followed dead on his path. Jack buried his head in the dirt, his heart triphammering as the thing walked right over him.

Bleeding, Jack counted to twenty before he breathed. Another ten before he looked. The massive spider padded its way through the green, turning left and right, listening. It skittered ahead and disappeared.

Jack pushed himself up, his face caked in filth. His blue eyes stood out in sharp contrast to the black mud, peering through the trees. Silently, he crawled forward, moving carefully away from where the attercop had gone.

It's over. The tunnel was over. Thunderbuck was gone. Hyena was gone. *All of it. Gone.*

He got to his feet, never blinking. He crept silently though the trees and saw the jungle break ahead. Jackal camp. *Home.*

Scanning left and right, Jack saw the jungle was empty, as was the camp. He wiped dirt from his face and slunk toward the closest clique.

Something hit him in the back and he went down splattering mud. He tried to turn, but found his legs and hips glued to the wet ground. He yanked, pulling the web loose, but only wound up wrapping himself in it. Winston crawled down from the trees, clicking that strange laughing sound the 'cops made when they got excited. *Kek-kek-kek.*

Jack stared into Winston's eight eyes and saw himself reflected there, eight little outlaws caught in a trap.

So close. We got so close.

Winston plunged his fangs into Jack's belly.

Gerba Whipmarples did not like visiting the camps. She had not been in Jackal since the early days when she and her team had fed dog meat to the yingcao flytraps to help them grow. Mixing directly with the students made her...uncomfortable. As such, she preferred to come with a companion that guaranteed her safety.

Iktomi, her gigantic mount, had a pedigree. It was the offspring of the spider-dragon Xeusia and would become a dragon itself in time. It might be decades before Iktomi traded webs for wings and took to the air, but for now it was a spider with a body larger than a carriage. Gerba enjoyed riding Iktomi; the hammerdwarves had constructed a magnificent saddle that affixed her to the spider at five separate points so she could travel up and down the Institute walls without fear of slipping. She had ridden Iktomi upside-down once and had found the experience exhilarating.

Padding beneath the canopy, she rode to the far side of Jackal camp, distant enough not to be seen. *Except by those who need to see me.*

Boss Mamba emerged from the jungle.

"I come bearing gifts." Gerba gently tossed down a brown paper package tied up with string. Mamba tore it open, revealing the new outfit she had created especially for his big day. A black shirt cut broad enough to accent his massive shoulders, tan pants, a wide belt, and hobnail boots the size of serving trays. "We must look our best when our guests arrive, mustn't we Mister Crait? The time is nearly upon us." *At long last.*

Mamba ignored his costume, as she knew he would. His temper flared hot, shouting. "When are you—"

Mind your betters. She pulled the reins and Iktomi reared up, bearing fangs as long as Mamba's arm. The big llystra froze. "No sudden movements, Mister Crait," Gerba warned. "It can startle Iktomi so. And we would not want that, would we?"

Mamba's chest heaved up and down. "I've done everything you asked. I've waited long enough." The big croc growled. "It's time you gave me what you promised."

Gerba smiled and glanced at the blue sky. *It is turning into such a lovely day.* "The seeds have been planted, the season is ripe, and our guests approach, ready for the feast. So yes, Mister Crait." She patted Iktomi on the back. "It is, as you say, time."

Chapter

20

TOOTH
= & =
NAIL

Razor blades and chainsaws
Axes and grenades
So many ways to kill you, children,
If you don't behave.

Anonymous

Oubliettes are designed for one purpose: to create pain. Much like water torture, the key component for creating sufficient agony within an oubliette is time. An oubliette exerts its slow pressure without cutting, crushing, or drowning; it is simply a hole in the rock. The prisoner is lowered into the hole, or sometimes thrown, into the exceedingly tight space below. Too narrow to lie down, the oubliette forces the prisoner to remain standing or squat hunched. Gerba Whipmarples' design for her oubliettes included an additional wrinkle, a floor shaped like a cone, so the prisoner could find no level footing. Some convicts would try to climb the walls, but they were too smooth and too high, and if they succeeded in reaching the top all they found waiting for them was a locked iron grate. At the end of the first hour, the prisoner's calves would ache from trying to fight the bad angle of their feet. By the third, their muscles would cramp. By the tenth, they would slump against the wall, incapable of rest, incapable of sleep, incapable of anything but agony.

Jack Swift made it thirty hours before his mind snapped.

At the beginning Jack screamed for someone to let him out. Later, he simply screamed, howling bitter anguish into the air. In the end, he merely whimpered. His back and hands were covered in scrapes and cuts from trying to climb the stone tube. His neck was sore from staring up into the dark, hoping the cover would open and let in some light. His naked feet were in constant contact with the previous occupant's bones.

He drifted. Alone, alone, alone. Solitary confinement. A lifetime of loneliness. There was nothing in his life, no one. Jack thought of his father, in Chicago, waiting for dinner at 6:00. He imagined his dad sobbing, his son lost forever. He tried to kill the thought, but it stayed with him like a phantom, Dad's shoulders sobbing. Jack cried then. Hot tears streamed over dirty cheeks. He would never see him again. Never see Rooker again. Nor Patch.

Not Leah, not Memphis, or Rajiv Banerjee. He'd never see *anyone* again. He was alone, as he always had been, detached from everyone and everything around him, isolated in misery.

Then came her face. That long horn bangled in gold jewelry. That tittering voice that felt like birdsong, if all birds were raptors.

(she's never going to let you go)

Jack felt the wolf's pelt brush against his feet. He spun, trying to find it below him, but the thing revolved just beyond his vision. It circled his legs, rubbing against him, pacing, prowling, hunting. He heard its cold voice like an icicle in his mind.

(she did this to you)

She did this to me. The thought circled Jack's brain, a vulture. She had robbed him of his dad. Robbed him of his life.

(you are her pet) The wolf sneered. *(her toy)*

Jack ducked his head, weeping.

(you are alone, boy. you have nothing left)

Tears drenched his face.

(and now you will end your days in the dark) He felt the wolf's bristled coat brush against his skin. *(with me)*

Lupine fear prowled his mind, looking for a warm spot to take up residence.

(you should learn to mind your betters)

Jack's face squeezed up into a knot. *Follow the rules, stay in line, keep your distance, be on time, come when I call, eat when I say, sleep when I say, do what I say. Be my puppet, be my slave. Work will make you free. Work will make you free. Work will make you free.*

He screamed. Somewhere nearby, his wolf snarled.

He imagined killing her, stabbing her, shooting her, watching her bleed. He imagined bashing her face in with a rock over and over and over, smashing it to bloody pulp and crushed bone. He ripped the horn from her snout and threw the bloody stump from the top of the Locke Institute. He set her body on fire and watched it burn, laughing, screaming, crying, howling.

That was how they found him when they finally opened the grate.

"Shut up!" yelled an acolyte.

Jack raised his head and roared, spittle streaming down his mouth.

"Dammit. You left him down there too long. Throw it."

Jack felt something hit his face. A fat rope, the kind they used in gym class. "Put the loop under your arms!"

Jack ignored them and doubled down on screaming rage, draining his lungs at the masked figures above him.

"Nope. He's gone." The acolyte turned away. "Fill it."

A *kunk* sound, followed by a hiss. Jack felt something spill over his feet. He stopped screaming and looked down as water flooded the tiny space. It rose over his ankles, his knees, his waist. As it reached his chest, his body became buoyant. In moments, the oubliette was filled with water. He rose, floating.

Another *kunk* and the water stopped near the grate. Acolytes grabbed Jack and pulled him out onto the floor, sodden and feral-eyed. He thrashed at them and found two spear tips at his throat. "Calm *down*," hollered an acolyte. "Get up!"

They led him down a lightless stone corridor and up a set of stairs to a room where a lean figure lay on the floor.

Rooker.

"Now." An acolyte stood over the pirate, his hands on his hips. "Tell me what you were doing in Hyena camp."

Rooker's voice was ragged. "Looking for yer mom."

Jack snorted. His feet ached, his back was sore, and his mind was cracked, but one laugh did the work of an hour's sleep. He eyed Rooker.

One friend left.

The acolyte sighed. "Okay. Do it."

Something flashed red in the darkness. Jack saw a thin line illuminate the room in crimson. The scarlet string came toward him, humming wickedly. Thin as a hot wire, the strand of light connected to a metal cuff that snapped around Jack's wrist. It burned sharply, then went cold. Rooker's wrist was bound with a similar manacle. Between them, the thread pulled tight, drawing them together.

Jack stared at the majik cord connecting his wrist to Rooker's. He pulled at his manacle and watched the red thread stretch. *Like one of those little dog leashes.* "What is this?" his voice sounded raspy and crazed.

"Making sure you two stick together," said the acolyte. "You got a few minutes before the presentation starts. Here." He threw a white linen shirt at each of them. "Get dressed."

Rooker yanked the chain, trying to break it. Jack was jerked toward him. The pirate scowled. "Get this thing offa me."

"Get dressed or we'll put you back in the hole."

"How?" Rooker barked. "Tell me how to put a shirt on when I'm chained to *him!*"

The acolytes glanced at each other. "The headmistress has the lightknife," one murmured. "I can't take it off now."

"Forget it, they can go bareback."

Jack heard the Great Bell begin to toll outside. The man shoved Jack toward the exit. "Move it, they're waiting."

The kid looks like a lunatic. Rooker eyed Jack, worried. *I don't look that bad, do I?*

As they were led to the great stone door, Rooker tested his manacle. He'd heard of lightchains before, but he'd never seen one. Once fastened, they were unbreakable, and could only be severed by a corresponding knife. He glanced at Jack again. The kid seemed like a wild animal; his eyes darted back and forth, feral. *And I'm chained to him.*

As the door opened, the sun shone directly in his face, blinding Rooker. He shielded his eyes, squinting, and heard the Great Bell toll over the assembly yard. The healing *wikk* flowed through Rooker. He had spent the last day on a prison cot, bleeding from the attercops' attack, but all that was suddenly washed away like a warm bath. His wounds healed shut, tickling as they closed. *Wonder who's getting executed today?*

Instead of a prisoner hanging by the neck, Rooker discovered Gerba Whipmarples pulling the bell rope. *Lord, she's wearing pink chiffon.*

All around the headmistress, all atop the butte, stood dozens of men and women, jaelin, dwarves, jinx, llystra and razorbacks, all dressed in the colorful finery of the upper class. Silks were in fashion that season, and many wore long scarves that fluttered in the wind like pennant flags. Elegant. Extravagant. Rich.

What the hell is this?

Rooker glanced at the assembly yard and found eight hundred unfamiliar prisoners. The faces he knew: Patch, Copper Dave, Fancy Nan, Ransom. But they were all scrubbed clean, not a speck of dirt on them. Their denims were washed, and each wore a new white linen shirt, spotless in the blazing sun.

The Agrat-ban-Haifa rang its final toll. The Headmistress of the Locke Institute opened her arms and smiled. "Refreshing, isn't it?"

The guests nodded, smiling as the last waves of healing majik flowed over their bodies. A few gaudily dressed debutantes on a lower balcony giggled loudly, whispering to themselves. Gerba's voice was sweeter than ever. "Welcome to the Locke Institute! With your help, my lords and ladies, we have collected over a thousand bandits, murderers, pirates, and outlaws from all over Keymark, and you should all be proud that the rehabilitation has begun!"

A polite smattering of applause echoed along the cliff. Rooker glared at Gerba. *Seriously, what the hell is this?*

"Each of these men and women was once a danger. But now, they are on their way to becoming productive members of society. Schooled in useful skills, and obedient in every way." Gerba raised her hand. "Kneel before your betters!"

All four camp bosses took a knee as if she had cracked a whip. Mamba, West, Hook, and Eightfingers lowered their heads and showed their necks. Behind them, the convicts eyed each other and followed suit.

Not a bad bit of showmanship. She must have threatened the bosses beforehand. None of those fellas wants to be controlled. Rooker enjoyed the moment. *But down they go.*

Nobles applauded with scant enthusiasm, unimpressed. Rooker had a feeling they were bored and wanted to get back to the wine.

"They are making our boots, providing our timber, filling our storehouses. Instead of stealing from us, they are giving *back* to society. In no time at all, the Locke Institute is taking those who were once as churlish children and transforming them into educated, responsible citizens right before your eyes.

"Of course, not all of them can be success stories." Gerba held up her hands for effect. "Some villains are beyond redemption. Some will never turn toward the proper path. Some have taken too much from too many for too long. For example!" Gerba clapped her hands together. "You may have heard the rumors that he is here, and for once the rumors are true. So, without further ado, the moment you have all been waiting for..."

O hell. Rooker felt an attercop push him forward into the sunlight.

"...I give to you, ladies and gentlemen, the most notorious out-law of all time, the legendary *Black Jack!*"

An excited wave of noise came from the crowd. On the wall, the nobles chattered to each other in exhilarated tones. In the yard, all the prisoners reacted, looking at Chicken Legs with new eyes, curious, cautious, suspicious. Rooker heard Jack take a sharp breath.

Kid, you just turned into a target for every convict on Huánghūn.

Rooker found Boss Mamba staring at the kid. A slow smile crept up the big llystra's saurian mouth.

Rooker glared up at the Headmistress. *We had a deal. I was supposed to get a chance at Nepenthe.* He redoubled his efforts to get the manacle off. *I have three days left, you dirty harridan.*

"Some say he ages backward," continued Gerba. "Some say he can't be killed. Peasant rumors say he fought at the Paladine Arch, but educated people know he was in Werrun Fell at the time of the battle, murdering the last heir of King David." A murmur from the crowd. "One thing is certain. He stole a ship's weight in gold from your families during the Black Accord and brought your noble houses to the brink of ruin. Now, here he stands, in chains!"

Applause thundered from the crowd. Several nobles pounded their fists while others hissed and booed. One threw a silver chalice from the cliff, nearly hitting Jack. Rooker snarled at the kid. "Stand further away, woodja?"

"Never fear, ladies and gentlemen, he cannot harm you. Shirt-less, barefoot, and chained to his filthy lackey."

Rooker grimaced. *Lackey?*

"I know you would like to see Black Jack punished for his crimes, am I right?" Cheers burst from the wall of the Institute. "So, ladies and gentlemen, before today's...education begins." There was some murmured laughter. "I would like to provide you with some light entertainment. Mister Crait!"

Dammit.

Rooker grabbed Jack and hissed in his ear. "We're dead."

"I am Mamba Crait!" The big llystra stepped forward, arms spread. "I have killed a hundred men and taken their power!" His voice thundered, loud enough to be heard all the way up the wall. "Today, I fulfill the promise of the Locke Institute! Today, my work will set me free! Today, I earn my freedom...by killing Black Jack for *you!*"

A thunderous cheer erupted from the wall.

"Dammit!" Rooker spat. Gerba had worked a loophole into her geas curse. He'd promised to deliver Nepenthe before the solstice, but Gerba had never promised him an opportunity to do so. *Damn my luck.*

"You want to be entertained?" shouted Boss Mamba at the nobles on the wall. "I will give you entertainment! I will show you there is only *one* Boss of Huánghūn!"

Rooker tried to break the lightchain with panicky strength. The giant llystra strode toward them, grinning. "Mamba. Big guy." Rooker tried a flattering smile and gestured at the kid. "Ya only want *him*, right?"

Jack glared at him; Rooker ignored it.

Mamba's tongue flicked his lip. "Rooker, I've been waiting two years for this." His massive tail dragged a thirty-foot circle in the dirt. The Crime King of Khandun stepped to the center of it and planted his feet. "Time to get what's coming to you."

Rooker looked up at the top of the butte and saw just a hint of a smile on Gerba Whipmarples' face.

Wasteka hag.

"Does this kind of thing happen here often?" Gerba heard Baronet Ket, a man whose noble blood went back nine generations, giggle like a schoolgirl. He threw back his cape and plucked a pair of opera glasses from his belt to get a better view. "This is wonderful."

Gerba smiled, enjoying his reaction. "Physical education is so important, don't you think?"

"Is he going to *kill* Black Jahk?" Ket's wife shivered with anticipation, knowing blood was only moments away.

Gerba shrugged. "Boys will be boys."

Below, the students formed a ring around the three combatants. Several nobles called cheers down on them, eager to see the fight. Money traded hands. Baronet Ket licked his lips. "I know men in Rimmy's Cull who would pay handsomely to see this."

Exactly what I wanted to hear. "Well then, sirrah." Gerba smiled sweetly. "We should get you a better seat."

She gestured. An attercop grabbed Ket and leapt from the wall. Screaming, he fell through the air, his wife plummeting beside him. They suddenly decelerated as the weblines came to an end and they were deposited, gently, on a large balcony thirty feet above the assembly.

Gerba mounted Iktomi, her baby spider-dragon, and descended the wall toward them. She tittered. "It takes a moment to get used to how we move about, here at the Locke Institute." The baronetess regained her composure before her husband did, straightening her gown as the baronet stifled his screams. "Vertical travel is a significant change in perception. But I think you will both agree it *is* exciting." Gerba smiled as she came to them. "Isn't that right, baronetess?"

"Exhilarating!" the baronetess clasped her chest. Baronet Ket smoldered anger, but his wife's enthusiasm embarrassed him into compliance. "Quite so." He nodded.

Gerba smiled her prettiest smile. *They're as easy to manipulate as the students.*

Baronetess Ket straightened her coiffure. "Now tell me the truth, Miss Whipmarples. Is that the real man? The one who robbed us all those years ago?" She fanned her breast. "Is it *really* Black Jahk?"

You will believe anything, dearie, if it is what you want to hear. Gerba nodded. "You may inspect the brand on his arm if you like. He is the genuine article."

"He looks so young," said the Baronet as he peered through his opera glasses. "And who is that *buffoon* with him?"

Rooker yanked the lightchain, tearing at the manacle on his wrist. "Come on, *come on!*"

"Come on." Mamba's eight-foot tail flicked like a hungry tongue.

"Jack!" Rooker hollered. "Do something!"

Jack still had that crazed look in his eyes, now augmented with terror. "Like *what?*"

Mamba lunged at them. Rooker went left, Jack went right. The lightchain pulled tight and jerked them both off their feet. A harsh bark of laughter rolled from both the nobles and the prisoners as they hit the dirt.

Jack scrambled to his feet. "Come over here!"

He's gonna get us both killed. "Sucks to that! Come over *here.*"

Mamba lunged at Jack, claws raking at his head. If the kid had been wearing a hat he would have lost it. The crowd cheered.

"Knife!" Rooker yelled at Jackal camp. "Give me a knife!" The prisoners eyed each other but no one dared help. "Damn you all!"

A *ptang* as a small stone blade hit the dirt and skidded toward him. Rooker looked up to see Patch Picaroon, her sheath empty. He snatched it and found the knife was only three inches long.

"Got anything bigger?" The lightchain dragged him off his feet and reeled him into the fight.

Mamba jerked the chain with his tail, yanking them both closer. Claws swiped at Rooker as he dove between Mamba's legs. Rooker rolled sideways, avoiding the foot that tried to crush him, and drove the knife into Mamba's thigh.

The blade deflected away, unable to pierce his crocodile skin.

Rooker tried to retreat, but the lightchain was too short and Mamba was too fast. Claws raked across Rooker's back, taking skin. The big llystra kicked Rooker flying. He skidded toward Jack and rolled to a dusty stop.

"Wrap the chain around his legs!" yelled Jack. "Get him down!"

"And *then* what?" Rooker ducked under Mamba's tail. "He'll just rip us to pieces on the ground!"

"Well I don't know, *you* come up with something!"

"What do I keep ya around for if I have to do all the thinkin'?"

Mamba swung low; Rooker went high. Claws slashed the air beneath him. Boss Mamba snatched the chain and yanked Rooker back to earth. The big croc spun like a hammer thrower and dragged them both into the air. Rooker and Jack bashed into each other as they hit the ground in a tangled heap.

The Crime King of Khandun roared.

Gerba stood on the balcony and listened to the shouts of the crowd. The nobles were having a magnificent time, cheering for the fight. But she wasn't watching them. She was watching Winston.

The spider stared at her, waiting. She nodded. *Now.*

The attercop skittered toward the ring, unbuckling the precious cargo from his pouch. Winston raced toward the fight, throwing convicts out of his way until he was almost in the ring itself.

Gerba's eyes narrowed. *Time to apply a bit of leverage.*

As the pirate dragged himself to his feet, she watched the attercop slip the single piece of Nepenthe into the man's hand. Rooker Flynn glanced down and froze. He shot a look up at her. *Good luck.*

No chance, thought Jack. *He's too strong.*

Flat on his back, Jack wiped blood from his cheek, watching the big llystra raise his hands in victory. Mamba knew the fight was won. He was grandstanding, drawing it out, savoring his triumph. *Maybe I can—*

Mamba's tail arced in and smashed Jack's ribs. His breath shot out and he hit the ground with a boneless *thub*.

No chance.

As Jack lay in the dirt, Rooker skidded to a stop at his side. He had a crazy smile on his face and shoved something into Jack's hand. "Okay, boychick. Time to turn the tables." Jack's hand closed around a familiar cylinder of wood. He tightened his grip and felt the thrum of *wikk* in his hand.

Nepenthe.

Rooker pointed. "Go knock his teeth out!"

Jack stared at the stick of bamboo, unbelieving. *Nepenthe. How did he—*

Rooker smiled, then Mamba was on him, punching the pirate into the dirt.

Jack got to his feet and gripped the wood tight.

Time slowed.

Above him, on the balcony, dressed in her finest pink chiffon, Gerba Whipmarples leaned forward, watching intently.

Rooker scrabbled backward in the dirt, his head bleeding.

Mamba raised his claws, ready to tear the pirate in half.

Jack clutched the bamboo in his fist. He moved his lips to call its name: *Nepenthe.*

Something moved in the shadows of the Institute wall. Something dark, something subtle. Jack spared it half a glance and suddenly realized the nearest balcony was packed with acolytes. A dozen longbows in their hands, a dozen bowstrings pulled taut, a dozen arrows ready to loose, all aimed at him.

He gripped the bamboo, feeling the power of it. The *wikk.*

He wanted it.

He needed it.

He'd kill for it.

Go down fighting.

The moment he called the staff, the arrows would fly.

And Nepenthe couldn't save him from that.

"Jack!" Rooker shouted. *"Summon it!!"*

Jack's eyes found Gerba Whipmarples. Not an hour ago, he'd been screaming in the oubliette. Cursing her, breaking her, killing her. Screaming.

If you do this, you give Nepenthe to her.

Steel crept up Jack Swift's spine. *Toughen up.*

He threw the stick away and charged at Mamba screaming.

Rooker couldn't believe his eyes. The bamboo stick bounced past him, useless, as the kid committed suicide.

Jack ran at Boss Mamba like a snarling wolf, his teeth bared like fangs. In that moment, he seemed more beast than man, a savage snarl on his lips, ready to kill or die.

Boss Mamba was happy to oblige him and raised one clawed hand wide.

If he goes, I'm next.

A decade aboard the *Venture Brigand* had taught Rooker Flynn a mastery of ropes, and he saw his opportunity. As Mamba lunged, Rooker flicked his chain over Mamba's wrist. The cord dragged tight around Mamba's waist, yanked Jack out of the way of the killing blow, and simultaneously yanked Rooker into the air.

He hooked his arm around Boss Mamba's neck and, for an instant, he straddled the llystra's shoulders like a bull rider. He whipped the chain around Mamba's neck. "Pull!" he screamed at the top of his lungs.

Jack yanked the cord tight. Mamba sputtered, his windpipe cut off. Rooker planted his foot into the back of Mamba's neck and pulled with all his might, choking the big llystra.

Mamba grabbed Rooker and threw him to the ground, but the big croc was tangled in the lightchain now, and every move he made dug the cord tighter into his neck. Rooker wrenched as hard as he could.

Mamba was jerked nearly off his feet. The big croc stumbled backward, off-balance.

Rooker screamed at Jack. "Pull, damn ya!"

Mamba turned on him, fangs bared, but he couldn't overcome the strength of both men working together.

Boss Mamba, the Crime King of Khandun, went to one knee. He flailed, choking. With a final sputtering *hurk*, he collapsed on his face, out cold.

Gerba Whipmarples' shoulders slumped, dissatisfied. "Well." She tried to keep the frown off her face. *After all, company is watching.* "That's that."

She gestured with one pinky.

Winston discharged a web and knocked Jack to the ground in a sheet of sticky silk. Other attercops sprang into action, webbing Rooker's face, his arms, his side, tangling him in snarling silk until he toppled and crashed to the ground.

"Well!" Gerba clapped. "That was exciting, don't you think?" Several nobles laughed, sipping from their silver chalices, applauding the show. *Not the grand finale I'd hoped for. But still. A good beginning.*

"Now." She snapped open her pink hand fan, waving it alluringly. "If you would like to step inside, I think you may be *extremely* interested to discover some new investment opportunities we are preparing at the Institute. Follow Portia if you please."

As acolytes escorted the nobles into the Institute, Winston came up the wall. Gerba held out her hand. *What a troublesome boy*, she thought, as Winston gave her the single joint of bamboo. She flipped Nepenthe in her hand and glanced at Jack, buried underneath a pile of webs. *You are still standing in my way.*

"Are you ready to concede our wager?" Cant lounged against the balustrade, his duster ruffling in the high wind.

Gerba had years of practice smiling at all the correct times. For once she allowed herself a moment without one. "Not quite yet."

"Very canny of you to use the archers. You could kill the doktar if he summoned Nepenthe and kill Boss Mamba if he didn't." The bounty hunter's eyes narrowed. "Either way you retained the advantage. And using Flynn to give him the weapon...I have to admit, I'm impressed." Gerba couldn't see the smile underneath Cant's mask, but she knew it was there. "It would have worked...if you hadn't made the boy hate you so much."

"No man can stand long on his own, Mister Naysayer." Gerba tucked Nepenthe into her handbag. "He has no more lies to hide behind. His people will turn against him soon. He is alone." She nodded. "It won't be long now."

Cant edged closer. "Double or nothing?"

At long last, Gerba smiled. "Triple."

Chapter

21

=TRIPLE=
DOWN

There is no comradeship except
through unity on the same rope,
climbing towards the same peak.

Antoine de Saint-Exupery

All right, convicts! Back to camp!" Winston yelled. "Get those shirts off, I want 'em back same as we gave 'em to you." As Winston barked orders, attercops corralled the cons, ready to quell any resistance. A few wrapped Boss Mamba up in webs like some gigantic fly and dragged him toward Jackal camp.

Rooker lay in the dirt, breathing slowly. *Why didn't he summon Nepenthe?* He stared at the blue sky. *I should be headed to the* Venture Brigand *right now. Right now.*

"You blew it, Flynn." Winston growled, hovering over him. "Your pal was supposed to put on a big show."

"Life's full of disappointments, ain't it?" Rooker felt Winston drag him to his feet. Immediately, he saw how many lingering convicts watched Jack. The kid stood like a statue in the center of the yard, staring at the ground.

Anger bubbled up inside Rooker. *All ya had to do was summon it!* He snatched Jack by the collar and dragged him toward the jungle. The kid offered no resistance, his face hanging slack. Some of the convicts followed them, all asking the same question: *Are you him? Are you Black Jack?* Rooker fled the questions and plunged into the jungle. After a few moments of halfhearted pursuit, the prisoners gave up the chase and headed to camp.

Reaching a secluded copse of palms, Rooker threw Jack to the ground. "What the hell's wrong with ya, boychick!?" He shouted at the top of his lungs. "Why didn't ya summon the whomping stick?"

Jack stared at the dirt. "She had archers on the wall."

"So?"

"It was the same as last time, with the dragon." Jack glared at him. "It was a trap. As soon as I summoned Nepenthe, she was going to take it away."

"So ya figured it'd be better to *die?*"

"What do you care?"

Ya cost me my freedom, that's what I care. Ya cost me the Brigand. "We're chained together!" Rooker hollered. "Ya wanna kill yerself? Go ahead, but don't take me with ya! Ya put *my* life on the line, and for what? A damn piece of wood!"

Jack got to his feet. He had a look in his eyes Rooker didn't like, hard, bitter, and cold. He spat and strode into the jungle.

Rooker spread his hands. "Where d'ya think yer goin'?"

"Back to camp."

Furious, Rooker jerked on the chain and yanked Jack off his feet. "Ya don't get it! If we go back to Jackal, we're dead. Soon as Mamba wakes up, he's gonna kill us both, Black *Jack*. And if he doesn't, there are a hundred cons in camp who will." He got in Jack's face. "Ya threw Nepenthe away! Ya *killed* us!"

"We'll go to Hyena." Jack's voice was cold, his eyes distant. "Barney and Yenrab weren't at assembly. They're probably already digging."

"For all we know, Barney and Yenrab are back in *Vulture!*"

Jack's eyes were hard. "They're with Thunderbuck. And Thunderbuck is in Hyena."

"Ya ever stop one time to think ya might be *wrong?*" Rooker shouted.

Jack stopped and turned, his cold eyes narrow. "How did you get your hands on Nepenthe?"

"Fell out of Winston's pack." Rooker lied. He tromped into the jungle and dragged Jack by the chain. "Come on, smart guy. Let's get to Hyena and find out how smart ya are."

"Jasper!" Ransom's eyes went wide at the sight of Jack. "Are you okay? I thought Boss Mamba was going to kill you!" He bounced back and forth, excited. "Are you *really* Black Jack? The headmistress said—"

"Shut yer clam, moron." Rooker eyed Hyena camp. *Loudmouth's gonna draw a crowd.* "Where are the twins?"

Ransom blinked. "The Red Dwarves? Yenrab is...well, he's been drunk since he got here. Barney's back in the—" He cut off. "Come with me, I'll show you. I thought Mamba was gonna kill you both, are you okay?"

Rooker kicked Ransom in the ass. "Now."

He led them around the jungle outskirts of Hyena, yammering about their fight with Mamba. Apparently, it had been one hell of a brawl. Rooker barely remembered half of it; all he recalled was the slight weight of Nepenthe in his hand.

They followed the tree line out to Hyena's midden pit; the offal stink assailed Rooker's nose. Swatting away the flies, Rooker came into a clearing and saw—

Boss West stood over Barney Bialik. The Red Dwarf was on his knees, hands clasped behind his back. West's claws were extended, his teeth bared, angry.

Ransom stopped short. "Boss? What's goin' on?"

West's eyes landed on the kid. "You want to explain your spies in my camp?" West snarled. "Black *Jack?*"

"What's it to ya, major?" Rooker snarled right back at him, eager for another fight. "Ya got what ya wanted. Go drink yerself to death."

West snatched something off the ground. "I caught your dwarf with *these.*" He threw two pickaxes at Rooker. They clattered to the dirt at his feet.

Dammit, this thing's coming apar—

"We're tunneling out," came Jack's hard voice.

Rooker shot a hairy eyeball at the kid. "Can't ya ever just shut u—"

"Tunneling?" Boss West stood straight. "No one can get through this rock, not even hammerdwarves."

"Not *this* rock," Barney broke in. Still on his knees, the Red Dwarf scooped up an egg-sized stone. "But *that* rock—" He squinted one eye and chucked the stone into a nearby depression.

Rooker watched the stone fall into a clump of bushes at the bottom of the sinkhole. The stone didn't bounce or ricochet, it simply vanished. After a moment, there was a *tik*, faint, followed by another, more distant *tok*.

Rooker heard Jack snort a sharp laugh. *"Ha!"*

West blinked, confused. Barney slid on one hip down into the sinkhole and pulled away the camouflage he had stacked there. Beneath it was a snarl of rock twisted together like snakes, with a man-sized cavity in the center.

"Took fourteen hours of pick work." Barney Bialik grinned gapped teeth. "But we got ourselves a hole."

Rooker blinked. *Fancy Nan's journal. Thunderbuck. The pick-axes. It all paid off. The kid was right.*

"So *that's* what you two have been up to," came a voice from behind Rooker. He spun to find Patch Picaroon leaning against a palm tree, a smile curled across her lips. "Sneaky little monkeys."

Not now. Rooker sucked in a breath to speak but Boss West stepped in. "Patch." His voice was soft. "What are you—"

"Hello, Bocephus." Patch smiled, easing into the light. "Mamba's boys are offering a pretty penny for whoever finds these two first." She cast an eye at Rooker. "And *he's* been talkin' about Hyena for a month."

Rooker scowled. "Patch, look—"

"Black Jack's secret is out." She folded her arms. "My leverage is gone. So either you bring me in on your little escape plan"—she flashed her teeth—"or I tell him where to find you."

This escape is the worst-kept secret I've ever—

"You can come with us," Jack said. Rooker turned to see the crazed look in the kid's eye, his hysterical grin. "You *all* can."

For once, Rooker Flynn was without words. All around him, the prisoners realized they were standing in the right place at the right time.

Rooker stared at the motley crew. *So this is it. A camp boss, his flunky, a picaroon, a redneck...*Rooker frowned, looking at Jack. *And him.* "Lucky bastards," Rooker growled. "Let's get in the damn hole before anyone *else* decides to join us."

"Get some rope!" Barney peered down into the hole. "It's deep."

Patch and West gathered vines as Rooker and Jack slid to the bottom of the sinkhole and peered into the blackness beneath them. *It's a real cave.* Rooker anchored the longest vine to a root. Barney snatched it and leaned back over the hole. "Great. Seeya." He dropped, and Rooker heard the dwarf slide down the vine into the darkness below. "C'mon, whippersnappers!"

Rooker stared down the hole and glanced at Jack. "Ya comin'?"

Jack held up the lightchain. "Where you go, I go."

Rooker dropped down the hole.

The cave was massive. Rooker hung suspended in the air, swinging on the vine. The lightchain's glow lit the area around him but there was nothing to see, just more blackness. Rooker lowered down the vine until he found the bottom. He snapped his fingers, creating a touch of flame.

He stood underground in a tunnel big as a house. The shaft stretched into the darkness on either side of him, the echoes long and deep. Barney grinned. "Lava tube."

"Pyroclastic vent." Jack landed beside him. Barney giggled and shook Jack's hand.

"Jack!" Ransom's face appeared in the hole above. "I'm gonna get some rope! You need anything else?"

"No. No, I'm…" Rooker watched Jack stare at the cave, his face exuberant. "No."

Kid's struck stupid. Rooker knew how he felt. Out of the sun and the sweltering heat of the jungle, this was the first time Rooker had felt cold since he stepped foot on Huánghūn. "Patch!"

She stuck her head over the side. "Yeah?"

"Drop us a torch."

"Torch? I—hang on." Patch disappeared from the lip.

Rooker eyed Barney. The Red Dwarf bounced back and forth from foot to foot, grinning like a little kid. He pointed down the tunnel. "That way. That way is the boats." He smiled gapped teeth. "There's light at the end of this tunnel." He slapped the kid on the back. "Ol' Black Jack, the man with the knack."

Sure, give him *the credit.* "Hey. What about yer brother?"

"Drunk as a skunk." Barney grinned. "Been at Thunderbuck ever since we got to Hyena." He chuckled. "Ol' boy's gonna have an apoplexy when he sees what we found."

Rooker scowled. "Is he sober enough to walk?"

"Heads!" Rooker heard Patch's voice and saw a crooked stick plummet toward him. Rooker snatched it out of the air, snapped his fingers and lit the bit of cloth tied around it. "Ain't much of a torch," he hollered up to Patch.

"Bitch, bitch, bitch," she replied.

Rooker's skinny torch illuminated the blackness. Oranges and yellows flickered along the craggy walls, making them come alive. The cave was rounded on all sides; the edges bowed with the flow of the lava that had once made a river here. The walls were pocked with hundreds of holes, varying in size from a teacup to a porthole. Some were just a few inches deep, some fathomless, and they were everywhere.

Jack stared at the walls. "This place is one big hunk of Swiss cheese."

"What's Swiss cheese?"

"Full of holes."

Rooker eyed his torch. It didn't have much life left in it. "We need lanterns," said Rooker. "And that rope."

"Yeah. Let's get back up top," agreed Barney. "We gotta plug that there hole before some Hyena sees it."

Rooker shook his head. *Not a chance, short stack.* "We're stayin' down here."

"Hah?"

"If we show our faces up there, we're dead. If Mamba finds us—"

Something skittered in the dark.

"—what was that?" Rooker spun.

Jack stopped cold. "What was *what?*"

Rooker held a hand up, shushing Jack. *Something moved.* Weak firelight flickered on the walls. At the edge of darkness, Rooker could just barely...*Is that thing moving, or is it the light?* He raised the flame. *Something*—

The torch went out.

Dammit, come on.

Rooker snapped his fingers and summoned his little flame.

The whole cave was moving.

Hundreds of shapes crawled silently over the rock toward them. Nearby, Rooker saw a yellow leg emerge from a hole, then another and another.

Shiq.

The torch died.

"Run!" came Barney's shout. Rooker saw Jack sprint for the vine, leap for it, and scramble skyward. Barney flew past Rooker and clambered up behind Jack. Rooker was left on the ground, the last man in the cave. *Don't leave me behind!*

Rooker snatched the rope and climbed. As his foot left the ground, Rooker saw half a dozen arachnids appear in the empty space below him. They withdrew, retreating from the column of sunlight.

The lightchain on Rooker's wrist drew tight as Jack clambered up the vine above. In the half-light, Rooker saw shiq skittering on the walls around him. He jammed his shoulder into Barney's backside. "Go, *go!*"

Above, Jack reached the top. "Patch! *Help!*"

Upside down on the ceiling, shiq climbed for the hole. One scuttled toward Jack. Rooker slipped Patch's little stone knife from his waistband and flung it. The blade embedded into the shiq's head and it dropped into the black. "Jack! Move!"

A spider landed on Barney. Screaming, the redneck lashed out his arm to knock the thing away

...and fell.

Barney's scream filled the cavern.

His flailing hands grabbed the lightchain.

Rooker felt it pull taut. *No—*

Barney swung and bashed into Rooker.

Above, a grunt as Barney's weight yanked Jack off the rope.

Rooker watched the kid fall, the lightchain hissing between them. He twisted his wrist, wrapping the vine around it. *If he goes—*

Jack's weight hit the chain that bound them.

Rooker was nearly pulled off the vine. He snarled as he felt the blood cut off to his wrist, trapped in the vine, knowing what would happen if he let go.

Barney grappled at him, terrified.

"Grab the vine, damn you!" Rooker yelled. "*The vine!*" Barney was too panicked to try, clutching the lightchain for dear life. He slid toward Jack and impacted with a thunk.

Another spider leapt from the wall. Rooker kicked out and punted it into the blackness. He spun in the air, Jack and Barney dangling below him.

Major West's paw flashed from the sunlight above, grabbed the vine, and hauled it up, dragging all three of them toward the surface. Rooker held Jack and Barney's weight by one arm. Straining, he grit his teeth. *Toughen up. Toughen up.*

Rooker slung one leg over the edge. "Help me!" he hollered, and West dragged him out of the hole. Rooker stuck his leg back in. "Grab it!" He felt someone clutch at his ankle and Jack dragged himself into the sunlight, climbing Rooker's leg.

The kid found purchase and plunged his hand into the hole. He pulled, and Barney's face appeared at the edge. The dwarf got a foot on the lip. "Ha!" Barney breathed a sigh of relief. He looked up at Jack, his eyes bright. "Ol' Black Jack—"

Yellow legs reached out of the hole, a dozen of them. They grabbed at Barney's arms, his shoulders, his face. Barney screamed as one spidery leg lashed over his mouth and he lost his grip on Jack's hand.

He didn't fall. The shiq dragged him sideways along the roof of the cave. Barney's fingers scraped the edge of the hole, then he was gone.

Only his screams made it out of the cave, and they were suddenly cut off, leaving nothing but an echo.

Rooker watched yellow legs extend from below, exploring the area around the hole, searching for more food.

An inhuman sound escaped Jack's throat. *"Nyuh!"* He grabbed a rock and hurled it into the hole, hitting one of the shiq. *"Nyuuh!"* He grabbed another rock. West put out a paw; Jack batted it away, screaming.

He's lost his damn mind.

Jack smashed a shiq leg with a rock. Another. Another. He howled like a maniac, crazy and shrill, a wild animal.

Rooker grabbed him. "Stop, stop, stop, *stop.*" Jack fought him. "You're too close, they'll drag ya down..."

Jack dropped to the ground sobbing. "We're never getting out of here!" Tears streamed down his face. "We're never getting out!"

"Wrong," came a voice from behind them.

Rooker spun and saw Patch and Ransom at the top of the sinkhole, their arms bound in webbing.

A dozen attercops lined the ridge.

"You get to leave when you die," said Winston. All around him, the cluster of 'cops broke out into hacking laughter. *Kek-kek-kek.* Winston lit a cigar, smoke curled around his head. "But don't worry, boys. Your time's coming soon."

PARADISE
ROAD

Criminals do not die by the hands of the law.
They die by the hands of other men.
George Bernard Shaw

Rooker Flynn felt stiff carriage wheels thunder beneath him. The stagecoach galloped at full speed, jouncing over every rut and pit the jungle road could offer. Fortunately, he did not have to worry about keeping upright in his seat because he was sprawled on the floor, gagged, bound, and blind.

Being bitten once was bad enough, but Winston's boys had left him littered in fang marks and flooded with poison. He was dimly aware he had spent a night, or maybe two, inside the Institute, and had only fully regained consciousness when the 'cops smacked his head while loading him into the carriage he now occupied. His stomach felt queasy, his neck was crimped, and his muscles knotted like walnuts. Webbing caked his eyes, his mouth, his hands and feet, turning him into a woozy sack of potatoes.

This exciting ride had gone on all morning and showed no signs of stopping. Above, Winston's whip came again as he drove the horses onward.

Paradise Road, Rooker thought. *Has to be. There's no trail on Huánghūn that goes on this long.*

Another bump and Rooker threw up. He gagged and spat half-digested galt through the webbing, feeling the acid burn his throat. Someone beside him moaned. At least three other people occupied the carriage with him, but there was no way to tell who. Judging by the lack of conversation, it was a good bet none were better off than him.

Once again, Rooker pushed his face against the door handle, trying to scrape the webbing off his eyes. *Wherever we're going, it's nowhere good.*

"Woah!" came Winston's voice from above. The carriage slowed to a canter then a halt. Rooker's head hit something and he heard the coach springs creak as the attercop crawled down. Sunlight flooded through the door. "All right, skags. End of the line." Rooker was dragged out of the coach and flung downward. Expecting mud or dirt, he was surprised when he landed on—

Grass? Rooker felt little soft blades brush against his face and tickle his nose. *There's no lawn grass on Huánghūn.*

Confused, he heard another carriage arrive. More doors opened. More attercops. More prisoners. As the noises continued, Rooker heard another sound, melodious and sweet.

A harp. Accompanied by a viol and a cello. Chamber music. *What the h—?*

Webs ripped away from his face, shredding his skin. Rooker opened his eyes to see a garden paradise.

The open lawn was bigger than the assembly yard, altogether green and dotted with manicured hedges. Nearby stood a trio of pretty white gazebos. Inside, musicians played formal music more at home at a debutante ball than a prison. Flamingos waded in a landscaped pond nestled against a wooden pavilion with an arching, ornamented roof, decorated with pennants flapping in the breeze. Littered on the deck were trays of iced fruit and fresh-baked bread. At the rear of the pavilion a suckling pig roasted on a spit.

We took a wrong turn and wound up in heaven.

Two dozen prisoners blinked, trying to get their bearings. All were bound by lightchains, paired off in groups of two. Patch and Ransom were chained together. Boss West was bound to a very upset Fancy Nan. Rooker realized Jack was standing right next to him. *Musta been him bumping me in the carriage.* The kid's face was pale, his eyes dazed; he looked ready to keel over any second.

"Get the blocks set up, please." Gerba wore a white garden party dress lined with blood-red piping. Her cartwheel hat had a lacey veil, her parasol matched the trim. "They will arrive soon. Chop-chop."

"All right, hump it, let's go!" barked Winston. Attercops drove the prisoners toward a dozen little platforms in front of the pavilion. Gerba stepped in front of Jack.

"Doktar." The headmistress unfolded her fist, revealing the pale rod of bamboo.

Rooker scowled. *It doesn't count unless I do it.*

Gerba Whipmarples leaned in close to Jack, offering Nepenthe. "This will be your final opportunity to summon Nepenthe. *Do* make it count." The kid looked at it, woozy-eyed. "Perhaps it is time to consider doing as you are told."

Jack barfed on her hand.

Screwing up her face, Gerba wiped the vomitus away with a dainty handkerchief. "Charming." She eyed Rooker. "Mister Flynn. You gave a disappointing performance, I must say. I thought you would exert more influence."

Out of the corner of his eye, Rooker saw Jack's brow furrow.

Rooker growled. "Look lady, I—"

"Where's Barney?!" cried an angry voice. Yenrab descended from a carriage, his face beet-red, drunk. Chained to the dwarf was Billy Pilgrim, his eyes wide and vacant, mouthing buh-buh-buh-*buh*. "Where is he?" thundered Yenrab. "Where's my *brother?*"

"Ah, the second Mister Bialik. Not to worry, you will be joining him shortly." Gerba gestured at Winston. "Silence him please." Winston shot a jet of webbing in Yenrab's mouth. The dwarf choked, tearing at it.

"*Whipmarples!*" came an angry voice. Boss Mamba emerged from the carriage behind Billy. He was chained to a small hammerdwarf who looked in danger of being trampled underfoot by the big croc. "Cut me loose, Whipmarples! This is enough!"

"It is indeed." Gerba faced Boss Mamba. Seeing them side by side, Rooker realized the headmistress was bigger than the llystra gangster by more than a head. "I have had quite enough myself, Mister Crait."

"I did what you said," snarled Mamba. Rooker imagined he heard a faint whine in his voice.

"You did, my dear sweet dumpling," Gerba cooed. "However, I did not tell you to make your little speech before the entertainment. I must admit, it was a bit upsetting. But you were right about one thing." She patted him on the cheek. "There is only one boss of Huánghūn."

Ornamented carriages thundered down Paradise Road, elegant in new white trim, led by horses decked in garlands. Gerba turned and clapped at the acolytes in the pavilion. "Places, everyone, places please!"

Rooker was forced toward one of the dozen platforms. Jack's voice whispered in his ear. "You made a deal with her?"

"I wouldn't deal with that harridan for all the spice on Chult." Rooker shot back. "She's crazy." *Almost as crazy as ya look.*

As Rooker and Jack were wrangled onstage, a dozen nobles exited their carriages. A wash of silk capes, white hosiery and velvet shoes crossed the manicured lawn. They took their place on the pavilion, making delighted noises as they sampled the food they discovered there.

Rooker tried to think what the little stages reminded him of, and it came to him in a flash. *It's an auction block.*

"You made a deal with her." Jack's voice was sharp this time.

Rooker shook his head. "Shut up. We got bigger problems."

"Gentlemen and lady." Gerba raised her hands, drawing the attention of the nobles. "Time is always a factor at the Locke Institute, so we must move along. We do not want to be caught out after dark, do we?" A series of nervous chuckles came from the pavilion. "The Locke Institute does appreciate your generous donations this morning, so let us see what your coins have purchased!"

One of the acolytes flicked her fingers; the air behind each auction block lit up with yellow symbols carved of illusion majik, numbers and names, glowing in the air behind each prisoner. *A scoreboard.*

Jack stared at the yellow numbers. "I'm worth a hundred points."

Rooker glanced over his head. According to the scoreboard, he was worth twenty. "Ya must be standing on the wrong side."

"As you can see, each outlaw is assigned a point value," Gerba continued. "And we *do* have some exciting participants for you today! Krom Hazard, who committed arson upon the manor of a doubleslash family in Reeds. Nancy Guinevere Mannus, née Fond-law, who murdered her family, including her three poor daughters, in a crime that shocked the Eynrys Plains. Major Bocephus West, traitor to the jinx raja. A conniving little bard who mocked Lordling Lund's family in the public houses of the Cull." She gestured to one of the nobles, who straightened, angry. "In a *series* of songs best left unsung. And...our headliner: the outlaw who stole more than a *billion* marks from the royal family, the legendary Black Jack."

The nobles clapped, eager. A dark duke whispered something in a viscountess's ear. She giggled and pushed him away, toying with her curls.

"Too bad." Jack broke into a half-mad grin. "You didn't even get a mention."

Rooker shot him a hard look.

"You may make your selections now." The nobles hemmed and hawed, clucking over their choices. Almost immediately four prisoners were led away from the blocks, dismissed. Gerba whispered to the Viscountess Jimenez. She listened, nodded, and gestured. More prisoners were led back to the carriages, including Patch and Ransom. Patch seemed relieved to be off the hook, but Rooker saw the look that passed between her and Boss West. *She knows something.*

Jack's ragged voice came next to his ear. "They're bidding on us?"

Rooker grinned. "Turns out, even you can be bought."

Soon enough, the field was whittled down to five pairs. Rooker and Jack, a yellow jinx chained to Hazard, West and Nan, Billy and Yenrab, and Boss Mamba with his dwarf.

"Very good!" Gerba clapped. "I applaud your selections! Now, gentlemen and lady, this is a timed event. You may select your instruments." The nobles opened the cases in front of them, revealing ash longbows and peacock-feathered arrows.

Rooker froze. *O bloody hell.*

Prisoners began to get the idea, shifting, nervous. "For each hit before your targets reach the end of the field, you will earn the corresponding points." Gerba smiled. "And before you ask, of course, every hit counts. Whoever scores the most will be crowned King or Queen of the Hunt! I wish the very best of luck to you all."

Gerba's eyes fell on Jack and Rooker. "Students ready!"

Rooker couldn't believe what he was seeing. *Nobles haven't done a thrill kill since—*

An acolyte struck a huge gong, the noise abrupt, loud and clear.

Hazard and his yellow jinx took off instantly, sprinting down the manicured lawn away from the pavilion. Most of the prisoners were caught flat-footed, not knowing what to do.

The yellow jinx suddenly sprouted an arrow in his back and went down screaming.

Jack's mouth fell open. "Holy s—"

"Wait for the *signal!*" Viscountess Jimenez shouted at Baronet Ket.

"I thought that *was* the signal," whined Ket.

Gerba laughed merrily. "You will know the signal when you see it, my lord! I should have been clearer! Do hold fire while they get a head start."

The prisoners glanced at each other and took off running.

Hazard scowled. Still bound to the corpse of the jinx, he picked up his dead companion and ran.

Rooker and Jack jumped off their stage and ran five steps before they got tangled in the lightchain. They went down in a pile of fresh cut grass.

"Match my stride!" Jack yelled.

"Match *my* stride!" yelled Rooker.

They ran for the tree line. The shimmering red chain sizzled between them. "Left, stay left!" yelled Rooker. Jack started to peel off and the chain drew tight, nearly yanking Rooker off his feet again. "No! *Stay* on *my* left! No switching, idiot, no crisscross!" Jack got the idea and drew up the slack in the chain. Their legs fell into a rhythm, a fleet beat-counterbeat.

"Where are we going?!" Jack yelled.

"Far side!"

"And here...we..." Gerba raised her thick hand, grinning anticipation. "...*go.*"

Yellow balls of fire exploded from the tentpoles of the pavilion, rocketing through the air. They burst into a flaming riot of blues, purples, and dark greens. Explosions thundered and blew apart into a thousand more fireworks. The nobles *oohed* and *ahhed* appreciatively. The hunt was on.

"Cut left!" yelled Rooker. Jack cut. At the pavilion, nobles drew their bows and fired. The viscountess screeched as her bow twanged out of her hands. Eleven arrows fell among the fleeing prisoners, digging into the dirt at crazy angles.

Hazard fell behind, weighted down by his dead chainmate. "Help me!" he yelled. "I di—" An arrow went through the back of his head.

"Right!" Rooker turned. Jack watched Hazard go down, the kid's eyes wide in shock. "Don't ya look at anyone else!" yelled Rooker. "Don't look at them! Ya match me!"

One of the nobility laughed as Hazard collapsed, stone dead. "I got him! Ha! Thirty points!"

Boss West ran with Fancy Nan, the big tiger easily the fastest of the group. Nan couldn't keep up so the major hooked his arm around her waist and ran for her. Boss Mamba was quick, but his hammerdwarf had short legs and slowed him down. Yenrab and Billy looked hopeless, barely able to figure out which way to go or how to get there.

West and Nan led the pack, a quarter of the way to the jungle and the safety of the trees.

"West!" hollered Rooker.

"What!?" the tiger hollered over his shoulder.

"Yer too easy to hit!" *The longer ya last, the less time they aim at me.* "Zigzag!"

West took an arrow in his calf. He cried out in pain and dropped to one knee. Fancy Nan stared at him, her eyes blazing panic. She lunged across his body and ripped the arrow from his leg. "Get up! Get up and run, you big pussy!"

West rose and ran, limping, an arrow landing in the spot he had just been in.

Mamba scooped up the hammerdwarf and carried him like a book. He picked up speed and ducked left. Arrows whistled past his head as the dwarf screamed.

Boss Mamba ran past Rooker and hurled the dwarf at him. Wide-eyed, the man hit the ground rolling. Rooker vaulted over the dwarf's lightchain but Jack's ankle caught. He went down and jerked Rooker to a dead stop.

Snorting, Mamba yanked his chain and reeled the dwarf back in. An arrow hit the big croc in the hunch of his back. Mamba didn't seem to notice.

Adding to the insanity, Billy Pilgrim started singing. He hadn't spoken a word in months, and what came out of his mouth now was a trilling series of notes like a bird with an excellent sense of melody. "Ta-*whe*-ba-*wha*!" The troubadour looked utterly mad, bare feet pounding over the manicured grass, his muddy hair in wadded spikes, sing-shouting senseless verse. Yenrab caught the idea and ran to the rhythm of Pilgrim's song, their strides matching the beat.

"Split up!" Rooker shouted. *Morons!* "Make worse targets, damn ya!"

Rooker cut left, West right. The big tiger leaned on Nan. Her face was strained in sweat, her tidy hair undone. Mamba took the lead, heading straight up the center, the dwarf tucked under his arm.

Somewhere behind them, Pilgrim's singing cut off.

"Spread out!" Rooker hissed at Jack, extending the distance between them. *Gotta get harder to hit!* An arrow skimmed Rooker's shoulder, drawing blood.

"*Hruh.*" West breathed heavily, blood matting his fur. Fancy Nan jabbed him in the side with a sharp fingernail. He snapped his head at her, roaring like an animal.

"Get mad, damn you!" she screamed. "Get mad and ru—" An arrowhead erupted from Fancy Nan's breast. Her face became a wide O of surprise and she hit the ground like a wet bag.

Boss West skidded to a stop and went back for her. Grasping Nan in his big arms, he lifted her and spun to run.

He got three steps before another arrow went through his thigh. He fell to his knees in agony, screaming. Another hit him in the back.

Rooker spared one last look at Major Bocephus West on his knees, a silhouette of bloody arrows. One more sprung from his neck and he went down. Back at the opulent pavilion, one of the lordlings popped a strawberry in his pink mouth and laughed.

"Drop behind me!" Rooker shouted. Jack tore his eyes away from West's corpse and pumped his legs, bare feet pounding turf. "Keep yer distance!"

Mamba was way out front, nearing the end of the killing field.

"He's getting away!" shouted the viscountess, pointing with a jeweled hand.

Another volley of arrows came. Most fell behind Mamba. One hit his shoulder. Another sprung from the back of his ankle. Mamba made it ten steps before he started to limp. He snarled, glaring at the hammerdwarf he carried. "You're too slow!"

The dwarf's eyes went wide. "Now d—" Mamba's claws slashed through the dwarf's wrist. His hand came off and bounced to a stop, splashing perfect grass with blood. "Wh—" the dwarf's eyes went wide as the manacle slipped off his bloody wrist and he tumbled loose. The big croc left him in his dust. "You bast—" An arrow skewered the dwarf's head.

Mamba grinned and picked up speed, almost free.

Rooker glanced back at the pavilion. "When I say cut, cut right *hard*!" he yelled at Jack. Rooker sucked air, not knowing if he would hear the twang of the bowstrings over the pounding of his heart.

Three arrows in his body, Boss Mamba sprinted for the safety of the trees. Thirty strides from the tree line, an arrow clipped his ear. At twenty strides, one cut through his bicep. Ten. Another in his back. Another.

Rooker heard it. The volley. A warbling of air as a dozen strings sang at once. "Cut!" He broke right. Jack nearly toppled trying to match him but kept his feet as a smattering of arrows fell upon their abandoned path.

The rest fell on Mamba. Ten feet from the green wall, half a dozen arrows hit him. His back, his shoulder, his leg, his arm. He cried out and fell, but forced his way to his feet. "I am Mamba!" He staggered to the tree line. "I am the Crime King of Khandun!" An arrow hit his lower back. "I am—" Another punched through his neck and he fell to his knees.

Dragging himself forward, Mamba watched his blood spill out on the turf. He tried to say something, but all that came was a bloody gurgle. *"Ahk. Am."* One hand reached out and grabbed a small tree. He tried to pull but his arm wasn't working any more. Another arrow missed, but it didn't matter. Mamba's last breath came as a dying, shuddering hiss accompanied by a bloody forked tongue.

Rooker sprinted.

"Hey, they're going the wrong *way!*" whined a lordling from the pavilion.

Mamba lay at the far end of the field, but Rooker's path went sideways. *They gotta recalibrate their shots, range and lateral. If we can get to the edge before they—*

Bowstrings thrummed. Arrows fell wide. Running short of breath, he felt the lightchain draw tight as Jack fell behind. "Move!" Rooker hollered.

Dragging Jack, Rooker sprinted for the edge of the field. Fifty strides.

Another volley hit the ground around him, closer this time. Rooker felt another arrow skim his arm. *Come on come on!*

Forty. A stray shaft thunked into the ground at his feet. Thirty. He pulled the lightchain, dragging Jack forward by the wrist. "Run!" Twenty. Ten. Five.

He crashed into the trees and heard a meaty thunk. Jack screamed. He went down on his face, chin first. *"Aiih!"*

Rooker hauled Jack into the trees. Dragging him, he stared at the kid. An arrow was punched through his side, where the fat would have been if the kid had any fat. *O Lord no.*

Blood blossomed from the kid's side. He kicked and struggled mindlessly, howling in agony.

Arrows clattered into the trees around them. Rooker grabbed the wooden shaft sticking out of Jack's back—*this is gonna hurt*—and ripped it through.

Jack howled. Rooker hooked an arm under the kid and dragged him to his feet. "Come on, kid. Don't die on me."

He dragged Jack into the jungle.

Chapter

23

THE
TIES THAT
BIND

In the struggle for survival,
the fittest win out at the expense of
their rivals because they succeed in adapting
themselves best to their environment.
Charles Darwin

C rashing through the branches, Rooker's skin was smeared in sweat and blood as he lugged Jack's dead weight. The kid's eyes were wide, alert and panicked. "Did it get my kidney? Did it get my pancreas? Rooker—"

I don't know what those things are. Rooker leaned him against a tree, ripped Jack's torn denims into a strip and tied it around the kids' gut, binding the wound. "Yer shot through the side, they didn't hit anything vital, now move." Rooker heard the calls of the nobles behind him, running across the lawn in hot pursuit. Somewhere in the distance, he heard the nicker of a horse. *"Move."*

Jack sucked air, clutching his side. "I'm bleeding a lot."

"I've seen worse. Forget it."

"Toughen up, huh?" Jack winced pain.

"Now or never." *Don't die on me, boychick. I can't carry ya that far.*

Jack nodded and took one step, then another. Soon they were moving, making their getaway from the killing field.

Shouts erupted behind them as silk doublets tore on thorns. Some nobles stopped at the border, others plunged on. "Now it's a good old-fashioned hunt, Lund!" Rooker led Jack through the trees, noticing how many bloodstains the kid left behind on the ferns. Catcalls came from behind them. "Hoo! Black Jahk! I'm gonna get a hundred points!" Rooker cut away from the voices. "Hey! There's blood! Hey!"

Morons couldn't find bread in a breadbasket and they're still right on our tail. Rooker lunged up an embankment, grabbed a tree root at the top, and slung himself up. Jack struggled after him as Rooker hauled the lightchain.

"Stop," hissed Jack, sliding backward. "I need my hand!"

Rooker glanced back. Three or four nobles braved the jungle, laughing and hooting.

One had a longbow aimed at him.

Dammit! Rooker ducked as the arrow passed through where his face had been. "They're here!" came the archer's voice.

Rooker grabbed Jack's waistband, hauled him up, and shoved him into the trees. Another arrow *thunked* into a palm beside him. *Damnit, kid! I can't drag ya through this!*

The other side of the hill was a vertical drop. Rooker sprinted along the ridgeline. It was a stupid idea, he made a fantastic target, but there was no other choice.

"Rooker, wait!" came the kid's voice. "Wait!" Rooker felt the lightchain grow taut as the kid dragged his feet. *"Stop!"*

Rooker skidded to a halt and realized the cliff was at an end. Rocks and pebbles bounced over the edge, plummeted into thin air, and struck against the few vines and tree limbs that hung over a stream below. *No luck at all.*

An arrow hissed past his head and he saw the archer, his fancy silks caked in mud, cursing his aim. Another arrived behind him. "Ha!"

Rooker stabbed a finger over the edge of the cliff. "That vine."

"Rook—"

"Onetwothreego!" Rooker sprinted for the ledge and jumped. Jack had no choice but to follow.

They hurtled into the air, legs pedaling. Rooker grabbed the vine. The kid hit, pawed at it, and latched on.

The vine broke.

Arms pinwheeling, they fell through the air screaming. A sudden jerk, and Rooker's arm shot up, nearly dislocating his shoulder as the lightchain caught on a branch. Jack smashed into him, spinning in midair.

"Gah!" yelled Rooker as he bashed into Jack again.

Two nobles arrived at the precipice, grinning like hyenas. The two outlaws hung suspended in the air, perfect targets. Laughter from the nobles as they drew their bows. "A brace of partridges!"

Rooker heard a bowstring creak taut. He raised his legs and kicked the kid in the chest, forcing them apart as the arrow loosed. He felt it skim between them as the chain slipped off the branch.

The kid hit the water with a splash. Rooker landed on top of him. Sputtering, Jack flailed to his feet, hauling air into his lungs. Blood poured from his hairline.

Rooker grabbed him and ran in waist-deep water, splashing toward cover.

Above, a noble hollered, "Follow them!"

"Are you out of your mind?"

As arrows splashed down in the water, Rooker threw Jack over his shoulder and staggered deeper into the palms.

Both men collapsed into the dirt. Rooker's chest roared like a blacksmith's forge. He glanced at Jack. The kid's face was covered in blood. "Here," Rooker grabbed some moss and forced it into Jack's hands. "Press this into the cut on your head."

Jack did, his breath coming in spasms. "My vision's all blurry."

"Yer the healer," Rooker panted. "Fix yerself."

"I don't—" Jack exhaled, out of breath. "How's my side?"

Rooker looked. Jack's wound was bleeding freely through the bandage. "Looks good." He grabbed some more moss and pressed it into Jack's wound, trying to staunch the bleeding. "This is hooga moss. The witches use it for healing." Rooker tried to pack the wound, but the stuff kept falling out. "Cures wounds fast."

"Really?" came Jack's hopeful voice.

No. "Yep."

Hoofbeats pounded toward them. Rooker's head shot up. "Ya gotta be kidding me." *We can't outrun a horse.* "Move. And stay low." Rooker hissed. He hauled Jack to his feet and ran straight at the sound.

A dun mare clopped through the jungle. Baronet Ket sat astride its back, a spear in his velvet fist. He stood in the stirrups, trying to get a better view through the rustling palms.

Rooker burst screaming from the underbrush right in front of his horse's nose.

Ket attempted to throw his spear, but the mare spooked and reared on two legs. Rooker flailed his hands at the horse's nose and rammed into its chest.

Rearing back, terrified, the horse threw Ket. The lordling hit the ground with a bone-rattling thud. Rooker ducked under the horse, got a foot in the stirrup, and dragged himself into the saddle. "Get on!" Jack clambered up the other side, the lightchain around the horse's belly. Rooker looped his chain around the pommel and slapped the horse's rump. *"Hyah!"*

Terrified, the dun took off at a gallop. Rooker stayed in the saddle, but Jack didn't make it. The lightchain dragged him, his feet skidding on the ground.

Ket shouted, grabbed his spear, and hurled it after them. It missed the horse by inches.

Rooker slung his other leg over the saddle and galloped into the trees.

Deep in the darkest jungles of Huánghūn, verdant life dominated all. Not a patch of dirt, not a fallen tree, nor a single stone existed that wasn't green. The world was layered in moss and lichen, feeding on itself in layers. Insects chirruped from their hiding places as they devoured each other by the millions.

The dun drank from a stream, guzzling water. Rooker and Jack remained in the saddle, fearing the thing would run if they didn't.

Jack's drag through the jungle had cost him some skin on his feet. Everything below his ankles was bloody. He winced, gripping the bandage at his side. "I...hate...horses."

"If it makes ya feel any better, she hates us," said Rooker.

Jack raised his shaking hand toward the sun, palm out, measuring. "We've got...two hours. Maybe three before..." he swallowed. "Before dusk."

They breathed.

Jack eyed Rooker. "We could...make it back to the Institute."

"Yeah," said Rooker. "Back to the Institute."

They looked at each other. Each waited for the other man to say going back was a good idea. The moment didn't come.

"Hey?"

"Hey?"

Jack took a breath. "You want to go for the—"

"Little cliffs on the bottom of the map?" Rooker shook his head. "No. All we're gonna find there is caves. And we already know what's in those."

"Fargil said there was a...building there."

"He said there *was* a building there." Rooker swallowed, panting. "Besides, it's too far off. And we don't know where it is."

"We're already twenty miles in. If the killing field is there"—Jack pointed—"and Paradise Road goes that way"—he made a line with his arm—"then the cliff is...that way." He stabbed a finger southwest.

Rooker eyeballed the sun. He moved Jack's arm slightly left. "*That* way."

They eyed each other. Rooker swallowed and glanced at the lowering sun. "Ya sure?"

"No. Are you?"

"No." Rooker eyed the chain that bound them.

Jack forced half a bloody smile. "You and me, yeah?"

You and me.

"Arright," Rooker jerked his chin up. "Let's take a crack at her and see what breaks."

Galloping through the dry riverbed, the mare's hooves clattered on stone. Rooker saw jungle he had never imagined. Bamboo trees too big to wrap your arms around. Tall conifers with yellow bristles, straight as a bottle brush. A copse of stooped willows that buried their limbs in the ground only to reappear halfway across the glade, ducking through the dirt like a sea serpent made of flickering leaves.

His chest clenched as the sun dropped lower. The moment it was gone, so was he. Trapped in the middle of Huánghūn with no yingcao between him and the shiq. Rooker tried to force it from his mind, but it was impossible. The darkness marched toward him.

They argued, bickering over which direction to take. Their discussion grew more heated as the sun lowered toward the horizon. Tempers flared, curses were exchanged, and without any other options, they rode onward.

At one point, the sound of huge wings beat overhead, a tremendous bird they could not see through the palms. The horse bolted, terrified, and Rooker almost lost control of the mare. The horse sensed the thing above them, frothing, eyes wide. It passed on, leaving them with one more thing to worry about.

Then they broke through a line of trees and there it was: a butte wall jutting out of the forest like the end of everything.

"Ha!" Rooker grinned. "Told ya it was this way."

The rock was shaped like an L. The stone face rose thirty yards in the air; the lower section was little more than the height of a man. Resting on the lower portion of the L was a small stone hut.

Rooker checked the sun. The bottom touched the trees, descending into the jungle for the night. "We're gonna make it." There was no response. Jack slouched in the saddle, blood dripping down his leg. Rooker scowled and kicked the horse's flank. *"Hyah!"*

Galloping against the sun, Rooker worked the horse into a lather getting up the rocks and followed a path toward the stone hut. It was a primitive little hovel, cobbled together a hundred years ago, before the shiq dominated Huánghūn. The roof was made of sheets of shale and scree, with a cracked chimney sticking out the top like a broken nose.

Rooker dismounted and slapped Jack awake. "Hey." He eyed the hut. There was an old wooden door, weather-beaten and cracked, but whole. Two open windows stared out at the jungle like black, vacant eyes.

Jack sagged in the saddle. "It's too...open."

Ya got another spot in mind? "We'll shutter the windows." Rooker staggered to the door and grabbed the handle. He struggled against it, then rusty hinges creaked as the door opened.

Rooker stepped inside and froze.

The hut reeked of ammonia. Yellow arachnid bodies littered the dark, hunched on the floor, the ceiling, the walls. In the corner, a big white egg sac the size of a sheep hung suspended in a mass of webbing, crawling with shiq the size of apricots. One of the big shiq came awake and realized he was there. It *churred*.

The others came alive in a mass of legs.

Rooker tripped backward. Shiq skittered toward him and he kicked the door shut. Yellow legs came through the window, grasping at him. Their bodies heaved through, then the shiq screeched as their skin hissed vapor. The spiders retreated from the toxic sun, escaping back inside the hovel.

Rooker sat on his backside, staring at the hut. Shiq legs pawed the door, slowed, then came to rest, twitching in anticipation.

Nowhere to go.

Rooker backed away.

Nowhere to go.

He could feel his heart in his ears. *Nowhere.*

Sunset's shadow slunk across the jungle canopy.

Retreating, Rooker mounted the horse. Jack grabbed his waist. "Where are we—"

"Hyah!" Rooker kicked the mare's flanks and rode away from the shadow along the base of the rock.

All around, the jungle fell to slow darkness. The sun dipped behind the butte and Rooker spied yellow legs flickering under the trees. At the hovel, the shadow passed over the rock and the shiq nest burst through the windows.

The mare's eyes went white, panicked. Foam dripped from her mouth, her coat slick with sweat. Dozens of shiq moved in the trees, crawling directly for them.

Rooker yanked the reins and veered closer to the rock wall, looking for a fissure or a crack big enough to fit in. *Come on! There's gotta be—*

A shriek exploded from the mare's mouth. Rooker spun to see a shiq hanging on to her hind leg. Rooker kicked at it. *Dammit!* The spider bit the mare's flank.

She screamed and went down.

Thrown from the saddle, Rooker hit the rocks. A second shiq jumped on the horse and bit its belly. A third wrapped around her face.

Jack screamed, stumbling backward. Rooker grabbed him and dragged him toward the wall as the horse's kicking legs disappeared under a tangle of yellow spiders.

(nowhere nowhere nowhere)

Heart thundering, lungs screaming at him, Rooker staggered toward a dark slash in the rock, dragging the kid by the chain. There was nothing...nothing...

There.

A crack.

Rooker dove at it and wedged himself inside. A narrow fissure went straight up like a chimney. He jammed himself in the gap and climbed.

Below, Jack howled panic. "Come on!" Rooker hauled the lightchain and dragged him up the crack. Jack scrambled after him, his eyes wide and terrified.

Rooker climbed the gap. As the *churr* of the shiq echoed in his ears, he saw a bigger gap ahead with a fat rock hanging over it. Rooker gripped the stone and monkeyed his way up the chimney.

He felt the lightchain go tight the same moment he heard the scream.

Rooker looked down to see Jack covered in spiders.

They bit at him, his legs, his feet, fangs sinking into flesh. An inhuman shriek sounded from the kid, a terrified wail unlike any noise Rooker had ever heard.

Rooker hauled at the lightchain, his strength spent.

Jack batted away one shiq and kicked another, flailing, screaming.

Rooker felt his head go light as he strained against Jack's weight. Stars danced before his eyes. *Don't pass out. Don't—*

Desperate, he jammed his foot against the overhang rock. It came loose and dropped a few inches, slipping sideways. Rooker felt Jack climb his hip, screaming. A shiq's legs tickled Rooker's foot.

He kicked the rock once more, and the thunder of falling stone split the world.

The boulder fell into the gap, jamming the fissure shut. He heard shiq crushed beneath the stone and heard Jack's ankle break along with it.

Rooker smashed the shiq crawling up his chest. Milky ichor sprayed over his body. He lunged forward and smashed the one digging at Jack's belly. Its body exploded, bursting like a grape. Another hissed and crawled over Jack's face, fangs bared. Rooker grabbed it under the neck and squeezed until its head popped off. Throwing the body aside, Rooker braced for the next one.

Nothing moved.

He lay there, panting, covered in shiq slime and blood.

Rooker glanced down and saw yellow legs squirming all around the boulder, prying, exploring, looking for a way in.

He breathed.

"Hey?"

He felt Jack move against his hip. "Hey?" The kid's voice sounded ragged, weak.

Neither of them spoke, just breathing. Rooker looked down and saw Jack bleeding from the bites. Yellow fluid leaked from the wounds. His ankle bent at an impossible angle.

"Everything's fine now." Rooker nodded. "We're...probably safe."

Jack grimaced. He looked down at the spider legs prying at the boulder, flickering over his twisted foot. "They're gonna...come through."

"Yeah." Rooker panted. "Don't worry, I'm sure you'll think of something." Rooker leaned back, closing his eyes. All he wanted to do was lie here. Forever. He took a long breath, relishing a moment of rest.

Jack's voice came from dry lips. "What...what did she offer you?"

Rooker blinked. "Huh?"

"Gerba. What did she offer you?" Jack breathed. "For Nepenthe?"

Rooker didn't have the energy to deny it. He shook his head. "How..." he gasped for breath. "How do ya build them?"

Jack raised his head, bloody hair hanging over one eye. "Build what?"

Rooker breathed, closing his eyes. "Mountains...out of mirrors."

"Mountai—"

"In Chegago."

He felt Jack's weight shift. "I don't—"

"She showed me." Rooker panted. "You and yer da. Mountains made of mirrors. The Tosh. Chegago. She showed me." Jack didn't say anything. Rooker nodded. "Guess we never really trusted each other, huh?"

Jack was silent.

"You and me, right, Jack?" Rooker chuckled.

"I thought..." Jack swallowed. "I thought if I told you...you wouldn't like me anymore."

"Well." Rooker nodded. "I don't like ya now."

Jack coughed. He wiped a finger against one of the bites, looking at the poison. "I don't think it's gonna matter long."

Rooker nodded. "You keep thinkin'." He struggled to his feet. "I'm gonna...keep movin'."

Jack held up the lightchain. "I'd say go on without me, but..."

"Yeah. Two peas." Rooker shifted and got his arm under Jack. The kid yelped in pain as his ankle brushed the rock. He leaned his weight on Rooker.

"My leg doesn't work."

"So...we've still got three legs." He raised his head, looking at the fading orange clouds above. "Four months I've been on

Huánghūn. Never once saw moonlight." He took a breath. "Let's go take a peek."

Rooker emerged from the top of the tunnel to find himself on a ledge at the top of the cliff wall. Here on the far side of the rock, a last few rays of sunlight caught the peak. In the darkened sky, the dim shapes of the two moons Anika and Gamilat looked down on them, not caring that the next few minutes would be their last.

Rooker peered down the ledge and saw the shadow of night creeping up the wall. With it came a million shiq, moving with the darkening edge.

He swallowed. The peak of the cliff would be the last thing to go, but there was nowhere left to climb.

"I can't...I can't feel my leg." Jack hobbled on one foot, blood soaking his denims.

"C'mon. We ain't done yet." Rooker heaved him up and ascended the narrow ledge, dragging Jack.

Sweating, Rooker watched the sun finally release her grip on Huánghūn. It disappeared beneath the horizon, abandoning the day, abandoning him.

As the cliffs gave up their golden glow, eight-legged shapes climbed over the top, flowing toward them.

Rooker heaved a breath. "They're coming over the wall."

Jack's ragged voice replied. "They're coming *out* of the wall."

Rooker turned to see shiq emerging from the cracks in the cliff face all around him.

Out of room, Rooker made his way onto a narrow edge that stuck out from the cliff, a peninsula of rock over a deadly drop. Shiq scuttled toward them from everywhere.

Rooker made his way to the edge. There was nothing left in front of him but open air.

He picked up a rock. "Okay. Let's make 'em work for their supper."

One jumped at Jack. The kid swung at it without strength. Rooker hit it with his rock, breaking off three legs, and sent it over the cliff edge.

Jack went with it.

—no—

Rooker dove, tried to grab Jack's hand, and missed.

Jack fell.

He hit the end of the lightchain and jerked to a stop. As the chain snapped tight, his weight nearly dragged Rooker over the cliff after him. He snatched an edge as Jack hung suspended beneath him, dangling over the drop.

Rooker's arm screamed pain. He bore Jack's full weight in his hand, and it was all he could do to clutch the ledge and hang on for dear life.

A shiq crawled up his leg.

Rooker roared, bellowing his final barbaric yawp at the world as the shiq swarmed toward him.

A chime sounded.

The single note cut the air like a razor, sharp and harsh. A rush of air thumped, rippling Rooker's shirt.

The shiq stopped, frozen in place for a moment, then fled.

Another sudden gust of wind.

Rooker's hair whipped back as he looked up at the sound.

His mind couldn't fathom it. All his brain managed was: *It's a flying spider.*

Xeusia flapped its wings again, immense, powerful, a nightmare silhouette against mismatched moons. Eight eyes gazed down at him. The spider-dragon's mandibles flexed, revealing fangs long as lances. It landed on the precipice in front of him and shrieked.

Rooker realized how small he was, how powerless, how frail.

In the darkness, a shadow detached itself from the saddle on the dragon's back. Stocky heeled shoes hit the stone and strode toward Rooker. Moonlight played over her face, her three horns, her sea-green eyes, revealing the headmistress of the Locke Institute.

There was no winsome smile on her face. No glint in her eye. Her face was cold as stone.

She gestured dismissively. The spider-dragon screeched once more, dove over the side of the cliff, and arced toward the mismatched moons.

Regaining their courage, the shiq moved toward her. Gerba Whipmarples flicked the brooch at her breast. It chimed again, discordant and grating, the sound of a dark, perverted *wikk*. The shiq drew away from her, repulsed by the dissonance.

Gerba tossed something at Rooker. He watched it skitter on the rock next to him. Gooseflesh flickered over his skin as he realized what it was.

A tiny crimson knife.

It was no bigger than Rooker's thumb, a hawkbill blade carried by sailors to cut rope. Its sharp edge scintillated red majik identical to the lightchain.

"Now." Gerba Whipmarples' voice came cold. "Let us see what happens next."

Rooker's eyes narrowed. Straining to hold on to the rock, he looked down at Jack.

He hung suspended from the lightchain, twisting slowly, boneless. His eyes drooped, his head lolled to the side. Blood caked his hair and shoulders, the arrow wound bled down his side, spider bites oozed yellow pus from his belly, his broken foot dangled below, useless.

Rooker strained, trying to pull him up. It was no good. He had no strength left. *I can't.*

He clenched his eyes shut. *I can't.*

"You can let him drag you down." Gerba whispered. "Or you can let him go."

Stop.

A familiar nightmare wrote itself on the back of Rooker's eyelids. A dock, a ship, a boy.

A wheelbarrow, filled with grain, food, a new coat.

(you and me)

Jasper Winegrad stared into Pip's eyes.

(you and me)

Rooker clenched his jaw.

No.

Jasper smiled, shaking his head in a mockery of pity.

(it's your turn, pip)

Don't.

(i gotta cut you lose)

Rooker felt his mouth move, forming the words. They hissed from his throat, a shattered whisper.

"I gotta cut ya lose."

Rooker Flynn gripped the red knife in his bloody hand and shouted as he cut the cord.

The lightchain split, disintegrating to nothing.

Jack's eyes flashed wide as he fell. He did not make a noise. He did not scream, did not cry out. He just locked eyes with Rooker, disbelief etched on his face. The last thing he saw was Rooker Flynn, holding the knife.

Rooker watched him plummet to the trees below.

And screamed.

Gerba Whipmarples' smile finally touched her eyes. It happened only rarely, on the few occasions when she was completely pleased.

The joy only lasted a moment, quick as a cord snapping.

Breaking an animal was always the best part. It had been so with the shiq, with the attercops, with the dragon, with the students of the Institute.

Breaking a person was the same as breaking an animal.

Isolate them.

Take away love.

Take away trust.

Take away hope.

She lifted her chin, raising her horn as Rooker Flynn screamed at her feet.

Once they've lost everything, then...

She smiled.

...then they belong to you.

END BOOK ONE

CONTINUED IN

THE TRIAL

OF ROOKER FLYNN

THANK YOU! PLEASE READ!

After years of dreaming about Rooker Flynn, the Isle of Huánghūn, and Gerba Whipmarples, they are finally made real with the help of *your* imagination.

I love that you have taken my hand and walked with me through the first part of this adventure in the Deep Blue South. It is your support that makes it possible for Keymark to exist.

Amazon gives you the opportunity to make your opinion known, so please take one second to <u>tap the stars</u>. Your rating makes it possible for this story to stand out among millions of books competing for your attention, and tapping those stars is the most powerful thing you can do to keep me writing. I love telling these stories. I would love to continue telling them, and only you can keep Keymark alive.

If you have the means, please gift this story to a friend. Most of the books I love came from someone who told me I *had* to read it. I hope you feel that way about this story. I sure do. And it only gets better from here.

Thank you for sharing my passion. I promise that I will keep telling you stories as long as you keep asking for them.

Your #1 Fan,
-Andy

ACKNOWLEDGEMENTS

*If you want to go fast, go alone. If
you want to go far, go together.*

I want to thank my editor, the indomitable Sarah Chorn, for wrestling with me through the early stages of the trilogy and helping pull all the strings of this story together into a single rope. Esmay Rosalyne Borst, Thiago Abdalla, and the Red Fury, Joshua Thompson, are heroes of Keymark. Their time, enthusiasm, and invaluable assistance made this story better than I could possibly manage without them. All of you are awesome and deserve more than I can ever give. I would also like to thank Dom McDermott for his spectacular proofreading skills and the unflagging support he lends to indie authors. In addition, I would like to praise Andrew Mattocks and Kayla Yetman for their steadfast encouragement and friendship. I want to thank every reviewer, reader and indie fan who has taken the time to discuss and promote my work; there would be no more stories without you. As always, I want to thank my mom and dad for encouraging me to follow my own path.

William, my dear son, you are a miracle.
And yes, I love you most of all, Glo.

ABOUT THE AUTHOR

A. R. Witham is a three-time Emmy-winning writer-producer and a great lover of adventure. He is the world's foremost expert on the history of Keymark. He loves to talk with young people and adults who remember what young people know. He has written for film and television, canoed to the Arctic Circle, hiked the Appalachian Trail and been inside his house while it burned down. He lives in Indianapolis, home of the greatest spectacle in racing.

If you would like a free short
story by A. R. Witham, please
sign up for his newsletter at
www.arwitham.com

Linktree: https://linktr.ee/arwitham